SOLD[IER OF] MISFO[RTUNE]

As a young man, in the hour of his country's direst need, he had made a decision to be a career soldier. But tragic events had conspired to end that noble choice. And, in a sense, it did not really end, because he still cherished beliefs like duty, honor and pride. Now, with those words ringing in his ears, Mack Bolan is called upon to make another decision: hunt and terminate a maverick faction in the U.S. military that is threatening America's freedom.

DON PENDLETON's
MACK BOLAN

A GOLD EAGLE BOOK

London · Toronto · New York · Sydney

All the characters in this book have no existence outside the imagination of the Author, and have no relation whatsoever to anyone bearing the same name or names. They are not even distantly inspired by any individual known or unknown to the Author, and all the incidents are pure invention.

The text of this publication or any part thereof may not be reproduced or transmitted in any form or by any means, electronic or mechanical, including photocopying, recording, storage in an information retrieval system, or otherwise, without the written permission of the publisher.

This book is sold subject to the condition that it shall not, by way of trade or otherwise, be lent, resold, hired out or otherwise circulated without the prior consent of the publisher in any form of binding or cover other than that in which it is published and without a similar condition including this condition being imposed on the subsequent purchaser.

First published in Great Britain 1988 by Gold Eagle

© Worldwide Library 1987

Australian copyright 1987
Philippine copyright 1987
This edition 1988

ISBN 0 373 61408 X

25/0288

Printed and bound in Great Britain by Cox & Wyman Ltd., Reading

There is no greater fatuity than a political
judgment dressed in a military uniform.
—Lloyd George, 1863–1945

I believe you do not mix politics with your
profession, in which you are right.
—Abraham Lincoln, Letter to
Gen. Hooker, January 26, 1863

A nation's first, *and* last, line of defense
rests squarely on the shoulders of her military,
on the spirit of soldiers dedicated and true. I
speak from grim experience.

—Mack Bolan

To the members of the original Delta Force

PROLOGUE

The night patrol had been a practice run, but it was turning into something else. The soldier had no fear of darkness, or the forest, but he didn't like the way his three companies had been acting. There had been none of the hilarity that usually accompanied their jungle milk runs, no suggestion that they ought to take it easy for an hour or two, then head on back to give the customary all-clear signal. Everybody knew the night patrols were basic drills that any trooper worth his salt had mastered long ago. The enemy was miles away—assuming that there *was* an enemy—and it would be a frosty day in hell before they got this far.

He didn't mind the night patrols... until this one. All day long the others had been looking through him as if he wasn't there, responding to his questions curtly, if at all. He wondered whether he had unwittingly stepped on someone's toes, or if he had begun to snore in barracks after lights-out. Anything, make it anything, as long as no one *knew*.

It had been stupid of him in the first place, poking his nose in where it didn't belong. His curiosity had gotten the better of him, and what curiosity could do for cats it certainly could do for men. In spades.

He hadn't meant to eavesdrop on the others. Not exactly. It was their fault for discussing private business in the latrine and forgetting to check out the stalls. So what if he had lifted up his feet the moment he'd heard them enter, praying that they wouldn't kick the doors back one by one? When it came down to lethal accidents, the crapper led all other sources by a mile.

But if he hadn't meant to eavesdrop—and he hadn't—he had to admit that what had happened next was certainly deliberate. You couldn't follow someone through the streets by accident, not ducking in and out of doorways like a frigging TV private eye, afraid that one of them will turn around and catch you at it, maybe notice your reflection in the windows of a shop or restaurant.

Okay, so he had followed them deliberately. Their conversation had raised some questions in his mind that wouldn't let him rest. Together with some incidents of strange behavior that he had observed from time to time—the pieces of a complex puzzle recognized subconsciously perhaps—the stolen snatch of conversation had begun to haunt him, made him wonder what the hell was going on.

The wise thing would have been to put it out of mind, of course. Wise and *safe*. And now he wished that just for once he might have opted for the course of wisdom. Too damned late.

There was a chance to save it even after he had followed them to town—not once or twice, but three times—if he had failed to put the pieces together or had simply kept the finished picture to himself. Approaching the CO had been a stupid trick; not only had he ratted on the men of his platoon, but it had gotten back to them somehow. He was convinced of it.

He could have sworn that the commanding officer had promised to investigate his charges in the strictest confidence. Of course, you had to figure that the old man wouldn't do it by himself, but you would still expect his chosen bloodhounds to be careful when they started throwing names around. Unless...

The sudden gooseflesh crawling on his back and arms bore no connection to the temperature, which seldom dropped below the seventies. The short hairs on his neck were standing at attention now, and he was acutely conscious of the fact that there were three of them behind him, armed and in a prime position if they meant to take him down.

"Let's take a break," DiSalvo called from somewhere close behind him, knowing they wouldn't be overheard.

"Sure. Why not?" The point man, Rafferty, was thirty yards ahead, but in the darkness he might just as easily have been standing right beside him, maybe with a Ka-Bar in his hand. "I've got a spot up here. C'mon."

On other night patrols, the break would be the high spot of their wasted evening. One of the others, usually Broderick or Steiner, would produce a couple of six-packs they had brought along in place of field gear, and they'd pass the cans around. It wasn't much, but it was a damn sight better than a ten-mile hike through jungle blacker than the inside of a coal mine, looking for an enemy who wasn't there.

Tonight, the soldier didn't think the others would be breaking out a six-pack. He couldn't be sure, but from the tone of conversation—or the lack of any conversation—it didn't take a genius to figure out that they were royally pissed. If he wasn't the focus of their anger, then he was free and clear. Next time a night patrol came up and they were teamed together, he would stand for sick call, shove a finger down his throat if necessary.

But he wouldn't fucking go out in the jungle with these guys again.

The spot that Rafferty had chosen was a marshy clearing, maybe forty feet across and twice that far around its kidney-shaped perimeter. It took a second, squinting look before he realized the center of the clearing wasn't solid ground at all, but some kind of bog with moss and shit covering the surface. Jesus, if a man blundered into that unknowingly—

The pain exploded in his kidneys and brought him to his knees before he knew that he was falling. In his sudden agony, he never felt the others pull away his M-16 or the survival knife he wore suspended upside down in shoulder rigging. By the time his guts stopped turning over, he was lying on his side, unarmed, the others looming over him like giants.

"It was stupid, man. You should've kept your nose clean," Steiner told him.

"Stupid," Rafferty agreed.

"The stupidest," DiSalvo offered.

"You're going to learn a lesson, boy."

"You're going to have an accident."

He didn't even try to match the voices with the speakers now, for they were all intent on killing him. He had to concentrate on getting them to reconsider while some hope remained.

"Wh-what's this all a-about?"

"You fucking spied on us, you shit."

"I didn't!"

And of course he had, but when your life is on the line you lie as if there were no tomorrow. He shuddered at the thought.

"Save your breath, man," Rafferty advised him coldly. "We already heard your story from the horse's mouth."

He knew that it was hopeless then, because the fucking CO had betrayed him to these animals, for reasons he couldn't fathom. Reasoning with them would be impossible; if he was going to escape the fate they intended for him, he would have to do it now, without resorting to words.

He rolled away from Rafferty and toward DiSalvo, groping for the man's ankles, jerking them from under him and bringing down his captor with a startled grunt.

A boot heel slammed between his shoulder blades and emptied out his lungs. He tasted dirt before another boot caught him in the testicles, and it was over. Curled into a fetal ball, unable to resist them as they hauled him to his feet, he knew that he was dead.

"Y-you can't d-do this," he stammered. "You w-won't get away with it."

"Won't get away with what?" one of them asked, sounding small and far away, beyond the curtain of his pain. "We told you to stick with us. It's not our fault you wandered off."

"We wasted hours lookin' for you," another voice chimed in. "Too bad we couldn't find a trace."

And he was moving now, too weak to struggle as they dragged him toward the marshy center of the clearing. For an instant he was curious to know how they would make his death look accidental, and at once he knew. It wasn't water underneath the moss and scum at all, but quicksand.

Somehow he discovered strength to struggle then, but it was feeble, and far too late. Another few strides and they were shoving him ahead of them, releasing him, allowing him to fall. His arms flailed madly for an instant, fingers clutching blindly for salvation, seizing only vacant air. He splashed down heavily, his face submerged, thrashing back to reach the surface, gasping desperately for air.

Don't struggle! He remembered that much about quicksand: if you fought and struggled, it would eat you quicker. There were ways to beat it if you kept your head. A lucid portion of his mind remembered stories of assorted victims who had saved themselves by floating or by swimming out of quicksand. Sure. Except he doubted they had been surrounded by four men intent on seeing them go under.

His equipment was dragging at him like a diver's weight belt, and his slimy fingers fumbled with the buckles while he tried to keep the rest of his body immobile. Before he even had the pistol belt unhooked, his boots had filled with mud, and now his legs were being drawn down inexorably. The suction made an aching bow out of his spine.

"Be seein' you," DiSalvo called. "You rotten shit."

The quicksand must be somewhere near his armpits now, for it was getting hard to breathe. No matter. He was worried most about the water that was lapping underneath his chin. It was the layer of water lying over quicksand that most often finished victims, he remembered. You weren't simply sucked away, you fucking drowned, sometimes mere inches from dry land.

Hopelessly, aware that there was no one in the world to hear him but his murderers, the drowning man began to scream. It took eight minutes for the marsh to silence him forever.

☆ 1 ☆

The viper hesitated on its perch, head slightly elevated, lidless eyes alert for any trace of movement while its forked tongue darted in and out to taste the air. A slender reptile, mottled green from nose to tail, it had been born for hunting in the trees, its form and function predetermined by a billion years of evolution. Its satin belly scales had never touched the forest floor below and never would unless the hunter lost its purchase in the canopy or was compelled to flee another predator by plummeting to earth.

The reptile sensed that something was amiss with its environment. It couldn't determine precisely the strange sensation, but it knew. Some of the viper's "modern" relatives possessed a facial organ capable of registering heat within a given range, thereby detecting prey and predators more easily, but they were creatures of the ground, competing with the mammals for their daily food supply. The arboreal viper had no warm-blooded natural enemies; its prey consisted of birds, amphibians and other reptiles, hunted by their scent, detected by the sudden movement of their flight. In mortal danger now, the viper was completely unprepared to face a different kind of enemy, completely foreign to its prior existence.

Secure in its speed, protective coloration and the venom in its fangs, the viper slithered forward, following the giant knotted limb, alert for any movement that was close enough to constitute a threat. The unfamiliar scent was stronger now, compelling in its promise of a feast to come. Days had passed since its most recent feeding, and the serpent's innate caution took a back seat now to gnawing hunger.

Sudden movement from above, a looming shadow closing swiftly, and the reptile had no time to coil or strike in self-defense. The needle tip of a commando dagger sliced through bone as thin as tissue paper, skewering the viper's brain and sinking half an inch into the bark beneath the viper's head.

Straddling the limb, Carl Lyons watched the viper thrash from side to side, impaled, the reflex action of its muscles taking over for a brain already dead. The hypodermic fangs could deal a lethal dose of venom even now, and he was cautious as he stretched to grasp the wriggling tail, his free hand wrapped around the dagger's grip, prepared to synchronize the move. In one deft motion, Lyons stretched the viper's body taut and pulled it toward him, pivoting the knife meanwhile until one razor edge was pressed against the reptile's neck. A twist and drag, a ripping sound and Lyons held three feet of headless snake in his fist, suspended forty feet above the forest floor.

He leaned out from the trunk, knees locked around the branch that was his sole support. He counted three and let the headless viper fall, its body twisting, wriggling as it pierced the nearest barrier of leaves and disappeared.

Five more seconds passed until he heard the sound of thrashing impact and muffled curses rising toward him through the verdant canopy. The Able warrior grinned, imagining the shocked reaction of his two companions as the viper had made its unexpected entrance from above.

They would be pissed, of course, when they discovered Lyons's prank, but they would soon get over it, and there was no harm done. He had been confident that they were too professional to open fire and give themselves away. If only Lyons could have seen their faces.

He worked the dagger free and flicked it sharply to his right, the serpent's mangled skull sailing through the leaves. Carefully he wiped the dagger's tip between two leaves, sheathed the weapon, double-checked his landmark, then began his slow descent. Decked out with lineman's climbing spikes and safety rigging, Lyons could have slithered down the rugged trunk in minutes, but he took his time, allowing those below to nurse their irritation.

At fifteen feet he saw them glaring at him through the leaves and lianas, the viper stretched out dead between them on a bed of mulch. When he had halved the distance, Lyons shook his safety rigging free, kicked off the spikes and did the final seven feet in free-fall, landing in a combat crouch one yard from his companions.

"That's some killer sense of humor," Hermann "Gadgets" Schwarz told him tersely.

"Yeah. A scream," Rosario "Politician" Blancanales commented, glowering.

"Jeez, I thought you guys could take a joke."

"I've got your joke right here."

"Guys, please," Pol Blancanales said, raising both hands in supplication. "Can we put the vaudeville routine on hold and concentrate on business?"

Lyons shrugged good-naturedly. "Why not?"

"I owe you one," Gadgets said.

"I'm quaking."

"Did you see it?" Pol demanded.

"Mmm? Oh, sure. Right where it was supposed to be. I'd estimate two klicks, southeasterly."

The landmark was a solitary mountain peak that thrust above the jungle treetops like a naked fang, apparently devoid of vegetation at its summit. Able Team would find its destination in the shadow of that mountain, two kilometers away.

"Okay." Blancanales checked his watch. "Let's figure four, four-thirty. We'll have time to kill."

"Suits me. I'd rather scan the place firsthand than trust those aerials," Lyons said.

"You'll get your chance. We need a recon on the compound anyway."

"So, let's get moving."

"Ironman," Gadgets said. "Sometimes I wonder if the guy who called you that was thinking of your head or your feet."

"What makes you think it was a guy, *compadre*?"

"I was betting the percentages."

"Let's move it, shall we?"

They had crossed the Rio Coco, from Honduras into Nicaragua, shortly after dawn. They had been marching south by southeast ever since, except for one midmorning break, the forest covering their tracks and letting them proceed without the threat of being spotted from above. The ground patrols were something else again, but fortune had been smiling on them so far. There had been no sign of scouts, although the probability of hostile contact was increasing with each stride they took in the direction of their final destination.

Able's target was a Sandinista base camp, eighteen klicks inside Nicaraguan territory. There were others like it ranged along the border with Honduras, granting rapid access to an armed frontier, but this camp had been rendered momentarily unique. According to the CIA's "informed" report, it was the one and only Sandinista base where field interrogations were routinely carried out on hostage VIPs before their one-way journey to the dungeons of Managua. And, again according to the Company, there was a client hostage currently in residence.

Their pigeon was a field commander for the counterrevolutionary forces, and he knew enough to seriously undermine the "Contra" government in exile if his captors managed to elicit full disclosure.

Able Team had been detailed to bring him out alive—or, failing that, to guarantee that he would not be talking under torture somewhere down the line. It was a dirty job, but one the Contras couldn't handle by themselves just now, with Congress arguing "humanitarian" appropriations versus "military" aid.

A bloody border incident could tip the scales decidedly in favor of the quasi isolationists, a fickle breed who balked at spending money to inhibit terrorism but were swift to call for economic sanctions aimed at friendly anticommunist regimes. In order to preserve "deniability" for Contra leaders and their sponsors in the CIA, Americans would do the dirty work in such a way that their involvement could be disavowed at any time. If one or all of Able's warriors should be killed or captured by the Sandinistas, they would be dismissed as mercenaries.

It was the kind of job that Lyons and the others understood from past experience. By definition, Able Team had been organized to cope with situations where the Oval Office dared not show its hand. The war on terrorism was a struggle against stiff opposition, foreign and domestic. Certain "friendly" nations placed their own self-interests over those of threatened neighbors, stubbornly refusing to participate in any hunt for border-hopping savages. In Washington, too many cooks had damned near spoiled the broth, with every freshman senator and representative intent on personally scrutinizing classified material, debating every move until the opportunity for action had been lost.

It was enough to make a warrior throw his hands up in frustration—or enlist with a contingent that was not afraid to bend the bureaucratic rules where necessary, shatter them entirely on occasion. Able Team was interested in results, and while they never viewed the ends as flatly justifying means, neither were the warriors sworn to honor any rules of parliamentary procedure.

The jungle was a second home to Lyons and his two companions. All had served in Vietnam, and each had seen his war extended into urban jungles with the ceasefire. Lyons had been working LAPD's orgcrime beat when he'd first met the Executioner, Mack Bolan, and the brief encounter had changed his life. When Hal Brognola started shopping for additions to his strike force, based in Washington, the blue-eyed sergeant of detectives was among his first recruits. The move to Able Team had been a natural for Lyons. It had meant personal commitment to an everlasting war against the savages, a war devoid of any hope of lasting victory, but Lyons harbored no regrets. A soldier did his best with what he had, and in everlasting war the battlefront was everywhere.

The men of Able Team had seen their share of action in Central and South America. It was a region that appealed to Lyons personally: the people poor but honest, for the most part working out their lives to make ends meet; the easy pace of life in Latin countries, where a man had time to think, to breathe; the macho men and doe-eyed women with their secret, inner fire. He loved the language, the cuisine, the climate, but he realized that there were serpents lurking in the garden. Of twenty-odd republics in the region, more than half were ruled by military juntas, left or right, and most were torn by some form of internal strife. Between the revolutionaries, death squads, Nazi fugitives and *narcotrafficantes*, there were enemies enough to go around, and then some. Communism had arrived at gunpoint and through "free" elections; some of its opponents, on the other hand, had proved themselves as ruthless and corrupt as any Moscow party-liner.

There were snakes aplenty in the Latin jungle, sure, and Lyons knew the kind that he had dealt with moments earlier would be the least of their concerns in Nicaragua. Reptiles killed for food, or in their own defense; the human vipers he was stalking maimed and killed their own in the pursuit of ideology, or simply for the sport of killing. Either way, they were a constant peril to their neighbors, threatening to spill across their borders like malignant cells invading healthy tissue. If and when he saw the opportunity to cauterize one of those running sores, the Able warrior would not hesitate.

The danger from patrols increased as they drew nearer to their target. Lyons took the point, his automatic rifle primed and ready to receive all comers. For their border crossing, Able Team had drawn Heckler & Koch G-11 caseless assault rifles from the Stony Man armory. Revolutionary in design, the weapons measured twenty-five inches overall and were constructed primarily from lightweight plastic. Because the rounds were caseless —4.7 mm projectiles set into solid blocks of propellant, with no empty cartridges to be cleared and ejected—the outer casing was uniquely free of openings. The G-11's only outer holes, in fact, were the muzzle and an ejection port, the latter provided for clearing the rare misfired round.

The plastic casing provided near-perfect protection for the firing mechanism against rough handling, immersion or fouling from outside contaminants. The weapon's single pistol grip was situated at the point of balance; its optical sight was built into a carrying handle mounted over the receiver. Utilizing "floating fire" to minimize recoil, the G-11 could achieve a cyclic rate of two thousand rounds per minute, ripping off a three-round burst before the gunner noticed any kick at all, but Able's weapons had been tuned to a more manageable six hundred rpm. As it was, a three-round burst departed from the barrel in the space of ninety milliseconds, and the 4.7 mm rounds could penetrate a combat helmet from five hundred meters out. The clincher had been portability and firepower: fully loaded with a hundred caseless rounds, the G-11 weighed in at a mere ten pounds.

They would be needing every bit of that impressive firepower, Lyons knew, if they were forced to storm the Sandinista base camp. There were other plans, but Able Team had been committed to a mission, and they had accepted, fully aware of the risks involved. If there was no way to remove their man, or silence him, without a major confrontation at the compound, they would have to take their chances. And they would be thankful for the G-11s if it came to that. As backup, Lyons packed his favorite Colt Python, with the six-inch magnaported barrel. Any Sandinista "liberation fighters" who got past the G-11's rain of fire would have a grim surprise in store for them when Able's Ironman treated them to a 158-grain hollowpoint at point-blank range.

Gurgling sounds announced the presence of a river just beyond his line of sight, and Lyons raised a hand to signal caution for his comrades. Anyone or anything might be discovered on a jungle riverbank, and if they clashed with Sandinista troopers here, their opportunity for a surprise assault upon the base camp would be lost forever.

Lyons stood still, listening and sniffing the air, alert for any telltale scent of gun oil, military webbing, human scent. In Vietnam the VC had boasted they could smell the American imperialists coming from a mile away, with their mosquito sprays and war paint, their equipment sleek and glistening with oil. It might have been an overstatement, but in time Carl Lyons learned that enemies *could* be detected by their scent in certain situations—sometimes by the smell of fear, and he had also learned to trust his senses on the firing line.

When he was satisfied that they weren't about to stumble over a patrol on bivouac, he pushed the clinging ferns and vines aside to scrutinize the river. It was narrow, nowhere more than fifty feet across, and Lyons's first impression was of shallow water moving rapidly downstream. Of course, he couldn't judge the depth with any accuracy; they would have a choice of gambling here, or wasting precious time in search of a better place to cross.

He waved the others up beside him to let them have a look.

"I'd figure three or four feet deep," he said.

Blancanales frowned. "Unless the bottom's worn away, or full of potholes."

"That current's fairly decent," Schwarz put in. "Without some solid footing, we could be in trouble."

"Lifelines?"

Blancanales scanned the opposite shore, eyes riveted on the encroaching tree line. "I'm inclined to go without," he said at last. "I'd rather take my chances with the river than be caught out there like mackerel on a string."

"Sounds reasonable."

Lyons ran a visual along the bank as far as he could see in each direction. "Zero crocogators visible," he said, grinning. "I know you love the scaly little devils, gentlemen, but I'm afraid we can't oblige this time."

"With my luck, it's piranha," Gadgets grumbled.

"Too far north. But there's a local variation on the needlefish you might be interested in. I understand it gets inside your shorts, and—"

"Are we crossing here today, or what?" Blancanales asked.

Lyons winked at Pol. "Just providing some enrichment for the tourists," he replied. "You know, many parts of a wader are edible."

"Eat this," Schwarz growled.

"I wouldn't want to rob the needlefish."

Again Lyons led the way, descending through a screen of reeds to reach the river's edge. The water's temperature was brisk, despite the muggy heat of the surrounding forest; Lyons felt his testicles contract, the gooseflesh crawling on his arms when he was only ankle-deep. He clenched his teeth and held the G-11 ready, trained upon the opposite bank, as water reached his knees, ascending slowly toward his groin.

They would be perfect targets now if hostile guns were waiting for them on the other side. A single burst of automatic rifle fire would chop them down like reeds before a scythe; they would be dead and swept away before they realized an ambush had been sprung. The water was around his waist now, lapping at his navel. He could hear the others at his back, resisting the persuasive current. It seemed warmer now, but Lyons knew that he was merely growing more accustomed to the water's temperature. Beneath his feet the silt and stones were shifting constantly, requiring him to think about each step before he was committed to the move. At midpoint Lyons longed to feel the relatively solid footing of the muddy bank that lay ahead.

He had been right about the depth. Aside from taking spray each time he moved, the Python in its shoulder rigging would be high and dry. Likewise the contents of his pack, including two days' rations, ammunition and assorted other fighting gear. If he didn't encounter any unexpected potholes in the final fifty feet, he would be free and clear.

The Able warrior found his footing on the far side and scrambled nimbly up the bank. Another moment and his comrades stood beside him, dripping wet, with Gadgets muttering about the river's temperature.

"Another klick and you'll be wishing you could soak in there all day," Carl told him. "But remember, when you start to sweat, it's not the heat—"

"It's the humidity," the others chorused back at him before he had a chance to finish. Scowling, Lyons plunged into the forest, following his compass south-southeast and picking up the pace. Within a hundred yards, the river's temperature was nothing but a fading memory.

They marched nonstop for ninety minutes more before they reached their destination in the jungle. Lyons smelled the cooking fires at the base camp from a hundred meters out; at thirty, he could hear the sound of human voices, muffled by the forest but distinctly audible. They covered the remaining distance at a crawl.

The Sandinista base consisted of a dozen corrugated huts inside a razor wire perimeter. The single gate was wide enough for flatbed trucks to pass, and there were lookout towers planted at opposing corners, east and west. Not that it mattered; from appearances, the towers were unoccupied just now, their mounted weapons unattended.

Lyons brought the glasses up and made a sweep from west to east, the single pass enough to let him memorize the layout. Half the buildings would be barracks for the troops in residence, and Lyons estimated that the compound would accommodate no more than fifty men. Fifty would be ample to derail their mission, sure, but at the moment it appeared the camp was understaffed. They might be running short of personnel habitually, or the others might be on patrol... in which case they could be expected back at any time. With no way to be certain, Lyons knew that there was little time to waste.

The other corrugated metal huts included a communications shack complete with tower, a generator shed supplying power to the camp, an armory and the commander's quarters. That left one, and Lyons knew instinctively that they would find their pigeon there, inside the smallest of the Quonsets situated in the center of the camp.

He handed the binoculars to Blancanales. "I figure twenty, thirty guns in camp right now. There may be others on patrol."

"That's it," Schwarz whispered from somewhere on Politician's other side. "Plan B."

"Well, shit."

"We've been all through it, Pol."

"I know, goddamn it, but I hate Plan B."

"Relax. You'll be a natural."

"My ass."
"We need the space."
"I *know*, goddamn it! You don't have to tell me that."
"They'll never know what hit 'em."
Politician glowered. "I hate Plan B," he said again.

☆ 2 ☆

Politician had good reason to despise Plan B, since it put his life squarely on the line. In simple terms, Plan B used Blancanales as a decoy, dressed in peasant garb and speaking Spanish, to distract the sentries at the gate while his companions found another means of entry. If anything went sour, he would be glaringly exposed, compelled to shoot it out at point-blank range with no real hope of finding any cover. And if things went well...then he was still exposed, the guy most likely to succeed in getting blown away by hostile fire.

Plan B was shit as far as Blancanales was concerned. But it was all they had. He had already shed his camouflage fatigues and replaced them with the faded linen pants and shirt that seemed to be the common uniform for farmers in the region. The serape would conceal his G-11 automatic rifle if he wore both items properly. His feet felt naked, painfully exposed to thorns and biting insects in the well-worn leather sandals that replaced his combat boots. He didn't bother trying on the tattered straw sombrero; it had never been designed to fit, although with luck it just might save his life.

In costume, Blancanales figured he could survive a cursory inspection by the sentries. He would never pass a close examination with his well-fed fleshy frame, the close-trimmed hair and fingernails. Short-term, the Able warrior knew that he could pull it off, but if the others were a trifle slow in gaining access to the compound...

He shrugged the thought away, prepared to confront that problem if and when it passed from theory into grim reality. Too many variables still remained: the empty lookout towers, roving guards, the nagging possibility that other troops might be returning from patrols at any time. So many possibilities for fatal error, but it didn't matter in the last analysis. Plan B was all they had.

Waiting was the worst of it, no matter how you trained your mind to cope with empty time, imagined dangers. It had been the same in Vietnam, but every mission now reminded Blancanales that he wasn't getting any younger. Still a long way from retirement dinners and the gold watch kiss-off, sure, and yet...

How many missions did this make? How many voluntary trysts with death? How many times could one man make that trip and count on coming back?

No matter. There were other things that a soldier did because they were his duty, and if he was worth a damn he didn't count the cost.

Lying outside the razor wire perimeter, they dined on jerky, waiting for the sun to set. The hour of dusk was minimal in any forest, with its looming trees and ever-present shadows; in the jungle this close to the equator, night literally fell as if a giant blackout curtain was briskly drawn across the sky.

It was dark now, and there had been no sign of any late patrols returning to the compound. Blancanales made another scan with the binoculars, confirming that the towers were unoccupied, the gates manned by a pair of sentries, other roving gunners on erratic foot patrol inside the wire. He was about to set the glasses down when sudden movement caught his eye from the direction of the camp's interrogation hut. The door was open, spilling yellow light into the compound, framing two figures in silhouette. They left the hut together, slamming the door behind them and cutting off his view inside, but Pol was much more interested in the men themselves.

One of them was Hispanic, dressed in olive drab and sporting tarnished captain's bars against a rumpled collar. His companion was a full head taller, blond and strapping, obviously Anglo. There were no identifying markings on his tiger-stripe fatigues, no way to eavesdrop on his conversation, but the very presence of a gringo in a Sandinista camp was ominous.

"Hey, check this out," he whispered, passing the binoculars to Gadgets, listening to his grunt of consternation, waiting while Carl Lyons had a look.

"You make him Soviet?" Lyons asked.

Politician thought it over, then finally shook his head. "Uh-uh. I make him Anglo."

"British or American?"

"No way to tell without an introduction."

"So let's introduce ourselves."

"Plan B."

"Don't rub it in, goddamn it!"

As they watched, the camp commander and his tall companion crossed the compound to the CP shack, remained inside for several moments, then retraced their steps to the interrogation hut. This time the door was open for a moment longer; Blancanales saw at least two other men inside, both dressed in uniform.

"They've got a party going on in there," Pol growled.

"You want to bet we know the guest of honor?" Schwarz said.

"Christ! How long have they been working on him?"

"He went missing Tuesday week."

"Eight days? They ought to know him better than his mama does by now."

"So we'll just have to see they don't communicate whatever they've found out."

"Plan B," Lyons repeated.

"Plan B," Politician grudgingly confirmed.

He got up slowly, knee joints popping, reaching for his G-11. With the sling diagonal across his chest, the weapon hung behind him, roughly in alignment with his spine but readily accessible. When Blancanales worked the poncho down around his neck, the piece was perfectly concealed and would remain so unless he was faced with more concerted opposition than the sentries on the gate.

For them, the sleek Beretta 93-R would be enough. With fifteen rounds and the selective option of an automatic mode with three-round bursts, the lethal handgun could be easily concealed inside Pol's sombrero, carried in his hands to show the peasant's proper deference for Sandinista troops. He double-checked the weapon, snapped the safety off and worked its slide to bring a live one up beneath the hammer.

"So let's do it."

"Give us five to get in place," Schwarz said.

"You've got it. Just don't dick around."

"We'll be there, man."

And they were gone, two shadows merging with the darkness. Barring any unforeseen disaster, they would be there when he needed them, Politician knew. For all their grousing, all their banter, neither one of them had ever let him down. Nor ever would, intentionally.

Blancanales gave them five, then made it six for safety's sake. Alone, he circled back in the direction of a rutted track that they had crossed in their reconnaissance, apparently the single access road connecting with the target compound. Jeeps could probably negotiate the path, but Blancanales wondered whether any larger vehicles had managed to survive the journey since the camp's original construction, finally deciding that it didn't really matter, either way. As long as no one drove up on his blind side tonight, he would be fine. Tomorrow they could run the frigging Grand Prix through this dump for all he cared.

The guards were careless. Neither of them noticed him before he closed the gap to thirty yards, and Blancanales could have taken both at that range. If everyone inside the compound was as laid-back as the men on guard, the Able warriors stood a decent chance of walking out of this one intact.

Once noticed, he was ordered first to halt, then cautiously approach the gate. The sentries covered him with their Kalashnikovs, eyes wary, scuttling around the dark perimeter in search of shadows. When the two of them were satisfied that Blancanales was alone, they started barking questions at him in rapid-fire Spanish.

When they asked his name, Politician told them he was called Antonio Alvarez. He was miles from home—a tiny village on the Rio Coco—walking to Managua on an errand of the utmost urgency. His brother had been a merchant in Managua but had lately disappeared, a fate he shared in common with a growing list of Nicaraguan citizens. Antonio's poor mother was despondent; she insisted that he leave their crop to rot and seek his brother in the distant city.

If the sentries were suspicious, nothing showed. In fact, they might have heard the story countless times before, for all the interest they displayed. Their faces were impassive until Blancanales asked for pity, then for food.

At once the bland expression turned to scowls, and one of them began to curse "Alvarez" bitterly, denouncing him as an ungrateful peasant bastard who thought only of himself, ignoring the requirements of his country. Blancanales took it, eyes downcast, already tuning out the diatribe and counting down the doomsday numbers in his mind.

Soon.

A burst of automatic fire erupted somewhere on the far side of the compound, followed instantly by other weapons and startled voices raising the alarm. The sentries wheeled in the direction of the gunfire, torn between their duty station and the obvious disturbance, one of them remembering "Alvarez" after it was far too late.

Politician had his Beretta up and tracking by the time his opposition noticed anything amiss. He took the older one first, a three-round burst chewing off the gunner's jaw and blowing him away before he had a chance to raise his AK-47. Number two was quicker in response, but it was still no contest. Blancanales shot him in the chest at point-blank range, the impact punching him around and out of action in a shattered heartbeat.

They had locked the gate, a simple hasp and padlock that couldn't withstand the close-range blast of Pol's Beretta. He was in and holstering the pistol, swinging up the G-11 from beneath his arm, before the troops in residence had time to realize that they were facing war on two fronts.

Downrange and to his left, a solitary uniform was scrambling up the ladder to his lookout tower. Now, with one of the attackers plainly visible, he hesitated on the ladder, hauling out an autoloading pistol, plinking desperately at Blancanales from the limits of effective range.

He pinned the gunner in the G-11's optic sight and stroked the trigger. His target was airborne in a boneless cartwheel, shrieking out his life before he hit the ground. There was a single, spastic tremor, and the twisted corpse lay still.

The fat was in the fire, and Blancanales had another reason to despise Plan B. He was alone inside the hostile compound, separated from his two companions by the body of a Sandinista strike force which, for all its ineptitude, still had the men and guns required to blow a solitary soldier's ass away. Whatever small security remained, Politician knew it lay in linking up with his companions, somewhere near the center of the camp.

He leveled two more soldiers with a blazing figure eight and double-timed for the interrogation building. Gadgets and the Ironman would be waiting for him there. If they were still alive.

THE FENCE HAD BEEN NO PROBLEM; it wasn't electrified, nor was it effectively patrolled. The Sandinista sentries used a kind of hit-or-miss technique, which mostly missed, and Lyons had no trouble clipping through the chain link with a pair of insulated cutters, opening a hole wide enough for Schwarz to wriggle through behind him. When they were inside, he bent a strand of the wire to secure the makeshift gate.

They moved out swiftly, circling behind the darkened, vacant barracks, playing tag with walking sentries who would never have survived a single night as stateside watchmen. Apathy had made them careless; carelessness would get them killed. All in due time.

Schwarz had been right about their pigeon. If eight days under torture hadn't made him spill his guts, the guy would never break, but they couldn't afford to take the chance. His captors might have everything already; they might also be reluctant to believe it. He might confess to anything; and they wouldn't know that most of it was crap until the analysts had time to pick it all apart. But the men of Able had a chance, provided that the commandant hadn't been sending out his information piecemeal. If the captain had his mind set on a solitary message, there was still a chance for Able Team to block transmission.

But it would require elimination of all witnesses.

Twenty paces from the interrogation shack, their luck went sour. A gunner coming back from the latrines apparently decided on a shortcut, rolling up behind them in the darkness. The trooper almost stumbled over Schwarz, recoiling, fumbling for his rifle even as he tried to find his voice.

He found them both together, and it was too damned late to shut him up. Gadgets had his rifle up before the gunner found his AK's safety, and one round through the face was all it took to blow the guy away.

"Let's shag it!" Lyons grated, painfully aware that they had lost the advantage of surprise. Somewhere on the perimeter, a nervous sentry opened up on shadows, riddling the night, and Lyons heard what might have been a fading echo from the general direction of the gates. The final rounds were parabellums, unmistakably, and that meant Blancanales had engaged the opposition. They were up against it now, with nowhere left to go but forward, down the dragon's throat.

The Ironman's G-11 chopped three gunners down before they reached the squat interrogation hut. He raked the front door high and low, went in behind a flying kick with Gadgets riding on his shirttails. There were five men in the room, but three of them were indisposed: two uniforms, preoccupied with dying at the moment, and a naked, mangled figure strapped atop a makeshift operating table. Lyons recognized the other two as the commander and his Anglo sidekick.

Recognition took perhaps a second. Time enough for the commander's bowels to empty, while his tall companion faded back a pace to stand beside the operating table. One hand was wrapped around a standard-issue .45, its muzzle pressed against the forehead of the battered hostage.

"Easy, boys," he cautioned. "Let's not lose our heads."

The bastard was American, and Lyons felt his anger trembling on the edge of overload. Still, the G-11 was rock steady in his hands.

The gunner didn't miss it as he spoke. "Don't try it, man. We're checking out of here together."

Lyons marked a weary resignation in the other's eyes, and he was almost ready for it when the gunner blew his captive's face off, whipping up his .45 to bring the Able warriors under fire. Almost. And even so, he might have lost it if the camp commander hadn't bolted, screaming, squarely into his companion's line of fire. Round two smacked into flesh beneath the captain's outflung arm, and he was sagging to his knees as Schwarz and Lyons brought their rifles into play as one, twin streams of fire converging on the tall man's chest. The impact lifted him completely off his feet and slammed him back against the corrugated wall.

"We bitched it," Gadgets muttered.

"Negative. We exercised the secondary option. Let's haul ass."

"Who *was* that guy?"

The Ironman played a hunch, their precious seconds slipping through his fingers as he crossed the room in four strides to stand above the fallen gunner. Reaching down, he ripped the tiger-stripe material aside and found what he was looking for around the dead man's neck. Disgusted, Lyons tore the dog tags loose and stuffed them in a pocket, turning back toward Schwarz.

"GI?"

"We'll know when we get home."

The Able warriors were preparing to evacuate when a familiar voice came from outside.

"You guys all done in there, or what?" Politician growled.

Another burst of automatic fire eclipsed his voice, and Lyons braced himself to take the threshold in a crouch. There would be time enough to think about the blond American when they were free and clear, provided that escape was still a possibility. The dog tags in his pocket might be souvenirs from Vietnam or peacetime service—countless veterans retained their tags on separation from the military—but a small alarm was chiming in the back of Lyons's mind. He didn't read the gunner as a wild-eyed veteran whose chain had finally snapped, and Lyons didn't want to think about the grim alternative.

There were more pressing matters on his mind right now, like twenty Sandinista troopers bent on blowing him away. He would have to deal with them before he could confront the problem of the blond American, and there was still a decent chance that he would never get that far.

Outside, the darkness was alive with deadly, winking fireflies. Rifle bullets drilled the corrugated metal walls around him, making them a jagged honeycomb. And there was no time left for speculation.

The Ironman cleared the threshold in a running leap, and he was firing as he hit the ground.

☆ 3 ☆

The point man called a rest stop shortly after noon, and Yakov Katzenelenbogen was relieved. They had been climbing steadily since breakfast, with a single fifteen-minute break at nine o'clock, and Katz was hearing protests from the muscles in his back and legs. He wasn't weakening, but all of them could use a rest.

McCarter waited for them twenty yards up slope, beneath an overhang that would protect their momentary bivouac from prying eyes. The countryside was wooded, lush with undergrowth, but Katz couldn't assume they were alone. In fact, he operated on the contrary assumption: that their enemies were close at hand, alert to any hint of hostile movement in the area. If he was wrong, if they were safe, another day was wasted.

He waited with McCarter while the others made their way up the slope. Encizo. Manning. James. Four men he trusted with his life, implicitly. They were professionals, the rough equivalent of modern samurai, and Katz had seen the men of Phoenix Force work martial magic. Sitting in the shade, his aching legs stretched out in front of him, the Israeli wondered if they would be able to produce the rabbit this time on command, with so much riding on the outcome of their mission.

Situated ten degrees above the equator, Costa Rica should have been a sweatbox, but the altitude together with the proximity of the Pacific and Caribbean, combined to offer sweet relief from scorching temperatures. The forest that surrounded them wasn't precisely jungle, but it fit the bill as far as Katzenelenbogen was concerned. A warrior weaned on sweeping desert combat, Katz felt slightly claustrophobic among the trees. It was a quirk that training had relieved, but which he probably would never fully overcome.

"How far to contact?" Calvin James inquired of no one in particular.

"If our informant was correct, we've got another four kilometers," McCarter said.

"I hope to hell he got it right this time. These little nature walks aren't exactly my idea of a rewarding afternoon."

"We'll find them, Cal. Don't worry."

"I'm not worried, man. I'm psyched. I wanna rock and roll with these jamokes."

"Be sure you save a dance for me," said Gary Manning. The Canadian was seated opposite James, his nimble fingers disassembling the Browning automatic pistol that he carried, reassembling the weapon perfectly without a downward glance.

"No sweat, my man."

Their target was a mobile column of insurgents, which had crossed the Nicaraguan border into Costa Rica late in February. Since that time, the hit-and-run guerrillas were believed responsible for several dozen violent incidents, including a grenade attack that had left a rural school in ruins, eighteen children lifeless in the wreckage. They had terrorized outlying villages, invading larger towns in groups of three or four to plant explosive charges, snipe at local politicians, ambush law-enforcement officers.

The Costa Rican government was ill-prepared to cope with terrorists who seemed to be well-disciplined, well-armed and well-supplied. The nation's army had been demolished in 1949, and since that time defense had fallen to the civil guards: three thousand part-time "soldiers" with a minimum of training and equipment that was generally obsolete. A backup force of twenty-five hundred rural guards were even less prepared to deal with cold professionals, their "training" limited to apprehension of assorted highwaymen and petty outlaws in the countryside.

Costa Rica's military weakness was the mirror image of its greatest strength. Established as a sovereign republic during 1848, the nation was apparently immune to the political disease of military rule, which plagued so many of its neighbors. Aside from twelve years of totalitarian control endured in the nineteenth century, Costa Rica had enjoyed one of the most democratic governments in all of Latin America. The army had been broken up in 1949 to keep that record safe, and there had been no major problems following disbandment of the military.

Until now.

It wasn't Katzenelenbogen's job to theorize about the motives of the terrorists he sought. He was content to let the deeds of savages define their words, fill in the gaps of logic that were ever-present in their stilted, semiliterate communiqués. It made no sense to think of armed guerrillas battling for "freedom" in a democratic nation, waging war against its children and elected spokesmen in the name of "liberation." Katz had seen enough of "freedom fighters" in his homeland: brutal men with lifeless eyes. They may have started out as soldiers of a cause, but somehow they had wound up killing for the pleasure of it, randomly selecting sacrificial victims to appease their own abiding rage.

The gruff Israeli knew that there was no negotiating with such men. They only understood one language, and the men of Phoenix Force were trained to speak that language fluently, conducting lethal conversations with their military hardware, pledged to have the final word with terrorists wherever they were found.

Costa Rica was a friend of the United States, a charter member of the OAS, but there was more behind the Phoenix mission than a simple offer of assistance to a neighbor in need of help. The fact that Costa Rica's enemies had come from Nicaragua, at a time when the U.S. administration was fighting for a green light to unseat the revolutionary Sandinista government, made all the difference in the world.

If solid evidence could be secured implicating Nicaragua in the violence aimed at Costa Rica, if the Sandinistas were themselves involved, it might persuade some undecided congressmen to vote appropriations for the Contra forces that were languishing for lack of arms and cash. A Sandinista border crossing into Costa Rica was as good as money in the bank to Washington, and Phoenix Force had been assigned to prove it...or, in the alternative, to find out what the hell was going on.

Katz had no vital interest in politics. He knew from past experience that there were decent men in every party, every movement, just as there were also rogues, embezzlers and scoundrels. The Israeli put his faith in people, rather than the cliques to which they periodically attached themselves. A man might change his politics from week to week, but he could never really change his soul.

Katz had no fear that two- or three-score terrorists would topple Costa Rica's government. He was concerned, instead, with the hell that they could raise before somebody finally brought them down. What worried the Phoenix leader was the shattered lives and broken dreams of common men and women caught up in a larger game that they could never hope to understand. How many times, on tours of the kibbutzim at home, had he seen men, women and children slaughtered by the homicidal pawns of men who lusted after power from a distance, men who wouldn't personally soil their manicured hands with Cosmoline and blood, but who were quick to order assaults, reprisals and wholesale murder of the innocents. His war was with those other terrorists, the twisted souls who kept the murder teams supplied with cash and weapons, but he knew that he could reach them only after dealing with their pawns.

The threat was here and now, in Costa Rica, and the men of Phoenix Force had been assigned to treat the lethal symptoms with a dose of cleansing fire. If they uncovered evidence that opened up another level of the lethal hierarchy, it would be a bonus. But for now, the shock troops took priority.

The warriors had been trolling for their targets, working sectors in the highlands for eleven days without a hostile contact. Twice they had discovered evidence of recent camps, apparently accommodating twenty men or more, and three days back they had discovered the survivors of a recent attack. The village, small to start with, had been whittled to a single shack when they had arrived, the others torched or shattered by explosive charges, thirty-seven corpses huddled in an overgrown ravine that had become their common grave. Survivors—four in all, with one of those severely wounded—told a tale of men in uniform who came by night, demanding food and shelter, sex, exploding into brutal violence when the villagers were slow to acquiesce. The massacre had taken forty minutes, start to finish, and its perpetrators had been three days gone when Phoenix Force had arrived.

Their break—if break it was—had been provided by a peasant whom they'd met by accident along a highland trail. The man had been hysterical with shame and rage, but Rafael Encizo's gentle questioning had pried his story loose. The terrorists had killed his brother, carrying away the dead man's wife and teenage daughter to provide themselves with some diversion on the march. He had pursued the killers, empty-handed, knowing it was useless, and had found the women where they had been left to die beside a mountain stream. His brother's wife had been dead already when he had reached her, but the peasant's niece had lived long enough to tell him of their ordeal...and to mention that the savages had named their destination. They were bound for La Mesa del Diablo— the Devil's Table—on an errand of such urgency that they had botched the job of murder, leaving her alive to reveal their secret.

Katz believed the peon's story, but that didn't mean he believed their enemies were waiting for them on La Mesa del Diablo. The terrorists had never settled anywhere for more then two or three days at a time, and they could easily have moved again before the Phoenix warriors overtook them on the Devil's Table. It would be a long shot, certainly, but it was still the only shot they had, and Katzenelenbogen realized that they couldn't afford to pass it by. If nothing else, another campsite might provide some indicator of the killer team's next target or their intended destination. And with that in hand, the men of Phoenix Force could be in place and waiting for them when the show began.

"That's twenty," David McCarter said. "Let's move it out."

Katz rose and flexed his shoulders, double-checked the metal tongs that were his strong right hand. The flesh-and-blood original had been a casualty of other wars, a different battlefield; its various prosthetic stand-ins served him ably and well. The current model was a stainless-steel clamp, mechanically articulated and controlled by Katzenelenbogen's biceps, honed to razor-sharpness on the "knuckles" to provide him with a lethal backhand. None of the Israeli's various acquaintances had ever dared to think of him as "handicapped."

They were approaching the Devil's Table from the south and running parallel to the direction of their enemies. According to the charts McCarter carried in his pack, the mesa's flattened summit covered slightly more than three square miles, its mottled woodland punctuated near dead center by a mountain lake. On colored maps it offered the impression of a blue eye, peering from the wilderness in vague confusion; on the black-and-whites, the tableland looked more like a doughnut. Or an asshole, Calvin James had pointed out: the perfect place to plant your nozzle for a 5.56 mm enema, reserved for terrorists.

In lieu of splitting up and covering the mesa individually, with all of its attendant risks, they would be making for the lake directly. Katz had reasoned that their quarry would prefer to camp near water, and if the Phoenix commandos found no spoor along the lakeside, they could always institute a wider search.

But they were getting close. The big Israeli felt it in his gut now as they hit the trail. It might have been a hunter's instinct, or a warrior's nose for carrion, but he could almost feel the bastards now, could almost smell them as Phoenix Force broke the crest of La Mesa del Diablo.

Here, the land began to level out beneath their feet. The upthrust soil was rocky, but it hadn't prevented trees and shrubbery from sprouting in profusion. They were covered well enough for now, unless their enemies had posted pickets, wired the game trails with grenades or satchel charges, maybe stocked up on the various security devices that were currently available. If they were dealing with professionals, as Katz believed, there might be foot patrols, or snipers posted in the trees.

In short, they would accomplish nothing short of suicide by charging pell-mell across the Devil's Table. Caution was required, and doubly so as they drew nearer to their enemies. Each member of the Phoenix team was conscious of the fact that death for one might doom them all.

It took another hour to reach the lake, a glacial pocket gouged from the earth before some other geological spasm had hoisted the plateau a mile above sea level. Fed by rains and possibly by springs from underground, the lake was full year-round and stocked with fish no longer found in lakes and rivers of the lowlands. Time had been arrested here, for all that fish and birds and reptiles knew, but man knew better. In man's eye, the past was dead and gone, the present veering dangerously into an explosive confrontation with the future. When they met, it would be time for Mother Earth to stand aside and wait to claim her dead.

The lake was dark and deep, though not particularly large—two hundred meters, perhaps, from north to south, and half again as long. There was no means of estimating depth, and Katzenelenbogen didn't care in any case. His quarry wasn't in the lake, but rather camped along its southern shore.

Against the tree line, safe from aerial reconnaissance and difficult enough to spot on foot, a dozen tents of camouflage material had been arranged in tandem, open flaps all facing toward the placid lake. The noonday cook fire had been doused already, wisps of steam still rising from a ring of blackened stone while several guerrillas cleaned their mess kits at the water's edge. Katz made a rapid head count, coming up with twenty-three; it fit the tents, provided one of the commandos slept alone or with a stockpile of equipment. That made twenty-five, to start; a troop of civil guards had gotten lucky three weeks earlier and had dropped a pair of terrorists as they were fleeing from the scene of an attack in Puntarenas.

"Twenty-three."

McCarter's whispered confirmation came from Katzenelenbogen's left. The others were spread out along a firing line to the Israeli's right, concealed by rampant undergrowth. The enemy whom they had stalked for better than a week was fifty meters away.

"We need to flank them," Gary Manning said, his voice inaudible beyond the screen of ferns that sheltered him and his companions.

"Catch 'em with their backsides to the water," Calvin James agreed.

"No time to lose." There was a special urgency in Rafael Encizo's voice, and Katz glanced down the line of faces, picking out the Cuban's profile. Something in his eyes, perhaps, the grim set of his mouth...

No time to lose. Encizo was correct on that score. The terrorists might begin to break camp at any time, and once they were in motion, setting up an ambush would be doubly dangerous. It could be done successfully, but

Katzenelenbogen hadn't reached his present age by courting needless risks.

He was prepared to give the order when a distant, droning sound distracted him. The others caught it simultaneously, frozen where they lay, eyes swiveled skyward toward the source of that familiar sound. An aircraft was approaching from the north and running low enough to beat the Costa Rican government's outdated radar gear.

McCarter spied it first, his index finger stabbing skyward toward the north end of the lake. The aircraft was a seaplane, fitted out with fat pontoons, and there could be no question now of a coincidental overflight. The terrorists had picked their bivouac with care, the lake performing double duty as a landing strip for their expected contact. Katzenelenbogen said a silent prayer of thanks—to providence, the fates, whatever—that they hadn't been delayed by hours or days to miss the covert rendezvous on the Devil's Table.

North meant Nicaragua or Honduras with a plane that size, and Katz was betting on the former point of origin. The pilot might be dropping off supplies or picking up evacuees, delivering fresh orders from Managua or retrieving battlefield intelligence collected by the terrorists along their bloody trek.

The plane touched down, white plumes of spray erupting underneath its wings as it began to taxi, slowing, veering sharply toward the line of tents on the shore. The pilot killed his engine as he reached the shallows; he could wade from there, provided he intended to come ashore at all. Two guerrillas were already splashing out to meet their guest, prepared to catch his mooring lines.

The cabin door swung against the fuselage, and Katzenelenbogen had the glasses firmly in his claw before a smiling face emerged. Its owner wore OD fatigues with military webbing wrapped around his waist, and he had a holstered automatic pistol on his hip. The stenciled name tag just above his heart read BAKER. He tossed an anchor line down to the members of his welcoming committee, waited while they made it fast, then joined them in the shallow water for a hike to shore.

"American?" McCarter's whisper was a rasp drawn roughly over Katzenelenbogen's nerves.

"Too early to be sure," the gruff Israeli answered. "Let's move out."

"But if he *is* American—"

"We're wasting time." His tone immediately canceled further argument. McCarter frowned but held his tongue, already moving out to flank the terrorist encampment. Calvin James was on his heels, Encizo following as closely as a shadow.

Gary Manning crouched at Katzenelenbogen's side, prepared to join the rest in taking up positions on the firing line. "It was a Yank," he said. "You know it was." And he was gone.

Alone, Katz double-checked the action on his Colt Commander, setting the selector switch for automatic fire. He knew, all right, but he refused to even think about the implications of that knowledge yet before he had more evidence to work with. An American in touch with terrorists was one thing; there were mercenaries everywhere, prepared to fight for nearly any cause that paid their tab. But an American supporting Sandinista terrorists was something else entirely...like a blend of oil and water, gasoline and open flame. Considering Managua's hard line on Americans, the two could never coexist, unless...

He squelched the train of thought before it could go any farther. He was needed on the firing line just now; there would be ample time for sorting theories later if they pulled the ambush off successfully. If not, then someone else could sweat the problem out another day. If Katzenelenbogen's ambush failed, the men of Phoenix Force wouldn't be cracking any mysteries in Costa Rica. They would simply be among the dead.

Katz wriggled backward through the clinging undergrowth to join his comrades on the razor's edge.

☆ 4 ☆

Rafael Encizo sighted down the barrel of his M-16, one finger curled around the trigger. From his new position in the middle of the firing line, he had an unobstructed view of seven tents and the men who moved around them with their weapons casually slung. It would be simple to annihilate them, hold the automatic rifle's trigger down and sweep from left to right, then back again, reloading and resuming fire until no one remained alive. So simple, yes... but he would wait for the Israeli's signal to begin.

Encizo felt an eerie hollowness inside, a kind of vacuum, and within that vacuum icy fingers gripped his heart. At some point, which he couldn't specify, his burning hatred for the animals in human form had died. In place of hatred there was only bitter cold: a grim, implacable desire to see the bastards dead before they could promote some new atrocity.

He knew the savages instinctively, although their paths had never crossed before this moment. Rather, Rafael Encizo knew their breed: the jackals born to prey upon society, devouring the weak, the helpless, forming packs to terrorize innocents at will. Devoid of conscience, any inkling of humanity was foreign to the cannibals who lived for violence. They were addicted to the thrill of murder, thirsty for the blood of victims they would never even recognize by name. They were beyond redemption, and the only way to exorcise their evil was through cleansing fire.

Encizo knew their breed from Cuba, where another "people's revolution" had been undermined, subverted from within by venal men who saw an opportunity to seize the reins of power. His parents and older brother had been murdered by the "freedom fighters" in an incident that was dismissed by Castro's courts as "self-defense." Encizo's two sisters and younger brother had been sent to "reeducation" centers, but Rafael had escaped to the United States. Along with thousands of other Cubans, Encizo had participated in the doomed Bay of Pigs operation. When air support was inexplicably withdrawn by Washington, the Cuban patriots had fought on against the odds and had been slaughtered like fish in a barrel. Wounded, Rafael had endured torture and extreme privation in Castro's prisons until he had finally escaped.

Stateside once again, Encizo had worked at various occupations—scuba instructor, professional bodyguard, insurance investigator—before joining Phoenix Force. No longer pledged exclusively to liberation of his Cuban homeland, Rafael would take on the jackals when and where he found them, using every means at his disposal to eradicate them from the earth. And if he had the opportunity to do some jackal-killing here, well, that was gravy on the side.

But he would wait for Katzenelenbogen's signal, and while waiting, there was time to think about the pilot of the seaplane. He was almost certainly American, and Rafael was conscious of a sour feeling in his stomach as he pondered the implications of that fact. Of course, there was no special pedigree for treason, and America had yielded up its share of Judases in recent years: the mercenary smugglers of arms to Libya's Khaddafi and the ayatollahs of Iran; the turncoat bastards who delivered classified material to agents of the KGB for cash or twisted "moral reasons" of their own; the neofascist crazies who pursued their "master race" philosophy with armed attacks against the media and law-enforcement officers. The cannibals had never been in short supply, and motives were primarily irrelevant to Rafael Encizo. It had always been enough to simply recognize the animals for what they were and act accordingly.

Encizo checked his watch again and burrowed deeper into his bed of moss and ferns. The signal should be coming any moment now, unleashing him against his enemies.

From somewhere to his right came the hollow crump of a grenade exploding, followed instantly by ragged screams, the telltale rattle of a Colt Commander spitting 5.56 mm tumblers. Before his targets could react, Encizo opened fire from ambush, milking short precision bursts out of his M-16. Downrange, the startled straw men toppled and sprawled in awkward attitudes of death. His armor-piercing rounds sliced through their tents as if they had been made of tissue paper.

Half a dozen fell before the others went to ground, returning fire with something less than perfect accuracy. After stitching one more line of lethal tumblers across their front, the Cuban knew that he would have to move before they found the mark. A few rounds had come dangerously close already, and Encizo had no wish to die here on the Devil's Table.

Shifting crablike to his left, he scuttled through the undergrowth on hands and knees while angry hornets swarmed above him, sometimes dipping close enough to singe him with their heat. The new perspective offered Rafael a different line of fire, but while the terrorists were furiously pumping rounds into his last position, he wasn't prepared to show himself just yet.

He fed the M-16 another magazine, then slipped a frag grenade from his waist. He yanked the pin, still holding down the safety spoon while calculating angles and marking the obstruction formed by overhanging branches. When he had set the move up in his mind, Encizo cocked his arm and lobbed the lethal egg, already lining up his rifle on the enemy before his pitch touched down.

Three seconds.

Two.

One of the tents erupted in a muffled thunderclap, hot shrapnel slicing into shrubbery and human flesh. There was an ugly writhing in the undergrowth before him, punctuated by the sound of panting screams, and Rafael began unloading on the wounded, knowing that a rabid dog was rabid until he died. There was no quarter asked or given in the hellgrounds, where the only mercy issued from the muzzle of a gun.

Encizo held the trigger of his rifle down, dispensing mercy to the cannibals.

KATZ RELEASED THE TRIGGER for a moment, his elusive targets having gone to ground behind a drift of fallen trees. Three crumpled figures lay between them in the no-man's-land that separated hostile lines, and there were others to the left where his grenade had served as an explosive overture to the attack. Surprise had let him take out half a dozen of the terrorists before they knew what was happening, but others had escaped his raking fire, and one of them had been the seaplane's pilot.

The Israeli wanted him alive, if possible, but there was little chance of taking any prisoners when you began with odds of more than four to one against you. It was not unheard of, but Katzenelenbogen knew from grim experience that any prisoners taken today were likely to be wounded and unable—or unwilling—to survive a rough interrogation. Maybe if they had an opportunity to check the plane there might be some solutions to the nagging questions in his mind.

A bullet clipped the fern that stood next to his face, and Katz ducked a second round, returning fire to keep the enemy in their place.

A terrorist erupted from behind the makeshift barricade, knees pumping as he broke for other shelter somewhere down the firing line. Katz led his target by a yard, sucked in a breath, released half of it, held the rest. His trigger stroke was gentle, and the three-round burst was gone almost before he felt its recoil. Forty yards downrange the gunner seemed to stumble, throwing out his hands as if to catch himself, except that he was spinning now, legs tangled in the undergrowth and going over backward.

The gunner might be dead, or merely wounded. Either way, he had effectively been neutralized until a mop-up party could be organized.

On the Israeli's left, incessant automatic weapon fire was battering the tree line, the guerrillas standing firm against their unknown adversaries. There were fewer of them now, however, and increasingly the stutter of their submachine guns or Kalashnikovs was overridden by the guns of Phoenix Force. Grenades were exploding along the battle line, a giant's fireworks peppering the undergrowth with shrapnel, and there seemed to be less hostile fire each time the thunder died away.

Katz freed a can of thermite from his harness rigging and held it in his left hand while he used his claw to jerk the pin. It was an awkward pitch, with an allowance for the slope that separated the Israeli from his target, but he didn't hesitate. A looping overhand, a burst of automatic fire to keep their heads down, and he watched the can thump down on target just behind the barricade of logs.

When the thermite detonated, smoking embers hot enough on impact to melt holes in tempered steel, arced skyward, streaming vapor trails. Before the roiling smoke from the initial blast had cleared, Katz saw the human torches up and running, weapons instantly forgotten as the white-hot coals devoured uniforms and naked flesh beneath.

Five times he locked the Colt Commander onto target, five times ripping off precision bursts that flattened human forms on impact. Five up, five down... and the Israeli knew there should have been at least one more. He double-checked, already sure, regardless of the drifting smoke and blackened flesh.

The seaplane's pilot hadn't been among them.

It was possible that he was still behind the barricade, killed instantly when the thermite can had exploded. Katzenelenbogen had to know for certain, and he broke from cover now, unmindful of the automatic fire that still played up and down the battle line.

Katz hit a combat crouch beside the smoking barricade, his rifle gripped in one hand, the prosthetic claw outstretched to steady him against the tumbled logs. A stench of burning flesh assailed his nostrils and made his stomach churn, but he couldn't seek cleaner air until he *knew*.

The Phoenix warrior made his move, hurdling the barricade with an agility surprising for a man his size and age. He held the Colt Commander ready to respond if any of the terrorists should still be capable of offering resistance, but there wouldn't be any opposition from the solitary man who shared his foxhole. From appearances, the thermite bomb had detonated almost in the dead man's lap; a dozen of the white-hot coals still smoldered in his clothing and flesh, but one that had struck him squarely on the nose had been enough. The center of his face was now a gaping wound, his nose and upper lip devoured by searing heat, together with a major portion of his cheeks. The guy's own mother wouldn't know him, but she would have known the smoking corpse had never been a blonde.

And he wasn't the seaplane's pilot.

The bastard had already slipped away before Katz had lobbed the thermite in. There was no other explanation, and he realized it must have been ridiculously easy in the firing and confusion. All he had to do was belly-down and worm his way through the encircling undergrowth. If he had been wise enough to keep his head and ass down on the way, there was no reason any of the Phoenix gunners should have noticed him.

Until he reached the plane.

If he escaped, Katz realized, their most persuasive piece of evidence against the Sandinistas would be lost. They could spend hours picking over corpses or examining Kalashnikovs and other arms that were a dime a dozen on the Third World market. But with the American in hand...

The Israeli heard the seaplane's motor cough and die. Again. He knew somehow that it would catch and hold the third time, that his quarry would be lost forever if he didn't move *right now*.

The Phoenix warrior was already on his feet and running, unmindful of the fact that he was now behind hostile lines with scattered firing still in progress. One of his men could pick him off as easily as any of the terrorists, but Katzenelenbogen had no time to waste. His quarry was escaping, and he wouldn't let that happen while he lived.

FROM HIS POSITION at the far end of the firing line, Calvin James was ready to cut off a terrorist retreat in the direction of the western shore. Not that the motherfuckers seemed intent on retreating at the moment; rather, their diminished ranks had been pulling back into a tight perimeter that almost cleared his line of fire.

Almost.

The Phoenix warrior's M-16 was fitted with an M-203 40 mm launcher, mounted underneath the rifle's barrel. With single-shot capacity and an effective range of some three hundred and fifty yards, the launcher let James drop explosive charges through the foliage from above, without the need for pinpoint accuracy. And it would bring the shrinking cadre well within his field of fire.

James fed a high-explosive can into the launcher, primed to blow on impact, cranked the muzzle skyward and squeezed off, already counting down the seconds until detonation. Sudden thunder ripped a patch of ferns and bracken from the earth and propelled the whole mess twenty feet into the air, a ministorm cloud raining mulch and sod. The hostile gunfire faltered momentarily, then cautiously resumed.

He had been too far left, and James corrected slightly, marking the position of the first explosion as he fed a fragmentation round into the launcher's smoking breech. No change in elevation; if the first round had come in a dozen paces to the right, it would have detonated squarely in their laps. Calvin braced himself to take the recoil, sighted, squeezed.

A different sort of blast this time, without the heavy baritone of high explosives. More a crack, if anything, and then the sound of countless razors slicing through the undergrowth, some of them smacking into tree trunks, others whining off stones. And many of them ripping into human flesh.

His enemies were screaming now... or some of them, at any rate. The hostile fire had faltered for an instant once again, and when it resumed, the ranks of operative gunners had been noticeably thinned. Their fire was still cohesive, still a threat, but they were being whittled down.

He worked another high-explosive round into the breech, squeezed off, already feeding in another when the smoky thunderclap erupted fifty yards away. For just a heartbeat, James was certain that he saw a human body airborne, tumbling like something from a circus acrobatics show... except that bits and pieces of this acrobat were gone, and he was trailing ugly crimson streamers as he somersaulted through the air.

Another frag round up the chute, another swarm of angry hornets overhead, and Calvin reckoned there could be no more than half a dozen gunners still responding from the hostile camp. He heard his comrades easing off their triggers at the same time, picking targets more methodically, with single rounds and three-round bursts.

He heard the seaplane's engine stutter into life and knew instinctively that something was about to go disastrously wrong. Katz had been interested in the pilot, more than anyone, and the Israeli would be pissed if the flier should somehow manage to escape the net. The engine was already revving, and there might be nothing James could do, but it was worth a try. And anything beat sitting on his ass while Katzenelenbogen's pigeon flew the coop.

He slammed a fresh mag home into the M-16's receiver, then cranked a buckshot round into the launcher's breech. The young black warrior was up and sprinting before the plane began its freedom run. James cleared the undergrowth and hit the rocky beach in double time, maintaining a rough collision course with the accelerating plane, continuing beyond the water's edge until he felt the slimy stones beneath his boots, lake water lapping at his groin.

The pilot saw him coming, tried to veer away and out of range, but it was too late. He was already hauling backward on the joystick, struggling for altitude, his pontoons skating on the surface, finally breaking contact. Calvin James was staring at the guy in profile as the plane flashed by him, and he gave the bastard everything he had. He heard the buckshot charge strike home amidships, watched a line of holes march down the fuselage as thirty tumblers raked the target, emptying the rifle's magazine in 2.5 seconds.

And for just a heartbeat, James was certain it had been too late. The craft was airborne, banking, drawing out of range. He couldn't bring the bastard back now; there was just no way. The Phoenix warrior cursed beneath his breath and resigned himself to watch the pigeon fly, when suddenly a plume of smoke erupted from the seaplane's undercarriage, reeking with the smell of oil.

"All *right*!" he shouted at the jungle, shaking one dark fist in the direction of the smoking aircraft.

There was still a chance the guy could pull it off of course. The seaplane's damage might not be critical; he might fly for miles before he lost it, if the thing came down at all. He might be safe across the border into Nicaragua by the time he had to land, and that would be the end of any hope of proving a connection with the terrorists.

But he would not.

As Calvin watched, dumbstruck, the seaplane canted sharply to the left, already losing altitude as it approached the north shore of the lake. It would be difficult for him to miss the tree line now, James saw. Unless he pulled up sharply, he was bound to lose it soon.

Instead of pulling up, the plane dipped even lower, seemingly resigned to answering gravity's demands. One wing tip grazed the surface of the water, and a graceful glide was instantly transformed into a crazy, screaming cartwheel, ending in the trees with an explosion that produced a rolling ball of oily flame. From where he stood, the Phoenix warrior could see trees and undergrowth in flames, ignited by the spill of burning gasoline and oil.

"God*damn* it!"

He had stopped the guy, all right, but he had stopped him too damned hard. He would catch hell from Katz when the gruff Israeli saw this mess. If Katz's pigeon hadn't died on impact, he was frying now, and they would need a dustpan for him by the time an extrication team could make its way along the lakeshore to the crash site.

It was over in the trees behind him, the reports of automatic fire already fading on a breeze that etched the lake with jagged ripples. Calvin James sloshed back to shore and sat down on a log at lakeside, thoroughly disgusted with himself.

They had neutralized the terrorists, but in the absence of persuasive evidence to mark the corpses as a Sandinista strike force, they were back at the beginning. If Managua chose to send another team of killers in next week, next month, the bastards would be innocent until someone collected evidence to prove them guilty.

Someone like Phoenix Force.

Dejected, even though there had been no immediate alternatives, James knew that he had blown it. Katzenelenbogen was approaching, storm clouds in his face, and Calvin braced himself to ride it out.

But Katz's anger was the least of it. The *worst* was coming back to do it all again because the evidence they needed had gone up in smoke and flames. The worst of it was knowing that their enemies were still alive and well despite the loss of valued pawns.

And, sure, the worst of it was knowing that each time you lost a little bit you lost it all.

☆ 5 ☆

The tall man stood alone, surveying the seemingly endless parade of headstones that stretched away from him in all directions. There were crosses, for the most part, punctuated here and there with Stars of David, all in pristine white, which pointedly belied their age. Some of the markers were made colorful by small bouquets of flowers, which would be removed before they had a chance to wilt. These graves were timeless, an eternal monument to human self-sacrifice.

Mack Bolan spent another moment in communion with the valiant dead of Arlington, Virginia. Buried here were countless men and women who had seen their duty and performed it under fire. From personal experience, he realized that few of them had cherished any thought of being heroes, and the unself-conscious nature of their sacrifice had made them all the more heroic. They had given up their lives for friends and allies who had depended on them, for the country that had nurtured them in freedom. And if freedom had been something less than perfect for a few of these heroic dead, if they had been reviled by fools at home because of race or creed, it mattered little in the end. These heroes had been large and wise enough to see the dream, sometimes obscured by sad reality, and they had pledged their lives to the preservation of that dream.

Bolan felt no apprehension in the presence of the dead. They held no terrors for him, cast no lurking shadows in his heart. He understood their motives, by and large, believed that they had done their duty as they had understood it, living up to values that had been instilled from infancy. And if a few of them had acted out of other motivations, seeking private gain perhaps, or searching out the killing grounds for darker reasons of their own, it mattered little in the last analysis. They had been gathered here because they had stood their ground and paid the price. And they were heroes.

Damn right.

For all his battlefield experience in Vietnam, the soldier knew that he would never rest among the peaceful dead of Arlington. His path had veered away from theirs, and Bolan had pursued his destiny to other hellgrounds, earning designation as an outlaw and a renegade. His private, everlasting war had violated the majority of civil laws in the United States and several foreign nations; when he finally met his end, the Executioner would die a hunted man.

But there was duty to be honored, all the same. As the respected dead of Arlington had seen their duty, followed it through hellfire and beyond, so Bolan recognized his obligation to the Universe...and to himself. He could no more forsake the everlasting war than he could voluntarily refuse to breathe. One course of action doomed the flesh; the other would irrevocably damn his soul.

He came to visit with the dead from time to time, as duty might allow, but on this afternoon he'd come to see the living. Bolan ambled past the rows of headstones, killing time until the scheduled rendezvous, unnoticed by the ever-present tourists and assorted mourners paying their respects. How many of the markers were inscribed with names that he would recognize on sight? Too many, sure. He meant to visit the memorial for casualties of Vietnam, if time and opportunity should ever coincide... but not today. For this one afternoon, the Executioner had seen enough of ghosts.

His contact was already waiting when he reached the Unknown Soldier's tomb. The honor guard ignored him as he sidled up to Hal Brognola, noting that the man from Justice seemed to be immersed in private memories.

"You're looking well," Brognola said when he became aware of Bolan's presence at his side.

"Must be the Geritol."

"I guess. It's been a while since we were here."

The Executioner didn't respond. Brognola was referring to a different sort of visit when the two of them had kept a life-or-death appointment with the renegade abductors of Hal's wife and children. Life-or-death could cut both ways, and their assailants had drawn the death card in a brief encounter that would never be inscribed in any tour guide of Arlington. It had been bloody work, and while it had turned out well enough for Hal and family, the man from Wonderland had changed somehow. A close examination might reveal new lines around his eyes and mouth, perhaps a few more graying hairs around his temples. He hadn't precisely aged, although that might be part of it, and none of them were getting any younger; rather, it appeared to Bolan that Brognola might have glimpsed his own mortality, the ultimate fragility of those he loved. The gruff Fed might not have seen his death, but he had come close enough to see its shadow, and that could be enough.

"I'm glad you could make it," Brognola said at last, emerging from his reverie.

Bolan waved a callused hand in dismissal.

"You have some time on hand?" Brognola asked.

"Depends."

"Okay." The man from Justice hesitated, then finally got it out. "I've got a little situation on my hands."

"I'm listening."

"Let's walk," Brognola said, sticking an unlit cigar between his teeth. "The doctor says I ought to give these up," he said, spitting out the shreds of the fine Havana leaf. "But I say what the hell. Nobody lives forever."

A faint alarm was chiming in the back of Bolan's mind. "But you've stopped smoking. Are you okay?"

"Mmm? Me? Oh, hell, it's not like that. I think it's being here, if you can figure that one. I don't like this place the way I used to."

"Understandable."

"I guess. About this situation..."

Bolan waited while his old friend hesitated, letting Hal get to it on his own. When he resumed, Brognola's voice and eyes were miles away.

"Have you been following the Nicaraguan situation?"

"Off and on."

"Okay. You know about the Contras, then, and all the flak in Congress over our continuing support. Some think it's Armageddon, others are afraid it's Vietnam revisited—or, anyway, the Bay of Pigs. Appropriations votes go up and down like fevers in the middle of a typhoid epidemic."

"So?"

"We've done some business with the Contra forces out of Stony Man," Hal told him. "Tagged a couple of their heavy hitters when they stepped outside Ortegaland, that kind of thing. You follow?"

Hal was nervous now, and Bolan didn't press him.

"Yes."

"Ten days ago your pals on Able Team went into Nicaragua to effect retrieval of a hostage. For the record, that's retrieval as in nab or neutralize."

The soldier understood that well enough. His first assignment out of Stony Man had been a similar retrieval, with a backup plan to execute the captive if it came to that.

"Go on."

"They found the mark, all right, but it was too damned late. Tough break, okay? The pisser was that an American was running the interrogation. Strike that. Not just an American—a goddamned *soldier*, Special Forces, out on furlough from his duty station in Honduras."

Bolan felt the short hairs on his neck begin to rise. A set of jagged fingernails were scraping painfully across a mental chalkboard, setting Bolan's teeth on edge and raising the alarm.

"That's double-checked?"

"No room for error. Ironman brought the bastard's dog tags out."

"There's more." And it wasn't a question.

Brognola nodded. "Tuesday afternoon Phoenix Force surprised a group of terrorists in Costa Rica. We were looking at them as suspected Sandinistas. Phoenix was assigned to confirm or deny."

Both men were conscious of the fact that Phoenix could accomplish neither prior to termination of the enemy. It was a given not worth mentioning.

"What happened?"

"Well, they bagged their men, all right, but not before the targets made connections with a Yankee pilot. Last name Baker, if you can believe the stencil on his uniform. As luck would have it, Mr. Baker and his plane went up in smoke before the boys could get a closer look. No hope of any positive ID under the circumstances."

"But?"

"Okay. His name and general description match another Special Forces trooper, also stationed in Honduras. He's been listed AWOL for the past two days, a no-show on a two-day pass. We've got a hunch they might as well stop waiting for him."

"What about the Sandinista linkup?"

"Nothing solid. Lots of surplus gear they could have picked up anywhere, some of it ours. A couple of them carried Uzis, but the standard arms were AK-47s. Zip again. Did you know you can buy Kalashnikovs right here in gun shops, if you settle for the semi-auto version? We import the goddamned things from China now—some kind of half-assed trade agreement."

They had reached the parking lot, and Bolan had no trouble picking out Brognola's four-door Chevrolet. It was the kind of unmarked car that city cops had finally given up because it was so obvious, complete with extra whip antennae for the two-way radio and special plates reserved for ranking government employees. All it needed was some touch-up paint, a red light mounted on the driver's side, and Hal would be prepared for hot pursuit of speeders.

"Take a ride with me?" Brognola asked.

For just a heartbeat, Bolan thought about declining, forcing Hal to state his business on the pavement, with the ranks of headstones visible across his shoulder. Anything could happen once he let himself be talked into the car. It might become his coffin if an ambuscade had been prepared. His options would be limited, his combat stretch reduced to maybe ten square feet, with that in motion. He would be a sitting duck.

Except that Hal wasn't a stranger. He was among the soldier's oldest friends, and Bolan trusted him implicitly. He knew that after everything they had been through together, after he had saved the big Fed's wife and children, Hal would cheerfully have died before he pulled a double cross. There was no guarantee, of course, that he hadn't been shadowed from his office. Anything was possible in Wonderland these days, he knew... but what the hell.

If Bolan couldn't trust Brognola, if he couldn't place his trust in someone, then his private war was all for nothing. And he wasn't prepared to face that possibility this afternoon, not with the heroic dead so close at hand.

"You working under cover?" Bolan asked, eyeing the Chevy.

Brognola scowled. "It's standard issue, I'm afraid. Austerity and secrecy don't always mix. It costs too much these days to travel incognito." The scowl became a sneaking grin. "Besides, she's got some extras that you won't find on the dealer's invoice."

And Bolan didn't need to ask about those hidden options as he slid into the shotgun seat. Brognola took the Chevy east on State Road 27 and caught the southbound ramp for Interstate 395. They drove in silence, Bolan keeping one eye on the sideview mirror, watching for a tail, relieved that there was none. Wherever Hal was taking him, he knew the man from Justice had his reasons. Neither of them said a word when Hal swerved sharply, cutting over several other lanes to catch the ramp for Alexandria.

The Little River Highway carried them to Cameron Station Military Reservation, but Brognola drove on past the gate and sentries, never glancing left or right as Little River crossed a tributary of the wide Potomac and was born again as Duke Street on the other side. Another mile or two, and Hal obeyed the signs directing him to the George Washington Masonic National Memorial. The parking lot was far from overflowing at that hour, but Brognola steered his Chevy to the outskirts of the lot and parked beside a solitary Continental, big and black, with deeply tinted windows.

"What's this?" the soldier asked, already certain that he knew the answer.

"Someone wants to see us."

"Hal—"

"I know, we've been through this before. But dammit, Striker, this is urgent. Top priority."

"It's always urgent."

"Give the man a chance, okay? The white flag's out. You walk away regardless. Can it cost that much to listen?"

"Hal, the horse is dead. Stop beating it."

"I wish I could, believe me." Silence hung between them for a moment, fragile as a pane of glass and tough as tensile steel. It took a lot for Hal to pierce that barrier, and Bolan heard the effort in his voice. "I know I've got no space to ask for favors after all that's happened, all you've done, but I believe this is important. If you'll listen to the man, I know you'll think so, too."

"And either way, I walk."

"You've got my word."

"No promises."

"Agreed."

Two husky men in carbon-copy business suits and mirrored shades had interposed themselves between the Lincoln and the Chevrolet. As Bolan and Brognola stood at ease, another gunner surfaced on the driver's side, his eyes invisible behind the standard-issue aviator glasses, hands concealed inside the car. He was the backup, Bolan knew, and even if they took the two in front somehow, he would be looking down their throats with something like an Uzi or a SPAS-12 riot gun, secure behind the armored Lincoln as he dropped them in their tracks. It was a decent system for a limited engagement such as this, but Bolan didn't plan on testing the odds.

Brognola passed his Smith & Wesson .38 revolver to the nearest suit and was discreetly patted down for any concealed weapons. Bolan watched his old friend's face for traces of offense but found only boredom and impatience there. The other bookend tensed as Bolan reached inside his jacket, hauling out the sleek Beretta, passing it reluctantly across as Hal had done. The soldier spread his arms, endured the probing hands and smiled when he thought of the reaction these college boys might have had if he hadn't been packing light.

When they were satisfied, the suits each nodded to their backup, and the third man spent another moment staring Bolan down, his eyes impossible to read behind the mirrored shades. "Okay," he said at last, and disappeared behind the wheel, prepared to cope with any unexpected incident inside the car itself.

One of the suits held Bolan's door, but he let Hal go first, following Brognola's backside like a circus elephant and settling into the empty jump seat, facing the Continental's stern. He recognized the Man on sight before Brognola spoke.

"Good morning, Mr. President."

☆ 6 ☆

"Good morning, Hal," the chief executive replied. He turned to Bolan with a smile. "The Secret Service hates it when I pull these little stunts."

"That's understandable."

"Of course. But there are some requirements of my office that cannot be carried out on national TV with agents lined up like the Rockettes in the background. If the press knew I was here, for instance, there'd be hell to pay."

"They won't be hearing it from me," the Executioner assured him.

"I'm aware of that. And please believe that I appreciate your coming here on such short notice."

Bolan glanced at Hal and caught him squirming in his seat.

"My pleasure, sir."

"I've been informed of your reluctance to resume our previous association. I respect your feelings in the matter, and I haven't asked you here to try to change your mind. But I'll be honest with you, sir. I need your help. America needs help."

The Executioner said nothing, waiting for the President to state his case. The reference to America didn't strike Bolan as corny or melodramatic; neither did it automatically commit him to the cause. He had already come this far, and he would listen to the man. No more, no less. If he decided to enlist for the duration, he would base his choice on facts and instinct, on the call of duty, rather than on trumpet blasts or the ruffling of flags.

"You filled him in?" the President asked Hal.

"Bare bones," the man from Justice answered quietly.

"All right. You know that we have evidence of personal involvement with the Sandinista forces by at least two members of the U.S. Special Forces stationed in Honduras. We're inclined to think there may be more."

He hesitated, putting on a frown that might have startled even hardened members of the White House press corps.

"No! I'm hedging, dammit, and we don't have time for games. We *know* there is a great deal more involved than individuals moonlighting with the enemy. If that was all of it, I'd have their asses slapped in Leavenworth before the sun went down, and we could all breathe easy. But it seems the turncoat bastards have support, including certain members of the general staff. You follow me?"

"I think so, sir."

And Bolan followed him, damn straight. The implication was that assorted covert contacts with the Sandinista forces hadn't come about by accident, but instead had been engineered by ranking military officers. But to what end? The army might have changed since Bolan had done his stint in Vietnam, but he wasn't aware of any socialists or bleeding liberals on the general staff, and the regime of Daniel Ortega in Managua was the next best thing to Castro when it came to boiling military blood.

"I've been aware for some time now of discontent among some members of the general staff, as well as ranking officers at the CIA," the President continued. "They believe we've been too soft on Nicaragua for too long. We're coddling the Communists, they say, and jeopardizing every friendly nation in the Western hemisphere."

The sentiment didn't surprise Mack Bolan. You could hear the same thing any day by turning on the radio or television, tuning in the latest news from Washington where hard-line congressmen were seeking more appropriations, butting heads with die-hard liberals propounding isolationism. Bolan would have been surprised if members of the military hadn't groused among themselves about the "fall" of Nicaragua and the rising tide of socialism elsewhere in Latin America.

"Our most recent intelligence seems to indicate a plan of sorts already in the works," the President continued. "Evidence collected by Hal's people in the field has helped to put the matter in perspective. How's your history?"

"I passed," the Executioner replied.

"You may recall the Reichstag fire?"

Mack Bolan nodded.

"Based upon our present information, I believe that certain members of the army general staff and the CIA are trying to create a situation that will force America to intervene with troops in Nicaragua. Not a Reichstag fire, perhaps, but something similar. An armed incursion into Costa Rica, for example. And it might have done the trick if certain unnamed individuals hadn't been there to pull the plug in time."

"You've spoken of intelligence and evidence," the soldier interjected. "If you have their names—"

"I have the names, all right...or most of them, at any rate. And you'll be hearing them if you decide to take on this assignment. As for evidence, let's say that I'm convinced, but it would never stand in court as is."

The Executioner could see assorted puzzle pieces drifting into place, and he was not excited by the prospect of the picture that was forming in his mind.

"You may not be aware," the President went on, "that Franklin Roosevelt was briefly threatened with a military coup in 1935. It's not the kind of thing historians are proud of. Certain members of the general staff convinced themselves that a continuation of the New Deal meant the ruination of America. Philosophies aside, I think we'll all agree it's best their putsch was quietly aborted in the planning stages. Later, John and Robert Kennedy had fears of covert military action in the missile crisis. Looking back at Dallas, who can say for certain they were wrong?"

"Seven Days in May," Brognola quipped, immediately looking sorry for the comment.

"Yes, except that that was fiction. We are forced to deal with facts."

"Is there some indication of a plot against the White House?" Bolan asked, his stomach knotting at the implications.

"Not as yet," the President replied, but Bolan marked a certain hesitancy in his voice. "But if the plan to light a fuse in Nicaragua should succeed—or if the plotters should be scattered somehow, rather than eradicated...well, who knows?"

Mack Bolan knew, damn right. He knew enough from grim experience to realize that ruthless and ambitious men would stop at nothing to achieve their goals. He knew the Oval Office wasn't sacrosanct to men—in uniform and out—who felt betrayed by federal policies. The sort of men who saw their tiny world turned upside down by forces they could never understand and reached for guns instinctively, believing they could change the course of history through violence. They might be correct to some degree, but Bolan didn't wish to contemplate the changes they might bring about within a democratic state. He had no wish to see the White House or the Bill of Rights set up as targets in a shooting gallery.

He was familiar with the sort of men the President described. In Colorado, years before, he had aborted the abduction of another chief executive, exposing a respected military officer with years of service on the firing line as the technician of the plot. It had remained for yet another confrontation at the White Sands proving grounds for Bolan finally to settle that account in full.

He was familiar with men like Thurston Ward, a millionaire and self-appointed "savior" of America whose master plan involved unleashing a mutant plague bacillus in the Caribbean. Men like General Jeremiah Blackwell, whose insane desire to be the King of Africa could only be expunged with blood. Men like Colonel "Can-Do Charlie" Rosky, veteran of Vietnam turned mercenary gunner in the interests of a holy cause. Men like Tate Monroe, a dying oil tycoon who used his final days to plot the overthrow of Mexico's elected government.

The world was filled with loony-tune messiahs. Their logic might be convoluted to the point of nonexistence, and their causes might appear pathetic on the surface, but such men were extremely dangerous. Their fierce commitment to ideals, which other mortals couldn't fathom, set such men apart; their willingness to kill whole populations in pursuit of nebulous nirvanas made them deadly.

Calculating odds and angles in his mind, already certain he would take the mission, Bolan said, "There's too much stretch. I don't see any way to roll them up without some members getting word of trouble and escaping. If I start in Washington, you're almost sure to lose the shooters. If we kick off in Honduras, you could lose the brains before we work back up the ladder."

"We've anticipated the logistics problem," Hal replied before the President could speak. "You'd work the Latin end exclusively, with Able Team and Phoenix Force as backup."

"I have other plans for those in Washington," the chief executive told Bolan vaguely. "When the time comes, they will all be taken care of, I assure you."

Bolan couldn't say precisely what that meant, but he decided that it didn't really matter in the long run. While their punishment might not be terminal, he had a feeling that the brains behind the plot in Washington would rather die than face whatever Hal Brognola and the President had in mind. But the consequences they would have to face would depend on the relative success of Bolan's mission to the south.

If Bolan failed to bag the military arm of the conspiracy, if even one or two hard-core conspirators escaped, the plot might roll ahead on automatic pilot...or it might be radically diverted toward a secondary target. Like the President himself, for instance, or any number of "defeatist" congressmen whose votes had stalled appropriations for the Contras, or members of the general staff who had abided by their oaths to serve the Constitution with their lives, or spokesmen for the media whose editorials had questioned the expediency of supporting counterrevolutionary actions in the western hemisphere.

There seemed to be no end of likely targets if the game went sour, and the warrior knew that it would be an all-or-nothing situation once he took on the mission. If even one of his opponents was permitted to escape, permitted to survive, he would have failed.

"I'll do my best," he told the President, and he could almost feel Brognola wilting with relief beside him.

"Excellent. The two of you can make your own arrangements. As for transportation, covers and the like, you have my full cooperation and assurance that the chiefs of staff will show you every courtesy."

"It doesn't reach that high, then?"

"No, thank God." The President held up a hand, his thumb and index finger separated by perhaps a millimeter. "But we came that close."

Brognola's voice cut through the momentary silence. "I've pulled in Able Team and Phoenix Force," he told the Executioner. "They're coming in to Stony Man, and you can meet them there. We'll cover all the players when you get together, lay out the logistics on this thing."

Brognola must have caught the look on Bolan's face; he got no further in his spiel before his voice dried up and blew away.

"At Stony Man?"

"Why not? It's totally secure, and Kurtzman's got his toys on-line to handle the intelligence we need. There's no place else where we can carry off a meet like this without some danger of exposure."

And of course Hal knew "why not," as Bolan knew that he would have to play along. The memories were painful, sure, but they weren't the open, bleeding wounds that they had been. The Executioner had come a long way from the grief that was a flip side to the coin of death. His heart had mended, and with any luck at all, it would be stronger at the broken places.

So it was Stony Man, and hell, why not? It would be good to see the Bear again, the men of Able Team and Phoenix Force. Too good, perhaps. The Executioner would have to keep his mind on track, remember that the mission was a one-time-only hit-and-git. He wasn't signing on for any long-term tour of duty this late in the game.

"Okay," he said, and let it go at that.

"It's settled, then," the President announced, his eyes returning to Mack Bolan's face. "I want to thank you personally for your help."

"Let's wait and see if thanks are necessary."

"I have every confidence. Of course, if something *should* go wrong, some leak, perhaps..."

"The White House has no knowledge of my presence in the area."

"Unfortunately, no."

The soldier smiled. "I wouldn't have it any other way."

The President looked momentarily confused, but it wasn't his favorite expression, and he quickly shifted back into the famous frown.

"I honestly regret your present circumstances, Mr. Bolan. Possibly if we had been in office when all this began..."

He let the statement trail away, already recognizing its absurdity. "All this"—the soldier's everlasting war—had been no more a White House problem at the outset than it was today. From time to time, the Oval Office occupants had tried to interpose themselves between Mack Bolan and his destiny. They hadn't been successful in the past, although his private duty sometimes coincided with the needs of public Washington, and the incumbent wouldn't be successful now. The Executioner was like a sentient force of nature, violating every law of physics as he constantly pursued the path of most resistance, homing on his targets as the need arose, as duty called. He had already tried the sanctioned route, allowing Hal Brognola and the White House to select his targets for him, and despite a string of hard-won victories against the savages, it hadn't worked. Betrayal from above had sabotaged the Phoenix program, costing precious lives and driving Bolan back into the wilderness, an outlaw hunted by both sides.

But he wasn't uncomfortable in the wilderness. He felt at home there, with the predators and prey around him, living on the edge from day to day. He was dependent now on no one but himself, and if he chose to work with allies—his brother, Johnny, assorted others—they were allies of his own selection, warriors he would trust implicitly with life itself.

In Vietnam, despite his leadership of a successful penetration team, the Executioner had done his boldest work alone, behind hostile lines. He operated best when he wasn't concerned about the safety—and the possible mistakes—of others, when his mind was free to concentrate upon the enemy and his destruction. Bolan was a living testament to what a single man could do with guts, determination and a driving sense of duty.

He dreaded going back to Stony Man, revisiting the slaughter pen where precious lives had been sacrificed to turn back the tide of treason. In vain? Perhaps. His late experience with Hal Brognola proved that there would always be more traitors waiting in the wings. If he took his business back beneath the government umbrella, Bolan would be rubbing shoulders with potential enemies each waking moment, constantly distracted by the thought that this one might betray him, that one might intend to sell him out.

Distractions of that sort could get a combat soldier killed, and while the Executioner wasn't afraid of death, he didn't court it foolishly. Whenever possible, he weighed the odds and angles in a given situation, opting out if there appeared to be no chance at all for victory.

Unless he heard the duty call.

Like now.

The odds against him in Honduras would be long and mean, worse still if he was forced to enter Nicaragua proper. From the moment he accepted the assignment, Bolan was exposed to danger both from enemies and so-called "friends," subjected to the possibility of leaks that were a way of life in Washington. If word of his involvement with the White House should get out...

But that would be the President's concern, and he was clearly willing to accept the risks. The Man was worried, Bolan knew that much. He might be frightened, but if so, it wasn't showing yet. Unable to succeed himself in office, he would have no problem at the polls if someone broke the story, but impeachment was another matter altogether. Personal involvement with the world's most-wanted felon should be adequate to crank the old heave-ho equipment up in Congress. Charges of obstructing justice, harboring a fugitive, complicity in murder and the like would certainly ensure conviction and removal from the highest office in the land. Once that was done, it would be time to file the criminal complaints and see about a term in federal prison for the one-time chief executive.

The President had obviously weighed those risks before he had placed his call to Hal Brognola, asking for a sit-down with the Executioner. The Man hadn't survived this long in politics by underestimating the potential dangers of a given hazard situation. If he thought the risks were justified, worthwhile, then who was Bolan to dissuade him?

Having made a life-style out of risking life itself, the Executioner could understand the mind behind that famous face. The Man had seen his duty, and despite all of its attendant risks he couldn't turn aside. The danger to his office, to the country that he served, wouldn't dry up and blow away spontaneously. Swift, decisive action was required, unfettered by procrastination in the courts. Sometimes—*this* time—it was enough to simply recognize the threat, to *know* of an atrocity in progress, and the President wasn't inclined to let a massacre proceed while agents tried to gather evidence for an indictment.

The President had seen where duty lay. The Executioner had known it all along. Together, with determination and perhaps a bit of luck, they just might make a difference in the scheme of things.

"I'll do my best," the warrior said again, and shook the strong right hand that was extended to him.

After retrieving their weapons, Bolan and Brognola stood together and watched the Continental disappear in traffic.

"I can wait while you get packed," Hal said.

"I'm packed right now."

"I'll drive."

"You bet your ass."

☆ 7 ☆

Shenandoah National Park lies along the crest of Virginia's Blue Ridge Mountains, sprawled between Front Royal to the north and Waynesboro to the south. From Skyline Drive, the only thruway running north to south along the Blue Ridge crest, tourists may observe the Shenandoah Valley to the west or the eastern coastal Piedmont. With scenery unparalleled throughout the eastern states, the park is heavily forested with hardwoods and conifers except for an occasional grassy meadow along the crest. Stony Man Mountain, one of the tallest peaks in the range at an altitude of 4,010 feet, overshadows Skyline Drive and broods above the Shenandoah Valley, eighty air miles west of Washington, D.C.

The valley's soil is steeped in blood and history. Here, Stonewall Jackson passed from glory into immortality with his classic Valley Campaign in the American Civil War. From 1861 through early 1865, the Shenandoah was a "valley of humiliation" for the Union troops who tried in vain to oust Confederates from their strategic strongholds. Here, for four long years, the simple courage of those men in butternut and gray withstood the power of a war machine impossibly superior in personnel and arms. It didn't matter in the end that they were fighting for a cause already lost, condemned by history as evil;

sometimes, in the heat of battle, honest courage justifies itself. The fighting spirit of those valiant men in blue and gray, the fallen warriors of both sides, had consecrated Shenandoah Valley and made the rolling countryside a living shrine to courage under fire.

With its proximity to Washington, its relative seclusion in the midst of so much tourist traffic, Shenandoah Valley was a natural location for the hard command post of Brognola's Sensitive Operations Group, aka the Phoenix Project. Nestled in the shadow of the peak from which it drew its name, Stony Man Farm was an enigma, melding modern high-tech expertise with mystery. The "farm's" location, even its existence, had been strictly need-to-know from the beginning; there were no more than twenty people in the whole of Wonderland who knew about the place at all, and less than half of those could point their finger at a map with any accuracy. The Phoenix base could run on its own in case of an emergency, but SOG wasn't a secret government unto itself. Responsive to the Oval Office, handling the dirty jobs that other agencies found inconvenient or impossible, the personnel of SOG were picked in equal measures for their loyalty and abilities.

There had been one brief problem, true, but it was never spoken of within the Stony Man perimeter. Survivors needed no reminder of the treason in their ranks, which had resulted in the loss of precious lives and the banishing of one among them into outer darkness. New additions to the team would never hear the story to begin with; it wasn't something they would need to know.

Observed by aircraft—or by satellite—the base appeared to be a rich man's hideaway, perhaps, or the executive retreat of some well-heeled conglomerate. The house was large—three stories—with a tractor barn and other outbuildings nearby, but even infrared photography wouldn't reveal the secrets locked away inside. A private airstrip in the northwest sector took advantage of the natural terrain; it had been built to handle whirlybirds and Lear-size jets, but it could take the latest navy-air force fighters as well. If tourists lost their way on Skyline Drive and happened down the narrow access road that served the farm, they might be treated to a scene of tractors in the field, or pastures lying fallow in the winter. If they tried to get beyond the barbed-wire fencing, they would see another side of Stony Man; a side that none would soon forget, provided they survived.

It was a hundred miles from Arlington to Stony Man by car, and the drive took Hal two hours with a stop for lunch in Warrenton. Mack Bolan ordered light and scarcely touched his food, preoccupied with private thoughts and memories, while Hal wolfed down his burger, fries and milk shake. They had driven almost fifty miles in silence, Bolan speaking only when Brognola spoke to him, his answers terse, distracted. Hal knew what the guy was going through, and there was nothing in the world that he could do to make it any better.

Going home again was never easy—some guys made a living out of telling others that it was impossible—but Bolan would be forced to try it all the same. Throughout the early days of his new war, the base at Stony Man had been his home, of sorts, and he had left a portion of his heart there. In the wake of everything that had befallen him, the Executioner had never contemplated going back until Brognola had played his hole card in the presence of the chief executive.

He might have felt betrayed, but somehow Bolan didn't. He and Hal went too far back to harbor grudges.

The man from Justice had a job to do, and he was in too deep. Instinctively the lifeline had been thrown toward Bolan, and the Executioner had picked it up, as Hal had known he must. It didn't matter that the men of Able Team and Phoenix Force could almost certainly have done the job without him. Bolan knew about the mission now and the stakes involved, and he could no more pass his turn than he could simply drop his everlasting war and walk away from it. At the heart of it, the mission and his war were inextricably entwined; suppression of the savages was what Mack Bolan's war was all about.

From Warrenton they followed Highway 211 on through Sperryville, in Rappahannock County, to the interchange with Skyline Drive. Their destination lay beyond the Blue Ridge crest, but Hal enjoyed the scenery, and he explained that driving south to Swift Run Gap and Highway 33 would put them at the farm no later— and perhaps a good deal sooner—than the lowland run down sinuous Highway 340. It didn't matter to Mack Bolan either way; with scarcely an acknowledgment, he settled back to scan the silent trees on either side of Skyline Drive.

Their turnoff was an unmarked access road, the entrance left deliberately overgrown with weeds and inhospitable in its appearance. It would take a foolish tourist or determined off-road sportsman to desert the friendly pavement for that one-lane track to nowhere. Several had tried, but none had ever breached the farm itself.

It had taken a traitor from within, the Executioner recalled, to break security at Stony Man and very nearly bring the Phoenix program down in flames. Experienced with treachery, the soldier had no difficulty in believing that a group of military officers might turn against the government they served, endeavoring to make new policy instead of merely taking orders from the chief executive. The problem lay not in believing, but in coping with the threat before it could be realized in further acts of violence.

Hal put his unmarked Chevy through the turn, and they bounced along for twenty minutes on a rutted road before they struck new pavement and the roadway widened once again. They had already passed two hidden checkpoints, Bolan knew. If they hadn't been expected at the first, a truck or tractor would have blocked their way before they'd reached the blacktop, gunners closing from the trees behind in case the "tourists" proved to be a threat.

But Hal had phoned ahead, of course, secure in his knowledge that the Executioner would not—could not—refuse the mission. Bolan might have been upset by Hal's presumption, but he knew the Fed too well to take offense, and there were other matters on his mind just now.

Like going home.

The trees began to clear, and Bolan had a glimpse of rolling meadows as the Chevy trundled downslope toward the farm. The one and only gate was situated at the northeast corner of the property, observed by cameras hidden in the nearby trees and patrolled discreetly by a "farmhand" who consumed the daylight hours, every day, with efforts to repair his pickup truck. In fact, the truck worked perfectly, as an intruder would have learned if he or she had tried to breach the northern fence. Because Brognola was expected with a passenger, the farmer had no qualms about admitting him this morning, never bothering to reach for the Beretta tucked inside the waistband of his overalls or the Uzi resting on the pickup's seat. To play it safe, however, he would radio ahead with the news of their arrival in case someone was dozing at the television monitors and missed the only action of the day.

The open fields were soon behind them, and they drove through scattered trees for half a mile before the manor house came into view. For just an instant—no more than a heartbeat, really—Bolan felt as if the intervening months had been erased somehow, and that he had never really left the farm for good. It was an eerie feeling, and he was uncomfortable now. It might not be impossible to visit home again, but he had no intention whatsoever of returning as a full-time tenant.

"The old town looks the same," Brognola warbled, "as I step down off the train—"

"You're no Tom Jones."

"I'm hurt. You've cut me to the quick."

"I seen me duty, an' I done it."

"Seriously, though, you'll find that things are pretty much the same, except for the additional security. We've beefed up the perimeter defenses, and we've also gone the extra mile on personnel. We put them through the polygraph and vocal stress evaluator, with the Pentothal as backup if we have the slightest shadow of a doubt. The shrinks and medics help us all they can. We test for drugs and mental aberration, with an in-depth physical from A to Z. We run a background check that would have weeded out J. Edgar Hoover, with a reexamination quarterly. There's no such thing as foolproof, but you're looking at the next best thing."

"I'll trust you," Bolan said...and meant it, as far as Hal Brognola was concerned. He knew some of the other personnel at Stony Man, the ones who had survived the assault, and he trusted them as well. As for the rest, the soldier didn't plan to be around that long.

Brognola pulled around behind the manor house and parked his Chevy near the tractor barn. It was a short walk back, but someone was already waiting for them on the wide back porch. The instant recognition brought a sudden lump to Bolan's throat. He swallowed angrily and forged ahead.

Despite confinement to a wheelchair, Aaron Kurtzman was a hulking figure. Dubbed "the Bear" in adolescence, when he'd been a member of his high school wrestling team, he had progressed to pumping iron as an adult. But Kurtzman's intellect had blossomed in proportion to his strapping body. Aaron was a genius with computers and communications, and with cooperation from the likes of Hermann Schwarz, he had designed or modified most of the high-tech gear in use at Stony Man. A charter member of the Phoenix project, he had proved himself invaluable to the team.

A bullet in the lower spine had taken Kurtzman's legs away from him, and now his wheelchair was another grim reminder of the treacherous assault that had almost finished SOG. Andrzej Konzaki, April Rose and others had been killed in the engagement that had left Aaron paralyzed below the waist, but the Bear had managed to survive his wounds and had come back on full duty once the therapists and surgeons had finally cut him loose. Kurtzman might not have legs to stand on, but maneuvering a wheelchair had already doubled his considerable upper body strength, and the computer whiz's mind was vibrantly alive, apparently unscathed by his near-lethal ordeal.

Bolan shook the hand that Kurtzman offered, doggedly refusing to surrender in the viselike grip. "Long time," he said at last.

"Too long."

"You're looking good."

"I feel like a half a million bucks."

"Not bad, considering inflation."

"Same old Striker."

"Same old Bear."

Kurtzman led the way inside, and Bolan noticed that he had resisted the temptation of conversion to a powered chair. As Bolan and Brognola trailed him, Aaron wheeled the standard model with a speed and effortless precision that belied his size and weight. The muscles of his forearms bulged like cables underneath the flesh, and Bolan noted also that his hands were bare, unlike so many occupants of wheelchairs who resort to wearing gloves. If Kurtzman had a choice, he would attack a problem in the hardest way imaginable, bending circumstances to his will instead of looking for the easy out. You had to admire a guy like that...and wonder, sometimes, how he pulled it off in spite of everything.

On entering the ground floor level, they found themselves in the dining room where Bolan had so often bolted hasty meals before departing for the hellgrounds. The dining room was empty, but before they had a chance to steer for the security HQ another member of the Phoenix team emerged from the adjacent kitchen, stopping dead at the sight of Kurtzman and his two companions.

"Oh, excuse me."

For an instant Bolan felt his heart freeze inside his chest, constricted by the sudden shock of déjà vu. When it began to throb again, the rush of blood was almost dizzying; he fought an urge to stretch a hand out and brace himself against the grips of Kurtzman's chair.

For just a microsecond there, he had believed that he was seeing April Rose. The hair was wrong, of course: ash blond instead of rich auburn. The face was different, if no less beautiful, and while the lady's jumpsuit did its utmost to conceal her figure, ample nature couldn't be disguised.

Kurtzman beamed at her. "No problem, Barb. In fact, I'm glad you're here. You know the boss, of course, but it's high time you met his sidekick." Aaron wheeled his chair around, half facing Bolan, a playful grin already crinkling his features. "Barbara, say hello to Colonel Phoenix. Colonel Phoenix, Barbara Price. My legs."

"They're looking better all the time," Brognola quipped.

The lady held a slim hand out to Bolan, and he took it gingerly, releasing it at once.

"A pleasure, Colonel Phoenix."

"That's *ex*-colonel. You can call me John."

And Bolan was surprised at just how easily it all came back—the cover name, the easy banter with his troops. Except that they weren't his troops, not anymore. He had divorced himself from Stony Man and SOG forever, kindling his bridges into flame deliberately with the white heat of his rage. The fire had faded over time, reduced itself to glowing embers, but it wouldn't do to think of this as home. The Executioner was merely passing through en route to Hell.

Before the lady could respond to Bolan, Kurtzman intervened. "I've got some business to discuss with Fearless Leader, Barb," he said, ignoring Hal Brognola's pained expression. "Would you show the colonel to his quarters for me? He's in number seven."

Hesitating for the barest fraction of an instant, Barbara Price responded with a smile. "Of course." She turned to Bolan, and the smile remained in place, although it looked a little strained. "Can I have someone get your luggage, Col—I mean—"

"I travel light," he told her simply. "This is it."

"Well, then, if you'll just follow me..."

He did, across the dining room and toward the entryway and its ascending staircase.

"We have elevators," she informed him, "but they're at the far end of the house. The stairs are closer to your room."

"I know."

She hesitated on the landing, glancing back at Bolan in surprise. "You've been at Stony Man before?"

"A time or two."

"I'm sorry, I assumed...that is...well, dammit, I don't know exactly *what* I mean."

They shared an easy laughter, and the soldier pulled himself up short again before he could allow himself to feel at home inside those walls.

"You thought I was some kind of drop-in VIP," he offered lightly, "kissing up to Hal for help on some pet project."

"Something like that," she agreed reluctantly, and Bolan saw the color rising in her cheeks. "You've found me out."

"Relax. I know the feeling. Amateurs get in the way, regardless of their good intentions. You don't strike me as an amateur."

They reached the door of number seven, and she lingered on the threshold while he checked the room, as if the act of entering might somehow have committed her to something more.

"We keep the bathrooms stocked with various necessities," she told him. "But you know that. If you think of anything at all that you might need..."

"I'm fine," he told her. "Thank you," he added, knowing he dared not face her as she closed the door behind her.

It wasn't the room that he had previously occupied, the bed where April Rose had come to him on nights when neither one of them could bear to be alone. He offered up a silent word of thanks to Kurtzman for the kindness. There were ghosts enough around the farm without inviting them to lie beside him in the darkness.

Bolan checked the closet and found a pair of uniforms already hanging there. They were his size: one khaki, one in olive drab. He smiled and closed the door again, then retraced his steps along the silent corridor and down the stairs to exit through the front this time. He needed time to think, and he made a circuit of the big house, lingering beside the tractor barn for several moments, listening to distant sounds of battle in his mind. For just a moment he could almost smell the gunsmoke, hear the small arms crackle as his men regrouped behind the barn and drove the enemy before them into bloody death. For just a moment he could almost feel the deadweight of a slender body in his arms.

Enough!

The Executioner had laid those ghosts to rest in fearful dreams that churned with smoke and fire until he'd woken up drenched in perspiration, fingers knotted in the sheets as if around the throat of some undying adversary. He had journeyed home to Pittsfield in his search for answers, finding some, but only on the razor's edge of death itself. The past had the power to haunt him still, but he wouldn't allow the ghosts to rule his life.

He heard the helicopter well before its silhouette was visible against the crystal sky. Company was on the way, but Bolan saw no need to second-guess identities. If it was Phoenix Force or Able Team, some others yet unknown to him, the Executioner would meet them in due time as their involvement in the mission was revealed. Brognola like to stage his introductions, and the Bear had already upstaged him once, with Barbara Price. It wasn't Bolan's place to write the script this time. He might have some revisions farther down the line, a few surprises up his sleeve for all concerned, but he wasn't about to tamper with Brognola's introduction of the cast.

All ghosts behind him for the moment, Bolan turned and started back in the direction of the house to meet the new arrivals. As he walked, he was surprised to find that he was looking forward to it, as a quarterback looks forward to the kick-off in a major game, as warriors in the midst of desperate battle eagerly await the chance to face their opposition.

☆ 8 ☆

It was Phoenix Force, arriving on a shuttle flight from Dulles with their gear. The sunburned warriors were unloading from a transport van when Bolan spotted them, and he descended from the ranch house porch to meet the team halfway. The gruff Israeli, Yakov Katzenelenbogen, an unaccustomed smile already brightening his weathered face, saw Bolan first. His good left hand was reaching out for Bolan's as the Executioner drew up beside the van.

"Brognola told us he was hoping you'd be in on this," Katz said. "I didn't think he'd pull it off."

"I didn't think so, either."

"Welcome back."

"We'll see."

He moved among the others, shaking hands and reaffirming bonds of militant camaraderie. The Cuban, Rafael Encizo, smiled so broadly that his face appeared in danger of exploding. Gary Manning, the Canadian ballistics and explosives expert, seemed relieved to find the Executioner on board. The former SAS commando, David McCarter, was reserved as usual, but his pleasure at their meeting was no less sincere. The newest member of the team was Calvin James, a burly soldier with the ebony complexion of his warrior ancestors. Bolan wondered briefly whether it was Calvin's relative position on the ladder of seniority or something else that made him seem so distant.

James had come aboard as a replacement for the only Phoenix warrior killed in battle to the present time. Keio Ohara had combined a martial artist's expertise with something close to wizardry in electronics. He had been trained in demolitions and as a paracommando...but none of that had made him bulletproof. His death in combat had surprised and shaken the survivors of the team; aware that it could happen anytime, to any one of them, the sudden shock of grim reality had given pause to Katzenelenbogen and his fellow warriors.

There had been no rivalry, no obvious resentment, when Brognola had selected James as Keio's stand-in. The Executioner had heard of Calvin James, the guy had proved himself repeatedly in battle, and there had been no complaints from any of the veteran Phoenix warriors.

Not your problem, Bolan told himself, and put the matter out of mind, returning to the manor house with Katzenelenbogen and the others. Kurtzman and Brognola were already waiting on the porch to greet them. Bolan caught a glimpse of Barbara Price beyond the open doorway, but she was obviously busy with other business, and she disappeared without a backward glance.

"We've got a big convention coming," Kurtzman told them. "Salesmen from Topeka. Some of you will have to double up unless you want to try the barracks."

"What?" McCarter feigned surprise. "No penthouse suite?"

"No penthouse, period," the Bear replied. "I've got you booked as follows: Manning and McCarter, number one, Cal and Rafael, next door in number eight, and Katz, you're alone in number two."

"How'd that work out?" McCarter asked.

"RHIP," James told him with a grin. "Rank has its privileges."

"That's bloody rank, all right."

"If you need any help with gear, feel free to lug it up yourselves," said Kurtzman. "All our porters are on strike, as usual."

"Last time I book this joint for a vacation."

One by one the Phoenix warriors disappeared inside until Mack Bolan, Kurtzman and Brognola were alone.

"That just leaves Able in the wind," Hal said. "I got a telex that their flight out of Los Angeles was held up on a technical. They'll be in late tonight or first thing in the morning."

"Lyons probably connected with some sweetheart," Kurtzman said.

"I wouldn't put it past him."

Silence spun its fragile web between them for a moment until Bolan broke the clinging strands.

"You've done a good job, Aaron."

"Nothing to it. After all the smoke cleared, we had money up the ying-yang for a while. The CIA was so embarrassed that they were offering to let us tap their secret fund carte blanche."

"It took a damn sight more than money, and you know it."

"Well...I had some help."

"Damned little," Hal put in. "The rest of us were marking time until they posted him for active duty," he informed the Executioner. "If something works around this place today, this guy is probably responsible."

"Go and pull the other leg," Bear said. "It couldn't hurt."

"I'm serious, goddamn it!"

"Well...I *did* have help. Keio and Gadgets helped me with schematics and the wiring. Everybody got his two cents in on hardware and security. I won't say that we're fail-safe, but we're tighter now."

"And will remain so, with any luck," Brognola told him, glowering. "The last damned thing we need is another raid on the farm."

"Agreed. But still, you never know..."

"Allow me some illusions, will you? Just this once I'd like to make believe things work the way they're supposed to."

"Sure, why not?"

"Where did you pick up your assistant?" Bolan asked the Bear.

"Who? Barb? She's MIT with honors, class of '84. If it has circuits and a keyboard, she can make the sucker walk and talk, I guarantee."

"How long's she been aboard?"

"Six months or so. She's clean, don't worry."

"Say again?"

"Her background check. We found a second cousin on her mother's side who got thrown out of Greenpeace in the seventies for advocating violence, but the family doesn't even talk to him these days. I trust her like she was my own."

"That's good enough for me."

The Bear appeared to have a sudden flash of revelation, staring hard at Bolan for a moment. "Hey, but if you'd rather she took a leave of absence for a day or two, I'll set it up."

"No need."

"Well, I just thought—"

"That was your first mistake," the soldier told him gruffly, but he couldn't hide the grin for long.

"So, everybody's a comedian these days. I don't know how the hell I'm supposed to get a job done in this three-ring circus."

"Take two Valium and call me in the morning," Hal suggested.

"I'd prefer to take a six-pack and forget the call."

"Sounds reasonable."

For the second time that afternoon, an aircraft engine broke the primal stillness of the valley, droning like an insect in the distance, drawing closer as they stood and scanned the far horizon.

"There," Brognola said, pointing toward a speck that had appeared above the distant treetops.

"I thought Able was delayed," Bolan said.

"They are," Brognola agreed.

"Could be some yokel trying out his toy," Kurtzman suggested.

"It doesn't feel right," Hal said. "Call up condition yellow."

"Way ahead of you," the Bear told him. "We stand on yellow from the moment we detect a possible intruder."

They could see the vaguest outline of the aircraft now, a single-engine prop. It had already crossed the farm's perimeter and had begun to circle over the protected airstrip.

"Let's go," Brognola snapped, but Bolan was already off the porch and circling the house with loping strides. He reached the Chevy first and was already seated when Brognola scrambled in behind the wheel. The engine caught on the first try, and they were digging for a moment, rear tires spewing gravel as the man from Justice powered from a standstill with the pedal on the floor.

"Goddamn it, if some local yokel picked today to be a smartass, I'll personally break his joystick off and shove it in his ear."

"That should be educational," Bolan quipped.

"You bet your ass."

Brognola covered the three-quarters of a mile in something under sixty seconds, rocking to a halt on the grass beside the east-west runway. Bolan noticed that the farmhand from the gate had fixed his pickup truck in record time, and he was with them now, parked near the juncture of the airstrip's runways with his door wide open and the Uzi visible across his knees. From somewhere in the trees, two men on horseback had emerged from different directions, closing on the private landing field, their carbines clear of saddle holsters by the time they reached ground zero.

Bolan slipped a hand inside his jacket, fingers curled around the grips of his Beretta, drawing comfort from the weapon's solid weight beneath his arm. He didn't clear leather, not yet, although Brognola had his snubby .38 in hand, half hidden on the seat beside him. They could see the aircraft clearly now—a Cessna Mescalero. With a thirty-six-foot wingspan, it was used primarily for air force training exercises. Capable of seating two, the plane was almost certainly unarmed... but even if it had been stuffed with high explosives, it was coming down too far from any target to inflict real damage on the farm.

And if the pilot *was* a local yokel, he was in for some unpleasantness, the Executioner reflected. Violating federal airspace was a felony, but prosecution was the least of it. The guy would be confronting half a dozen guns and one infuriated Hal Brognola. Of the choices offered, Bolan knew that he would personally have preferred the guns.

The Mescalero's pilot touched down lightly, throttled back at once and was taxiing before he reached the midpoint of the east-west runway. Bolan took his time in exiting the Chevy, anxious for its cover if the Cessna proved to be a kamikaze, but Brognola was already homing on the plane, his .38 held close against his leg and out of sight. The others took no pains to hide their weapons, covering the cockpit fore and aft, alert to any sudden, hostile movements by the pilot.

Even with the tinted windows, Bolan realized that they were dealing with a single man. The second seat was empty, and unless the pilot had a backup gunner lying on the floor, he was alone. As Bolan watched, the human silhouette unbuckled safety harnesses, shut down the engine and retreated toward the exit hatch. Brognola was already waiting for him on the ground when he emerged.

"God*damn* it! Will you look at this, for pity's sake?"

"I'm looking," Bolan told him, closing rapidly to shake the outstretched hand of Jack Grimaldi.

"Bet you thought I wasn't coming to your party."

"Last I heard," Brognola said, "you weren't invited."

"Technicalities. How are you, Sarge?"

"I'm hanging in. And you?"

"The same."

Grimaldi had been Bolan's wings in the early days of his one-man war against the Mafia. A veteran of Vietnam who had sold his talents to the highest bidder and become embroiled with members of the syndicate, Grimaldi had been more than ready to defect when Bolan had come along and offered an alternative. For months he had served as Bolan's eyes inside the Mob, reporting on the travels of assorted gangland VIPs. When the Phoenix team was organized at Stony Man, Grimaldi was among the charter members, and his expertise with aircraft had seen Mack Bolan through a number of his worst campaigns against the savages.

"I understand we're cooking up big medicine," Grimaldi said.

"I'd like to know where that came from," Brognola growled in answer.

"Yeah, I'll bet you would."

"Goddamn it, Jack—"

"Hey, mellow out. I'm here, okay?"

Brognola scowled. "Okay."

"That's the spirit. Nice of you to offer me a lift."

"I ought to let you walk."

"Ah, but you won't."

"Get in the car."

Brognola stowed his .38 and slid behind the wheel. They made the short drive back in silence and found Kurtzman waiting for them on the porch.

"Hey, Jack," he called. "I wondered when you'd get here."

Hal was glaring back and forth between them, but the look was losing some of its ferocity. "*You* called him in?"

"Seemed like the thing to do," Bear answered. "What's a family reunion without the black sheep?"

"Is that some kind of ethnic slur?" Grimaldi asked.

"Christ, I give up." Brognola was already clumping up the stairs when laughter hit him like a wave. He hesitated, glanced from one brave warrior to the next and finally joined them, a bemused expression on his face as if he couldn't quite believe himself. "Well, now that you're here," he said at last, "we'll have to find some quarters for you."

"Got it covered," Kurtzman interjected. "Jack, you're booked in number four."

"Surrounded by conspirators," Hal grumbled, and that set the laughter off again. It broke at last when Barbara Price emerged onto the porch, a curious expression on her face.

"Is everything all right?" she asked.

"I wonder," Hal replied offhandedly. "Come on, Jack. Let's go up and get you settled."

"Thought you'd never ask." Grimaldi winked at Barbara as he passed, causing her to blush.

When they were alone, she turned to Bolan hesitantly. "I'm afraid I owe you an apology."

"Oh?"

"I didn't recognize your name."

"No problem. I do that myself, sometimes."

"No, honestly... I should have put the two together. Colonel Phoenix, as in *Project* Phoenix."

"It's still John," he said. "No point in hashing over ancient history."

"We study your campaigns, you know. As training when we enter SOG."

"That must be tedious."

"Oh, not at all... I mean..."

The color had returned to Barbara's cheeks, and Bolan let her off the hook. "How long have you been interested in computers?"

"All my life, I guess. I got a small one for a birthday present when I was in grade school. It was just a toy, of course. You asked it certain questions, and a little voice would answer. But it got me started."

"And the rest is history?"

She smiled. "I guess so. Yes."

"You must be lonely here," he said, and wondered where the hell those words had come from.

Barbara pinned him with her eyes for just a moment, and he noticed for the first time that their color was a deep, disturbing gray. "It's not so bad," she said at last. "We have a furlough system, as you know, for R and R, but at the moment I prefer my work with Mr. Kurtzman. He's a genius."

Bolan grinned. "He'd have a cow if he could hear you call him that. The 'mister,' not the genius."

"I suppose you're right." She grinned. "He makes me call him Aaron. I can't bring myself to call him Bear."

"It's just as well. Will you be backing up our little party here?"

She nodded. "Yes. All leaves are canceled as of Tuesday last. We'll be on full alert here from the time you leave until your safe return."

Or otherwise, he thought, and saw that the alternative had occurred to her as well. Her eyes were briefly downcast. When they rose to meet his again, there was a sadness in them that reached out to Bolan and touched him.

The words were forming on his tongue, demanding that he tell her she reminded him of someone, when he realized it wasn't true at all. Aside from the coincidence of sex and setting, Barbara Price bore no more natural resemblance to April Rose than any other woman Bolan might encounter on the street. Why should she, after all? Because he had expected something of the early magic to remain at Stony Man? Because, in spite of everything, his resolutions firmly made, the Executioner had hoped to find a time machine of sorts, some way of taking back the pain?

Forget it. There was no room in his world for miracles or grand delusions. A combatant who couldn't accept reality was doomed before he took the field, and Bolan knew that he would need his wits about him in the coming days. As for the woman, she was simply one more member of the staff that Kurtzman had assembled, trained to do her job and keep her mouth shut when she left the farm.

And yet...

There was a trace of magic in her eyes, a spark, perhaps, which might be kindled into open flame with some attention. If he only had the time and opportunity.

"How old are you?" he blurted, then mentally kicked himself. Dammit, had he forgotten how to talk to a woman?

"I'm old enough," she told him. The penetrating gray gaze didn't waver once from Bolan's face.

I wonder, Bolan thought. She had never killed, he could tell that much. Most likely she had never been in danger of her life, although the day might come if she remained at Stony Man.

"I'm sorry," Bolan said. "I don't know why I asked you that."

"I think you do."

"Well, then, you've got me."

"You were wondering if I could cut it," she continued. "If a 'kid' like me could really understand this game and make it work."

Which game, he almost asked, but left the words unspoken, settling for repetition of his previous apology. "I'm sorry. I was out of line."

"I disagree."

"How's that?"

"From what I understand, your life is riding on this mission. You have every right to know the quality of your support."

"I have no doubt about your competency," Bolan told her frankly. "Kurtzman tells me you're the best."

"He said that?"

It was Bolan's turn to nod. "You may have noticed that he's not exactly loose with compliments."

"I noticed. Thank you."

To the west, the Blue Ridge Mountains were devouring the sun, the shadows growing longer across the open ground of Stony Man, impenetrable darkness pooling beneath the trees.

"It's getting late. We'd better hit the chow line."

"Wait. You haven't told me yet."

"How's that?"

"Apology accepted?"

Bolan grinned. "Let's make it mutual."

The lady's smile was dazzling. "I think I'd like that," she replied, and she was gone before the Executioner could think of anything to say. He hesitated for another moment, then followed her inside.

☆ 9 ☆

The Phoenix war room occupied the northeast quarter of the ranch house basement level. Soundproof and secure against intrusion from outside, its Spartan furnishings consisted of a conference table and a score of wing chairs. Twelve of those were occupied at 4:00 p.m. on Bolan's second day at Stony Man. At the table's head sat Hal Brognola, leafing through a slim manila folder labeled CONFIDENTIAL. Aaron Kurtzman's wheelchair was positioned to Brognola's right, and Barbara Price was seated on his left. The men of Phoenix Force were ranged along the conference table's left-hand side, with Able Team's three warriors seated opposite. The Executioner sat at the far end of the table, facing Hal Brognola, with Grimaldi on his right.

An air of silent expectation hung in the room. Only Barbara Price seemed nervous, sitting in at Kurtzman's personal request for her first combat briefing. Bolan and the other warriors were accustomed to the waiting, but a certain edginess was evident in several of the battle-hardened faces. Of them all, Grimaldi seemed the most relaxed. He hadn't been invited to the meet, and while the others knew that he would never exercise the option, he was free to walk away from the impending mission.

Brognola cleared his throat and put the ball in play. "Except for Jack, you each know parts of this already.

What we're looking at now is the overall, with a proposed solution." He hesitated while he put his thoughts in order, then he forged ahead. "Twelve days ago we got a squeal from contacts in the Contra movement that a VIP from their side had been bagged by Sandinistas on a border crossing. They were hot to go in after him, but Washington persuaded them to put the matter in our hands, preserve deniability...you know the drill. The bad news is our Latin clients blew five days before they tipped us off. When Able reached their man, he had been undergoing stiff interrogation for at least a week."

"That's bad," McCarter said.

"It's not the worst," Brognola told them. "An American was running the interrogation for Ortega's team."

"A mercenary?" Katzenelenbogen asked.

"That's negative. We have a positive ID on Pommeroy, James G., a sergeant in the Special Forces, stationed in Honduras. He had two days left on furlough when the Ironman pulled his tags."

If Lyons felt the others watching him, he gave no sign. His face was grim, impassive, as he listened to Brognola, waiting to hear something he didn't already know.

"What kind of background do we have on Pommeroy?" Bolan asked.

"The usual. He was a model trooper in the middle of his second tour. No indication of subversive tendencies or sympathy with any Third World revolutionary movements. All concerned are stunned, unquote."

"There's more," Grimaldi said, and when he spoke, it didn't come out sounding like a question.

"Yes. While Able was involved in Nicaragua, Phoenix Force was hunting terrorists—suspected Sandinistas—in the Costa Rican highlands. They made contact Tuesday morning, just in time to see the targets make connections with an Anglo pilot. His description and the name on his fatigues are both consistent with another Special Forces trooper—Baker, Thomas A., already listed AWOL on a weekend pass. They had to smoke him."

"*Calvin* smoked him," Gary Manning said, enjoying the discomfort of his comrade.

"Dammit, how did I know he was going to crash the plane?"

"Whatever." There was tension in Hal's voice, and suddenly the banter died away. "Costa Rican rural guards recovered the remains, and we now have a firm ID from dental records. Here's your man."

Brognola pulled a glossy eight-by-ten out of the file and handed it to Katzenelenbogen. The Israeli glowered at the photo for a moment, then nodded. "Yes."

The black-and-white was passed around the table. In a moment, Bolan found himself confronted by a smiling, almost boyish face, the eyes obscure behind dark glasses. Dead now. Smiling from the grave.

"Baker's seaplane was reported stolen in Miami eighteen months ago," Brognola said. "God knows who's had it in the meantime. It was painted, with a half-assed stab at altering the numbers."

"Can we link the two?" McCarter asked.

"Affirmative. They knew each other, but were not considered special friends by anyone who's still alive and talking. That's the public version, anyhow. We must assume that someone's covering."

"No other unexpected MIAs?" Pol asked.

Brognola frowned and shuffled through the papers in his open file. "We *do* have one more trooper unaccounted for, but I'll be damned if I can see a similarity. A Special Forces heavy weapons man named Charbonneau, Paul J. He turned up missing on a night patrol three weeks ago, and no one's seen or heard from him since then. The other members of his team report he broke formation for a nature call and never made it back. They beat the bushes for an hour or so, then packed it in and filed an MIA report. The CO organized a more extensive search and came up just as empty. At the moment, Charbonneau is listed as a possible deserter."

"Something stinks," Grimaldi said.

"I smell it, too," the man from Wonderland agreed. "But there's been nothing we could put a finger on, besides the fact that all three men were Special Forces."

"Let's stick to what *do* we know," Katz suggested.

"Right." Brognola spent another moment staring at the file in front of him. When he resumed, his voice was strained, low-keyed. "The Oval Office has uncovered evidence of a conspiracy involving members of the army general staff and CIA covert operations. It's designed to foment border incidents between the Sandinista government and neighbor states, ideally stirring up a situation where the Pentagon will have to intervene with combat troops. Potentially we're looking at another Bay of Pigs."

"It sounds more like another Vietnam," McCarter growled.

Brognola's frown carved lines around his mouth and eyes. "The White House is determined to prevent the situation from advancing to that point. No effort will be spared to stop this operation cold before it gets completely out of hand."

"Where do we start?" Schwarz asked.

Carl Lyons made a sour face. "The top, where else?"

Brognola shook his head in an emphatic negative. "The names in Washington and Langley aren't important," he informed them. "They'll be dealt with by the President. You'll be concerned with operations in the field, which mustn't be allowed to pass beyond their present state."

"What do we have," Encizo asked, "besides two dead men and an MIA?"

Brognola riffled through his file again and came up with two flimsy sheets of paper. "The man on site appears to be a brigadier," he said. "McNerney, Michael John. A thirty-five-year man, enlisted out of high school just in time for the Korean War. He saw the worst of it at Pork Chop Hill and came out with a battlefield commission. Doug MacArthur was impressed enough to take a personal interest, and McNerney was a major by the time the cease-fire rolled around. It's all uphill from there until the early 1960s. He was stationed briefly in Berlin around the time the wall was going up, but he was reprimanded under JFK's administration for permitting distribution of extremist literature on base. He was whipping up some of these leaflets on his own, importing others from the Birchers, Minutemen, you name it."

"Was he busted?" Bolan asked.

Brognola shook his head. "They wrote it up as reassignment. After Dallas, when things started heating up in Vietnam, he got the nod for a position under General Westmoreland. Decorated twice for valor under fire. He's not your average rear-echelon CO. The final pullout—or the sellout, as he called it—shook McNerney up so bad he started writing to the White House, begging for another chance to win the war. Instead, he got another reassignment—to Honduras. If it was designed to force him out, it didn't work. At fifty-four, he's hanging tough. McNerney was involved in planning the Grenada operation, and before that we have indications of a covert link with the CIA in the Allende overthrow. Our boy's been busy...and we now have reason to believe that he's been working overtime."

"I can't imagine Special Forces troopers dealing with a brigadier directly," Bolan offered. "Not in something of this magnitude."

"Agreed. There has to be a buffer, some chain of command. Unfortunately we have no idea which officers are working with McNerney on the side. We might be looking at a handful, or the whole damned shooting match. As for the line troops...well, who knows?"

"How long has this been going on?" asked Hermann Schwarz.

"The Nicaraguan phase is relatively recent, but the ranking members go back twenty years or more together. Some of them were tied in with the Bay of Pigs in '61."

"And no one caught a whiff of it before?" Grimaldi asked. "That's unbelievable."

"Not really. Think about what's happened in the meantime, Jack. The missile crisis. Dallas. The Dominican Republic. Vietnam and Watergate. Beirut. Grenada and Iran. The OPEC squeeze. Khaddafi and his cast of thousands. We've been through five presidents in twenty years, and they've had better things to do than look for traitors in their own damned government."

"Okay," Grimaldi said, "I get your drift."

"We're fortunate to know this much, but I can guarantee it's not enough." He scanned the table, steely-eyed. "You all know well enough from personal experience how one or two bad apples can disrupt an operation."

"Roger that," Blancanales said. "How do we play it?"

"Striker will be going back on active duty," Hal replied. Beside him, Barbara Price appeared confused until she saw the others turn toward Bolan. "We've prepared a jacket for him that should cover all the bases—combat record, decorations, recent disaffection with the trends in foreign policy."

"How solid is the cover?" Bolan asked.

"It ought to hold. We've got the joint chiefs backing us on this one, and your opposition shouldn't be too choosy. They've been coming up shorthanded lately."

Bolan nodded, satisfied. He had gone into other missions with as much at stake and less behind him in the past. If worse came down to worst, he would revert to instinct, play the rest of it by ear.

"That leaves the rest to us outside," Politician interjected.

"Not exactly," Hal replied. "We've got a special job for you. There are some indications that the local Contra hierarchy may be tied in with McNerney. We need someone on the inside to confirm, if possible, and mark the players if it's true."

"Plan B," Carl Lyons said, chuckling and his laughter was immediately joined by Gadgets Schwarz. Pol glowered at his fellow Able warriors and shot them both the finger as they shared a private joke at his expense.

"I ought to let you jokers handle it," he growled.

"No hablo español, señor," Schwarz answered, dabbing at his teary eyes.

"I've got your *español* right here."

"All right." Brognola raised an open hand to still the spreading laughter. "Now the rest of you will be on-site, but undercover, in Tegucigalpa. Keep the profiles low until we need you. If the opposition hits on Striker, we're in business. If they pass, we'll have to see what Pol comes up with on the other end."

"And if we miss on *both* ends?" Gary Manning's tone was cautious, falling somewhere short of outright skepticism.

"Then we'll be forced to wait until they make their move," Brognola said. "If it goes that way, we could lose it in the stretch."

"What's my end of the action?" Jack Grimaldi asked.

"You weren't expected," Hal replied. "We're looking at a crowd scene as it is."

"Give me a break," Grimaldi said. "One body, more or less, won't make a difference."

"So, stay home."

"Goddamn it—"

"I could use a lift," the Executioner suggested, interrupting Jack before the argument could hit its stride.

"We've taken care of that," Brognola answered, eyes still fixed upon Grimaldi. "You'll be traveling by military transport with the regular replacements."

"It'll need a pilot."

"I believe they have a few on staff these days."

"He might be useful," Bolan said.

"Hell, yes," Grimaldi said, beaming. "You never know."

"All right, all right." Brognola raised his hands in mock surrender. "I'll arrange it. Anybody *else* have problems with the way things stand?" When no one answered, Hal seemed satisfied. "Okay, let's wrap this up. You're outbound first thing in the morning. I suggest you take advantage of the time remaining for some R and R."

They left the war room in single file, with Bolan bringing up the rear. He hesitated briefly for a word with Hal. "Jack won't be any problem."

"Christ, I hope not. I don't want to read about a one-man air strike on Managua in my morning paper."

Bolan smiled. "Except as absolutely necessary."

"Right." Brognola found the smile contagious and matched it with his own a moment later. "Right," he said again. "But I don't want him going near Havana."

Bolan had his supper early, dining alone in the mess hall. Afterward he spent an hour wandering around the grounds, across the fields and through the trees that ringed the farmhouse, sheltering it from the weather and from prying eyes. He tried to concentrate on the mission, but his mind kept drifting back to other days, other battlegrounds and the origin of Stony Man itself.

America had been besieged by terrorists when Bolan had launched his bloody "last-mile" blitz against the Mafia. It was a six-day razzle-dazzle aimed at mopping up the largest fragments of a broken syndicate, presumably delaying its revival for a year or two and giving federal prosecutors time to win indictments on a number of the highly placed survivors. In retrospect, Bolan knew his optimism had been premature. The Mafia was down, all right, but it was far from out, and there were times when Bolan worried if he might have been mistaken, changing tacks the way he had before the job was finished.

When those doubts arose, the soldier told himself that it would never have been finished, not if he had blitzed a different family every day, year-round, for fifty years. The Mafia was like a cancer, spreading, changing, virtually before the surgeon's eyes. The savages who filled its ranks were like malignant cells, regenerating constantly, a hundred born for every one destroyed. And Bolan knew the Mob was here to stay until such time as every man and woman in the nation recognized its danger, finally demanding its destruction. While John Q. Citizen continued patronizing prostitutes and bookies, buying stolen goods at "discount" prices, renting bootleg videocassettes and lining up for pornographic movies, there would always be a syndicate. It was free enterprise in action, the immutable law of supply and demand. And it was well beyond Mack Bolan's reach.

At best, his "victory" against the Mafia had been a temporary one, but at the time he had been grateful just for that. Brognola had arranged a secret pardon for the Executioner, conditional upon his "death" and subsequent "rebirth" as Colonel Phoenix, spearhead of the SOG's new war on terrorism. Given all the evidence of daily headlines, it had seemed the thing to do, another angle of attack against the savages who preyed on humanity around the globe. It was another war devoid of any possibility of final victory, but he had known that going in, and Bolan had approached the problem with his eyes wide open, knowing he could fight a holding action. But in the end...

There was no end of course. No end to terrorism, as there was no end to syndicated crime. He might as well have tried to stop an avalanche with a plastic pail and shovel, but the ultimate impossibility of a decisive win didn't intimidate the Executioner. His war wasn't a futile effort. One man could make a difference, and if he saved a single life, undid a single rotten scheme before they cut him down, then he had done enough. Sometimes it was enough to make your stand regardless of the final outcome. Others might be moved to stand by the example of a single sacrifice, and Bolan knew that his crusade had altered other lives—some for the better, some for worse.

It would not do to think about the dead just now, not with another confrontation looming on the horizon. Concentration on the fallen was the first step in defeatist thinking, and he knew that frame of mind could get him killed. The Executioner wasn't afraid of death—had been prepared for it from the beginning of his private war—but neither did he court the Reaper needlessly. The soldier knew that he would need a mental edge for the assignment that awaited him, and he wouldn't allow preoccupation with the past to dull that edge.

Time to concentrate on here and now, he thought, his steps already turning back in the direction of the ranch house. By this time tomorrow he would be among the enemy, two thousand miles from Stony Man. Two thousand miles from *home*?

Not anymore. As Bolan scanned the grounds, he felt a certain bittersweet nostalgia, tempered with the barest trace of longing, but the farm was no more home to Bolan now than Pittsfield, Massachusetts, where he had been born and spent his childhood, where he had buried his family. Home is where the heart resides, according to the poets, and Mack Bolan's heart was on the firing line, committed to the struggle that had chosen him so long ago. There might be fleeting sanctuaries in the hellgrounds, but he knew there could be no final resting place while he survived. His destiny was written on the wind, in battle smoke.

War everlasting with no holds barred, no quarter asked or given. No retreat and no surrender. War to the knife, and the knife to its hilt. Mack Bolan's war was to the death, and if, inevitably, that must spell his own destruction, he was ready.

Someday.

But not tonight.

The sun had disappeared while Bolan prowled the grounds alone, replaced by winking stars and a moon that fell just short of being full. He walked by moonlight, comfortable with the darkness, conscious of the fact that he was doubtless being scrutinized by sentries, television cameras and electronic sensors. Kurtzman or his staff would know the soldier's every move while Bolan roamed the grounds, but he didn't begrudge them their security. It was a necessary fact of life for stationary warriors, minimal insurance that the sun would rise again for all of them tomorrow.

Bolan let himself into the farmhouse, and the door locked automatically behind him. Every guest in residence and member of the staff possessed a key, which never left the grounds; they would be counted in the morning prior to departure, and a missing key would bring the bloodhounds out in force. However trivial it seemed, the key check was a symptom of the necessary paranoia that was part of life at Stony Man. The house crew, like Mack Bolan, lived within a world where one mistake could get you killed; the only difference was that Kurtzman's team had no real combat stretch, no place to run.

He climbed the stairs, turned left, then right, to reach his room. The others might be in the dining room or den below, but Bolan wasn't feeling social at the moment. Sometimes on the eve of mortal combat, it felt good to be alone.

He hadn't bothered locking the bedroom door; it opened at his touch, and Bolan left the lights off as he padded toward the bathroom for a shower prior to turning in. He couldn't wash the smell of death away, of course—it was a part of him by now, exuded from his pores—but showering would help him to relax. He turned the water up as hot as he could stand it and stood beneath the scalding spray until the pent-up steam began to threaten suffocation. Then he cut off the hot water and switched back to cold, which raised gooseflesh on his arms and chest. When he was shivering, he killed the shower, stepped outside and pulled a towel down from the rack.

A rustling sound from the direction of the bedroom froze him in his tracks, the towel still dangling from one hand. He blinked away a couple of droplets that were trickling into his eyes. The bathroom lights were on, the bedroom in darkness, and the Executioner felt suddenly exposed, intensely vulnerable.

Bolan dropped the towel and lunged for the light switch in a fluid motion that took him through the doorway, ending in a combat crouch beside the bedroom chest of drawers. His eyes would need another moment to adjust to the darkness, if he had the time. Moonlight filtering through the curtains enabled him to make out traces of a shape beneath the rumpled blankets of his bed.

"I hope you're not about to shoot me," Barbara Price informed him from the bed.

He straightened slowly, and the tingling that raced along his nerve ends now was unrelated to the icy shower or his momentary fright. "I wouldn't dream of it," he said.

"I'm sorry if I startled you."

"I'll live."

"I hope so." Silence spun between them for a moment, finally broken by a voice that demonstrated equal parts passion and embarrassment. "You really ought to be in bed."

"My thoughts exactly."

In the time it took for him to cross the room and slip into bed beside her, Bolan made his mind up that it wasn't necessarily the best idea to spend the eve of battle in a solitary contemplation of potential death. Sometimes it was enough to live the moment, share it with a willing comrade and forget about tomorrow.

Sometimes, like now.

☆ 10 ☆

"That slob-ass bastard! Didn't he learn anything from Pommeroy? Goddamn it, if he didn't have the common sense to keep himself alive this close to zero hour, I hope he rots in hell!"

The white-haired officer sat back, endeavored to relax and spent a moment smoothing wrinkles from the decorated tunic of his uniform. The outburst had been therapeutic in its way, releasing tensions that had threatened to evoke a screaming migraine. Now he felt the rage subsiding, bleeding slowly out of him as if a drain had opened somewhere in his psyche, letting anger, disappointment and assorted other mental garbage sluice away.

"Forget about that now," the general ordered. More than thirty years of military service had conditioned Michael John McNerney to command others. He was good at it; more to the point, he loved it. "We can run this drill shorthanded if we have to, but you might as well be on the lookout for replacements."

"Yes, sir." Major Anthony Falcone knew his place, and clearly realized that his commanding officer was in no mood for arguments this morning. "We have some replacements coming in tomorrow afternoon, including Special Forces. I'll put Rafferty to work as soon as they arrive."

"Be careful, Major. I don't want another foul-up like the mess with Charbonneau."

"I've got it covered, sir."

"I hope so, son, for your sake. Be on notice that this operation will proceed on schedule, regardless of any obstacles. Am I clear on that?"

"Yes, sir."

"We will proceed on schedule if I have to take the field myself with you beside me. Clear?"

"Yes, sir, I understand." The major's strained expression indicated that he understood McNerney's words all too well. "On schedule."

"No slob-ass bastard's going to prevent us from achieving our objective, Major. Not if every mother's son goes down in the attempt. We will succeed, and I will not be fucked around by anyone."

"No, sir."

McNerney's jaw muscles rippled when he thought of how he had been fucked around by experts in the past. But he had taken all he could stomach. From the day of his enlistment, it had been the same: the fucking spineless politicians shook their heads and mumbled into microphones on radio or television, trying to convince the populace that this or that war was, in fact, "unwinnable," a "quagmire," sapping the American vitality. Somewhere along the line, McNerney's enemies had been converted into "freedom fighters," Communist guerrillas openly compared to Washington and Lincoln in the left-wing press. The mass of voters—spineless slob-ass bastards—ate it up and howled for more, demanding cease-fires or troop withdrawals when the fighting men who risked their lives for God and country were within a few short yards of final victory.

McNerney had observed the syndrome first in the Korean War as a recruit of seventeen. He was a private when the yellow hordes came screaming up the slopes of Pork Chop Hill. When they retreated for the last time, broken, he had been among a handful of survivors, and the CO had commissioned him as first lieutenant on the spot. General MacArthur had confirmed his battlefield commission when he had pinned the Silver Star on Mike McNerney's uniform.

The general had made a little speech about the Communist threat to freedom, and he had allowed as how it would require more soldiers like McNerney to contain that threat and eliminate it from the earth. They would have done it, too, if Harry Truman and his crew of goddamned pinks in Washington had let MacArthur do his business. After Truman had relieved MacArthur of command, the war had been as good as lost. And for Mike McNerney's beloved America, it had been the first time in a hundred and eighty years.

McNerney hadn't been the only soldier who was bitter after Panmunjom. Enough of them had still believed in victory to see potential in a first lieutenant who had earned his bars on Pork Chop Hill. Promotions had come with startling rapidity: he was a captain nine months after cease-fire, a major six months later and a colonel two years after that. He had kept his nose clean and had waited for the day when he would have another opportunity to face the godless Communists in mortal combat.

There had been fleeting hope in 1952 when Truman had decided not to run for another term. General MacArthur, now retired, had been McNerney's candidate for President that year, but all the slob-ass liberals had pooled their strength against him, calling him a would-be dictator, comparing him to greaseballs like Perón in Argentina. It had broken Doug, the lies and slanders that were thrown at him in '52, but Eisenhower was a soldier, too, and any fighting man was better than a candy-assed civilian in the Oval Office. So McNerney had expected decent things from Ike.

So much for expectations. Under Eisenhower, Cuba had been lost to Castro. Truman had allowed the goddamned Soviets to steal the atom bomb, but it was Ike who had let them take the lead in space, outdistancing America with Sputnik and their cosmonauts. The frigging U-2 incident had been a national disgrace, and it was symptomatic of an era when Americans had lived in fear of Khrushchev's threat to bury them alive. While Eisenhower had used the army to protect black children in the schools of Little Rock, the Russians had massacred Hungarians and secretly supported Ho Chi Minh in his campaign against the French in Indochina. Revolution was a firestorm, circling the world, imperiling the very way of life Americans had come to take for granted through the years.

One benefit *had* come to Mike McNerney in the Eisenhower years. He had been named a brigadier in 1960 and posted to Berlin, where he could stare across the frigging wall and see the fruits of socialism every day. Sometimes there would be scattered gunfire and a body hanging on the wire, another bid for liberty snuffed out while the Americans stood back like Pontius Pilate, scrubbing at their hands.

In 1960 General McNerney had supported Richard Nixon. It had been common knowledge in the Pentagon that Nixon had had a plan for liberating Cuba, and his mini-brawl with Khrushchev had impressed McNerney all to hell. There had been rumors of irregularities in Nixon's campaign fund, some hints of underworld associations, but McNerney didn't give a shit if Nixon paid his taxes or went drinking with Italian jailbirds on weekends. Back then, as now, he'd only been interested in turning back the tide of communism before it drowned the nation that he loved. When Nixon had lost to Kennedy, General McNerney had settled in to suffer through the years of Camelot.

The Kennedys had gone ahead with Nixon's plans for Cuba...to a point. The exile army had been armed and trained by Special Forces and the CIA, but at the crucial moment, after they were on the beaches at the Bay of Pigs, the White House had denied them vital air support. Survivors of the bungled raid had rotted in Castro's prisons while the Oval Office had hedged around the question, trying to preserve deniability, admitting to involvement in the raid when it had become apparent everyone had known the truth for months. The Bay of Pigs had been another in the string of shameful episodes that had finally convinced McNerney that his country, proud America, was very likely doomed.

The pamphlet incident had followed naturally, although McNerney hadn't been braced for the fury it had evoked in Washington. With Russian missiles planted ninety miles from Florida and brushfire revolutions blazing all around the globe, McNerney had seen it as his duty to provide some education for the soldiers under his command. Countless groups had emerged in the early 1960s, born in self-defense against the President's advance toward socialism, and their literature had been readily available.

McNerney had sampled widely from the John Birch Society, the Christian Anticommunist Crusade, the Minutemen and the Sons of Paul Revere. He had stayed away from outfits like the Klan, which had already earned a place on the subversive list, even though he had privately agreed with their positions on the issues. His discretion had only proved that Mike McNerney was a reasonable man—a moderate, in fact. The furor over distribution of "extremist literature" had taken him completely by surprise, and it had very nearly ruined his career. At the same time, though, what had begun as a disaster had finally proved to be the most important moment of the general's career.

McNerney had been posted briefly to the Pentagon before his transfer to the south, and he had been approached by fellow officers who had shared his view of world affairs, specifically the role of the United States in stopping communism before it had a chance to devour the world. He had learned that they were organized and had been discussing means and options since before the Bay of Pigs. They had been opposed to Kennedy's pathetic stance in Vietnam and his concentration on the cause of civil rights when everybody had *known* the Reds were backing Martin Luther King. A change was coming, and America would one day soon regain its primacy among the other nations of the world, but she wouldn't achieve that goal without some sacrifice.

The sacrifices had begun in Dallas, and while Mike McNerney had been surprised by Kennedy's assassination, he hadn't shed any tears. The man had been a gigolo, at best; at worst, he'd been a dupe of leftist forces bent on the destruction of America. There might be certain questions of propriety regarding Lyndon Johnson, but there was no doubt about the Texan's grit and his willingness to tackle dirty jobs and see them through.

The dirty job in 1964 was Vietnam, and it had been too long deferred already. After Tonkin and Pleiku, when

Johnson had committed ground troops to the fighting, General McNerney was among the first to volunteer for Asian duty. Friends in Washington had helped arrange the transfer, and for seven years McNerney had done everything within his power to win a war devoid of clearcut enemies and battle lines. Again, as in Korea, spineless politicians had lacked the courage to declare a state of war, but when your ass was on the line and hanging out a mile, you had no doubts about precisely what was happening. If Calley and his boys had gotten somewhat overzealous at My Lai, you had to understand the enemy was everywhere, concealed behind each passive face. You never knew for sure until they pitched a hand grenade or came out shooting, and by then it was too late.

They might have pulled it off in Vietnam but for damned civilian interference. His health in ruins, Lyndon Johnson had begun to weaken after Tet, and his successor, Richard Nixon, had proven to be no more consistent. Every escalation of the bombing had been immediately followed by a cease-fire, which Americans had observed without cooperation from the enemy. With Watergate and ruination looming just around the corner, Nixon had set out to earn himself a reputation as a statesman, visiting the goddamned Communists in Moscow and Peking, negotiating trade agreements when he should have been at home, lining up preemptive strikes against the enemy. That crap about a "peace with honor" had been aimed at pacifying voters, but it hadn't cut a bit of ice with fighting men in Vietnam. McNerney had lingered in Saigon until the bitter end, attempting to convince Westmoreland—anyone—that they should stand and fight.

In retrospect, it was undoubtedly his telex to the White House that had done McNerney in. He didn't feel that he had overstepped himself in speaking generally of sabotage and treason; what else do you call it when a nation's leader tramples on the interests of his people, selling lives for votes in a pathetic bid for reelection?

It had been the telex, almost certainly, that had gotten him posted to Honduras, but McNerney hadn't minded in the long run. Pausing briefly at the Pentagon to get his final orders, he had learned that certain officers agreed with him in principle, and while they wouldn't jeopardize their stars by speaking out, they had some concrete strategies in mind. A man like Mike McNerney could be useful to them in Honduras, the way things were shaping up in South America. Allende's revolution of the ballot box in Chile had been the overture for general upheaval in the Latin countries, and Americans committed to the preservation of democracy would have to act, regardless of the President's reluctance to involve himself.

The ousting of Allende had been a masterpiece of strategy, arranged by members of the military, the CIA and certain heavyweights from State. McNerney had been placed in charge of general coordination for the project, overseeing shipments to the rightist factions that had opposed Allende's socialist regime, coordinating transport during the revolt and afterward. He had been waiting just offshore the day Allende had been murdered, and he had gone in with a team of crack interrogators to congratulate the victors and offer them the full assistance of their grateful neighbor to the north. In Washington, his efforts had been recognized and filed away for future reference. He had convinced himself that he would soon be going home.

The monumental fuck-up generally known as Watergate had changed everything, of course. If Nixon had fought to keep his office rather than retreat in the crunch, McNerney might have made it stateside after all, but abdication had closed the door, perhaps forever. Gerald Ford hadn't been about to raise Allende's ghost with an election in the offing, and his loss to Jimmy Carter had sealed McNerney's fate. The peanut farmer had known enough about McNerney's past to recommend that he be left on-station in Honduras, permanently. As it turned out now, the spineless wimp had actually done McNerney a tremendous favor, leaving him in place to meet the challenge of a lifetime.

Nicaragua was the Cuba of the 1980s. With Somoza's overthrow and the imposition of the Sandinista revolutionary government in 1979, Castro and his Russian sponsors had their long-awaited foothold on the mainland. Reagan's team in Washington had severed diplomatic ties with Nicaragua during 1981 and thrown their weight behind the Contra forces, but the Sandinistas still found ways to arm guerrillas in El Salvador.

The White House might not have sufficient evidence for the United Nations, but McNerney and his backers knew the truth. Unless Ortega's dogs of war were muzzled permanently, they might spark a conflagration that would leave scorched earth and misery below the Rio Grande. With Congress waffling on appropriations for the Contras, backing off from the American commitment to defend its allies in a crunch, the stage was set for a catastrophe that might eclipse the hell of Vietnam.

It would be preferable, in McNerney's view and that of his associates, to face the bastards now, while they were small and relatively weak. Whenever Mike McNerney thought about the possibilities, all missed by careless, venal pigs in Washington, his pulse would hammer wildly. The doctors warned him about getting riled that way, but there were some things that naturally enraged a man.

Like watching long-haired boys and filthy girls make out in public.

Like turning on your television set and finding some damned fool soliciting your hard-earned cash to feed the starving hordes of Africa and Asia.

Like submitting to the orders of a slob-ass bastard in the White House who was busy grabbing all he could with both hands, selling out his country in the process.

It was too damned late to rewrite history in Cuba or in Vietnam. McNerney recognized that fact, although it ate at his stomach when he thought about it. There might be time for Nicaragua, though... provided that the operation he was working on came through on schedule, with the players carrying their own respective weight and doing what was necessary.

His associates had learned enough from Vietnam to realize that Congress needed provocation, something that the liberals could get their teeth into, before it would allow for military intervention. Something on the nature of a Tonkin incident, but camouflaged securely enough so that their design wouldn't be exposed before the goal was achieved. If the Ortega forces—or a close facsimile—were caught making war against their neighbors, crossing borders with a flagrant disregard for sovereignty and human rights, it would be easier to win approval for retaliatory strikes in Nicaragua. In the present get-tough atmosphere of Washington, emboldened by the airborne raid against Khaddafi, such a punitive assault might be expanded to include elimination of Ortega and the Sandinista party in Managua. There were several Contra leaders who had demonstrated promising potential in their counterrevolutionary struggle with Ortega's forces. Any one of them would do, as long as he remembered his responsibilities and obligation to America.

So far the plan had been proceeding more or less on schedule. A group of "disaffected" Green Berets had put out feelers to the Sandinistas, offering their part-time services, and the Ortega team had swallowed it without apparent reservations. The abduction of a ranking Contra strategist had gone down smooth as silk... at least until the final stages of interrogation had been interrupted by a force of unknown size and strength. There had been no survivors at the border camp, and one of those who fell had been Jim Pommeroy, a mover for McNerney's team. His disappearance might have been concealed indefinitely, listed as an AWOL or desertion, if it hadn't been for fuck-up number two.

Creation of a small guerrilla force in Costa Rica had been easy. Using mercenaries fitted out with uniforms and gear to match the Sandinista pattern, Mike McNerney's secret team had launched their campaign in the highlands, branching out from time to time and bringing bloody action to the cities. It had worked like a charm until the strike force had found itself outgunned at the Devil's Table and another of McNerney's crew had been eliminated by a faceless enemy.

The brigadier was no believer in coincidence. He thought the Contras might have wasted Pommeroy and company, although the operation had been conducted with a precision and a certain style that the native insurrectionists were sadly lacking. As for the Devil's Table, Mike McNerney didn't have the slightest idea what had happened. He was certain that the Costa Rican rural guards had surfaced only after it was over, picking through the ashes and identifying Tommy Baker's pitiful remains. And McNerney was equally convinced that *someone else* had done the killing, ruthlessly, efficiently, without attempting to secure prisoners.

An execution squad, of course...but whose?

The question haunted Michael John McNerney, but it didn't sway him from his course of action. He was totally committed to the overthrow of Sandinista rule by any means, and it was too damned late for outside interference to disrupt the operation now. Anyone who stepped in front of the McNerney war machine was going to get flattened like a bug.

The worst scenario, unthinkable at this point, would involve exposure of the operation at the top, with a reaction from the President that might include suspensions and arrests. It was preposterous, of course...but if the unimaginable should become reality, McNerney was prepared to play his hand alone and take it to the limit.

He had been silent and subservient for too damned long. He was fed up with taking orders from civilians who possessed no understanding of the global stakes involved, the life-or-death importance of their relatively "small" decisions made in Washington. If only Doug MacArthur could have been elected back in '52. If only things were different, safer, as they had been when Mike McNerney was a boy.

But the United States had never been secure, not really. Open any history book and you would find the nation threatened by subversives from within and enemies without. It took intrepid men of vision to defend America against her countless foes, and Michael John McNerney saw himself as such a man. He was prepared to sacrifice himself for the glory of his native land. And if some others had to be eliminated in the process, if the Bill of Rights was necessarily curtailed along the way...well, sometimes ends *did* justify the means. A fool could see that with his eyes closed.

"We go ahead on schedule," he repeated, talking to himself as much as to Falcone. "Pass the word."

☆ 11 ☆

"That's all for now, LaBoeuf. You'll pick up your assignment from the duty officer."

"Yes, sir." The soldier snapped to attention, ramrod straight, his brisk salute a textbook study in precision. Captain Fletcher Crane's salute was casual, a gesture of dismissal, and he watched the new replacement go with no emotion other than a mounting disappointment. He would have to pass on Sergeant Everett LaBoeuf.

The next file up was number five of seven that had landed on his desk that morning, one for each replacement from the stateside garrisons. He had arranged them alphabetically, as always, perfectly predictable in the routines that kept his office running smoothly. Crane hadn't perused the files beforehand; he would skim the contents one by one before each interview to give himself a feeling for the man he was about to meet. Thus far he had been interviewing soldiers who were competent within their specialties, apparently content with military life—at least for the duration—anxious to perform their duties as required. But there had been no spark, no hint of anything extraordinary in their files or in their faces. They were men who followed orders and kept their personal opinions to themselves.

He knew at once that number five was different.

Crane took his time examining the record of LAMBRETTA, FRANK. It wouldn't hurt the man to cool his heels outside awhile, and if the wait produced a flare of temper, offering Crane a glimpse of what was on the inside, well, so much the better. Settling back into his swivel chair, the captain started over from the top.

Lambretta was a lifer in the Special Forces with a double hitch in Vietnam behind him. He was rated as an expert with both light and heavy weapons, demolitions, all the tools of Armageddon. After Nam, he had been stationed for a while in Thailand, helping counter Communist incursions from Cambodia and Laos. He had gotten into trouble there, the first time, for conducting border crossings of his own, to punish Red guerrillas in their sanctuaries. It was readily apparent that Lambretta's CO had been sympathetic, letting him off with a reprimand, but there had been no covering the second incident. Lambretta had assaulted anti-U.S. demonstrators on the street in Bangkok, and he had been given ten days in the brig with loss of pay.

The soldier's stateside reassignment should have been a natural. Lambretta had been posted to Fort Benning, training new recruits for Special Forces duty, specializing in guerrilla warfare and survival skills. He had been rated highly for his skills as an instructor in the field, while drawing reprimands for certain lectures that described the past four presidents as "soft on communism." Ordered to delete the editorials from classroom lectures, he had demonstrated insubordination to superiors by stepping up his diatribes. Confronted with the choice of punishment or transfer, the commander at Fort Benning had had Lambretta's walking papers ready when everything had blown wide open in the Caribbean.

Lambretta had been in his element with the Grenada operation. When the Cuban forces had made their final stand outside St. Georges, it was Frank Lambretta's A-team that had outflanked the enemy position. Lambretta had killed seventeen of the "advisors" personally, capturing a dozen more for the interrogators and pulling in his second Silver Star for bravery under fire. He had been slightly wounded in the battle, but there seemed to be no permanent effects; the doctors who had listed him as clear for active duty noted that their patient had seemed disappointed with the swift conclusion of the fighting in Grenada.

Stateside once again, Lambretta was a warrior needing only war to make him come alive. Unsuited to civilian life, he stayed in service out of habit, but he obviously longed for action. When he couldn't find it on a foreign battlefield, he sought it elsewhere, and compiled a record of disturbances in cheap saloons. The final incident had taken place in a Vietnamese café; Lambretta, roaring drunk, had trashed the furnishings and worked his way through most of the employees by the time MPs had arrived to haul him off. He had served thirty days, with loss of pay, and when he had still refused to pull the pin, his CO had decided to export the problem.

Lambretta would be Fletcher Crane's concern from here on out... and that might be a blessing in disguise. He leaned across his desk and punched a button on the intercom. "Send in the next one, Corporal."

"Yes, sir."

Frank Lambretta's full description had been printed in his file, but Captain Crane was still surprised by the soldier's appearance. The man looked ten years younger than his age. His dark hair was combed back from rugged features that Crane thought some women might find handsome, even irresistible. The man exuded power from his chest and shoulders, from the biceps straining at his sleeves... and from the eyes that were now fixed, almost defiantly, on Fletcher Crane.

"Lambretta, sir, reporting as ordered."

"Sit down," Crane ordered, waving toward a straight-backed wooden chair that none of the preceding soldiers had been asked to occupy.

Lambretta sat, legs crossed, his right hand resting on the upraised ankle. Crane immediately noted that the sergeant's fist kept clenching and unclenching, as if subconsciously Lambretta was preparing for a fight. Aside from that apparently unconscious gesture, he seemed perfectly at ease.

"I've just been looking through your file, Lambretta."

"Yes, sir."

"Double tour in Vietnam. Distinguished service in Grenada."

"I got lucky, sir."

"I see. Apparently, you lucked into the Silver Star on two occasions."

"Anybody could have done the same," Lambretta said.

"Of course. But anybody didn't, Sergeant. *You* did."

"Yes, sir."

"You were an instructor in survival and guerrilla tactics up at Benning."

"Yes, sir."

"From all appearances, you did the job enthusiastically."

Lambretta smiled. "I got my tit caught in a wringer, yes, sir."

Crane didn't return the smile. "Do you believe it is the military's role to pass on foreign policy?"

"I never thought about it that way, sir. I've seen some policies I'd like to *piss* on, though."

"I'll tolerate no insubordination, Sergeant."

"No, sir."

"You've compiled a record of intoxication and disturbances in public places, Sergeant. May I trust that's all behind you now?"

"I'm not an alcoholic, sir."

"I know that. If I thought you were, I'd kick your ass on the first plane back to the States."

"Yes, sir."

"We walk a tightrope here, Lambretta. For the average Honduran citizen, we are the face of the United States. Our conduct must be constantly above reproach."

"I understand, sir."

"Indiscretions of the sort I notice here," he hesitated, drumming fingers on Lambretta's file, "are dealt with more severely than they might be stateside."

"Yes, sir."

"Am I getting through?"

"Yes, sir."

"You are aware of our position vis-à-vis the Sandinista government in Nicaragua?"

"Yes, sir. We look the other way while they do Castro's dirty work."

"We follow orders, Sergeant. To the letter. Are we clear on that?"

"Yes, sir."

"I've been in combat," Crane informed the new replacement, "and I know that rush that it can give you. It's a feeling like no other, am I right?"

"I don't know how to answer that, sir." Suddenly Lambretta looked uncomfortable, eager to be gone.

"I mean to say that sometimes there are difficult adjustments to be made in peacetime. Sometimes fighting men are forced to go against the grain and sublimate their interests in pursuance of their duty."

"Yes, sir."

"We are in a situation that demands supreme discretion, Sergeant. We will not be jeopardized by individuals who feel the world is out to get them."

Frank Lambretta frowned at that. "I'm not a paranoid. Sir."

Crane let it pass, continuing. "If there should come a time when we are ordered into confrontation with the Sandinista forces, I believe you would be a valuable addition to our team."

The frown became a cautious smile. "Thank you, sir."

"No thanks are necessary, Sergeant. Your record speaks for itself."

"Sometimes I think it says too much, sir."

"You are not on trial here. I anticipate no problems. Do your job and keep your nose clean, Sergeant. You'll do fine."

"Yes, sir."

Lambretta was immediately on his feet, and the salute he flashed to Crane in parting was a rather different gesture than the last one, sharp, respectful. Captain Crane returned it briskly, watched Lambretta close the door behind him as he left.

It would have been presumptuous to think that he had won Lambretta's confidence in one short conversation. Crane had been engaged strictly in planting seeds. The sergeant had a history of insubordination toward superiors, but only those who treated him as something less than the committed warrior that he was. When he was sidelined, forced to tow the line and parrot policies prepared by ineffectual civilian leaders, Frank Lambretta strained against the leash. The sergeant's sense of duty ran too deep for him to pull the pin on his career, and so he lashed out at the world in other ways, through barroom brawls and petty acts of disrespect that marred his record but allowed him to preserve his place within the military structure.

Frank Lambretta was a warrior waiting for a war, and there was every chance that he might not be forced to wait much longer. If the old man's operation went ahead on schedule, there would be ample opportunity for each and every one of them to meet the enemy, up close and personal. Lambretta's file revealed an independence that might be the root of trouble, but it also demonstrated that the sergeant had ability to work as one component of a fighting team. He hadn't lived through Nam, through the invasion of Grenada, by embarking on a one-man war against the enemy. When Frank Lambretta understood his orders—and approved of them—he spared no effort to achieve the ultimate objective. He might be perfect for the old man's operation...or recruiting him might prove to be an absolute disaster. Either way, the credit or the blame would fall on Fletcher Crane and no one else.

The captain needed to be sure before he passed Lambretta's name on up the ladder of command. If only there had been more time, an opportunity to test the new arrival, put him through his paces prior to making a decision. They were locked into a deadline now; the old man was determined to proceed no matter what went down. Crane understood the rationale, of course. He was aware, historically, of military operations that had failed because commanders in the field were too conservative in their approach. If called upon, he could have rattled off the dates and code names for offensives that had fallen short of victory in Vietnam because the officers in charge had procrastinated, wasted precious hours or days before deciding on a course of action.

Still, he wished there was more time.

The others were especially on edge since Charbonneau. They could have lost it there if another officer had occupied Crane's chair when Charbonneau had come rolling in with his report of treason in the ranks. If Crane hadn't been privy to the operation, he would certainly have launched his own investigation, carrying the word on to Falcone for transmission to the top. And then what? Would Crane suddenly have vanished, as Charbonneau had? Would they have been able to explain the disappearance of a captain with the same bullshit they had used to lose a corporal?

There were ways and means, of course—Crane knew that going in—and the old man would know them all. A captain could be made to disappear, and while his passing wouldn't be ignored, neither would it ultimately have to be explained.

Crane knew that he was vulnerable, and the knowledge meant as much as his commitment to ideals when it came to listing reasons for remaining on the old man's team. If Crane had cherished any suicidal urges, there were better ways to go than crossing Mike McNerney and the men behind him.

He had never doubted for a moment that the old man had substantial backing. No one but a psychopath would try to stage this kind of operation on his own, and Crane would never have enlisted on the project if he thought McNerney was a raving wacko. There were other men behind him—in the military and the CIA, perhaps at State—and you could rest assured that none of them were lightweights. Crane would never know their names, could never prove a thing against them if he did, but you could bet your life that if he tried to rabbit, they would come down on him like the crack of doom itself.

Crane stayed because he had no choice... but he was also a believer. He believed that communism must be brought up short before its agents devoured the western hemisphere. He was convinced that there could be no higher calling than eradication of the menace from the East. He was afraid of General McNerney, granted. But he also knew the man was right.

He punched the intercom again and waited for a responce.

"Yes, sir."

"Dismiss the other men to quarters and reschedule interviews for 0900 hours, tomorrow."

"Yes, sir."

"I need to meet with Major Falcone, ASAP. Reach out for his adjutant and make the appointment."

"Yes, sir."

Crane sank back into his swivel chair and closed his eyes. Falcone would know what to do about Lambretta. They would lay it out together, balancing the operation's needs against the risks and the potential benefits involved. If Tony thought Lambretta looked unstable, Crane would let it go at that. But if he liked the sergeant's style as much as Crane expected he would...well, they would have to find a way to bring Lambretta in before the operation ran its course without him.

And it all came down to time. They had a week at most, and you could never really get to know a man in seven days. You might acquire a feeling for him, but it would take a damn sight longer to be certain that a man would stand and die on your command if he was called upon to do so.

Frank Lambretta had already proved himself to some extent. His valor in Grenada and in Vietnam had demonstrated that he wouldn't cut and run when it was in the fan. He wouldn't flinch from combat if he understood the stakes.

It would be Fletcher Crane's responsibility to pass upon the new man's level of sincerity, his gut commitment to a cause of which he was, at present, absolutely unaware. No easy task, but Crane had noted something in the sergeant's manner, in his eyes. And he was betting that Lambretta would enlist without a second thought. Hell, he would probably demand a piece of the action. They would have to fight to keep him out of it, once he was privy to their plans.

And that would be the problem. The moment of exposure when their man might eagerly embrace the cause, or cut and run. If Crane misjudged Lambretta, if the sergeant cherished any hidden scruples that weren't apparent from his past performance, they would have an ugly situation on their hands.

No. Crane would have an ugly situation on *his* hands.

Lambretta was a mortal man, and there would be ways of taking him if it came down to that, but he wouldn't go quietly, like Charbonneau. Lambretta was a different breed of cat, and he would take a lot of killing. There might very well be other casualties in the attempt, and Crane wasn't encouraged by the prospect of attempting to disguise a wholesale massacre. Each man they lost before the operation actually began reduced their odds of victory, and they were missing two already.

Frank Lambretta might be able to replace the missing warriors on his own. A two-time combat veteran, he had experience that no amount of training could supplant. There was a chance the others would mistrust him, but they would abide by orders from above.

Crane realized that he was being premature, imagining reactions of the other troops to Frank Lambretta when he hadn't even cleared the first recruiting pitch with his superiors. Assuming that Falcone liked Lambretta's looks, it would be passed upstairs for ultimate approval by McNerney. That accomplished, Crane would be assigned to bag their man and guarantee his loyalty to the cause.

In the meantime he would wait and try not to remember that they were all running out of time.

☆ 12 ☆

"Cerveza, por favor."

Rosario Blancanales waited for his beer and paid with two lempiras when it finally arrived. Predictably the beer was warm and flat, the atmosphere inside the small cantina thick with smoke and sweat, but Blancanales hadn't chosen this particular saloon for its aesthetic qualities. In fact, he hadn't chosen it at all. He had allowed his contact to select the meeting place, and if the rendezvous worked out, Pol knew that they wouldn't be staying long.

The bar was one of countless similar establishments that jammed the red-light district of Tegucigalpa. Prostitutes were taking care of business on the street outside, their customers consisting primarily of Americans in uniform and tourists dressed in noisy floral-patterned shirts. Patrolmen on the beat appeared to take no interest in the lively trade, but rather occupied their time by hanging out on corners and glowering at passersby. A pair of them were bellied up against the bar right now, already working on their second round of beers and whispering to one another, glaring daggers at the barkeep if he came too near before they called for more.

It hadn't been difficult to get in touch with spokesmen for the Contra movement. Nicaraguan exiles in Tegucigalpa had achieved the status of celebrities through media reports of their unending war against the Sandinista

Front. The leaders of the movement had been publicly identified for years, but rank and file soldiers maintained a lower profile, thinking that surviving relatives in Nicaragua might be placed in danger if their counter-revolutionary actions came to light. Recruiters theoretically observed security precautions specially designed to rule out infiltration by the enemy; in practice, natural attrition had already thinned the Contra ranks dramatically, and new recruits had little difficulty finding a position in the motley ranks. There were formalities to be observed, of course, and Blancanales—aka Rosario Briones, Nicaraguan exile—knew that he would have to sell himself before the Contras would accept him.

He had acquired a straw sombrero with a scarlet hatband to identify himself, but now, as Blancanales glanced around the crowded bar, he noted several other peasant-types with headgear similar to his. No matter. Pol had followed his instructions to the letter, right down to the time and tiny corner table. If his contact couldn't recognize him, he would be forced to scratch the meet and try again tomorrow.

The Able warrior drained his beer and ordered another from the hard-faced waitress. He was sipping at it slowly when a slender man with pockmarked cheeks and beer in hand sat down across from him, not waiting for an invitation. He examined Blancanales for a moment, silently, and then leaned forward, speaking loudly to be heard above the din of conversation in the bar.

"I am Raúl."

"I am Rosario."

His contact raised the bottle of *cerveza* in a toast. "Managua."

"Soon," Pol answered, clicking bottles with the stranger, drinking deeply after he had finished the simplistic recognition signal.

"Come with me," Raúl instructed, rising and moving toward the exit, trusting Pol to follow him without a backward glance. Politician took his beer along; he wasn't thirsty now, but if there was an ambush waiting for him on the street outside, the bottle would do double duty as a weapon while he scrambled for the .38 revolver tucked inside the waistband of his faded denim pants.

The well-worn side arm wouldn't have been Blancanale's choice, but Nicaraguan drifters in Honduras had no access to the high tech weaponry of Stony Man. Believability was crucial, and he had been forced to compromise, hand-picking the revolver from a cache of throwaways, then field-stripping it and testing it for accuracy on the firing range. Politician was content when he could cut a two-inch group of six from thirty yards, but he had backed up the .38 with a six-inch switchblade just in case. It was a street tough's knife, and while he would have felt more comfortable with a Ka-Bar, Blancanales knew he could do the job with what he had.

Outside, the street was bright with gaudy lights, alive with party sounds. Raúl was waiting for him on the curb, and they set off together, Blancanales bringing up the rear, alert for any sign of treachery. They brushed past uniforms, police and military, jostled tourists and were jostled in return. The prostitutes ignored them, conscious of the fact that local peasants and assorted hardluck drifters had no extra cash to spend on pleasures of the flesh. The profits lay with Europeans and Americans, all suet-pale beneath their gaudy clothes, who sought adventure for an evening in the willing arms of a *latina* tigress. Locals would be going home to wives and children, while the drifters sought a place to sleep where they wouldn't be rousted by police or washed out by the frequent rains.

Raúl made no attempt at conversation, pacing off the blocks with Blancanales like a shadow on his heels. Soon they left the garish red-light district, plunging into mud and darkness as the sidewalks and streetlights petered out together. From skid row, they had moved on into the slums, a feature of all Third World cities. Blancanales grimaced at the stench of ancient garbage, open sewers, human bodies alien to soap and water. Scrawny animals moved in and out of shadow here; Pol hoped they were cats and dogs, but some of them bore a resemblance to enormous rats, apparently devoid of hair.

A lifetime of experience made Pol examine every shadow as he passed along the putrid street. It was an educational experience, but one that Blancanales would have waived with pleasure. The houses here were little more than tin and cardboard. There seemed to be a good-sized pile of garbage every block or so, aswarm with children seeking castoffs that might still be edible.

Some of these were Nicaraguan refugees, Pol knew, but most would be Honduran citizens. The yearly income for Honduran workers averaged less than seven hundred and fifty dollars, and for thousands in the cities there was no employment currently available. They lived from hand to mouth, when they survived at all, and when they died there were a hundred others waiting to replace them in the reeking slums.

They never saw a penny of the aid dispensed from Washington, in excess of a hundred million dollars every year. That money went for national defense—the arms and uniforms and training necessary to defend Honduras from her neighbor to the south. If thousands lay down hungry in Tegucigalpa every night, at least they would be reasonably safe against invasion by the Sandinista Front.

Their destination was a darkened warehouse, obviously out of use for years. It had been stripped of signs, the walls defaced and windows pelted out by vandals. Blancanales was relieved when Raúl kept going past the loading dock and giant doors, around the side and past the office entrance, homing on a flight of stairs affixed to the exterior in back. Above them, on the narrow landing, yet another door stood waiting, this one seemingly undamaged.

Following Raúl, Pol reached the landing in another moment and found the metal door to be a relatively new one, painted gray to match the drab warehouse exterior. Before he got around to knocking, Raúl turned back to face Politician. He was good, the Able warrior had to give him that. The automatic pistol had appeared from nowhere, with its muzzle aimed directly at his forehead.

"You are armed?"

There seemed no point in lying, after he had come this far. "I am."

The pistol didn't waver as Raúl searched out the .38, examined it and tucked it in his belt. He found the switchblade on his second pass and slipped it into the pocket of his faded dungarees. When he was satisfied, the Contra runner made his automatic disappear and rapped a coded signal on the warehouse door. It opened silently a moment later to reveal a hard-eyed sentry leveling an Uzi submachine gun. He ignored Raúl but scrutinized Politician closely, spending nearly half a minute on his scan before he stood aside and let them pass.

The door banged shut behind them, double locked, and they were lost in darkness. Blancanales stood rock-still until the lights came on around him, naked bulbs suspended from the ceiling in a narrow corridor that seemed to run across the whole rear of the warehouse. A line of doorways opened on the left, in the direction of the warehouse proper, and he trailed Raúl along the corridor until his contact found the one he sought.

"Wait here," Raúl commanded, disappearing through the doorway. Pol was left alone with the impassive sentry, conscious of the Uzi's muzzle leveled at his spine. Too far to reach in an emergency, but maybe with a backward roundhouse kick...

His train of thought was interrupted by Raúl's emergence from the room. The Contra runner nodded toward the open door. "Inside," he ordered.

Blancanales found himself inside a Spartan office. Plate glass windows overlooking the expansive warehouse had been boarded up, securing the room and any occupants from chance discovery by squatters camping out below. The desk and filing cabinets had been shoved against one wall, a wooden table flanked with folding chairs positioned in the center of the room.

One chair was empty, facing toward the other three and waiting for Politician to arrive. He sat down gingerly, examining the Contra warriors even as they studied him.

The central figure was a rigid military type with rugged features, back-combed hair revealing gray around the temples. On his right, a slim, athletic-looking man regarded Pol with evident hostility, his deep-set eyes suspicious, angry. On the leader's left, a striking woman met the Politician's gaze with cool directness, hesitating for a moment, then finally permitting the suggestion of a smile. All three were decked out in civilian clothes devoid of any rank insignia, but Blancanales knew that he was looking at the leaders of the local Contra cell. He also knew, without a second glance, that he was in the presence of a sensual, well-built female.

"Name?" the leader asked.

"Rosario Briones."

"You are Nicaraguan?"

"*Sí.*" He volunteered no information, making his interrogators work for everything they got.

"Your village?"

"Agua Verde. Ten kilometers below Granada. It was leveled by the Sandinista pigs four years ago." That much, at least, was true.

"Your family?"

"Wiped out."

"How many?"

"Seven."

"You escaped." It didn't come out sounding like a question, but he read suspicion in the Contra's tone.

"I had gone in to market," he explained. "The thing was done when I returned, but I had no idea who was responsible. When I sought help from the authorities, I was arrested and thrown in prison."

"Where you stayed until last June."

"Correct. They took me on a work detail with thirty, forty others, all in open trucks. I saw an opportunity and ran."

"You were pursued."

"A short way, yes. I managed to avoid them in the forest, and I started walking north."

"How long have you been in Tegucigalpa?"

"Thirteen days."

"You wish to join us?"

"I will kill the pigs who massacred my family. If you would like to help me, fine. If not, I do the job alone."

"You are impertinent," the slender Contra snapped.

"Silencio," the leader cautioned both of them. Again to Pol, "Do you have military training?"

"Sí. I spent four years with General Somoza's civil guard."

The leader raised an eyebrow, obviously pleased and curious. "You did not flee the Sandinistas with Somoza and the others?"

"Agua Verde was my home. Why should I run away from animals?"

"I am Luis Machado," the commander said. "You have already met Raúl Gutierrez. Esperanza is his sister and a loyal combatant for the cause." He turned back toward the slender, scowling figure on his right. "My second-in-command, Anastasio Ruiz."

Pol shook hands with each in turn, beginning with Machado and moving down the line. Had he imagined that the woman pressed his hand a bit more firmly than was absolutely necessary? There was no imagining the anger radiating from Ruiz; he scarcely touched Pol's hand, and Blancanales caught the burning look that Anastasio directed toward the woman. Careful there, he thought. It would be dicey if he stepped into some kind of love triangle while pursuing other goals, and yet...

The woman could be useful to him. She had the leader's ear, and there was every chance that she might have some knowledge of a Contra linkup with the rogues from Special Forces. If he could insinuate himself into her confidence, he might gain access to that information and place himself in a position to disrupt the hypothetical connection.

Careful.

Love and honor were regarded by Hispanics with the utmost seriousness. If he tried to put a move on Esperanza—or respond to any moves the lady might initiate—

he would be dealing both with a potential jealous lover and the woman's brother. It was risky, sure...but risk was what Plan B was all about.

He might come up with nothing, Blancanales knew, and it wasn't his mission to disrupt the Contra movement. They were sanctioned out of Washington with full support directly from the Oval Office, but it was possible that certain Contra elements had slipped the leash, as certain members of the Special Forces obviously had. If trained Americans—and general officers at that—were actively conspiring to subvert the foreign policy of the United States, why should the Contras flinch from underhanded dealings in the war to liberate their homeland?

Pol could sympathize, but he could also recognize the danger posed by independent operators. If Brognola was correct, McNerney and his men were looking forward to another Vietnam in Nicaragua. But if they overreached themselves and agitated Sandinista allies to the east, they might be stirring up a different kind of conflagration altogether.

World War Three, for instance.

Would Moscow stand and fight for Nicaragua? Would it make a difference if the Cubans intervened and U.S. forces lowered the boom on Fidel? What *would* it take to make someone on either side reach out and push the doomsday button? Pol didn't know the answers to those questions, and because he didn't, he was doubly determined to prevent their being asked aloud. If someone in the Contra movement was about to raise the ante here, employing extralegal aid from members of the U.S. military, it was time to ring the curtain down and stop the show.

It went against Politician's grain to interfere with righteous freedom fighters, all the more so in an age where they had been preempted, for the most part, by a flock of terrorists and mercenary killers totally devoid of ideology. But there was more at stake this time than simple opposition to a dictatorial regime. When local freedom fighters threatened to ignite a global conflict, it was time to reassess their cause and intervene, if necessary, to prevent catastrophe.

But he was being premature, he realized. Politician made his mind a blank. Idle speculation wouldn't help at this point, and it might prove detrimental later if he was locked into a theory unsupported by the facts. The only way to play it was to keep his eyes and mind wide open, searching for the truth until he found it. Or until he proved that there was nothing to be found.

And in the meantime there was always Esperanza.

"If you are interested in joining us," Luis Machado said, "I feel that we can guarantee full vengeance for your family, in time."

"I would be honored," Blancanales told him, turning toward Esperanza and looking deep into her eyes. "The pleasure will be mine."

☆ 13 ☆

"You want a good time, *si*? Ten dollars, American."

The girl was no more than seventeen in Bolan's estimation, but her face already showed the scars of living on the streets. If he could glimpse her soul, the Executioner was certain he would find it callused, like a peasant farmer's hand. The light of youth and joy was missing from her almond eyes.

"Not now," he told her brusquely, pushing on, ignoring her as she began to bargain for her wares.

"Six dollars? Gimme six, you get a half-an'-half that make you loco."

Bolan closed his mind to her and concentrated on his destination, three doors farther down the block. Aside from dialects and accents, certain cooking smells, he could have been in Saigon rather than Tegucigalpa. Red-light districts were essentially the same throughout the world: congested, frantic, throbbing with an urgency that passed for passion, even love, if you were desperate enough. The blaring music, uniforms, the women showing off their bodies in revealing clothes, were all familiar to the Executioner from other duty stations, other wars. In Vietnam, between engagements with the enemy, he had been known to patronize establishments of easy virtue on occasion. It had offered him diversion, but the grim realities of war and death were always waiting for him when he stepped outside again.

And it was funny how life insisted on demanding your attention. Every time you slipped away, reality came back to haunt you, dredging up the ghosts and memories of failures that were never quite forgotten. Standing on the main drag of Tegucigalpa's red-light district, rubbing shoulders with the uniforms and tourists, prostitutes and pushers, Bolan knew that in a way this *was* reality. His war was here, among the seedy bars and cribs, as much as in the steaming jungle to the south. No matter how you sliced it, Bolan had to get a handle on the situation soon before he lost his chance forever.

Three days into it, and the mission simply wasn't taking off. So far there had been no proposition from the enemy, and Bolan had begun to wonder if the prior disruptions, carried off by Able Team and Phoenix Force, had put the opposition on its guard. McNerney and his team wouldn't ignore the incidents, of course, but Bolan had been hoping their commitment to the cause would make them forge ahead, regardless of the risks involved. Without a deadline, Bolan had no way of knowing what their schedule might be, but instinct told him that he didn't have much time. Two lethal incidents within as many weeks—or three, if the suspicious disappearance of another Green Beret was added to the equation—told the Executioner that there was more to come.

It was entirely possible that Bolan's adversaries had decided to proceed with what they had, eliminating risks inherent in recruitment of additional participants. If so, then he would have to find another way inside, but he wasn't ready to give up just yet. He had a reputation to uphold, as Frank Lambretta, and he was prepared to give the troops a show they wouldn't soon forget. With any luck at all, he might arouse some interest from a member of McNerney's group...enough, at any rate, to make them take a closer look.

"Lambretta" had already asked around the base and learned that there were three cantinas catering primarily to U.S. servicemen. The first had been a rude surprise, its clientele predominantly black and universally indignant when the Anglo sergeant had shown his face inside. Devoid of racial prejudice himself, the Executioner was well aware that "Frank Lambretta" and the men he sought would not be likely to associate with blacks off duty, and he had retreated without ordering a drink.

The second joint had been a quasi disco, heavy metal music blasting from giant speakers mounted every yard or so along the walls. It seemed as if two different albums might be playing simultaneously, but no one seemed to mind. The crowd was young, composed primarily of two- and four-year enlistees, their rented women and a scattering of tourists who appeared confused, disoriented. Conversation was impossible, and Bolan had been forced to order by gesture. The place didn't feel right to Bolan, lacking the depressing atmosphere familiar to him from the countless other bars where soldiers congregated to lament unfinished wars. This place was upbeat, flashy, overpriced—the absolute opposite of what the Executioner was seeking.

On his third try, Bolan hit the jackpot in a dive where ceiling fixtures were discreetly tuned to twilight hues and oldies from a decade past were playing on the jukebox. As he entered, Barry Sadler was just winding down his "Ballad of the Green Beret." Bolan took a look around and guessed that Sadler got a lot of play from this crowd, consisting as it did of veterans in knife-edged uniforms, assorted prostitutes and B-girls, with a smattering of locals who resembled cheap Chicago gangsters from the 1950s.

Bolan ordered a beer and found himself a table in the middle of the room. There was no dance floor—these men came to drink and brood, uninterrupted by the sounds of celebration—and he had an unobstructed view of both the entryway and bar. When he was settled in, the Executioner began a secondary scan...and struck pay dirt immediately.

Leaning against the bar, a Special Forces sergeant by the name of Rafferty was downing beers like there was no tomorrow. Bolan knew him from the base—they had been introduced and hadn't spoken since—and Rafferty was one of those the soldier had been keen to watch more closely. Tall and muscular, a lifer in his early thirties, Rafferty had ten years on the average trooper stationed in Honduras.

With a handful of selected friends—DiSalvo, Steiner, Broderick, some others—he apparently was at the core of an elitist clique on base, their camaraderie excluding even other Green Berets. The group wasn't especially popular, but they were universally acknowledged as the best at what they did: specifically, instruction in guerrilla warfare and the latest counterrevolutionary tactics for the local military under terms of an assistance treaty. Bolan knew that all of them were combat veterans with service in Grenada, Vietnam, or both. Their training was the best, refined by battlefield experience...and if the Executioner was right in his suspicions, he would have to face them all before his mission in Honduras was completed.

At the moment, Rafferty was drinking like a jilted lover trying to forget his sorrows, glancing neither left nor right. When he had put away five beers, by Bolan's count, he took a breather, ordering another one but merely sipping at it for the moment, turning from his place to scan the crowded, smoky room. His eyes were dark, suspicious slits, his mouth turned down into an angry scowl. Whatever had been bothering the sergeant, he was plainly working up his anger and his nerve to share it with the world.

"I dunno 'bout the rest of you," he growled to no one in particular, "but lately I've been wondering just what the hell we're doing here." He scanned the silent faces, holding their attention now, and sipped his beer again before continuing. "I mean, do you believe they packed us off down here so we could sit around and watch the fuckin' Sandinistas use the border like it was a revolving door?"

A murmur arose from a group of uniforms positioned near the door. They might not be acquainted with the speaker, but he had already touched a nerve.

"Containment," Rafferty informed them scornfully. "Assistance short of personal involvement. And what kind of chicken shit is that? How many of you think Ortega and his fuckin' terrorists are gonna be contained so long as they're alive?"

No hands were raised.

"You bet your ass they won't!" the sergeant bellowed. "We've been sitting on a fuckin' powder keg down here since 1981, goddamn it, and there's people in Managua who would love to light the fuckin' fuse. If they could blast us out of here tomorrow, they'd do it. Am I right?"

"Tha's right!" a solitary voice chimed in from somewhere off on Bolan's right. He didn't bother tracking down the voice's owner.

"Bet your ass, I'm right! I dunno 'bout the rest of you, but I'm a fighting man. The U.S. government has spent a bit of money teaching me to fight guerrillas, terrorists, the kinda scum you got in uniform across the border there. I'm tellin' you, they spent a fortune teaching me to kick some ass, and now I gotta sit on mine while fuckin' terrorists do anything they goddamn please and get away with it. I dunno 'bout the rest of you, but I'm pissed off!"

"Damn straight!"

"Fucking-A!"

It suddenly occurred to Bolan that the sergeant had preempted him. He was performing "Frank Lambretta's" act, preempting Bolan as a drunken rabble-rouser. If the Executioner should chime in now, he might antagonize his would-be contact. If Rafferty was running down an act to draw "Lambretta" or recruit new members for McNerney's team, it wouldn't do for Bolan to attack the bait with too much zeal. His record as a loner was available to anyone with access to the files, and he couldn't afford behavior that was out of character. If Rafferty's performance was sincere, however, then there might be time. If he was seeking gunners to replace the dead and missing, Bolan could approach him later when they had more privacy and try to strike a deal. It would require discretion, extraordinary care, and Bolan knew that any slip he made from this point on could be his last. A simple word in passing might be adequate, next time they met on base, or if the opportunity arose this evening...

"I'll tell you what's the matter," Rafferty began again, his tone increasingly belligerent. A cocktail waitress blundered into him, approaching from his blind side with a tray of brimming mugs and glasses. Staggered by the impact, she released her tray; it fell with an explosive crash, warm beer and wine deluging Rafferty below the knees.

The sergeant stood and gaped for several seconds, color rising in his face until his cheeks were darker than his ruined khaki pants. "You stupid bitch!" he bellowed, whirling on the frightened waitress and flinging the remainder of his beer directly in her face. He followed with an open-handed slap that drove her to her knees.

Bolan thought Rafferty would continue his assault, but a native macho man was suddenly between them, shouting back at Rafferty in Spanish and shoving him away. The sergeant staggered, hesitated, and a wicked grin replaced the brooding storm clouds in his countenance.

"You want a piece of this, José?" he asked.

"Chinga tu madre, gringo!"

"Bring it on to papa, greaseball."

With a shout of rage, the local rushed at Rafferty, both hands outstretched as if to throttle him. The sergeant ducked beneath those hands and cut his adversary's legs away with one deft kick, allowing him to fall facedown beside the bar. Before the local could recover, Rafferty was on him, kicking at his back, his legs and buttocks, bending down to hammer at the unprotected skull with angry fists.

No less than half a dozen uniforms were on their feet, restraining Rafferty before the beating could become a murder. Bolan kept his seat while others scooped up the bloody victim, dragged him to the doorway and dumped him on the sidewalk just outside. The battered waitress, grateful to have been forgotten in the chaos, had already cleared the floor of broken glass and disappeared behind the bar, refilling orders for the tables in the rear. She didn't look at Rafferty as other servicemen surrounded him, congratulating him on work well done. The barkeep, a Honduran native, kept his face impassive and his opinions to himself.

"There's nothin' to it," Rafferty was telling one of his admirers as they ordered up another round of beers. "We could go through the fuckin' Sandinistas just like that if someone up in Fairyland, D.C., had guts enough to give the go-ahead."

Bolan nursed his beer and watched as Rafferty was gradually deserted by his rooting section, troopers drifting back to tables they had occupied before the fight had erupted. Rafferty didn't appear to miss them, concentrating on his drink and strangely silent in the wake of his preceding outburst. Had the rush of combat sobered him enough to realize that he was talking out of turn? Maybe he had gone too far already, spelling out the feelings common in McNerney's group in front of an audience that might contain informers? Or were beer and battle simply combining to create fatigue?

It was already after midnight, and the Executioner had duty early in the morning. He would stick with Rafferty a short while longer, trusting in his intuition, to see if anything further would transpire.

As if in answer to his thoughts, the sergeant downed his final beer and pushed a pile of currency across the bar, retreating toward the exit. Several of the others offered him a round of weak applause, but Rafferty ignored them, homing on the doorway and the street outside. The Executioner was well aware that any sudden move could blow his cover, but he couldn't afford to let the sergeant slip away just yet. If Rafferty was going back to base, so be it; Bolan would be naturally heading in the same direction, thankful for the rest. If not?

There had been no cessation in the action on the street. If anything, the pimps and prostitutes had sent for reinforcements, nearly doubling their numbers. Bolan glanced in both directions, picking up his quarry on the second try, already halfway down the block and moving rapidly despite the quantity of alcohol he had consumed. As far as Bolan could determine, Rafferty was heading for the base.

Bolan set off in pursuit of Rafferty, ignoring hookers and the junk men who emerged from darkened alleyways with bags of pills and marijuana, quoting prices on the run. Ahead of him, the Special Forces sergeant was running a gauntlet of his own, pausing long enough to dicker with a greasy-looking pimp before his mood abruptly soured and he shoved the man away. Mack Bolan half expected some retaliation from the pimp, but if he carried any grudge, the weasel didn't show it, backing off and seeking other customers. As Bolan trailed him from a distance, he saw three men fall in step behind the sergeant, closing fast. Despite the angle, one of them was easily identifiable as Rafferty's assailant from the bar.

The battered man had picked up reinforcements, burly toughs who swaggered as they walked, dressed like a stateside street gang circa 1960. Stepping up his pace, the Executioner spied two more leather jackets in front of Rafferty, already veering on a rough collision course. That made it five, and Bolan wondered if there might be others salted through the crowd or waiting in the nearby alley's mouth. Whatever, Rafferty would have his hands full, and it might still work out to Bolan's personal advantage.

He couldn't hear a word above the blaring music and exaggerated laughter that surrounded him, but from the visuals alone he knew when Rafferty's assailant hailed the sergeant. The man in khaki grinned in recognition of the man who had intruded on his reverie and kept on grinning when he saw the flankers. Other words were passed, inaudible to Bolan, but the sergeant's posture made it clear that he wasn't averse to taking on three men at once. And it was also clear he never saw the other two, approaching swiftly on his blind side.

One of them clubbed Rafferty behind the ear as his companion drove a fist into the sergeant's lower back. The khaki soldier folded, but he never hit the sidewalk; eager arms were open to receive him, bearing him away in the direction of the darkened alley. In their wake, the business of the streets continued unabated as if nothing had transpired.

Bolan had a choice to make. If Rafferty was maimed or murdered in the alley, the Executioner might lose his only hope of making contact with McNerney's team. So far he had no evidence of Rafferty's involvement in the plot, no "proof" beyond his intuition that the guy was dirty. If he let it go at that, abandoned Rafferty to face the jackals on his own, he would be relinquishing the only chance to prove his hunch. And once that opportunity was lost, there might not be another.

One part of Bolan would have been content to walk away and let the street thugs deal with Rafferty as he had dealt with others. But another part—the cold, pragmatic part where logic lived and strategy was born—demanded that he intervene, make something of the situation if he could. And if his instincts were off base this time, if Rafferty had no connection with the plotters... well, at least he would have tried.

The punks had left a sentry at the alley's mouth so that they could deal with Rafferty in private. The guy was slender, hatchet-faced, one eyelid drooping where a knife or razor blade had severed muscles in some other confrontation. Both eyes were on Bolan as he approached the alleyway, the weasel's sensors picking up an urgent danger signal, urging him to cut and run.

He stood his ground, and Bolan gave him credit for remaining at his station. Not a word was spoken as the Executioner approached the alley's mouth; his opposition moved to intercept him silently, one hand tucked inside the pocket of his leather jacket, fishing for a weapon.

The soldier never gave him time to find it, lashing out with a surprise snap kick that took the sentry low and solid, crushing genitals between the boot and pubic bone. The weasel doubled over, gasping, both hands visible and reaching for his wounded privates as Bolan finished with a chop behind one ear. The lookout folded like a sack of dirty laundry, and the way was clear.

The soldier glanced back once in the direction of the lights and traffic, knowing this might be the last street he would ever see. He shrugged the morbid moment off and concentrated on his mission, merging with the darkness of the alleyway.

☆ 14 ☆

The sounds of thudding feet and fists were Bolan's guide until his eyes adjusted to the darkness. Moving cautiously, in case the toughs had placed a backup sentry somewhere in the shadows, Bolan homed in on the spot where Rafferty or one of his assailants was receiving what sounded like a vicious beating. From the muffled curses and accompanying grunts of pain, he had no doubt that Sergeant Rafferty was on the receiving end of the punishment.

A naked bulb was mounted just above the exit of a pawnshop butting on the alley, and the toughs had brought their victim here to work him over, shielded from the street by garbage Dumpsters and a right-hand corner of the alleyway. Approaching as silently as possible, with gravel, broken glass and trash spread out beneath his feet, the warrior risked a glance around the corner prior to barging in.

The sergeant hadn't lost his fighting spirit yet, but stunning blows and too much beer robbed him of coordination. Bolan watched him try to throw a side kick at the tallest of his adversaries, but the punk stepped out of range, his three companions darting in like jackals from the flanks to strike at Rafferty with sticks and chains. A club glanced off the sergeant's skull, with other blows impacting on his back and shoulders, driving Rafferty to all fours amid the litter.

Something rolled beneath his heel, and Bolan stopped to heft the length of pipe. If used correctly, it could be a lethal weapon, and he needed every edge that he could get just now. The punks were occupied with Rafferty, too distracted with their captive gringo to be conscious of a shadow closing in on them. Incredibly, as Bolan fell among them, he achieved the victory of absolute surprise.

The nearest adversary had his back to Bolan, one boot raised, already lining up a solid kick at Rafferty. The force of Bolan's cudgel ramming home against his kidney brought the tough guy to his knees, a breathless gasp of pain escaping from his throat before the pipe made solid contact with his skull and squelched the sound.

The others spun to face him now, surprised to find another enemy among them but determined to proceed. They fanned out, circling Bolan, Rafferty forgotten for the moment as he lay amid the garbage, moaning. "You have made a bad mistake, *señor*," the battered barroom patron told him, smiling wickedly. "We still have business with this one."

"I'd say you're finished," Bolan countered, glancing at the fallen sergeant. "He looks worse than you do, right?"

"Ees not enough," the local told him, playing with the length of chain he held in both hands now. "You gringos need a lesson, eh? Find out that you do not own this country. You treat our men like peasants, and our women worse...like whores. This time, I think we make you pay."

The soldier sidestepped, edging outward from the grimy wall behind him, looking for some combat stretch.

He took the precious time to cast another glance at Rafferty.

"He's paid already," Bolan told the spokesman for the gang. "I've got no quarrel with you."

"But I believe *I* have a quarrel with *you*," the leader of the toughs replied. "*¿Quién sabe?* Who knows? You all look alike to me."

The others brayed with laughter, the sound cut off with guillotine precision as they rushed at Bolan simultaneously, chain and bludgeons flailing. Bolan took the leader first, going low beneath the whistling flail of stainless-steel links as he brought up the length of pipe into crushing impact with his adversary's groin. The tough guy staggered, lost his balance and curled into a fetal posture on the filthy ground. The nearest of his comrades stumbled over him and fell, rebounding from the alley wall face first, an outstretched arm too late to save his nose and cheek from grating contact with the brickwork.

Bolan spun to face his third assailant just in time to take a jarring blow across one shoulder from the tall man's salvaged table leg. The Executioner ducked a second blow, his free hand lashing out to clip the brawler's chin and snap the man's head back sharply while the small end of his pipe made jarring impact just below the sternum, emptying his adversary's lungs. The guy was doubled over, gasping desperately for air, when Bolan whipped the pipe around and down against his unprotected skull with enough force to knock him out.

There were awkward stirrings in the scattered rubbish behind him. Bolan turned to find the other leather jacket on his feet, still daubing at the wet abrasion where his cheek had been sandpapered against the wall. His nose was bleeding heavily, the crimson streamers trailing from his chin. A spark of savage anger, verging on irrationality, was visible behind his eyes. *"Está muerto,"* he declared, and spat dark blood at Bolan as he worked up nerve to make his move.

"Come on," the soldier taunted him. "We haven't got all night."

The punk snarled and came at Bolan in a rush, with no clear thought of strategy or timing. Bolan stood his ground until the final instant, feinting left to throw the human juggernaut off-balance, fading right before his adversary could correct, the backhanded swing already whistling toward impact with that snarling face.

The brawler's bloody nose and front teeth went together with an ugly crunching sound, his upper body frozen by the impact while his legs kept running, losing traction when the torso failed to follow. The adversary stretched out at Bolan's feet.

A scraping sound from Bolan's flank distracted him. The leader of the gang had struggled to his feet, still nursing wounded genitals and standing slightly knock-kneed, braced against the pawnshop's wall. He held a broken bottle by its neck, the jagged end extended like a stubby rapier toward the Executioner.

"It's over," Bolan told him simply. "Let it go."

His only answer was a ragged, wordless cry that carried him toward Bolan in a clumsy rush. The soldier could have stepped aside and let his adversary stumble into impact with the opposite wall, but now he stood his ground, the length of pipe gripped firmly in both hands. Enraged, his enemy thrust forward with the broken bottle, straining in his urgency to slice the soldier's flesh, and Bolan found his opening.

He raised the pipe and brought it whistling downward in a single, fluid motion, shattering the knuckles in his adversary's outstretched hand. Momentum kept the startled, gasping man in motion, and there wasn't even time for him to scream before the soldier caught his windpipe, pinched it off without apparent effort and lifted him completely off the ground. The length of pipe descended on his skull, and he was limp in Bolan's grasp before the warrior let him fall.

Beside a battered, leaky Dumpster, Rafferty was stirring fitfully, emerging from semiconsciousness. The sergeant's face was caked with blood and refuse from the alleyway, swollen out of shape, and his uniform was a grimy write-off. Bolan helped him to his feet, intent on getting out of there before a chance police patrol had time to spot the sentry's body on the sidewalk and decide to check it out. There would be questions when they reached the base, but that was one thing; spending time in a Honduran jail was something else entirely. The Executioner had work to do, and whether Sergeant Rafferty was part of Bolan's mission or a cheap distraction, Bolan couldn't operate—couldn't protect himself—inside a cell.

"I know you." Rafferty could barely speak through cut and bloodied lips. His voice was distant, dry and strained.

"We'll talk about it later," Bolan told him, steering for the sidewalk with the sergeant's arm around his neck, supporting Rafferty until the disoriented noncom found his legs and started helping out. No sooner had they cleared the alley than an ancient taxi rumbled into view, the driver trolling apathetically for fares. He did a double take when Bolan flagged him, clearly tempted to abandon these bad-news GIs, but money talked, and he could charge them double for a run back to the U.S. military base.

They settled into the tattered seat, with Rafferty half turned to stare at Bolan through the eye that wasn't swollen shut. "Why did you do it, man?"

"Why not?"

"Don't get me wrong, okay? I'm frigging glad you butted in, but what I just can't figure out is why."

"Let's say I didn't like the odds."

"Okay. You recognize the leader of the pack back there?"

"I caught your floor show, yeah."

"You figured he'd be laying for me."

Bolan shrugged. "I figured it was time to get some air."

"I owe you one." He squinted at the ID plate on Bolan's khaki shirt. "Lambretta, right? I owe you one."

"Forget about it."

"No way, man. No way at all."

They finished the trip in silence, giving Bolan time to wonder what the duty officer might think of Rafferty's condition. Coming back to base in tatters was a damned sight better than returning under guard, but if the locals raised a beef about the action in the alley, it wouldn't take Sherlock Holmes to pin the rap on Rafferty. And if it came to that, the sentries would remember who the sergeant had been leaning on when he returned. It would be worth the risks if his mark was on the inside with McNerney's operation. But if Rafferty was clean... well, Bolan thought, it might work out to his advantage, anyway. The word would get around that he had helped a fellow soldier out of trouble with the locals. It couldn't hurt, assuming always that the renegades were shopping for replacements in the first place. If they were determined to proceed with what they had, then it would matter little if the sergeant was among their number or a simple drunk, attracting problems like a human magnet.

Bolan kept his fingers crossed as they approached the base. He had the cabbie pull up to the curb a block before they reached the gates, then pushed a handful of lempiras at the driver, letting Rafferty negotiate his exit for himself. The sergeant was regaining his strength, his swagger, but he would require a bath and change of uniform to really pull it off. At least he didn't need to lean on Bolan as they walked the final block together, moving slowly as the sergeant favored aching muscles, bruises hidden underneath his clothing.

"I hope you've got your story put together," Bolan muttered as they drew up to the gates. A solitary sentry had already seen them coming, taking up his place with automatic rifle held at port arms, ready to receive them.

"Never fear," the sergeant croaked. "I've got it covered." Lurching toward the gate, he raised one hand and called out to the ground, "Hey, Vince, you got a six-pack on you?"

Closer, Bolan recognized the sentry now. He was a crony of the sergeant's, name DiSalvo.

"Jesus, Raff, what happened, man? You look like shit."

"I feel like shit," the battered sergeant told him in reply. "You gonna let us in, or what?"

"You guys together?"

"For the moment," Bolan told him.

"Bet your ass we are," the sergeant answered, more emphatically. "They'd have me in a cell downtown, or in the cold room, if Lambretta hadn't pulled my chestnuts out."

"What happened?" Vince DiSalvo asked again.

"A little rumble with the locals," Bolan said.

ROGUE FORCE

"A *little* rumble! Listen to him, will ya? It was like the fuckin' Alamo, for crissakes."

"I've seen worse," the Executioner replied.

"I'll bet you have, ol' buddy. I'll just bet you have at that."

"You'd better shag ass back to quarters, man," DiSalvo cautioned Rafferty. "The DO gets a look at you, there won't be any way that I can cover for you."

"Never mind the fuckin' DO, Vince. You know we got this place sewed up."

"You're drunk, man. Better watch that mouth."

The sergeant stiffened, seemed about to answer back, then reconsidered, clamming up. DiSalvo passed them through the gate, and Bolan walked with Rafferty in the direction of the barracks that they shared. It wasn't much, but there was something in the tone that Rafferty had used and the reaction of DiSalvo to his words.

We got this place sewed up. A reference to their covert link with General McNerney? Indications of a wider plot? Or was it just *cerveza* talking, amplified by ego?

Bolan couldn't answer any of those questions yet, but he could watch and wait. Whatever the McNerney forces had in mind, they weren't going anywhere tonight. Tomorrow he just might have another shot at Rafferty, an opportunity to loosen up his tongue.

The barracks were in darkness as they entered, both men heading for the latrine and showers. Bone tired, Bolan knew a shower would relax him, help him sleep, and it would also flush the pungent odors of the alley from his pores. Inside the confines of the barracks, he could smell himself, and Rafferty was ten times worse. Unless the laundry could work miracles, the sergeant could forget about his uniform for good.

The two of them were stripping down for showers when another pair of soldiers entered the latrine. A glance was all it took for Bolan to identify them: Broderick and Steiner, two more buddies of DiSalvo and the sergeant.

"What the hell did you buy into?" Steiner asked.

"A little disagreement with the local greaseballs, eh, Lambretta?"

Broderick glanced at Bolan, frank suspicion in his eyes. "You in on this?"

"I caught the last act," Bolan told him.

"Shit. He saved my bacon," Rafferty declared. "Those bastards would have had my ass fileted if this boy hadn't come along."

"You get their names, Raff? Faces? We can go in town tomorrow and mop 'em up," Broderick offered.

"Forget it, Tim. Their mamas wouldn't recognize those faces now."

Steiner laughed, a sound like dead leaves scraping on the sidewalk. "Guess you showed 'em pretty good, eh, Raff?"

"*He* showed 'em," Rafferty responded, nodding toward the Executioner. "I took the first one off okay, and then they japped me. Listen, I been thinkin' we could use Lambretta, here, and—"

"Easy, Jason." Broderick's voice was stern, a warning. "You could use some sleep."

Chastened, the sergeant nodded grudgingly. "I guess."

"We'll talk about the rest of it tomorrow, 'kay?"

"Okay."

He limped away in the direction of the showers, leaving Bolan on his own with Broderick and Steiner. Silence hung between them for a moment, finally broken by the slim blonde.

"We appreciate your helping Raff," Kurt Steiner said. "You gotta understand, he rambles sometimes when he's had a few."

"I figured."

"Solid. You're okay, Lambretta."

"Frank."

"Okay. We appreciate it, Frank."

"My pleasure."

"Yeah. Sleep tight."

They left him, fading back into the barracks proper, leaving Bolan alone in the latrine. Behind him, he could hear the rushing of the shower and Rafferty still muttering beneath the spray.

It was a start. The sergeant had distressed his friends, not once but twice, with his allusions to some covert bond between them. Bolan's gut was nagging at him, warning him of danger, but there was nothing firm for him to go on yet. For all he knew, the four might be involved in some illicit operation on the side—diverting arms to outside dealers, possibly, or dealing rations to the locals on the sly. They might have no connection whatsoever with the operation that McNerney and his backers had already set in motion.

Still, he felt it in his bones, along with weariness from the encounter in the alleyway. The four were dirty, and he would have bet his life that they had been tight with Pommeroy and Baker when the renegade Berets were still alive and kicking. As for the missing Charbonneau... well, he would have to wait and see.

A shower first, and then some sleep. Perhaps the answer would be waiting for him in restless dreams. If not, the Executioner would have to find it for himself tomorrow.

☆ 15 ☆

"You must have patience. Nothing happens overnight."

"Perhaps. But I grow tired of waiting."

Blancanales drained his beer and flagged the waiter for a refill. Seated opposite, the woman known as Esperanza watched him thoughtfully, a small frown altering her beauty but incapable of hiding it.

"You are impetuous, Rosario," she said. "Ortega's prisons taught you nothing."

"Oh, they taught me something," he responded, contradicting her. "They taught me that tomorrow is not guaranteed to any man...or woman. Those who would succeed make opportunities. They do not wait for chance or fate to deal a winning hand."

"You are a soldier in the people's army now. You do not have the luxury of acting on your own."

Politician spread his hands. "I simply wish to act."

At 10:30 p.m. the restaurant was crowded, patrons following the Latin custom of dining late. The place was not Tegucigalpa's most expensive—Pol was masquerading as a Nicaraguan exile, not a Texas millionaire—but it would do. Esperanza had been suitably impressed by his impulsive invitation, seemingly impressed by his selection of a restaurant. She might not dine in such surroundings often, but a survey of the other diners reassured Politician that she was the most attractive woman in the room.

Two days had passed since Blancanales—as Rosario Briones—had enlisted with the Contra team. As yet, he knew no more about their U.S. military links than he had at the beginning. There had been no further contact with Machado, the commander of the group, and the Gutierrezes, Raúl and Esperanza, answered all his questions with the vaguest generalities, while Anastasio Ruiz regarded him with frank suspicion and dislike. Pol dared not push too eagerly for information, knowing that the Contras lived in constant fear of infiltration and destruction by their enemies. He had mixed motives for the dinner invitation that had placed him in this restaurant, with Esperanza seated opposite: aside from the desire to speak with her in private and extract such information as he could, Pol was excited by her closeness, by the sensuality that she exuded without trying.

She was a sexy woman, and her allure was undiminished by her obvious intelligence. She understood the stakes in Nicaragua and Central America, had obviously considered her options before joining her brother in the Contra movement. Esperanza was committed to the liberation of her homeland from an ideology that she abhorred, and Blancanales knew that she had risked her life in combat situations more than once in that pursuit. That told him zip about Luis Machado's possible involvement with McNerney and the others, though. If the commander was in league with certain military renegades, how many of his aides were privy to the secret? Would Esperanza know, or would Machado keep her in the dark for reasons of enhanced security?

Politician realized that he was reaching now, attempting to absolve her in advance. He was attracted to her and he didn't want to count her with the opposition—didn't want to kill her—but he couldn't let his gonads do his thinking for him, either. If the Contras were involved, if Esperanza was among those dealing with McNerney's team, he would be forced to deal with them as enemies, regardless of the opposition's sex or sex appeal. It wouldn't be the first time that a soldier's duty ran against the grain, against his heart, but Blancanales was a soldier first and foremost. He would do his duty if it killed him.

The Contras were a tight fraternity, as secretive in operation now as Daniel Ortega's Sandinista Front had been before the downfall of Somoza. Secrecy was paramount for any group outnumbered and outgunned from the beginning of its struggle. Knowledge filtered through the ranks on the basis of a need to know, and it was possible that Esperanza was unaware of a connection with McNerney and the other renegades, assuming such a link had been established.

Pol was wandering in mental circles, and he knew it. There were too many wild cards in the game for him to bet his life on anything. And yet, he had already done precisely that. The ante in this game was life or death, and every moment that he spent among the Contras raised the stakes. Inviting Esperanza out to dinner was a risky proposition in itself, inviting trouble from the likes of Anastasio Ruiz. Machado's slick lieutenant obviously wanted Esperanza for himself, and while she seemed oblivious to his desires, that didn't make the man less dangerous. If anything, her cool response appeared to make him want the lady even more, and if Ruiz began to think of Blancanales as a rival, it could lead to serious trouble.

So be it.

Pol was braced to use whatever weapons came to hand, emotional or otherwise, to break this thing wide open. If it took dissension in the ranks, then he was ready to oblige. And if the lady took a fancy to him in the meantime... well, far be it from the Able warrior to discourage her. The information gained through pillow talk could be invaluable to an agent in the field, and if it took romance to make the lady drop her guard, Politician was prepared to do his utmost for the cause.

Blancanales could have named a dozen things that he would rather do than tamper with the lady's feelings, but he had to play the circumstances as they came. She was available, and she was highly placed within the local Contra infrastructure. It was even money she would know about a deal with Mike McNerney's troops, if such a deal existed. Barring revelation of a better source, Politician would be forced to run with what he had.

"You've heard the story of my life," he said when they were finished with their salads. "How about yourself? What brings you to the movement?"

Esperanza thought about her answer for a moment, and her eyes were far away as she began to speak. "Raúl and I were raised outside León," she said. "Our father had a small plantation there. We were not wealthy, mind you, but we were not poor, as many of the people were and are today. Our parents sent us both to school, we had new clothes and decent food to eat, a home with walls and roof."

"The peasants envied you," he said.

The lady shrugged. "I did not understand this envy as a child. I knew my father dealt with President Somoza on occasion, that he offered information on the Sandinistas when guerrilla troops initiated their campaign around León. We recognized the danger, but it was an abstract thing. Our father did not seem to take it seriously. Why should we?"

She paused and sipped her wine while Blancanales waited for her to continue. He could predict the story's end already, but he sensed that Esperanza had to get there on her own. How long had it been since she dared to share the pain with anyone besides her brother? Might confronting it not help to wipe away the bitterness that he had sensed about her from the moment of their introduction?

"In the spring of 1980, after President Somoza fled, guerrillas came to see our father. They informed him that he had been charged with treason, and our mother had been named as his accomplice. They were shot before our eyes. Raúl and I were taken to a camp that offered social and political 'reeducation' to the chosen few. The officer in charge was a widower and very lonely. I was seventeen years old."

She didn't need to spell it out for Pol to get the picture. Esperanza sat with eyes downcast, and she avoided looking at the waiter when he brought their entrees.

"You got out," the Able warrior cautiously reminded her. "You're free now."

"Am I? Is it possible to shed your memories, your past, the way a reptile sheds its skin? Sometimes I feel that I have never left León, that I am still a child in the reeducation camp. Sometimes...I think that I may never put the blood and bitterness behind me."

"Why put yourself through all of that again?" he asked, sincerely curious about the lady's motives now.

"I owe it to my parents," she replied. "Until I have avenged their death and helped restore the freedom of my native land, I cannot rest."

"At least you're not alone. I mean, you have your brother, Anastasio, the rest."

Her smile was dazzling and somehow very sad. "Each of us is finally alone," she told him. "As for Anastasio...he looks for things that are not there."

"I'm glad to hear it."

"Are you?"

Blancanales nodded. "Yes. It gives me hope."

"Of what?"

"That you may be mistaken. Finally, we may not be alone."

"I knew you were impetuous," she said, "but I did not imagine you would be presumptuous, as well."

"Forgive me if I have offended you. I meant no harm."

"What did you mean?" she asked, and there was something playful in her eyes this time.

It was Politician's turn to shrug and smile. "We are engaged in a crusade that may require our lives," he said. "It seems a shame to die without experiencing life."

"Are you a man of no experience?"

"There are varieties, degrees," he told her in response. "A man who has consumed one apple may find others sweeter still."

"You are a man of many talents. First a warrior, now a horticulturist."

"You mock me."

"No. Well, just a little. But I meant no harm."

They laughed together, and he took her hand, surprised when she returned the gentle pressure, blushing. "We must eat," she said, "before our food gets cold."

"Don't worry," he replied. "It's warm in here tonight."

And it would be a great deal warmer soon, he thought, if things worked out. He'd need caution with the woman. She might be tough as tempered steel when making life and death decisions for the Contra troops, but she was fragile on the inside, and he didn't wish to be responsible for any damage there. At some point, the demands of duty trespassed on a soldier's conscience, and he had to make a choice before he trampled roughshod over other lives. Whatever followed naturally from their contact here tonight, Politician was prepared to see it through. But he was *not* prepared to sacrifice the lady needlessly.

Perhaps, he thought, the lady was prepared to use him, too. And that was fine, provided that he read her accurately, understood her well enough to recognize the risks involved and cope with them in time. If not, the give and take might get him killed, and Pol wasn't prepared to die. Not yet. Not here. Survival was the top priority, and he would cling to it by any means available, but there might be an opportunity for stolen comfort in the meantime. It wasn't often that you found an opportunity for recreation on the eve of battle, and if Pol could mix a little pleasure with his lethal business, he was game. And if it paid off for his mission, then so much the better.

ANASTASIO RUIZ was waiting, watching, when they left the restaurant. He had been with them from the time Briones picked up Esperanza at her lodgings, clinging like a shadow in the streets. While they were dining, he had waited in the darkness, raging silently against the stranger who was threatening his world. Fists clenched, he peered through the lighted windows at the patrons in their finery and wished them dead.

Ruiz had been in love with Esperanza from the moment she had first approached the Contra organizers with her brother. Bold, determined, she had touched Luis Machado with the story of her family's tragedy, but it had been her beauty that had impressed Ruiz. Beneath the dirt, the baggy clothing, he had seen a woman of incredible appeal. A bachelor all his life, convinced that he would never love or marry, Anastasio had been astounded by the depth of his emotion.

Esperanza had been something less than innocent, of course—he knew the story of her time in the reeducation camp—but still, Ruiz had treated her with absolute respect. Another man might have declared himself at once, attempting to seduce her with his wit and charm. Ruiz had neither, and he knew it. At night, when he was left alone to brood about his life, he realized that romance hadn't simply passed him by. It had retreated in a rush on each occasion when he had tried to find female companionship. The Contra soldier had no way with women, and before Luis had recruited the Gutierrezes, Anastasio had worried that he might grow old and die alone.

There were the prostitutes, of course, and anyone could be successful on the streets. The whores had never turned Ruiz away, although they had infected him with syphilis on two occasions. At the time, he hadn't minded; it had been worth the extra cost. A furtive moment of companionship, away from wars and talk of wars.

But Esperanza had changed everything. She treated him with kindness, smiled at him from time to time, and didn't flinch away on rare occasions when their hands touched accidentally. She brought a gentleness into Anastasio's existence, and he loved her all the more because she did it all unconsciously, completely unaware of her effect upon him. He had never dared to voice his feelings, always waiting for the perfect time, which never quite arrived.

On one occasion he had written her a letter, struggling through four drafts before he had gotten it right. He had walked three blocks to find a mailbox, quarreling with himself en route, one part of him afraid to mail the envelope, another portion burning with desire. As soon as he had released the letter, heard it drop into the mailbox, he had known that it was wrong somehow. She would be horrified—or worse, amused. He had strained to get the letter back, one arm thrust down the box's tight, unyielding throat, but all in vain. At last he had been compelled to drastic action. Sprinting back to his apartment, he had secured a handful of incendiary sticks, retraced his steps until he had reached the mailbox, primed the slender flares and thrust them down the box's open maw. He had been a block away and weeping bitterly before the box had begun to melt.

The incident had made him realize that he would have to take his time. There was no point in rushing into anything before he was prepared; he had already learned that much from military strategy.

Ruiz was barely competent in the performance of his duties, and in combat he was every bit as timid as he had been in his dealings with the ladies. Awkward—some said *ugly*—as a child, he'd borne the derision of other boys who had taunted him unmercifully. In time he had learned to shut them out, and when that blank stare appeared on his face, they had gone in search of other fools to torment, leaving Anastasio alone. In certain ways the solitude had been infinitely worse, and there had been days when he had wished for playmates to belittle him, make jokes about his posture, his complexion—anything. At least while they had jeered at him, it had meant that they had recognized the fact of his existence.

It was his fault, of course, as it had always been his fault. In social situations, Anastasio invariably put his worst foot forward, bringing ridicule and shame upon himself and his companions. When the Contras needed someone to present their cause in public and Luis was unavailable, they canvassed members of the rank and file, ignoring Anastasio, forewarned by past experience. They knew the way he froze in crowds, the way his tongue refused to follow orders from his brain when he was called upon to speak in public. None of them referred to Anastasio's affliction when they passed him over—none of them would dare—but neither would they offer him the rostrum while a viable alternative remained.

Sometimes the speaker's duties fell to Esperanza, and on those occasions Anastasio was more than happy as a member of the audience. It granted him the opportunity to stare at her, unashamed, pretending he was fascinated by her speech instead of by her face, her almost otherworldly radiance. She had the ability to charm the crowds, and contributions doubled after Esperanza took the dais with her stories of the living hell that Nicaragua had become. There wouldn't be a dry eye in the house...except, perhaps, for certain fat cats who were wondering what Esperanza would be like in bed.

Let them wonder, as long as none of them made any effort to find out. Ruiz would gut them like the pigs they were and hang them up to bleed if any one of them should dare to lay a hand on Esperanza. She was his, although she didn't know it yet.

Of late, since the appearance of Rosario Briones, Esperanza had been taking on another form before his very eyes. Ruiz couldn't be sure of what was happening, but he had dark suspicions, and the evidence appeared to bear him out. Where Esperanza had remained aloof from men before, he often caught her examining Briones from across the room now, intent on every word the new man said. He had surprised them in the midst of conversation more than once, and he wasn't deceived by their attempts to steer the topic back toward military strategy.

For three years Anastasio had yearned for Esperanza, and now she was lavishing her attentions on a stranger. Was she sleeping with him yet? Ruiz dared not confront the question, knowing it could snap his mind. If Esperanza had betrayed him, he would kill her. No, not that... but he *might* kill her lover. And if the deed was done before Briones actually became her lover, why, so much the better.

It would be difficult, of course. Not the mechanics of the thing; life was a cheap commodity throughout Honduras, with supply far greater than demand. But the logistics would be something else entirely. If Briones simply disappeared—or worse, if he was cut down on the street, like something from a Yankee gangster film—there would be questions. From Luis. From the authorities. From other members of the Contra team. Ruiz had made no secret of his feelings toward the new recruit, and he would be suspected instantly... unless Briones was exposed for what he was: a threat to the stability of everything that they had worked for through the bitter years.

How best to do the job? What sort of planted evidence would be required to paint Briones as a traitor to the cause? Whatever was required, Ruiz would spare no effort in his drive to save the movement, save his woman. Save himself.

Esperanza and the stranger emerged from the restaurant, laughing underneath the streetlights, and she had one hand looped through the bastard's arm as if they were embarking on a promenade. Ruiz felt sick, light-headed, and he locked his teeth against the scream that threatened to erupt from his throat. He let them lead, already conscious of their destination, trailing at a distance, one more shadow in the night. He stood across the street from Esperanza's lodgings while they huddled in the doorway opposite, all lips and searching hands until she called a breathless halt and broke away. Despite the darkness and the distance, he could see the flaming color in her cheeks and felt himself responding, stiffening, but there was no time now for fantasy.

Ruiz had two alternatives: he could confront her now and force her to acknowledge him, his love...or he could trail Briones and attempt to gather evidence against the stranger who was now his mortal enemy. Considering the options, it was really no damned choice at all. He dared not bare his soul to Esperanza, even now. If she rejected him in anger—worse, if she should *laugh*—Ruiz would be destroyed.

Briones, then. He let the slick *pendejo* put a block between them, falling into step and running parallel along the other sidewalk. Streetlights here were few and far between; if Anastasio's quarry turned and tried to catch Ruiz in action, shadowed doorways could conceal him in an instant. Nothing could go wrong.

Briones walked for half a mile or so in the direction of his rooming house before he veered off track along a narrow, darkened side street, picking up the pace. Ruiz was momentarily afraid that he had blown the tail, but there was no sign from Briones. Anastasio proceeded with caution, one eye on his quarry while the other scanned for any hostile movement in the shadows. When he satisfied himself that there was nothing, he proceeded with alacrity, intent on closing the gap.

Downrange, a dark sedan had nosed into the curb beside Briones, and the man was hesitating, glancing back along his path suspiciously. Ruiz ducked back into the shadows of a vacant doorway, praying he hadn't been seen. Another moment, knowing that he might have lost his prey already, and he peered around the corner, risking everything.

A rear door of the car was opening. Briones scrambled inside. The dome light showed two more faces. The driver was a blonde, perhaps American. The second man had dark hair, Anastasio could see that much, but then his features were obscured by Briones's silhouette.

Ruiz exploded from the doorway, sprinting after them, bent low to make himself a smaller target if they saw him coming. He wouldn't attempt to stop them, but the dark sedan was moving now, and he had no means of identifying them for future reference. If he could just get close enough, before they pulled away...

At thirty yards, he knew it was a rental, branded with a sticker in the window. Twenty yards, and he was close enough to read the license plate, already dropping to a crouch against the curb, committing it to memory as they accelerated and disappeared around the corner.

Strange, indeed. The meeting might not be incriminating in itself—a number of the Contras ran illicit operations on the side, returning portions of their income to the movement—but the rental plate would be worth checking out. He wouldn't do the job himself, but there were ways. Too late for any action now, but in the morning...

In the morning, yes, Ruiz would have a word with Travers and put the wheels in motion. If Rosario Briones had a secret, it would soon be placed beneath a microscope for all the world to see.

☆ 16 ☆

They had been stalking Bolan since an hour after sunup. Of the four who had started out on the hunt, he had eliminated only one. Four hours. At this rate it would take all day to clear his backtrack, if they didn't tag him first. He checked his weapon, counted four rounds left, together with the extra load. It ought to be enough if he conserved his ammunition and chose his targets carefully.

The forest was alive with rustling sounds and dancing shadows, tempting him to fire on anything that moved. It would be easy to expend his small supply of ammunition, but experience in jungle fighting had prepared him for the wait. If they were looking for him, they would find him; he had left a subtle trail designed to lure his pursuers into range. It had already worked with one of them, and it would work again unless they saw through Bolan's strategy. Unless they took him by surprise somehow.

The jungles of Honduras brought back vivid memories of Vietnam. The latitude and climate were enough like Southeast Asia that the countries could have passed as twins, until you met the natives. Even then, there were dramatic similarities: the prevailing agricultural economy; uneven distribution of wealth; pervasive poverty afflicting the majority of citizens; a history of military occupation. Dialects and racial strains might differ, fauna might not coincide, but the Honduran peasant would be quick to understand his Asian counterpart if they were ever face-to-face.

Just now, the forests brought back other memories, of being hunted by a killer force intent upon the Executioner's destruction. Bolan had been through it time and time again. He had survived thus far by virtue of the fact that he had never taken survival for granted. If the Executioner knew anything, he knew you had to work at living in the hellgrounds, every day and every minute. If you let your guard down, you were finished, and the jackals would be gnawing on your bones.

Perched above the game trail, lying prone along a massive limb, concealed by leaves and vines, he heard the hunters coming. One of them, at least, had found his trail. The man was moving stealthily, employing every trick he knew, and he was almost good enough.

Almost.

At twenty yards the soldier knew for certain that his adversary was alone. He couldn't see the hunter yet, and Bolan spent another moment making sure that the others weren't flanking him. Clearly they had separated, opting for a sector search that let them cover ground in shorter time. It also left them vulnerable, as the new arrival was about to learn.

Ten yards, and now he knew that it was Steiner on his trail, a thatch of Nordic wheat protruding from beneath his green beret, the cold blue eyes intently scanning Bolan's track. The guy was good. He hadn't missed a trick so far, remaining on the scent like a determined bloodhound. There was no way Steiner could have known he had already blown it, that the Executioner had traveled arrow-straight for fifty yards beyond his present vantage point, then doubled back along a different course to take up his position in the trees. There were no clues for Steiner to interpret, nothing to alert him as he did the only thing he could do.

Bolan let the hunter pass directly under him, content to watch and reassure himself that there would be no reinforcements closing in to box him when he made his move. The trail behind his adversary was deserted, and he couldn't hear any sounds of parallel pursuit on either side.

He rolled out and dropped ten feet to make a perfect touchdown on the forest floor. Already in a crouch and sighting into target acquisition, he was squeezing off as Steiner spun to meet his doom. A single round exploded in the hunter's face, erupting in a crimson shower, speckling the jacket of his camouflaged fatigues.

"You're dead," the Executioner informed him, rising from his crouch. "Go home."

"God*damn* it, I was sure I had you." Steiner grinned through lips and teeth made hideous by Bolan's killing shot. The air gun's pellet, filled with paint, was soft enough to burst on impact, but it must have stung in any case. The soldier rubbed his cheek with one hand, smearing phony blood on face and fingers, then withdrew a mourner's armband, hoisting it around his sleeve to indicate a walking corpse. "I'm out of here," he said, good-naturedly. "We'll catch you at the rendezvous."

"So long."

The game had been proposed by Jason Rafferty at breakfast, following their confrontation with the street toughs in Tegucigalpa's red-light district. Bolan and a couple of the others had been tied down with assignments for the afternoon, but they had wriggled out next morning on the pretext that their game was a survival training exercise. Aware that he was being tested, Bolan had gone along with Rafferty's suggestion that he play the fox against four hounds.

"We used to have a couple of other guys who liked to play," the sergeant had informed him, "but they had an accident. The fatal kind."

"Tough break."

And standing in the forest clearing, Bolan could recall the sergeant's total absence of emotion as he had shrugged it off. "They come and go," he'd said, and that had been the end of it.

There had been suspicions that the others might have found him out somehow. If they knew of Bolan's mission, if Brognola's allies back in Wonderland were playing both sides of the fence, he was as good as dead. The game would offer Rafferty and friends a perfect opportunity to silence him, with only minor questions if an accident should suddenly befall the new boy. He thought of going armed with more than just a pellet gun, but finally discarded the idea and settled for the Ka-Bar on his belt. If one of them was packing, he would have to deal with it as best he could. Thus far his fears hadn't been realized.

And it was time for the Lambretta fox to teach the hounds precisely what it felt like to be hunted. They would be expecting him to run, or stand and fight if he could find a suitable redoubt, but they wouldn't be braced for a reversal of the roles that Rafferty had chosen. Bolan would be "it," but with a difference; he would be pursuing his pursuers, doubling back to hunt them down like animals.

Bolan started working back along a path that paralleled his former trail. He took his time, preferring silence to the extra speed he could gain by throwing caution to the wind. Whatever else they might be, Bolan's adversaries were professionals, and they would seize upon his smallest error. If he was to win their trust and admiration, it was necessary that he win this game with no holds barred. Annihilation was the ticket, even if it was a simulated slaughter this time out. Next time, he knew, the circumstances might be decidedly more deadly.

Half an hour later, Bolan spotted Broderick. The trooper had declared a unilateral time-out, relaxing with his back against a tree trunk, smoking. Bolan did a silent recon, making certain that he wasn't being suckered, with Rafferty waiting somewhere to effect the kill. In fact, it seemed that Broderick was simply taking five, relying on the fox to be away and running while he broke formation. It was careless, and it said a lot about the man. It was about to get him killed.

Bolan noted the pistol in his adversary's lap before he made his move. He knew that Broderick would respond efficiently to any sign of danger, and he also knew that lag time would prevent the guy from making it in time. Without a miracle to tip the scales, it would be virtually impossible for Broderick to defend himself against an ambush. Bolan had the firm advantage of surprise...until he showed himself.

Before he cleared the wall of ferns and creepers, Bolan's adversary was already scrambling to his feet, the cigarette forgotten, both hands digging for the weapon in his lap. Before he had a chance to line it up, a crimson pellet spattered on his forehead, staining his beret and blinding him with dye. He stumbled on a root and sat down hard, rough knuckles grinding at his eyes until they cleared.

"What kinda shit-ass trick is that?" he growled.

"The kind that wins. You're dead," the Executioner reminded him.

"Some kinda smartass," Broderick muttered, but he pulled the mourning armband on, retrieved his weapon and moved toward the game trail in a sulk. "Raff's gonna drop you, guy."

"We'll see."

Three down, and one remaining in the bush. DiSalvo and his sidekick, Steiner, had been trackers, homing in on Bolan's trail while Broderick had opted to relax and sit it out. If Bolan read the sergeant right, he would be working on another angle of attack. If he had double-timed, for instance, he could be ahead of Bolan now, expecting company along the trail. It would be an audacious move, and risky: if he stayed in place, "Lambretta" might not pass his way, and if he put himself on roving stakeout, they could miss each other just as easily.

It would be Bolan's task to guarantee they didn't miss each other. He would have to find the sergeant's trap and spring it, with enough room left to turn the setup around and make it work against his adversary. It would be simple. Just like falling off a cliff.

Reloading, Bolan mulled over the countless possible locations for an ambush. The whole damned forest was a hiding place, but Rafferty wouldn't be trying to conceal himself so much as he would be intent on flushing out his prey. His choice would have to be a relatively obvious position...obvious to Bolan as a "safe" retreat, that is. The sergeant would be courting disappointment if he hid himself too well, because no one was looking for him.

Bolan finally opted for the trail he had been following throughout the day. There had been ample time for Rafferty to cover ground and find himself a hiding spot, waiting for the fox to make himself available. He might have counted on "Lambretta" setting up an ambush of his own, eliminating one or more of the pursuers prior to moving on. If true, it meant the sergeant was prepared to sacrifice his men if it would help him draw the winning hand. It wasn't the strategy they taught at Benning, but his quarry wouldn't pass for average or normal in the Special Forces. Thousands of the Green Berets were dedicated to their country, prepared to die in her defense. Of those thousands, half a dozen had apparently gone sour at the urgings of an overwrought commander whose dreams were nibbling away at hard reality.

The fault wasn't with Special Forces, Bolan knew. It lay with General McNerney and his handful of superiors, men who should have been removed from office years ago. Somewhere along the line those men had lost the meaning of America, her Constitution and the Bill of Rights. They had presumed to think and act for every man and woman in the nation, and along the way they had seduced accomplices who shared their hopes and fears, their paranoia.

It was Bolan's job to stop them, but he had to start with Rafferty. Right now.

The trail ran serpentine for fifty yards, then straightened on the downslope toward a river. When he heard the water, Bolan knew instinctively that he had found his man. Not literally, of course... but Rafferty was there. He felt the sergeant's presence, just as the predatory cat sometimes feels its prey.

But this rat wouldn't budge until Bolan showed himself and offered his quarry a target. He could search the trees and riverbank for hours, days, without discovering the sergeant's hiding place, but if he seemed to let his guard down, then Rafferty would come to him.

There was a possibility that Bolan's prey would simply cut him down from ambush and emerge from cover only once the kill had been confirmed. It was the cautious way to go... but Bolan didn't read his adversary as a cautious man. The sergeant would be eager for a taste of blood by now, albeit artificial blood. He would surmise from Bolan's presence that the others had been circumvented or eliminated, and he would be anxious to redeem the honor of his team. But most of all, he wouldn't like to lose.

It would require split-second timing, and Bolan would be hampered by the fact that Rafferty could strike from any of a hundred hiding places, firing before the Executioner could take evasive action. Somehow he would have to see it coming, give himself the edge required to take his adversary down without himself becoming a statistic of the game.

He broke from cover, edging down the riverbank, pretending relaxation that he didn't feel. He held the air gun casually, its muzzle pointed toward the ground as if an ambush was the last thing on his mind. The warrior's combat senses were alert to any hint of sound or movement in the undergrowth, prepared to strike.

He knelt beside the stream and pretended to examine muddy soil for traces of his quarry, knowing Rafferty wouldn't be fool enough to leave his prints behind. The soldier drew a breath and held it, straining to hear anything beyond the pulse drumming in his ears.

Out of the corner of his eye, he saw a flicker accompanied by the whisper of a weapon rising and brushing through the overhanging ferns. He kicked back, rolling clear as Rafferty squeezed off, imagining that he could feel the pellet brush his cheek before it plopped into the stream, imparting murky color to the water. As he pivoted to bring his adversary under fire, he slid the air gun out to full extension and squeezed off at speed until the magazine was empty. Ferns and tree trunks speckled crimson, like the figure rising out of cover, smiling through a mask of camou war paint.

"You got lucky, man." The recent corpse was checking out his "wounds," a smear of paint across one shoulder and another on his thigh. "Rules say a solid hit is fatal, period. If this was all for real, I'd still be after you."

If this was all for real.

"Sometimes the rules are helpful," Bolan told him.

"Sometimes," Rafferty agreed. "But most times they're just in the way."

They walked back to the rendezvous in silence and found the others waiting with their camou paint and stage blood cleaned away. When they were all assembled, Broderick produced a six-pack and the cans were passed around.

"You did all right," DiSalvo said.

"All right? He took us all," the sergeant interjected.

"Some kinda fucking Jap or something, sneaking up that way," Tim Broderick growled.

"Will you grow up?" Kurt Steiner's voice and glare were withering. "You think he's gonna send a telegram ahead?"

"He cheated!"

"Shit."

"Will you guys can it?" Rafferty had moved to stand between them like a referee. "We're not out here to argue with each other, okay? Let's stick to business. And for future reference, Tim, I felt like taggin' you myself, the way you had yourself laid out. This wasn't supposed to be a fuckin' bivouac."

He turned toward Bolan, leaving Broderick to fume alone. "I'll tell you right up front. I've had a look inside your file."

"That's confidential," Bolan answered, hoping that he looked surprised.

"I didn't say I took an ad out, man. Let's say I was interested in your background, okay?"

"How come?"

"We're into something here that's gonna make a difference for the future, for America. We had a coupla other guys, but they got tagged while they were in the field. We're looking at a deadline now, and we could use another hand."

"You don't give much away."

"We can't afford to, man."

"What kind of operation are we looking at?"

"The details aren't important now. Let's say we're setting up Ortega and his Sandinistas, fixing things so Uncle Sam will have a prime excuse to kick some ass."

"What makes you think that I'd be interested?"

"I told you, man, I've seen your file. Remember Thailand? Hell, you shoulda had a freakin' medal for the way you tracked those zipperheads to Laos, but they hit you with a reprimand instead. Don't tell me that it doesn't frost you, either, 'cause I've been there. And I know about the rest of it—at Benning, in your classes, all of that reeducation work you've done in bars and honky-tonks. I've *been* there, man."

"I'll need more details on the operation."

"When you're on the inside, man. Right now, it's need-to-know."

"Hey, Raff, forget this guy."

"Shut up, Tim!"

Bolan glanced at Broderick and read the animosity behind his eyes. The soldier was a rotten loser, and he obviously held a grudge. He might be perfect as a human wedge between the other members of McNerney's fire team. Once the shooters were taken out of action, he would have the time to deal with their superiors.

"Suppose I pass?" he asked the sergeant.

Rafferty was deadpan. "We forget the whole damned thing," he said. "You've got no evidence against us. We're home free. Let's say I trust you not to squeal."

Like hell. If Bolan passed the offer now, he could expect to play the game of fox and hounds again, this time for stakes of life and death. He wondered whether Charbonneau had been approached, if he had turned the plotters down, but it was futile speculation and he gave it up at once.

The Executioner didn't intend to turn the offer down. He had been looking for precisely such a handle on his mission. Whatever happened afterward, he would be going in with both eyes open, braced for anything.

"Okay," he said. "I'm in."

☆ 17 ☆

"The bloke's moving."

Yakov Katzenelenbogen didn't turn immediately, appearing to ignore McCarter's warning. He was dawdling along the sidewalk like a tourist, oblivious to the pedestrians and traffic all around him. Those who took the time to notice would have seen a man of average height with graying hair and hearing aid. American or European by the look of him, undoubtedly on holiday. None would have guessed that he was armed, or that the "hearing aid" was actually a small receiver, mated to the miniature transmitter that he wore—disguised as a Masonic pin—on his lapel. And if he muttered to himself from time to time, a casual observer might ascribe his strange behavior to the eccentricity of tourists.

Katz could see his mark now, a distorted image in the plate glass window, passing on the far side of the street. Ruiz had spent an hour in the bar beneath McCarter's watchful eye, and the Israeli had been on the verge of ducking in to find some shade when the former SAS commando had advised him that their man was on the move. Katz hoped that he was going somewhere for a change.

Five days on station in Tegucigalpa, and the men of Phoenix Force had come up empty. They had staked out local Contra leaders and shadowed them around the clock without discovering a link to General McNerney and his coconspirators. While Katzenelenbogen and McCarter followed Anastasio Ruiz, Gary Manning and Encizo were assigned to Luis Machado. Calvin James was odd man out, detailed to follow Raúl Gutierrez as best he could. The Phoenix warriors cheerfully agreed that Blancanales had the woman covered well enough already.

They had been on-site and waiting when Politician had made his contact with the Contra forces. The Stony Man team was set to pull him out if anything went sour, but Blancanales had come through in style. The woman, Esperanza, was a beauty, and the chemistry had sparked with Blancanales from their first encounter. Katz had felt a pang of envy, sure... until he remembered where their game was heading, toward inevitable violence of the body and the soul. If they were wrong, if local Contras had no linkup with McNerney's rogue machine, then Pol would still be forced to disengage himself from Esperanza. And if they were right, then the lady might be part and parcel of the problem.

Katz felt a sneaking admiration for the Contras and their lost crusade. As an Israeli, old enough to recall memories of Palestine when it was still part of Britain's empire, he could sympathize with anybody fighting to regain their homeland. As a warrior who had seen the Sandinista Front in action, Katzenelenbogen wished the Contras well. But if their war had crossed the line, subverting U.S. military missions and corrupting personnel, then he would strike against the local Contras with the same ferocity reserved for terrorists in general. Emotions had no place in plotting strategy.

McCarter had emerged from the cantina, glancing right and left before he fell in step a block behind Ruiz.

Katz had already tagged their mark across the street, prepared to intercept in case of any unforeseen emergency. Ideally they would simply tail Ruiz, observing any contacts, noting any drops or pickups, and with any luck at all they would be able to find out what he was doing. And if luck held up, he might be doing more than simply killing time.

A phone tap could have saved some time, but Katz had scrubbed the notion after learning that Machado and his people used pay phones exclusively. If several calls were necessary, Anastasio, the woman or her brother made the rounds, calling from successive booths until the circuit brought them home again. If they received an urgent call, they would respond by reading off the number of the nearest kiosk, and one of them would be there, waiting when the caller dropped his second coin.

That left the roving tail, and so far it had come to nothing. From appearances, the Contras lived inside a bubble of their own creation, shunning any social contact with the locals, cleaving to their fellow refugees when it was time for R and R. They were a closed community, at least until Politician had slipped inside—and so far he hadn't produced a shred of evidence to link them with McNerney's operation, either.

Perhaps today.

Ruiz was making for a restaurant, McCarter on his heels. Katz started for the corner, then changed his mind and cut across in front of traffic, dodging as a taxi driver held the pedal down without attempting to decelerate.

"He's going in," McCarter said. "I'm on him."

Do it, the Israeli thought . . . and realized that he had actually spoken when an aging female tourist froze beside him, one hand raised to flag a taxi, staring at him curiously. Katz pushed on, determined to cover Ruiz in case he stopped for something other than an early lunch.

The Phoenix warrior sensed that they were running out of time. He couldn't have explained the feeling if his life depended on it, but experience had taught him to respect his instincts. They were working on a deadline, and the fact that they were ignorant of any limitations on the game would only make the play that much more dangerous. McNerney and his troops, Ruiz and his companions, might be on the verge of pulling something off tonight, tomorrow, which would take the SOG force by surprise. And in a combat situation, Katzenelenbogen knew, the slim advantage of surprise could make the difference between survival and sudden, violent death.

The restaurant was cool and dark inside. He spied McCarter in a tiny booth perhaps five meters from the table where Ruiz was seated with a tall American. Katz didn't recognize the contact, and he dared not push his luck by asking for adjacent tables. They would have to split the tail now, one of them remaining with Ruiz, the other on the tall man when he left. Katz waved the waiter off and found an empty bar stool, cranking it around until he had a glimpse of Anastasio Ruiz and his companion from the corner of one eye. He ordered a beer and settled down to wait.

LANE TRAVERS hated dealing with his contacts in public. It violated every standard rule of operations taught at Langley, and it made him nervous, wondering who might be watching, listening, recording every word he said. The restaurant, for instance. It was nice enough, as foreign squat-and-gobbles go, but was it secure? He would have needed wire men, all the slick technicians who were readily available back home, to sweep the place and finally pronounce it clean. Of course, Lane Travers had no wire men or technicians at his beck and call. He had a staff of twelve, including secretaries, and a rather more extensive net of contract agents who were constantly on call. They served him well enough on simple break-ins, or to handle the elimination of an enemy from time to time, but they were strictly second-class.

Travers missed the States and drew no consolation from the knowledge that his present mission might be vital to American security for years to come. A ten-year man with the CIA in foreign posts, he knew how words like "national security" were tossed around to justify the most outlandish operations. Castro was a prime example. When they couldn't kill him, Langley's brains began extracting new proposals from the Twilight Zone. They made plans to sprinkle a depilatory powder on his clothes, to blitz the famous beard, to impregnate his cigars with LSD or to wire a clamshell to explode while he was swimming in the area. It was the kind of thinking that had made the Agency a laughingstock for years, and Travers was immediately cautious when the men upstairs began appealing to his love of country, Mom and apple pie.

The Nicaraguan deal was different, however. Three years in Honduras had convinced the Company that Daniel Ortega and his Sandinista Front were hell-bent on expansion. Soon, inevitably, they would cross the border, north or south, and start to gobble up their neighbors. When it happened, the United States would be confronted with another Vietnam in its own backyard. The Langley brains had hammered out a plan that would eliminate the middleman and take out the Sandinistas before they had a chance to call the play. Travers was enthusiastic when he learned that members of the army general staff were backing up the Agency, but his enthusiasm had been tempered by his first encounter with Brigadier General Mike McNerney.

Travers wouldn't say the man was absolutely nuts, but there was something in McNerney's eyes, his voice, that smacked of raw fanaticism. Travers dealt with him infrequently, preferring to receive instructions and relay his answers through subordinates whenever possible.

The plan had sounded clean and simple at the outset. All they had to do was strike a spark and let the Sandinistas run with it, provoking an American reaction before Ortega's forces were strong enough to wage a protracted war. It would be like Grenada—in and out before the bastards knew what hit them. Stars and stripes forever, bet your ass. But somehow, over time, the plan had begun to change. Instead of waging war against the Sandinistas, one of Mike McNerney's boys was helping them interrogate their prisoners—in Nicaragua, yet. Another of his guys was playing footsie with guerrillas in the Costa Rican highlands, and who knew where it all would end?

For Pommeroy and Baker, it had ended with the grave, and Travers had been sweating ever since the word had come down. Two friendly dead, in separate operations, miles apart. Unless you were a firm believer in coincidence, you had to figure something had gone wrong, but it didn't deter McNerney from proceeding with the plan on schedule. Phase three, the final stage, was set to run the day after tomorrow, and here Travers was, killing time in a café with Anastasio Ruiz.

He didn't like the Contra second-in-command. The guy reminded Travers of a weasel, with his beady eyes and pointed nose. Each time they met, the man from Langley half expected Anastasio to have some chicken feathers dangling from his mouth. The other Contras were okay—and Travers wouldn't have objected to some undercover work with Esperanza what's-her-name—but he wouldn't trust Anastasio Ruiz out of his sight. For all he knew, the weasel might be working for Ortega's people, masquerading as a Nicaraguan patriot.

"Let's keep this brief," he said before Ruiz was even settled in his chair. You had to show the natives who was running things. "I've got a shitload of appointments, and I don't have any time to waste."

"I shall not waste your time, *señor*. I think you will be grateful that I called."

"Get on with it."

"Luis has taken on a new man named Rosario Briones."

"So?"

"He is not what he seems."

Lane Travers felt his stomach tighten, just a twinge at first, but there was worse to come. "Go on."

"I was suspicious of this new one when Raúl presented him to Luis. Last night I followed him."

There was an undercurrent to the Contra's tone, betraying some unspoken animosity, but Travers wanted solid information, and he didn't give a damn about emotions in the long run. "What's the punch line?"

"Punch?"

"Where did he go?"

"A rented car was waiting for him on the street. Calle Rivera. Two men in the front, one of them blond. American, I think."

"I don't suppose you got the license number?"

Ruiz held out a slip of paper. Travers took it gingerly, avoiding contact with the Contra's hand. It was a local plate, and there would be no problem making a connection to the rental agency. From that point on, however, he was likely to be dealing with an alias and phony address. Still, it was the only lead he had, and he would have to check it out.

"What tipped you off to this Briones?"

"His behavior," Anastasio replied. "The inappropriate advances that he makes to one of his superiors."

The woman, Travers thought, and in a flash he knew Ruiz wasn't concerned about the operation or Luis Machado's personal security. He had the hots for Esperanza, dammit, and the new man was about to beat his time. Ruiz pretended that he thought his rival might be pumping her for information, but if Travers knew his man, it was a different sort of pumping that the weasel had in mind. He was about to tell the bastard off... but what if Anastasio was right about the new boy? What if the rental car checked out? Could the covert meeting, the appearance of a new man on the scene, have any bearing on McNerney's plans?

It was a long shot, but the man from the CIA couldn't afford to let it slide without a closer look. He thought of Pommeroy and Baker, felt his stomach doing barrel rolls at the suggestion that their deaths might be connected with Ruiz, his unknown contacts in Tegucigalpa. If there was concerted opposition to McNerney's scheme, and if that opposition had progressed this far, all holy hell was going to break loose within the next two days.

Lane Travers didn't need this kind of grief. He definitely did not need another meeting with McNerney, not this close to the old man's explosion after Baker had bought the farm in Costa Rica. He would run the plate this afternoon and see where that might lead before he started blowing any whistles. In the meantime, Anastasio could keep an eye on this Briones character and tag him if the guy got too far out of line.

"Have you discussed this matter with Luis?" he asked the weasel.

"No. I did not wish to burden him with such a matter."

"Good idea," he said, and thought, You greasy bastard. Are you playing both ends off against the middle now? "You'll keep in touch?"

"Of course, *señor*."

He left a few lempiras on the table, trusting in Ruiz to separate his payoff from the waiter's tip. The weasel had a knack for taking care of number one, but he was getting too ambitious for Lane Travers's taste. Luis Machado was a patriot, committed to the liberation of his homeland and afflicted with the sort of tunnel vision that was not uncommon in the ranks of revolutionary freedom fighters. Focused on the common enemy with such intensity that he couldn't detect ambitious would-be traitors in the ranks, Machado might turn out to be an easy mark for someone like Ruiz. McNerney's operation could provide the perfect background for some sudden changes in the Contra leadership, and Travers cringed at the idea of Anastasio Ruiz in charge.

If things began to lean that way, he might be forced to take a hand, but there was time yet. This other matter with Briones required his more immediate attention. If he couldn't sort it out himself, he'd have to run the problem past McNerney, and he knew what that would mean.

Two days remaining. Travers wondered if his aching gut could take it, or if it would turn upon him like some kind of gastric Frankenstein and eat him up alive. Of course he had no choice. The man from Langley was committed. He had paid his money, and his ticket had been punched. Lane Travers was riding to the end of the line.

"STAY ON RUIZ. I'll take the stranger."

Katzenelenbogen's quarry was already half a block away before he reached the sidewalk, veering right and falling into step. If he maintained his course, the mark would pass directly through downtown Tegucigalpa.

Katz had given up on guessing at the man's identity. He was American—that much was obvious. He wore a business suit despite the heat, which placed him in the realm of government or business. From his appearance, he might have been a junior diplomat or the assistant manager of a department store. Katz wasn't banking on the latter possibility, but anything was possible. In 1954 the CIA had helped to overthrow the Guatemalan government at the behest of the United Fruit Company. Twenty years later, in Chile, the price of copper had as much to do with the Allende ouster as did socialism and the specter of a Cuban foothold on the mainland. You could never tell, and Katz was making no assumptions as he trailed his quarry through the noonday traffic toward the heart of the Honduran capital.

It would be simpler if Katzenelenbogen's mark turned out to be a private citizen, with no connection to McNerney or the rest of it. Assorted U.S. businessmen were known to help out the Contras with gifts of cash, equipment and the like. Ruiz might very well have been arranging for a fresh donation to the coffers...or his meeting with the slim American might have a more insidious interpretation. Either way, the Phoenix warrior had to satisfy himself before he closed the book on Anastasio Ruiz.

And if the mark turned out to be a U.S. agent, it would still prove nothing. The American involvement in support of Contra forces was an open book. Indeed, it would have been surprising if Machado's team didn't have contact with the local embassy. A simple meeting would establish nothing with regard to Mike McNerney and his rogue commandos, but it might supply the Phoenix soldiers with a name, a place to start with their investigation.

Once again he was oppressed by the conviction that they must be running out of time. For maximum effect, McNerney and his crew would need to move before the final votes were cast on the appropriations bill in Washington. If they could light the fuse while Congress was debating future funding for the Contra movement, they would have a captive audience. A border incident precisely timed—or, better yet, a border war—would force the undecided senators and representatives to make their choice, and it would doubtless swing a number of the "nay" votes over to the Contra side. Without a schedule or a blueprint of McNerney's plans, the gruff Israeli might be flying blind, but he had learned to trust his hunches in a combat situation, and this time out he knew for certain that the enemy was primed to strike.

The mark had reached his destination, disappearing through the double doors of the Honduran version of a high rise. Katz picked up his pace and was in time to spot his man before the elevator doors slid shut. The setup was Honduras "modern," with a pointer mounted on the wall above the elevator doors, which indicated six floors. The Phoenix warrior's man got off on five.

Katz doubled back to the directory, which he had passed on entering. The first three floors were occupied by lawyers and accountants. Number four was roughly split between an advertising agency and an investment firm. The fifth floor had a single occupant, identified as International Security Consultants: InterSec. And it was making sense already.

Katz didn't have to check the daily codes to know that InterSec was a facade for local operations of the CIA. The guy, whoever he might be, was working for the Company.

That complicated matters, but it didn't make the job impossible. He had contended with the CIA before, on friendly terms as well as under hostile circumstances, and the tough Israeli wouldn't mind if he was forced to step on Langley's toes. In fact, if any of the local spooks were dealing with McNerney on the side, Katzenelenbogen might enjoy it.

Hal had warned them from the outset of a CIA involvement with the Nicaraguan scheme. It came as no surprise, therefore, to learn that grass-roots agents might be implicated, but it would be Katzenelenbogen's task to estimate the level of involvement on the part of station personnel, then decide on the appropriate response. In short, he would be forced to make a choice on who should live and who should die.

Before he could perform that function properly, Katz knew that he would need more information. He could hardly run a questionnaire past InterSec's executives, but there was always an alternative. Perhaps Brognola...

Hal had assured them of support and promised them cooperation at the highest levels. Someone must be able to obtain the names and mug shots of the staff at InterSec. The Phoenix warriors would then at least be able to identify their enemies on sight...assuming that the InterSec connection traced back to McNerney and his rogues.

Assumptions. Katz was sick and tired of playing mind games while the clock ran down to zero hour, when there was necessary action to be taken.

Soon.

But in the meantime he would have to play the waiting game and stretch their forces even thinner, covering Ruiz's contact while maintaining a constant vigil on the Contras. For the moment it would have to do. And if the whole damned thing blew up in Katzenelenbogen's face... well, he would make the best of it and take as many of the bastards with him as he could. But first things first. And at the top of Katzenelenbogen's new agenda was a rush communiqué to Wonderland.

☆ 18 ☆

"You say we have a problem. Spell it out."

"I said we might be looking at a problem, General. Nothing's been confirmed."

McNerney waved his hand in a dismissive gesture. "Never mind the confirmation. Give me what you've got."

Lane Travers cleared his throat and shifted in the straight-backed wooden chair. He looked uncomfortable, and McNerney hoped that looks were not deceiving. As a military officer, accustomed to the open battlefield, he was suspicious of the CIA in general, uneasy with Lane Travers in particular. McNerney was convinced that Travers lacked the nerve to make a first-class fighting man. He worried that the man from Langley might fold when things got rough, his weakness jeopardizing everything McNerney and the rest had worked for through the years. It would have suited Mike McNerney to dispense with the CIA entirely, but the damage had been done.

"I got a call from Anastasio Ruiz last night. At home, if you can picture that." The agent shook his head, as if disgusted with the Hispanic's inability to follow protocol. "We met this morning."

"So?" McNerney made no effort to conceal his irritation as the agent worked his way around to what was on his mind.

"Machado has a new boy on the team these days. Guy claims to be Nicaraguan. Calls himself Rosario Briones, but Ruiz thinks he's a phony."

"Why?"

"Too slick, for one thing. Like he knows the ropes before he's even in the game."

"Go on."

"Some of it's personal, I think. Briones and Ruiz have a hard-on for the same *muchacha*, and Ruiz is losing out."

"Goddamn it, Travers, if you're taking up my time with pussy talk, I swear I'll see you on a walking beat in the Aleutians."

"No, sir." Travers had gone pale. "There's more."

"Well, spit it out, for crissakes. I've got things to do."

"Ruiz was curious enough about the new boy to initiate a tail. The first night out Briones met with two men, one of them a definite American, the other probably. Ruiz took down the number of their rental car."

"Is there a point to this?" McNerney asked.

"Yes, sir. I ran the plate through local channels, and it came back registered to Avis. On their sheet they list the client's name as Eric Larsen from Los Angeles. He's booked into the Sheraton, room 415."

"I'm listening."

"Well, uh...that's it. I mean, they've never heard of him in California or at Langley. Nothing with LAPD, the FBI or DEA. We're digging for a tax return right now, but if the guy runs true to form, he's never filed with IRS."

"A cover?"

"Yes, sir. I believe it must be."

"Who?"

"Your guess would be as good as mine."

"My *guess* would be worth shit, goddamn it! You're supposed to know these things."

"We think he might be independent, sir. We're elbow-deep in mercenaries since the operation in Grenada. They've been dealing weapons to the Contras, running border operations on their own for private parties, offering their services to anyone with ready cash."

"That covers Larsen—maybe. What about his sidekick?"

"Zip. We've got no name, no clear description from Ruiz. He thought the second man looked Jewish, maybe Arab."

"Jesus Christ! You're telling me we've got Mossad on this? Or maybe it's the fucking PLO!"

Lane Travers shook his head, dejected. "We believe the second man is an American. We simply haven't pinned him down as yet."

"Forget him. What about Briones?"

"Once again, there's nothing in the files, but with an alias there wouldn't be."

"So what this all boils down to is you don't know shit."

"I wouldn't say that, sir. We have eliminated several possibilities."

"I don't care squat about your fucking possibles," McNerney snarled. "Your job is to eliminate the problem. Are we clear on that?"

"Yes, sir."

"I hope so, mister. We are set to roll in two days' time, and I will not be fucked out of this opportunity by some slob-ass incompetent civilian. Are you reading me?"

"Yes, sir."

"All right, then. Do your duty, and be quick about it. I don't want to know the details, but I want this thing cleaned up before it snowballs. Understood?"

"Yes, *sir*."

There was the faintest trace of insolence in Travers's voice, but Mike McNerney let it go. The boy was getting mad, and that was fine. It would require some righteous anger—or some fear—to get him off his ass and into action. If he feared McNerney, so much the better. Never much concerned with winning friends, McNerney needed soldiers now, combatants who weren't afraid to kill—or die—if called upon. They were so very close now, and he wouldn't let a sniveling civilian spoil the shining opportunity of any warrior's lifetime.

It was troublesome, this word out of the Contra camp, but it was nothing that couldn't be put to rights. If Eric Larsen and his friends were mercenaries, they wouldn't be missed in time to raise a hue and cry. If they were dealing on the wrong side of the law...well, they might not be missed at all.

And if they were employees of some federal agency, unknown to Travers and his slick computer system? If their deaths should sound some kind of general alarm? Then what?

No difference.

The operation would proceed no matter what might happen in the interim. McNerney was committed to success or absolute annihilation, as he had been on the slopes of Pork Chop Hill, and later, in the reeking swamps of Vietnam. He would succeed because his cause was just and honorable. He was standing for right against the evil minions of destruction, chaos and despair. No matter that the slob-ass pinko bastards up in Washington were all infatuated with détente. McNerney would prefer a slow and painful death to kissing Moscow's ass.

For over thirty years McNerney had been proud to stand up in America's defense. When others had burned their draft cards, run away to Canada or Paris, he'd been on the firing line with gallant boys who hadn't been afraid to pay the price. Sometimes at night he saw those trusting, boyish faces in his dreams and woke up bathed in sweat, his throat constricted in a silent scream. How many lives, and all for nothing? He would do the same tomorrow, if the goddamned politicians were restrained from meddling in military business, putting in their two cents worth without a vestige of the expertise or common sense required to run a battlefield campaign. Limp-wristed bastards that they were, you could have hanged them all and Mike McNerney wouldn't have missed them.

He would show them this time, though. When he was finished here, the nutless wonders would be forced to recognize his insight into world affairs. How could they question him, his motives, when the evidence was laid at their feet? There would certainly be some dissent. He couldn't count on a unanimous ovation, not while spineless liberals were trumpeting the Kremlin's party line from San Francisco to Manhattan, but he would secure the majority that mattered in the end. And when the cleanup was completed... well, it might be time to think about retirement. Perhaps a fling at politics, while Mike McNerney's name was still a household word.

God knows that military victory had paved the way for other occupants of 1600 Pennsylvania Avenue. From Washington to Eisenhower, it had never hurt to have a war behind you, a defeated enemy beneath your heel. If Doug MacArthur hadn't been prohibited from winning in Korea, he would certainly have occupied the White

House in his time, but slob-ass politicians had betrayed him. They wouldn't do the same to Mike McNerney.

He wasn't concerned about a few deaths within the Contra movement. They were volunteers who knew the score, and they were dying every day. His interests lay not in the people, or in Nicaragua, but in halting communism where it stood, containing it as a preliminary move toward rolling back the crimson tide of history, recapturing the sacred ground that Marx's bastard offspring had defiled. Nicaragua was as good a place to start as any, from McNerney's point of view. Next up, Havana, and from there...

Why not?

America had never really done its share in the support of freedom fighters who opposed the Communists. A great deal more could be accomplished for the bold mujahedeen in Afghanistan, for instance, and the nationalist Chinese could be encouraged in their righteous dream of taking back the mainland. Few Americans were even conscious of the small but vital White Russian movement, Narodno Trudovoy Soyuz, which had been a thorn in Moscow's side since 1917. For every revolution carried off by Communists and sympathizers, there were freedom fighters waiting to reclaim their birthright, their ancestral homes. In Vietnam. In North Korea. Laos. Cambodia. The fucking Ayatollah had his problems in Iran with freedom fighters, too, and one day soon a sniper might be looking at his turban through the cross hairs of a telescopic sight. There was a world to win, normality to be restored, a cancer to be ruthlessly excised, and no one used a scalpel quite like Mike McNerney.

"...right on it," Travers finished, his voice jarring McNerney back to reality. "If I have any problem with Ruiz—"

"You won't. He may be pussy-whipped, but he knows who his friends are."

Travers rose to leave. "I'll keep you posted, sir."

"You do that."

Travers would complete his task; McNerney had no doubt of that. The man believed in what they were about to do, but he was also frightened, and the combination should be adequate to keep him loyal for the duration. After they were finished...well, a witness to the inner workings of the operation might become a walking, talking liability. But there were ways to deal with liabilities.

The general rocked back in his reclining chair and dreamed about a world devoid of revolutionaries.

AS ALWAYS, TRAVERS WAS RELIEVED to have his meeting with McNerney finished. There was something in the old man's eyes these days, a kind of madness, that was terrifying. When McNerney leaned across his desk, eyes flashing, Travers would have sworn that he was a human time bomb, ready to explode.

Sometimes in his more optimistic moments, Travers thought the bastard might be working toward a coronary. It would have made the agent's life a great deal easier, but he had never been a lucky man. McNerney would outlive them all, and if the operation blew up in their faces, he would find a way to pass the buck. The old man wouldn't bat an eye at sacrificing soldiers in the field—or agents in the street, if it came down to that—but he would have a nice escape hatch all prepared for number one if things went sour.

Lane Travers didn't fancy himself as a human sacrifice. He still believed in what they were about to do, but lately he had harbored doubts about the operation's feasibility. The more he thought about it now, the more he was convinced that something would go wrong. The plan looked as slick as snot on paper, but they had already lost two men, and who knew what might happen in the next two days?

The man from Langley liked his operations safe and simple. Backing up the Contras was a case in point: the Agency could funnel guns and money to the Nicaraguan rebels for a hundred years and never lose an agent in the field. If they got lucky and the Sandinistas folded, great. If not, well, there would always be another load of guns, another suitcase full of money. They could run the Sandinista forces ragged, kicking ass until the cows came home, and it would never really cost the Company a thing.

As for McNerney's plan, well, once the cards were dealt this time, America would have to raise or fold. You couldn't cling to status quo with hostile forces on the wrong side of the border; failure to respond would be the same as defeat. And once the fighter jockeys started making border runs, you had to raise and raise again, continually beefing up the stakes to stay in play. The damnedest thing about it was you never knew who else might want to join the game.

The Cubans were already in, of course. "Advisors" now, but it wouldn't take long for Castro to supply an expeditionary force if things got tight. The Russians would be interested observers, but they might accept an active role if Sandinista leaders asked them nicely. And if Moscow bought a hand...well, Travers didn't even want to think about the ante in that case.

The Company was interested in Nicaragua as a test of strength, an exercise in feasibility. It had been years since Langley actually overthrew a government; their recent Third World efforts had been pitiful, and everyone, from the director down, would be encouraged by a victory. Of course, McNerney's game had never been proposed to the director or the top men in Clandestine Ops. It was strictly without official sanction, and heads would roll if word leaked out before the coup was an accomplished fact. Heads might roll anyway, but it was always easier to seek forgiveness than it was to get permission.

The logic was impeccable. Create a border incident that would destabilize the region, thereby forcing Washington to move decisively. Once U.S. troops had been committed, Sandinista forces would react accordingly, the violence escalating into full-blown war. Once in, the White House would be free to pull out all the stops, matching rhetoric to action for the first time since Grenada. And with friendly forces in control once more, there was no end to the intriguing possibilities.

It might be worth a second glance at Cuba. The Company had taken quite a drubbing at the Bay of Pigs and later, when the Kennedys had pulled the plug on operations aimed at Castro personally, but important people in the CIA were still concerned with the disposal of Fidel. With Nicaragua back in friendly hands, there just might be a way to pull it off, preserving some small measure of deniability. He could already picture the scenario: the Contras would be so ecstatic over liberation of their homeland from the Sandinistas that they would move against Havana voluntarily. Of course, it would require encouragement, material support, and they would have to take it slowly, building up a head of steam, but it was possible.

Lane Travers thought of Rosario Briones. Travers wouldn't have to lift a finger there; Ruiz had volunteered to take the new boy out already, and he was only waiting for the go-ahead. He might be wrong about Briones. Nothing in the files simply meant nothing; it certainly didn't mean conclusive evidence of guilt. As generally fucked up as Third World operations often were, there was an outside possibility Briones and his contacts might be working for the Company on something Travers didn't "need to know." He was assistant to the station chief, but he wasn't naive enough to think that he knew everything the Company was doing in Honduras, even in Tegucigalpa.

And the station chief was shrewd. In his darker moments Travers wondered why McNerney and the team at Langley had selected him instead of starting at the top. Someone had chosen Travers on the basis of his record. He had been flattered at the time, excited by the prospect of a major covert operation, and he would have thanked the individuals who had picked his name. These days, however, Travers would have had to flip a coin first: heads, he would have thanked them; tails, he would have blown their fucking brains out and been done with it.

But Lane Travers had realized too late that he wasn't a soldier. He was a planner, fascinated by logistics, strategy, the *why* of operations that succeeded or went wrong. He wasn't meant to carry weapons in the trenches, spilling blood and having his blood spilled. Allowing for the fact that it had always been a dirty business with a fair amount of risk, he still believed that it was possible to reach retirement with his ass intact. It would require some skill, but Travers was a clever man. At least he'd seen himself that way until he'd been embroiled in the McNerney operation, strapped into his roller coaster seat with no alternative except to hang on for dear life. The best that he could hope for now would be to cover for himself and pray for victory.

After Ruiz took Briones out, there'd be two more assets left in the bush. His reference to a second man might be the truth, or simply an attempt to make the truth more interesting. Whatever, if he learned that Anastasio had lied to him, the man from Langley was entirely capable of taking sweet revenge. For now, his mind was occupied with the elimination of a man—or men—whom he had never seen.

There were assorted contract agents who would take the job, but Travers had to choose his gunners carefully. There was no telling how much "Eric Larsen" knew about the plan, but it was still imperative that he be silenced. While the team was at it, they could take out any partners or associates in the immediate vicinity, shooting for a clean sweep. And if someone wriggled through the net ... well, by the time he spilled his gut, it would all be over. His announcement would be too damned late to change a thing.

Unless, of course, some outside force had known about McNerney's plan from the beginning. It wasn't impossible, the man from Langley knew. But would they let things go this far, allowing men to die when intervention might have saved those lives? Had the old man and his associates been cunningly manipulated all along? By whom? And to what end?

There was no end to questions, and he gave it up and dismissed the doubts as budding paranoia. In the Agency, you lived with an assumption that the world was out to get you, and if you were in Lane Travers's place, assumption might brush shoulders with reality. Sometimes the whole world—or at least the Eastern Bloc—*was* out to get your ass, and you could only save it by remaining one step in front of your pursuers. When the time was right, *you* would be running with the pack and snapping at *their* heels.

Poetic justice, sure. It was the name of the clandestine game, and Travers was a junior master of the sport. Just now, however, he was wishing that the master might resign his post or seek a transfer to New York, Los Angeles—hell, Butte, Montana, would be preferable to his present situation. Travers knew that it was strictly fantasy; if he should bolt now, the old man's gunners would eventually track him down and close his file for good.

The man from Langley had no options left. The only path lay straight ahead, to the end of the line.

☆ 19 ☆

"You'll like the CO, Frankie." Rafferty was driving, glancing frequently across his shoulder. "He's our kinda guy."

"A real American," DiSalvo added from the shotgun seat.

Wedged in between Steiner and Broderick, aware of the resentment radiating from the soldier on his right, Bolan asked, "Is he the man in charge?"

"No way," DiSalvo answered. "Hell, we got ourselves a whole chain of command."

"You talk too much, Vince." Broderick's voice was hard and unforgiving.

"Off my case, man."

"Can it, both of you," the sergeant ordered, glaring from the rearview mirror. "We've got enough enemies without you starting on each other."

They were encroaching on Tegucigalpa's red-light district, narrow streets with garish advertisements for cantinas, tattoo parlors, pawnshops and cheap hotels. The main drag was alive with tourists and the creatures of the night, exchanging cash for company or chemicals in furtive hit-and-run transactions.

"Funny place to meet the CO," Bolan offered.

"Can't be too damned careful these days," Rafferty replied. "First whiff of anything peculiar, the friggin' CID would have us on the carpet, spoilin' everything."

"You ever hear of undercover agents?" Broderick asked the sergeant, eyes fixed firmly on the Executioner.

"Get offa that for crissakes, willya? I been through his file."

"I've seen files doctored up before."

"*You've* seen? Who the hell are you, James Bond?"

"I'm telling you—"

"*I'm* tellin' *you* to let it rest, okay? The CO has his say, we live with it. If that's not good enough for you, I'll let you out right here."

"Relax." The sudden hint of nervousness in Broderick's voice implied that backing out would carry consequences more severe than walking back to base alone.

Unconsciously the soldier's words had come uncomfortably close to Bolan's secret. If the others had believed Tim Broderick, if Bolan hadn't found a friend in Rafferty, they might have turned on him here where he had no damned combat stretch at all. They still might, depending on the word from their mysterious CO, the man who was in charge but not in charge.

He put the riddle out of mind and concentrated on the street signs as Rafferty left the main drag, negotiating side streets that were narrower and darker. Pallid, ghostlike faces watched them from the crypts of shadowed doorways, bony hands outstretched and beckoning them back to taste the pleasures—and the terrors—of Tegucigalpa's dark side. Bolan had already seen enough of urban misery since his arrival, and he focused on the landmarks, mapping out a mental route against the possibility that he might have to cut and run.

He was unarmed, at Rafferty's insistence. Whether Broderick and the others carried weapons, Bolan couldn't say, but he had followed orders as a show of faith. If they were planning to surprise him with an ambush at the meeting site, he was as good as dead, but Bolan didn't read the team that way. Tim Broderick might have killed him cheerfully, but Rafferty and the others seemed to have accepted him, within established limits. If he passed the scrutiny of their commanding officer tonight, they might trust him with details of their operation—or enough, at any rate, to institute a counterstrike before it was too late.

And if the CO turned thumbs down? Then he would have to play the rest on nerve alone until he could secure a weapon or make contact with his backup. If the meet went sour, Bolan's chances of survival ranged from slim to none, but he wasn't a pessimist. The Executioner had walked away from traps before, and he was none the worse for wear. If he was forced to fight his way out, he would do his best and take as many of the bastards with him, depleting their forces to the point that D-Day might be necessarily postponed.

The sergeant nosed his car into an alleyway beside a small hotel, so dark and dingy that it lacked the usual complement of whores out front. They locked the car, and Rafferty flagged down a passing youth, informing him in broken Spanish that he needed someone to protect his vehicle. The sergeant tore a couple of lempira notes in half and passed them to the boy, explaining that the other halves would be forthcoming if the car survived an hour free from damage.

When they entered the hotel, they strode past a greasy-looking night clerk glued to a girlie magazine. Instead of using the ancient elevator, they took the stairs. A rank, pervasive stench of sweat and urine wrinkled Bolan's nostrils. From appearances the place hadn't been painted since construction, and he didn't even want to think about the linen, or what might be dwelling there.

Third floor, room 305. The sergeant knocked, a simple coded signal. Bolan didn't bother memorizing it; if they were smart, the signal would be changed from one meet to the next.

The door swung open, and he recognized the CO instantly as Captain Fletcher Crane. So much for all the pointed warnings in his new-post interview with "Frank Lambretta." Crane was Rafferty's connection with the high command. McNerney wouldn't waste his time—or risk himself—by dealing with the grunts directly, not with so much hanging in the balance. If the deal went off the rails somehow, Crane could be eliminated to preserve deniability, allowing officers of higher rank to evade the blame. DiSalvo had implied a wider knowledge of the hierarchy, but he might be engaged in speculation leading nowhere.

Bolan let it slide. He needed names, and never mind the sort of evidence required by courts of law. His chief concern was that the net should cover everyone, with no odd stragglers running free to strike up operations on another front. The Executioner was shooting for a clean sweep. Annihilation. And there was no room for hit-or-miss in his game plan.

When they were seated, sipping beers provided by DiSalvo at the captain's order, Crane looked long and hard at Bolan. "You've decided to come in with us, I understand."

"Yes, sir."

"I trust the nature of our mission was explained to you?"

"I got the gist of it. No details."

"And the 'gist,' as you interpret it?"

The soldier shrugged and spread his hands. "We give Ortega back a taste of what his troops are dishing out to peasants in the countryside. We kick some ass, and if the government gets shaky, that's a bonus."

"Simply put, but basically correct. You have no qualms about covert activity?"

"I'm here. You've seen my file."

"Of course. You were selected on the basis of that file... but sometimes people change."

"If I could change that easy, I'd be riding desk at Benning."

"Fine. If the alternatives have been explained to you—"

"I told your boy I'm in." He caught a glimpse of color rising in the sergeant's face. "I don't need threats to make it stick."

"That's fair enough. I have to tell you that your mission may be rather different from the one you had in mind."

"Oh? Different how?"

"Your target won't be Nicaragua, not directly." Bolan waited, let the captain give it to him in his own words and his own good time. "In covert operations things are rarely what they seem to be. In this case we intend to stage a border incident that'll create a negative reaction toward the Sandinista Front and bring about concerted action to eliminate the threat."

"What kind of border incident?"

"A mercenary force has been recruited from the local population and fitted out with Sandinista arms and uniforms. On D-Day they'll cross the Honduras border at a preselected point in choppers that'll pass for Soviet ones if no one gets too close. They'll raise some hell, withdraw and any casualties they leave behind will be identified as Sandinistas. Washington will have its first-time-ever confirmation of a border crossing, and a punitive reaction will be indicated. Any questions?"

"Yes, sir. Where do we come in?"

The captain smiled. "I thought that would be obvious. Our mercenary team will be in need of expert guidance. Timing, target options, all that sort of thing. You'll be going in with the assault force."

"And if one of us checks out? Are we supposed to pass for Nicaraguan natives?"

"Hardly. We expect you to survive, but just in case, you'll be carrying the normal ID tags and papers of a *spetsnaz* trooper. If you buy it, it'll be at the expense of Mother Russia."

The plan was clever, Bolan had to give them that. It almost seemed a shame to waste the slickest part of their production, and he wondered if some member of the team had been selected in advance to buy the farm, deliberately leaving "evidence" of Russia's special shock troops on Honduran soil.

"The ID might be solid, sir, but what about our faces? Fingerprints? We're all on file with Special Forces and in Washington?"

"You *were* on file, Lambretta. As of this time yesterday, your prints and dental records have been substituted with a casualty from Nam. Your prints and records don't exist. Not here, and not in Washington."

"That's pretty slick."

"We've thought of everything," the captain told him, with a touch of pride.

"I do have one more question."

"Certainly."

"When do we move?"

"The day after tomorrow," Fletcher Crane replied. "At 0500 hours on Sunday."

Bolan's narrow smile concealed a multitude of doubts. So soon. Would he be able to touch base with Able Team or Phoenix Force? If not, he would be on his own against a force of unknown strength and capability, embarked upon a suicidal mission in the jungle. It was obvious from Crane's synopsis that the plan demanded casualties; without the evidence of corpses, uniforms and weapons taken from the dead, there would be nothing to connect the Sandinistas with the raid. Without a body count, the exercise would be a waste of time. He wondered whether Rafferty or someone else had been detailed to guarantee the body count, to add a bogus *spetsnaz* corpse or two along the way. The odds in favor of betrayal were substantial, but the Executioner would have to take it in his stride.

There could be no turning back from this point on. The Executioner wasn't intimidated by the thought of fighting on his own. His everlasting war was calling him.

"IT'S CLEARED," Lane Travers said. "You're free to tag Briones at your own convenience."

Ruiz sat back and sipped his beer, amazed that it could be so simple. Obviously Travers or the members of his network had discovered something serious about Machado's new recruit. But it didn't matter to Anastasio. He wasn't concerned with details. The elimination of his rival was enough, on any pretext, and he would be happy to oblige.

A sudden problem crossed his mind. "The others?"

"Taken care of," Travers told him. "That's not your concern."

"There may be questions," Anastasio replied, and cursed his hands for threatening to tremble as he raised his glass. Why was his nerve deserting him just now, when everything was going as he wished it to?

"I'll handle the PR," his contact said. "Your problem is Luis and the reaction of his people when you pop Briones."

"They are not *his* people."

"Suit yourself. I don't care how you handle it, as long as there's no backlash on the Company. You lead the dogs to me, I'll have to cut you loose."

There was no question in Ruiz's mind that Travers meant precisely what he said. And termination, in the parlance of the Agency, meant more than two weeks' notice with a severance check. When you were terminated by the likes of Travers, there were no second chances. You might disappear, or suffer any one of several lethal accidents, but the results would be the same. You were no more. A cipher. Gone.

Ruiz wasn't afraid of Travers personally, but he feared the shadow government that Travers represented in Honduras. They were capable of anything, it seemed, except perhaps for the expulsion of Ortega's Sandinistas from his homeland. Soon, however, even that might be accomplished, barring interference from a traitor like Rosario Briones, a pig who wooed Esperanza for selfish ends and conspired with gringo agents to betray Machado and the rest. It was Ruiz's patriotic duty to eliminate the Judas before it was too late. In another day they were scheduled to begin their final move against the Sandinista Front and maintain their rendezvous with destiny. No man—no traitor—must be given opportunity to interfere.

"I've gotta run," the man from CIA informed him, rising as he spoke. "A busy day tomorrow."

"Sí, señor," Ruiz agreed. "A very busy day."

After Travers left, he flagged the waitress and was about to have another beer when he decided something stronger was in order. Opting for a bottle of tequila, Anastasio Ruiz sat back to ponder the elimination of Briones. It would be foolish to initiate an action that he couldn't follow through. If he was going to eliminate his rival, he must do it swiftly and without arousing the suspicions of Luis Machado. He was confident Luis would go along with his decision once the facts were laid before him, but there was no time for a debate just now. If the intruder was allowed to have his way with Esperanza, worm his way into the inner councils of the movement, he could do irreparable damage by the time Luis was made to see his treachery. Immediate elimination was the answer, and Ruiz would have to take the weight of that responsibility upon himself.

In time, he knew, the other members of the movement would be thankful for his courage and determination. They would praise him as a hero when they finally knew the truth about Rosario Briones.

It disturbed Ruiz a little that he didn't know the truth himself. Perhaps Briones was working with some faction of the CIA, but would Lane Travers not be conscious of the fact? Some other agency might be involved—Ruiz was well aware of how clandestine services waged war on one another in America—but he couldn't begin to guess which group might seek to undermine the Contra movement. If Briones and his friends were mercenaries, they might have a wide variety of motives, but Ruiz wasn't prepared to waste his time on all the various considerations. The moment Briones made his move on Esperanza, he had crossed the line of no return. It might be unprofessional to let emotion overrule his mind, but there was no alternative. Ruiz was blind where Esperanza was concerned.

He recognized the weakness in himself, this pitiful dependence on a woman, but the Contra second-in-command couldn't deny his heart. For better than a year now he had pined in silence, waiting for the moment when his true love's eyes would open and recognize his devotion. He refused to give up hope despite the absence of encouragement from any source outside his own imagination. When Briones had interfered, Ruiz had known it was time to act.

Approval from the Agency was helpful, but he would eventually have gone ahead without it. Travers had supplied the necessary shout of courage that Ruiz required to make his move... although some more tequila would not do him any harm. A soldier on the brink of an irrevocable action needed all the courage he could find.

He checked his watch and decided it was too late to eliminate Briones tonight. But the tequila would console him, and tomorrow would offer endless opportunities. Ruiz would call in sick, avoiding an appearance at the office that Machado had rented from an ally of the movement. Anastasio would have all day to weigh his options, choose his weapons and prepare himself for the eradication of his enemy.

Ruiz had killed three men of whom he was aware. The first had been a beggar in Managua, in the days before Ortega and his Sandinistas had seized control. The man had been all rags and running sores, trailing Anastasio and his companions down a lonely street, one hand outstretched, demanding alms. Instead, Anastasio had hurled a brick that had cracked the beggar's skull and left him dying on the pavement. His comrades had congratulated him, but he had spent the night hunched over a commode, his stomach rolling at the mental image of a body crumpled on the sidewalk. Sometimes, in his nightmares, he still saw the beggar's face.

The other two were Sandinista pigs, encountered on a border crossing with Machado and a dozen other Contras. Anastasio had found them sleeping at their post outside an enemy encampment in the forest. He had stood above them, trembling, with his rifle pointed at the forest floor, until he had heard the crack of small arms fire around him, signifying that the battle had been joined. The sentries had stirred, and only then had he been startled into swinging up his AK-47, holding down the trigger, hosing them with eyes shut tight until his magazine had been empty and the two of them had lain deathly still in the grass.

The Sandinistas didn't come to Anastasio in dreams, but he had managed to avoid participation in any other combat missions up to now. He played the role of master strategist, more valuable to Machado and the others at his drawing board, preparing plans for future raids against the traitors who had captured Nicaragua. No one had suspected that he feared to face the enemy in open battle. No one, save perhaps for Esperanza. If she recognized his cowardice, she gave no sign...but might it not account for her aloof behavior in his presence? Might the smell of fear repulse her?

Perhaps. But all of that would change when he had dealt with the traitor in their midst. Elimination of Briones would reveal Ruiz to Esperanza in another light. When he was able to display his evidence before her, she would see him as the hero that he was. And she might love him just a little.

But first things first. He must assume his adversary would be armed and dangerous. The man exuded violence, radiating menace like an unexploded bomb. Ruiz would have to take him by surprise if he was to succeed without endangering himself. It would accomplish nothing for the movement if he died without eliminating the intruder, leaving Briones to fabricate some story and deceive the others with his lies. Ruiz would have one chance and one chance only. If he failed, there would be no escape.

The tequila had begun to numb his face, as if a dentist had injected novocaine between his eyes. It was enough. He pushed the bottle back and left a crumpled handful of lempiras on the tabletop. His legs felt disconnected as he stood up and headed for the door.

He needed sleep, a chance to clear his head. There would be enough time tomorrow to prepare his strike against Briones. Anastasio decided that he might stop by the office, after all, and question Esperanza—subtly, of course, about her schedule for tomorrow night. He had no doubt that she would spend the evening with Briones, possibly in bed.

So much the better. Anger would prevent his hand from shaking when he pulled the trigger. It would give him the resolve to face his enemy and do what must be done. Or, if he found a chance to shoot Briones in the back, it would be all the same to Anastasio Ruiz. The Contra second-in-command was proud of being flexible.

He flagged a taxi, gave the driver his address and settled back into an alcoholic haze. Until tomorrow, when the traitor would be his.

☆ 20 ☆

"It is a sin to feel this way. I know it."

Bundled up in sheets and blankets, Esperanza stretched languorously, snuggling back against Pol Blancanales when she finished. He was giddy with the fragrance of her and the recent frenzy of their coupling.

"It may be sinful," he replied, "but I prefer the way I feel right now to pious suffering."

She giggled. "So do I. That's what makes it sinful."

She was teasing him. He knew enough about the woman now to realize that she didn't adhere to any organized religion. Childhood faith had been seared out of her by her experience in the reeducation camps, and Esperanza had no use for plaster saints or the trappings of devotion. She was a believer in the rights of man, in human dignity at any cost. She had already paid her dues, and still the lady was prepared to keep on paying, with her life if necessary, for the final liberation of her homeland.

Pol respected her for her determination and ideals. He hated using her, without her knowledge, as a pipeline to Luis Machado's inner sanctum, but his mission was the foremost problem on his mind. Slowly he had begun to pick her brain, eliciting such basic information as she cared to part with on their short acquaintance. Now that he had talked her into bed, he thought the take might turn to something more substantial.

There was nothing yet to link Machado's operation with the plans of General McNerney, but a nagging apprehension wouldn't let Politician rest. The local Contra band had too much cash, too many weapons for their size. In other districts larger cadres were reduced to begging aid from Washington, but hard times hadn't laid a finger on Machado's people. Clearly they had found themselves a covert source of money and material, one that hadn't been available to others of their kind. It was Politician's job to trace that source, identify it, and—if it turned out to be McNerney or his covert allies—shut the pipeline down.

"I need a shower," he informed her, feeling guilty. "Join me?"

"In a moment."

Sliding out of bed, he started picking up his scattered clothing from the carpet, making sure the .45 was tucked inside his folded shirt before he headed toward the bathroom. It was force of habit, but a savvy warrior stayed alive by taking care of details. As a warrior in her own right, Esperanza wouldn't begrudge him the precaution—if in fact she noticed it at all.

Inside the bathroom Blancanales piled his rumpled clothing atop the toilet tank, within easy arm's reach of the shower. Turning up the water temperature as hot as he could stand it, taking it as therapy and as a form of punishment for his betrayal of the woman in the other room, he stepped beneath the spray and closed the sliding door. As steam began to infiltrate his sinuses, he threw his head back, closed his eyes and willed his knotted muscles to unwind.

Their sex had been fantastic, physically exhausting, but it had left him somehow unfulfilled. Beneath the weariness of bone and muscle, nagging guilt had kept his nerves on edge. If only there was some way to reveal himself, to put his trust in Esperanza, tell her of his mission...

Blancanales turned around and let the water pound his shoulders, sluicing down his spine in steaming sheets. There was no way at all, he realized, to justify enlightening the woman. If Machado was connected to McNerney's rogues, the strong odds had her privy to the deal. If she was ignorant of an existing link, the revelation of his double role or Machado's lack of trust in her might spark an unpredictable reaction. He couldn't spare any time to soothe a woman scorned, nor could he risk the possibility that she might blow his cover.

She didn't love him yet, he could be thankful for that much. When he was forced to reveal himself, there would be pain, resentment, but he wouldn't break her heart. She would find strength within her anger, her devotion to the Contra cause... provided he could let her live that long.

Politician was prepared for every possible scenario, and in the worst of them he would be forced to take the lady out along with her associates. He didn't relish the idea, but there was more at stake this time than any single life. Pol knew he was expendable, and so was Esperanza, in the larger scheme of things. If she was part of the McNerney operation, if she tried to stop him when he had to pull the plug, then Blancanales would react accordingly.

But he would hate it.

In other circumstances he might cheerfully have stood beside the Contras, joined their fight to liberate a captive homeland, but the cards hadn't been dealt that way. His mission interdicted theirs, and while he understood their motives perfectly, he wouldn't subjugate his logic to misguided sympathy. The Contra movement had its rotten apples, just as they were found in every other group composed of human beings. Some were brutal, others avaricious, and a few would sell their brothers down the river for a song. If it could happen to the Phoenix team at Stony Man, he knew damned well that it could happen to anyone. And when power-hungry rogues took control and cast all honor to the winds, the cause no longer mattered. No one cared today if early members of the Ku Klux Klan had *really* meant to serve as honest vigilantes, curbing violent crime, before extremists took control and steered the outfit into racial terrorism as a way of life. It didn't matter in the least if Lenin and his Bolsheviks had cherished bright ideals in 1917, before the bloody purges changed utopia into the gulag's stark reality.

The only true reality was here and now. Motives mattered only when you had the luxury of sitting down to put the pieces in their place for a debriefing. Everything fit perfectly in retrospect, provided you lived long enough to see it.

Between the steam and morbid thoughts, he had almost forgotten where he was. When Esperanza came to join him, sliding back the shower door, his first reaction was to hit a combat crouch and lunge for his weapon, hidden in the rumpled pile of clothing. Secondary recognition hit him like a fist between the eyes, and he could feel the color rising in his face, his cheeks on fire, as she flinched back from him.

"I'm sorry." It was all that he could think of, and he added lamely, "You surprised me."

"It is I who should apologize. I know the risks of startling a warrior." She slid in beside him then closed the sliding door to trap the steam inside.

"It's a good thing that I wasn't armed," he muttered, feeling foolish.

"Ah, you underestimate yourself." She found him with her hand, and he responded instantly, as if on cue.

"You may be right," he growled, and pulled her close to him beneath the shower's spray. He let his doubts evaporate in the surrounding steam. For the moment, the reality of Esperanza in his arms was truth enough.

ALONE IN THE ELEVATOR, Anastasio Ruiz withdrew the Llama .45 caliber automatic from his belt and double-checked the load, confirming a live round in the firing chamber. He was nervous, and he cursed the trembling hands that made it difficult for him to tuck the pistol back inside his belt. God knows that he couldn't have tagged a moving target over any kind of distance. If Ruiz intended to survive this night, he must rely on point-blank range and the automatic's rapid rate of fire.

Throughout the morning and afternoon he had pursued Rosario Briones. Always one step ahead of him, his nemesis had given Anastasio the slip...until tonight. There was no doubt that he would be with Esperanza, and although Ruiz was loath to spill the traitor's blood in her apartment, even though he didn't wish to see the two of them together, he would have to seize the opportunity or watch it slip away.

The elevator shuddered to a halt at Esperanza's floor, the double doors hissed open, and he lurched into the corridor, unsteady on his trembling legs. His body was betraying him, his stomach rolling sluggishly, but Anastasio was pledged to see his mission through. No childish queasiness would stop him now.

He must be strong. For Esperanza. For the movement, which depended on his expertise, his knowledge of the enemy. Machado might be furious at first, enraged by his deliberate circumvention of the normal circuits of command, but when Ruiz explained himself, Luis would understand. They all would understand, including Esperanza. She would finally forgive him when she realized Briones was a traitor to the cause, a Judas who had used her mind and body to betray the sacred homeland.

It would all be so ridiculously easy to explain, as soon as the intruder had been permanently silenced. When he thought of all the information that Briones might have leaked to hostile ears, Ruiz was livid, and the anger made him stronger. Thankfully the traitor had known nothing of the vital mission scheduled for the day after tomorrow.

He froze outside Esperanza's door, and now his hands were trembling again. Unless, of course, Briones had been briefed by Esperanza, burrowing into her confidence as he had wormed his way into her bed. She was a woman, and never mind the warrior trappings she affected. Anastasio was well acquainted with the weakness of the female. In a man's world women were for pleasure and for procreation; it was a mistake to trust a woman with the secrets of a military cadre. If he hadn't been in love with Esperanza, he would have protested vehemently when Luis had included her among his top lieutenants. As it was, Ruiz had been content to see her on a daily basis, basking in her beauty and forgetting for the moment his opinion of the weaker sex.

It was her sex, her weakness, that had made her vulnerable to Rosario Briones. There could be no doubt that he had played upon her vanity, deceived her with his lies and flattery to make her fall into bed with him. It was ironic. Anastasio had loved her from a distance, worshipped her as if she were a frail Madonna, all without the slightest sign of recognition on her part. Then came a ruffian from God knows where, all jagged edges, peasant dirt beneath his fingernails, and she had fallen for him like a schoolgirl on her first romance. It was enough to make Ruiz despair of ever understanding womankind... but there were more important tasks at hand.

The most important mission of a lifetime rested on his shoulders now, dependent on Ruiz alone to guarantee security. He had to plug the single glaring leak before it was too late. When Esperanza had composed herself, she would agree that he had done his duty for the movement. For the cause.

Immersed in thought, he almost passed her door before he caught himself. He glanced up and down the hallway, then eased the Llama from his belt, taking care to switch the safety off. He thumbed the hammer back and cringed as if the other tenants might somehow have heard it locking into place. He smiled self-consciously. If that hadn't woken them, perhaps the fireworks he had in mind would rouse them from their apathy.

He hesitated, then finally pressed his ear against the door, but could detect no sound. They would be in the bedroom, almost certainly, and he could take them by surprise if he was swift and silent enough. Fishing in his pocket, he withdrew the key he had duplicated when Esperanza had let him use her car on Contra business. It had been a childish thing to do, of course; he had never meant to use the key, but he drew pleasure from its presence in his pocket, feeling smug as if they shared a precious secret. Tonight, ironically, the key would serve him well...but on an errand of destruction rather than a rendezvous with love.

Ruiz had never tried the key, and momentary panic gripped him as it refused to turn. He tried again, deliberately relaxing, rewarded by the soft metallic sound of tumblers falling into place.

A latch chain barred the door, treating Anastasio to a narrow view of half the living room. He froze, expecting angry voices, but the room beyond was empty. Cautiously he slipped one hand inside, his fingers groping for the latch. If they were watching him, it would be the perfect time to strike. A shoulder block against the door would snap his wrist like kindling, pinning him in the doorway while Briones found a weapon and came to finish him. He gripped the Llama tighter in his left hand, ready to squeeze off directly through the door. Perspiration beaded on his forehead, trickling between his eyes.

He found the latch, released it and pushed the door wide open, panning the empty living room with his pistol. Beyond an open doorway, he could hear the shower running, muffling the sound of voices. The woman's heady scent assailed his nostrils, his senses, and he had to shake it off before proceeding toward the bedroom to find the source of mocking laughter.

He hesitated in the bedroom doorway, giddy with the unmistakable odor of their union. Rumpled sheets, still damp with perspiration. Scattered clothing on the floor, draped over chairs. A shoulder holster crumpled on the floor beside a nightstand. Empty.

Would Briones take his weapon to the bathroom with him? It was possible, or it might be concealed beneath a pillow, close at hand while he enjoyed the miracle of Esperanza's flesh. Unwilling to accept the risk, Ruiz crossed to the bed and threw back the sheets and blankets, scanning for a pistol, wrenching bleary eyes away from evidence of their illicit lust. He ran a trembling hand beneath the pillows, then finally hurled them to the floor. He found nothing.

Deafened by the pulse that hammered in his ears, he almost missed the sound of naked feet on tile behind him, hesitating in the doorway leading to the bathroom. They had found him, made a mockery of his surprise, and he could only act on instinct now, put conscious thought on hold.

He spun to face the enemy, raising the Llama, squeezing off before he had the muzzle locked on target, blinded by the angry tears that filled his eyes. A blur of naked flesh appeared above the gunsights, and the .45's report battered his eardrums, roaring like artillery inside the confines of the tiny bedroom. Anastasio was roaring with it, bellowing his rage, aware of Esperanza screaming in the middle distance as he pumped another bullet through the figure driven back through the bathroom entrance.

THE FIRST REPORT of gunfire startled Blancanales. It brought him lurching from the shower stall as Esperanza screamed. A moment earlier she had been in his arms, retreating with a playful smile that told him he would find her waiting in the bedroom. In the intervening seconds, something had gone terribly wrong, irrevocably wrong, and Blancanales felt his stomach rolling as he fished beneath his rumpled clothing and found the automatic pistol hidden there.

Another burst of rapid semiautomatic fire followed the first, and Esperanza's body vaulted backward through the open bathroom doorway, toppling a laundry hamper on her way to touchdown, sudden scarlet speckling the tile. Instinctively, Blancanales knew she was beyond his help as he flattened against the wall, his primed autoloader angled toward the doorway. He might be able to defend his tenuous position briefly, but Politician had no time. Already neighbors would be answering the sound of gunshots, calling the authorities or moving in to check it out, perhaps with weapons of their own.

The Able warrior snared his crumpled clothing from the toilet tank, edged closer to the doorway and pitched it underhand. The unseen gunner fired instinctively, popping Blancanales's chinos with projectile impact. At that moment Politician made his move, before his adversary could discover the mistake. Going long and low beneath the line of fire, he slid naked on a slick of Esperanza's blood, erupting through the doorway with his pistol braced in both hands, searching for a target.

There was a heartbeat left in which to recognize his enemy before Pol started squeezing off in rapid-fire. Ruiz danced and jerked with the impact of the parabellum shockers ripping through his rib cage as he reeled backward toward the bed. The Contra gunner's nose burst when a killing shot exploded in his face, and his body was lifted completely off its feet and draped across the mattress.

Pol rose on rubber legs and stood above his fallen adversary, side arm leveled at the sunken ruin of the gunner's face. The guy was dead as hell, but Blancanales hadn't reached his present age by taking chances. Stooping to retrieve the dead man's .45, its slide locked open on an empty chamber, he stepped back and tossed the piece across the room.

Backtracking to the bathroom, Pol knelt down beside the lady, feeling for a pulse and finding none. On hands and knees, he pressed an ear against her breast, heard nothing, felt no rise and fall of respiration. She was still warm, but it wouldn't be long before her body temperature began its final plunge.

Rising, Blancanales realized that he was smeared with blood from cheek to ankles. There was no time for another turn beneath the shower, but he hooked a towel off the rack and moved to stand before the full-length mirror, brusquely scrubbing Esperanza's essence from his skin. The towel was clotted with it when he finished. He let it drop and went in search of his discarded clothing. Tugging on the chinos, he was conscious of a draft and poked his fingers through a bullet hole beside the fly. He ran the zipper up, pulled his shirt on and stepped into his loafers without socks.

Emerging from the bedroom, Blancanales found the outer door ajar, a key protruding from the lock. He didn't stop to ponder Anastasio's possession of the key; the Able warrior was beyond all caring now. What mattered was the possibility that he was blown, that Esperanza hadn't fallen victim to a would-be lover's jealous rage. If there had been a defect in his cover anywhere along the line, then Schwarz and Lyons were in jeopardy as well. Ruiz couldn't have visited them—Gadgets or the Ironman would have chewed him up and spit him out again—but others might be backing up his play, coordinating strikes against the different members of the team.

Outside, he heard a rising babble as the neighbors worked their courage up, believing in the false security of numbers. Blancanales fed his pistol a replenished magazine and hit the doorway with determined strides, making no attempt to hide his face from the collection of uneasy men and women huddled two doors down.

"There's been a shooting," he informed them, squeezing off a round above their heads for emphasis and watching them scatter back to their respective rooms. He questioned whether any of them would remember him with the precision necessary for a decent suspect sketch, and if they did, the police would still be groping in the dark with several thousand local residents who fit his general description.

Blancanales concealed his pistol as he hit the stairwell, rapidly descending to the street. The aging desk clerk had his back turned and was muttering into the phone as Politician slipped past unseen. His first priority must be to put some ground between himself and Esperanza's flat. Next, he had to get in touch with Schwarz and Lyons and warn them to be ready for a possible attack. They had been coasting up to this point, covering surveillance, taking his reports, secure in the belief his cover would protect them all.

Three blocks away he found a phone booth, ducked inside and riffled through his pockets for the necessary coins. The hotel operator hesitated when he asked for Lyons's room...or was it only his imagination? After an eternity, the phone was answered by an unfamiliar voice.

"*¿Hola?*"

"Room 513?"

"That is correct. Detective Sergeant Alizondo speaking. May I have your name and number, please?"

Blancanales cradled the receiver, then slumped against the glass wall of the phone booth. A detective sergeant in the Ironman's room meant trouble, and he couldn't begin to sort it out without endangering himself as well as any possible survivors. For now, he had no choice but to anticipate the worst.

And somehow he must get in touch with Katzenelenbogen. Tonight. If Able Team was blown, so might be Phoenix Force. He didn't even want to take the notion to its logical conclusion, didn't want to ponder whether Bolan might be blown.

Politician sorted through his dwindling supply of coins and fed the telephone again. Against all hope of saving anything from the disaster, he began to dial.

☆ 21 ☆

Finished thumbing through the magazine, Carl Lyons dropped it on the floor. He eyed the bedside telephone uneasily, relieved that there had been no call and at the same time eager for some contact with the world outside. A call would mean that there was trouble, but the Ironman felt restricted by the confines of his hotel room. The television was a write-off: ancient movies from the States, all dubbed in Spanish, or atrocious horror films from Mexico, in which the mummy, vampire or whatever had to cope with leaping acrobats and hulking wrestlers. The laughs wore off after an hour or so, replaced by tired monotony.

It was already dark outside, and he had been expecting Gadgets back by now. The fact that Schwarz was late didn't necessarily spell trouble, but it was one more sliver of anxiety wedged underneath the Able warrior's fingernails. It had been two days since any solid contact with Politician, and now Schwarz was late from his appointed meeting with the point man out of Phoenix Force. It seemed to Lyons that the Latin *mañana* mentality had somehow polluted their mission, forcing everything to happen in slow motion.

Still, Pol hadn't been exactly slow in lining up a lady for himself. She was an eyeful, too, and Lyons wondered how she was in bed, but decided he was better off not knowing. Sex could fuck up an operation—he smiled at the pun—if the several parties didn't keep their wits about them. Once emotion entered the scene, you had a world of trouble to contend with: jealousy and guilt, regret and longing, a desire to help your bedmate even when the mission was at stake. The Ironman had been there, sure... and he had learned from his mistakes.

A decent combat soldier cherished love in abstract terms, like God and country, motherhood and apple pie. The moment love became concrete and personal, the soldier had a fatal weakness; he was vulnerable to the enemy if they should tap that wellspring of emotion, trace it to the source and use it as a weapon of the soldier's own destruction. Lyons thought of Flor Trujillo, saw the ghostly image of her smile before he slammed that mental door and threw his weight against it.

Love's memories could get you killed, if you indulged yourself too much, and Lyons made a point of clinging to reality. Whatever pain might be involved, he could endure it. They didn't call him Ironman for nothing.

He slid the six-inch Python out of side leather, broke the cylinder and spilled six Glaser safety slugs into his palm. Ironically nonlethal in appearance, looking more like rubber bullets than the sure-fire killers that they were, the Glasers were renowned for one-shot stopping power. Pellets of number twelve shot, suspended in liquid Teflon, were designed to blow on impact, savaging the flesh of any living target, wreaking havoc on internal organs, arteries and such. The "safety" designation indicated that a Glaser round wouldn't pierce doors or walls, endangering the innocent, but there was no such safety net for anyone who stopped a Glaser round. No one had ever managed to survive a head or torso wound from one of the explosive rounds, and even relatively minor wounds to the extremities might kill in time as liquid Teflon traveled through the bloodstream, homing on the heart and clogging the valves.

Carl Lyons always treated Glasers with respect, aware that the smallest flesh wound might have permanent results. He alternated ammo in accordance with his task, the Python feeding anything from hollowpoints to armor-piercing loads, but in a down-and-dirty confrontation, Glasers gave the Ironman something extra up his sleeve.

He checked the Python's action, spun the empty cylinder and decided he had time to strip and clean the piece before Schwarz got home from the meet with Phoenix. He was halfway to the closet and his cleaning kit when something made him hesitate. A sound? A feeling? What?

There was an insistent rapping on the outer door. Lyons fed the Glasers back into the Python's cylinder and snapped it shut, his index finger circling the trigger as he stepped into the parlor of his suite. He made no further move in the direction of the door.

"Who is it?"

Heartbeat hesitation, then: "Room service."

Lyons felt the short hairs lifting on his neck, the fight-or-flight response already pumping out adrenaline. "There must be some mistake," he called. "I didn't order anything."

"Compliments of the management, *señor*."

Really. After five days, he didn't believe the hotel would be sending flower baskets. Lyons sidled over to the couch, crouching behind it with his gun leveled at the door. "I'm not dressed. Leave it in the hall."

They would be forced to move or lose it now, and he was ready when a burst of automatic fire chewed through the woodwork, shattering the double locks. A heavy boot heel slammed the door wide open, and he caught a glimpse of three or four assailants dressed as bellhops, crowding close before another string of parabellums raked the air above his head.

One round to let them know that he was in the game, and Lyons saw the stucco sprout a fist-sized hole before he ducked for cover. Wriggling along the floor, his face pressed into heavy shag carpeting, he heard the sofa taking hits. The bastards were inside, and he would have to deal with that before they encircled him and pinned him up inside a box that would become his casket.

Lyons reached the far end of the sofa, easing back the Python's hammer as he risked a glance at his attackers. One of them was plainly visible, intent on pumping bullets through the sofa, too damned confident to imagine that his target might have moved. It was an easy shot from Lyons's prone position, and he punched a Glaser through the gunner's rib cage, blowing him away before the guy had time to realize that he had made a terminal miscalculation.

Lyons backed it up as angry autofire converged upon his new position, shattering the sofa's arm and spewing cotton stuffing in a frenzied blizzard. He was incongruously reminded of Bing Crosby, dreaming of a white Christmas, and the mental image made him bray with sudden, unexpected laughter. Startled, his assailants hesitated as they heard their target laughing in the face of death.

He could have used a frag grenade or two, but a lull in hostile firing was the best that Lyons could expect. Some fifteen feet of empty space lay between the Ironman and his bedroom door. The stucco walls were thin, but they provided better cover than the leaking couch, and he was running out of time.

The Able warrior erupted from his questionable sanctuary in a combat crouch, backpedaling in the direction of the open bedroom doorway, squeezing off his four remaining Glaser rounds in rapid-fire. A lamp exploded, furniture and fixtures went to hell, but he was finally rewarded on the last round as one of his assailants toppled backward, crimson spouting from a ragged shoulder wound.

The two survivors were unloading on him as he reached the doorway, parabellum stingers gnawing on the woodwork, plucking at his clothes. A white-hot lance drilled through the fleshy part of Lyons's side, above his belt line, and he staggered, stumbled out of range and collapsed to the floor as searching rounds explored the space that he had occupied mere heartbeats earlier.

No time to staunch the flow of blood from what he knew to be a flesh wound. He could judge a wound's severity these days by pain; he would survive this one, provided he didn't make a habit of absorbing lead this evening.

He broke the Python's cylinder and dumped the smoking empties, feeding in another load of Glasers, then locking down. The shooters couldn't have much time to spare; they had already suffered casualties, and they were making enough noise to raise the dead. Police would be along within the next few minutes, but the Ironman hoped that he wouldn't be forced to answer any of their questions. He wasn't prepared to finish out his mission in interrogation rooms, or at the prison ward of a hospital.

A rush of feet on carpeting, and Lyons knew that they were coming for him. Swiveling to let his Python clear the doorjamb, Lyons sighted on one of his attackers. The shooter had an Ingram MAC-10 submachine gun, and he held the trigger down as he advanced, one-handed, free arm cocked as if he were about to pitch a baseball. Lyons didn't have to guess what he was carrying; he ducked a string of parabellum rounds and slammed two Glasers home into the gunner's stomach. Gutted, dying, his assailant still had enough strength to make the pitch, and Lyons was already moving out when the grenade rebounded off a nightstand, wobbling across the carpet toward his hiding place.

The closet was his only hope, and Lyons hit the sliding doors full tilt, the inner rack and hanging outfits coming down on top of him. Knees pressed against his chest, eyes closed, he rode the thunderclap that rocked his bedroom, lying deathly still as shrapnel ripped the walls above his head.

His ears were ringing and his wound was burning, bleeding steadily as Lyons scrambled out from under cover, searching for a target with his Python. Three down, one to go.

SCHWARZ KNEW THAT IT WAS LATE, but it couldn't be helped. The men of Phoenix Force were spread so thin in their surveillance that his contact, Gary Manning, had been late for the meet, apologizing with the explanation that he had been following Luis Machado on his rounds and compelled to wait for Katzenelenbogen to relieve him. It was the Israeli's news that interested Schwarz the most; perhaps disturbed was a more accurate description of his feelings, after listening to Manning for the best part of an hour.

There was still no evidence connecting any of Machado's Contras with McNerney's operation, but Machado's second-in-command, one Anastasio Ruiz, had met that afternoon with an apparent senior agent of the local CIA. There hadn't been an opportunity to tap their conversation, but Ruiz was under scrutiny, and Katz was juggling their numbers, trying desperately to cover his connection with the Company.

It came as no surprise for Contras to be doing business with the CIA. The Agency had backed their play from the beginning, openly at first, and then through different proxies as the mood in Congress had gradually begun to change, inclining more toward a selective isolationism. It was only natural for the Machado troops to have their tie-ins with the Company, and yet...

The timing worried Schwarz. They had a man inside, already living on the razor's edge, and any alteration of routine at this point was a cause for deep concern. He knew about Ruiz from Pol: the Contra's obvious infatuation with the woman, Esperanza; his apparent jealousy of Blancanales. What that meant in concrete terms, or how it might connect with CIA, was anybody's guess. There was a chance Ruiz might try to intervene in Pol's relationship with Esperanza, or he might back off and let it lie. Whichever, Schwarz was agitated by the sudden contact with a troubleshooter for the Agency.

It would be helpful to identify the man from Langley, and Gadgets understood that Katz was working on that now. A firm ID could always be relayed to Wonderland, where Hal might have an opportunity to match the name against his list of coconspirators. If Anastasio's connection was a part of the McNerney game, they had their link. If not...then they were right back at the drawing board.

Schwarz checked his watch and cursed beneath his breath. He would catch hell from Lyons, nervous as the

Ironman seemed to be these days. He knew that Carl was worried for Politician's sake and by the blurry nature of their mission, overall. They were on standby, serving as reserves for Bolan if he needed them, but they had no real grasp of Bolan's situation, even his location from one moment to the next. For all they knew, he might have slipped across the line and into Nicaragua; by the time they missed him, it would be too late.

And if they lost him? Then what? Gadgets knew the answer even before the question finished coalescing in his mind. If they lost Bolan or any of the others, they would forge ahead. As long as one of them was still alive, the mission was a go. They were committed, and surrender wasn't part of the vocabulary taught at Stony Man.

The hotel loomed ahead of him, and Schwarz ducked through the swinging doors, relieved to find the lobby almost empty. In a corner chair a meaty tourist type was browsing through the local paper, and a well-dressed couple kept the desk clerk busy, signing in and waiting for a bellhop to assist them with their luggage. Gadgets flipped a mental coin, deciding on the elevator. Riding up alone and humming to himself, he tried to find the perfect phrasing to begin his apology to Lyons.

Every thought of conversation vanished as the elevator doors hissed open on a roaring battlefield. From somewhere to his left, the sound of automatic weapons rattled in the corridor, eclipsed and punctuated by the booming answer of a Magnum handgun. Digging for the Beretta 93-R beneath his jacket, Schwarz knew instantly that there could only be a single explanation for the racket. Someone had seen through their cover, and the opposition meant to close their show with a bang.

As if in answer to his thoughts, a muffled blast sent shock waves rippling through the floor beneath his feet.

Downrange, the ceiling released a misty rain of plaster. Schwarz was closing on the room he shared with Lyons, saw the door was standing open, gnawed by point-blank rounds, when a disheveled figure stumbled through the smoky portal. He was dressed like a bellhop, but the automatic weapon that he carried wasn't standard gear for any hotel concierge.

The hitter sprayed another burst into the suite, retreating toward his death as Schwarz lined up and slammed a double punch between his shoulder blades. The gunner dropped, triggering a last reflexive burst that carved an abstract pattern on the wall. Schwarz put another round behind one ear to pin him there for good and swiveled, tracking, as another tattered figure cleared the doorway.

Carl Lyons looked like death warmed over, blond hair tousled, his sport shirt saturated on one side with seeping blood. The Python's muzzle locked on Gadgets for a moment, then slipped to Lyons's side.

"Looks like I missed the party," Schwarz quipped.

"Better late than never."

"Yeah. I take it that we're checking out?"

"I'd say. We'll touch base with Pol when we get clear."

"You need a medic."

"Never mind," the Ironman growled. "It's in and out. A compress ought to do it."

Schwarz wasn't convinced, but he wasn't about to start an argument with doors already easing open and frightened faces peering up and down the corridor.

"You packed?"

"You're looking at it," Lyons told him, shrugging on a jacket that he carried in his free hand. They were leaving everything behind, but none of it was irreplaceable. Mobility was crucial to an operative in the field.

"Who blew us?" Gadgets asked when they were safely in the elevator.

"I was hoping you'd tell me."

He thought about it while they passed two floors. "Machado's right hand had a sit-down with a spokesman from the Agency. There might be some connection."

"That's Ruiz?"

"Uh-huh."

"He wants Pol's ass. How does that lead him back to us?"

"I haven't got a damned idea. I'm fishing."

"Shit. We've gotta find Pol before somebody makes a move on him."

"I hear you."

Still no action in the lobby, indicating that their fifth-floor neighbors hadn't yet found the courage to call for help. The well-dressed couple had already disappeared upstairs, and the desk clerk was busy with his register. On Schwarz's left, the tourist-type was still concealed behind his paper. Reading? Dozing?

"Watch that dude."

"Got him."

There was thirty feet between them when the backup gunner dropped his paper, rising from the easy chair and digging for the automatic hidden in his waistband. He wasn't even close when Schwarz and Lyons gave him three rounds each, the impact toppling the man and chair together, leaving their assailant on his back. The desk clerk dropped from sight as if he himself had stopped a round.

Holstering his Python, Lyons pushed ahead of Gadgets through the swinging doors. "No class," he growled when they were on the street. "I hate these fucking amateurs."

"Let's not be disrespectful of the dead."

It was the living that concerned Schwarz now, and Blancanales in particular. If they were blown, it stood to reason that their inside man had been identified and marked for termination. He might be done already, but if there was any chance at all, they had to try to pull him out.

That was the catch, of course: if there was any chance at all.

The Able warriors might be out of chances, out of time. Unless they touched base with Katzenelenbogen and found someplace to shelter while they put their feelers out to Pol, they were as good as dead themselves.

And dead, in Schwarz's mind, was no damned good at all.

☆ 22 ☆

Lane Travers slammed the telephone receiver back into its cradle, cursing under his breath. The late returns were in, and it was obvious that he had blown it. Ruiz had bagged the woman, Esperanza, but he had missed Briones, getting dusted in the process. That was bad enough, but Travers's "professionals," the hit team he had sent to mop up "Eric Larsen" and his sidekick in their hotel suite, had bought the farm. All five of them were stretched out in the morgue downtown, and there was no sign of the marks. No frigging sign at all.

Travers wasn't looking forward to delivering the news. McNerney would be livid, and the man from Langley wondered if the days of killing messengers who brought bad news were truly past. God knows the old man had his heart set on proceeding with the plan, on schedule, but if they were penetrated, it was tantamount to suicide. The raiding force might be destroyed. The *federales* might be waiting to spring a lethal trap on all concerned.

It struck him suddenly that Mike McNerney wouldn't care. It didn't matter in the slightest if his expeditionary force was cut to ribbons. The Contra troopers and their mercenary backup would be dressed as Sandinista regulars; the four or five Americans involved were going in as Soviet commandos, *spetsnaz* shock troops. They would certainly be missed, and someone—at the base or in the media—was bound to put the pieces back together, but in the interim there would be time for Congress and the White House to react effectively. The doves in Washington would all be pregnant by the time they realized they had been screwed.

It barely hung together, but a suicide mission hadn't been what the man from Langley had in mind when he'd signed on. He had imagined a deception utilizing some finesse and style, and if a few stray Nicaraguans bought the farm... well, that was life. Anticipating dead Americans was something else entirely. Travers had no moral qualms in that regard—the idiots were volunteers—but it was so damned risky. Dead Green Berets in *spetsnaz* uniforms would raise a hellish stink in Washington, and there would be calls for a congressional investigation once the smoke finally cleared. If it came down to that, his ass was in a sling, and he couldn't depend on Mike McNerney for relief. He knew the old man well enough by now to realize that he was looking out for number one exclusively.

Or was he?

Was McNerney mad enough to still believe that it could work? Did he imagine that congressional investigators would ignore his role in the fiasco, finding scapegoats in the lower ranks? It was a possibility, of course—they had employed the usual buffers, blinds, and proxies—but Travers didn't intend to bet his life on Mike McNerney's instinct or his ability to bluff the whole damned world.

The more he thought about it, Travers was convinced McNerney didn't care what happened after they were finished sorting out the dead. By then, if everybody took the bait, there would be troops en route to Nicaragua, and with victory as an accomplished fact, the congressmen who made it happen might be loath to wave their dirty laundry in the headlines. He was stretching it, of course, but Travers thought he had finally begun to see the operation through McNerney's eyes. Security was less important than success. You didn't have to hide your tracks unless you planned to lose.

And if they blew it? How would McNerney's clique react to failure, or if Washington refused to press the issue with Ortega, even in the face of massive provocation? Were the turks at the CIA prepared to climb out farther on their limb, then saw it off behind themselves? It worried Travers when he found he couldn't answer any of those questions. Suddenly it seemed that he had bet his life on strangers, risking everything on behalf of men who might be suicidal in their zeal.

The hard-core team at the CIA were true believers; Travers knew that much. For all of their maneuvering, for all their special interests, they *believed* that Daniel Ortega was a menace to American society, if not the Antichrist. They believed that Sandinista forces would eventually capture all of South America if they weren't destroyed in a preemptive strike, that history would finally absolve them, prove them heroes in the struggle to preserve civilization.

McNerney, likewise, was a true believer. He was dangerous specifically because of his commitment to an ideal. McNerney's perfect world would be devoid of Communists and socialists and "pinks," a vision Travers had been able to appreciate before he'd realized the cost. He could recall the Tet offensive in 1968, when Charlie's screaming legions had entrenched themselves in Hue outside Saigon. Artillery was used to root them out with the result that Hue was leveled and turned into a common grave. Before the smoke had settled, newshawks had aired an interview with one of the artillery commanders in the field, and Travers still recalled the soldier's chilling words: "It was necessary to destroy the town in order to save it."

And that, he surmised, was McNerney's vision of the world at large. The Sandinistas were a menace to their neighbors, to the very people of their homeland. If it took a bloodbath to eliminate the threat, then so be it. If it was necessary to destroy the Nicaraguan populace—in their defense, of course—McNerney and his troops would do what was required. They were prepared to leave scorched earth and carnage in their wake, annihilating friend and enemy alike in the pursuit of their ideal.

It was too late to call off the operation, and in any case Travers didn't have the necessary pull. He might have thrown a roadblock in the way, delayed McNerney from achieving his objective, but it would have cost his life, and he wasn't prepared yet to pay that kind of tab. Desertion was a possibility, but it was premature to think of bailing out just yet. No groundwork had been laid for his escape, and if he disappeared before the strike, McNerney's hitters would be after him before the sun went down. The Agency would offer nothing in the way of sanctuary if he broke and ran; there were too many rogues, too well concealed, for Travers to have faith in any of them.

If he ran, he would be on his own, and that knowledge kept the man from Langley at his desk when every basic instinct told him he should be en route to the Tegucigalpa airport. He was trapped, and he would have to see the operation underway, at least, before he made his break. Once the battle had been joined, there was a chance that he could take advantage of the general confusion and slip away unnoticed.

But first things first. And number one was carrying the news of failure to McNerney. There was still an outside chance that the old man might panic and call off the operation when hostile penetration of the Contra forces was confirmed. It was a futile hope, Travers realized...but at the moment it was all he had.

In his rookie days, when he was fresh out of Camp Peary, Travers had believed that he, the Company, could handle any given situation that arose. He would be one of the manipulators, writing history behind the scenes, directing lives so subtly that the players never even realized that they were being used. In retrospect, Lane Travers saw that he was little better than a puppet. They had put him through his paces, played upon his limited ideals, and suckered him into a box from which there seemed to be no exit. He was at their mercy now, and they were seldom merciful.

He didn't have to think about the consequences if this operation blew up in his face. McNerney and the Agency would cast about for scapegoats, losers who could take the heat while those above walked out unscathed. McNerney's subordinates, Crane and Falcone, were naturals to fill a scapegoat's role, but they wouldn't be going down alone. The Company would need its share of sacrificial lambs as well, and Travers could already feel the bull's-eye painted on his back. The men at Langley would discard him like a worn-out pair of shoes to save themselves...provided he let it happen.

There were ways of taking out insurance, though, and Travers knew them all. His journal, in a safe deposit box with copies stateside, spelled out details of the mission, complete with places, dates and names. Whenever feasible, he had recorded conversations with the principals involved: McNerney, Crane, Falcone, intermediaries for the Company. The diary would be opened and excerpts published in the case of any sudden accident to Travers. His attorney was instructed to provide the media with copies of the tapes in the event of Travers's death. Nobody knew of his insurance policy—not yet—but if they took it in their heads to rub him out, the man from Langley wasn't going down alone.

Revenge was one thing, but it couldn't hold a candle to survival. Travers knew his business well enough to trust his own abilities, and he was a survivor. If he continued taking care of business in the usual way, as a professional, he just might survive.

Still, McNerney would be furious at the snafu. But there was nothing to be done. He couldn't turn back the clock. If it wasn't too late already, he might be able to launch another strike against the targets, provided he could discover where they were of course. And that, he knew, would be no easy task.

He had no further contacts in the local Contra movement, and he dared not tap the Company's files to see if there were any other men in place. There was no time to turn a working mole at this late date; he would be forced to make the best of an atrocious situation with his people on the street.

And he would have to deal with Mike McNerney. Now. The longer he delayed, the worse it looked, and bad news should be broken quickly, just like ripping off a Band-Aid. Any longer, and the old man might suspect that Travers was covering for someone, possibly considering a break, betrayal. That would never do, not if the man from Langley planned on living out the night.

He would rely on his insurance, try to make the old man understand that it wasn't his fault. And, in the meantime, he would do his best to make it right.

The enemy would still be somewhere in Tegucigalpa. All he had to do was find them and pin them down before they had a chance to blow the game sky-high. There were only half a million people in the city; how long could it take?

Lane Travers didn't plan to be among the casualties when the smoke cleared. Reaching for the telephone again, he started marshaling his troops for battle. If the man from Langley went, it wouldn't be without a fight.

"I'D LIKE TO HAVE the medics take a look at that," Katz said again.

The Ironman waved him off. "It's fine. The bleeding's stopped already. Let it go."

With the exception of Blancanales, who still hadn't touched base with members of either team, they were huddled in a room secured by Katzenelenbogen after he'd received the call from Schwarz. The rooms already occupied by Phoenix Force were two floors up and empty at the moment. Lyons's wound was fresh in everybody's mind as they discussed what had happened and Pol's failure to appear.

"Could be the shooters muffed it," said David McCarter. "They get overanxious, go in blasting. Bingo! Two for one. It's bargain night."

Lyons shook his head. "It doesn't wash. I believe Pol was tailed."

"And if you're right," Katz said, "then what?"

"Then you all have a fifty-fifty chance of being free and clear," the Ironman answered. "It led the shooters back to us and maybe got Pol killed. You had no contact with him after he went under, am I right? And I can guarantee nobody followed *us* tonight."

"You hope."

"I'd bet my life."

"You have," McCarter said. "And now you're betting ours."

"So, what's the problem," Lyons growled. "Are you on board to break this thing or just take notes?"

"Goddamn it—"

"That's enough!" Katz snapped. "We have no time for juvenile distractions. Pol may be alive. We'll have to wait and see. The mission stands unchanged. Our top priority now is touching base with Striker, warning him that Able's net has broken down. Suggestions?"

"Yeah, I've got one." All eyes turned toward Calvin James, who had been silent until now. "Somebody fix me with a uniform, and I'll tell Striker anything he needs to know."

"Why you?" Schwarz asked.

"Hey, look around. You're blown, *compadre*. Show your face around McNerney's playpen, and somebody's bound to shoot it off. Your partner's blown *and* wounded. David and Katz would be conspicuous, you follow? No one really notices a black man on a military base these days. Hell, we're like furniture."

"Makes sense to me," the Ironman grudgingly conceded. "Anyway, I hate to argue with a coffee table."

"You're too kind."

"I'm working on it."

"If we can put the vaudeville routine on hold," Katz interrupted, "I agree that Calvin should make the touch with Striker. Be damned careful, though. You've got no solid cover if you draw attention to yourself."

"I'm the soul of discretion."

"That anything like soul food, Cal?"

"I've got your soul food right here, Ironman."

Katz continued as if he hadn't been interrupted. "I'd advise a touch off-base, if possible. Too late this evening, but I'll have your uniform and basic paperwork first thing tomorrow. You can check the night spots first and fall back to the post as a last resort."

"I'll handle it."

"You know we're running out of time," Schwarz said to no one in particular.

"Did Pol come up with something on the deadline?"

"No, I would've passed it if he had. It's just a feeling that I can't get rid of."

Katzenelenbogen knew the feeling. It had been haunting him for days. Without a single shred of solitary evidence to back it up, he knew the hostile operation must be coming to a head, and soon. With recent setbacks, most especially with the latest violence, Mike McNerney and his team couldn't afford to postpone zero hour any longer than was absolutely necessary. If McNerney knew that operatives were breathing down his neck, he had two choices: scuttle, or proceed with deliberate speed. Katz knew what he would do if he was in McNerney's place, and he assumed the rogue commander's zeal was equal to his own.

The enemy would be redoubling its efforts, working toward a deadline that was still unknown to Phoenix Force. When it came down to that, the plan itself was still unknown. McNerney's team might strike at any target, any time. They had no choice but to pursue surveillance on Machado's group and hope that Calvin James could find the answers they so desperately needed.

If he failed to contact Bolan—worse, if Bolan had been tagged by hostiles—then the Phoenix team would be required to act on instinct, moving to preempt a strike that they couldn't predict with any accuracy. If Machado's people were involved, as Able's late misfortune seemed to indicate, a forceful move against their base of operations might derail the secret operation, or at least demand postponement while McNerney went in search of reinforcements. On the other hand, he might be using mercenary troops or relying on the Contras as a backup.

There were far too many questions still unanswered for the gruff Israeli to pretend that he had matters well in hand.

Right now they needed who, what, where and when. Without the basics, they were groping in the dark, compelled to wait and mount an unprepared reaction to the enemy's eventual assault. It was a situation Katzenelenbogen didn't relish, and he knew that it was troubling the other members of his team as well.

There had been no word of Bolan in five days. If he had run into a major obstacle, the warrior would have been in touch by now, assuming he hadn't been tagged already by the enemy. They could only wait and hope, while taking every possible precaution in the meantime, drawing meager consolation from the fact that it couldn't go on much longer.

And either way it played, Katz knew that they were bound to have the answer soon. He only hoped it was an answer he could live with. Otherwise, Tegucigalpa should be gearing up to face the firestorm of a lifetime.

☆ 23 ☆

Dawn found Bolan wide awake. A fitful bid for sleep had gotten nowhere, and the Executioner had used the quiet hours to best advantage, laying out contingencies and making rudimentary battle plans. So much depended on the enemy at this point; there was so much that he didn't know about the coming strike. They would be keeping him deliberately in the dark, of course, but perhaps he knew enough to bring the operation down without the final details. Zero hour was a closely guarded secret, but he knew the day, and he was privy to the target.

They were rolling out tomorrow against an unarmed village twenty klicks south of Tegucigalpa. San Felipe was a trading center for surrounding settlements, and Fletcher Crane—or his superiors—had timed their move for Saturday when business would be at its best, with peasant farmers and their families collected in the central marketplace. Crane's team would be flying in from the south, and making certain that their choppers were observed—too late—on radar screens. A strike force armed with automatic weapons and grenades would turn the festive afternoon into a bloodbath, wreaking havoc on San Felipe's hapless population.

Bolan realized that he had to connect with his backup team soon, but it wouldn't be easy. He knew that Rafferty and friends would be observing him with extra care while they counted down to zero hour. He couldn't risk any phone calls from the post, and with his allies spread too thin already, they wouldn't be sitting by the telephone. Somehow he had to get off-base before the final call-up, find a way to contact Able Team or Phoenix Force. The passing of intelligence would only take a moment, but the intervening hours might constitute a lifetime. And if McNerney's raiders caught him at it, it could be the end of Bolan's life.

He had no doubt that they would kill him to protect their mission. Broderick might do it just for sport, if he decided that the odds were on his side. If they couldn't arrange an accident, straightforward violence would do just as well. And either way he cut it, Bolan ran an equal risk of losing it before he could derail the master plan.

Would it postpone the operation if he forced their hand in public? Bolan couldn't say for certain, but he would have bet that the arrest of four or five Berets wouldn't derail McNerney's scheme. The body of his force had been recruited elsewhere, and they would be standing by to sweep down on San Felipe to complete their mission. Removal of the Rafferty contingent might result in some peripheral confusion, but he couldn't count on scuttling the plan so easily. To break the raiders, it would take a hot reception on the ground.

Which brought him back to Able Team and Phoenix Force. He knew their basic game plans, knew that Pol had been assigned to penetrate the local Contra team, but otherwise he had no inkling of their progress, their security. For all he knew their covers might be blown by now. If Hal or someone in the White House had been sloppy in their preparations, it could all be over but the dying.

Bolan pushed the defeatist train of thought away, refusing to be cowed by long-shot possibilities. If worse came down to worst, he was prepared to tough it out alone. They would be counting on a turkey shoot, without resistance from the peasants, never counting on a wild card in the ranks. Alone, he still might have the slim advantage of surprise. It wasn't much, but it could buy him precious numbers when the chips were down and it was killing time. One man could make a difference, sure, and if the Executioner couldn't prevent a massacre at San Felipe, then perhaps he could arrange for roughly equal body counts on either side.

It was a kamikaze game that he was contemplating, but it might turn out to be the only game in town. If he couldn't reach out to any of his outside contacts, he would have to take the play by ear, relying on his instincts in the clinches. The Executioner wasn't afraid of death, but neither was he looking forward to the prospect with anticipation. When it came to banzai missions, Bolan knew the drill, but he would bide his time until the other possibilities were thoroughly exhausted.

Bolan showered, shaved and dressed for breakfast underneath the watchful eye of Jason Rafferty. The sergeant lingered close to him, like a self-appointed officer in charge of Bolan's personal morale. His other purpose, that of keeping Bolan under constant scrutiny, was shared throughout the day by members of the inner circle.

Steiner sat with Bolan during breakfast, griping animatedly about the quality of food available on-base, soliciting "Lambretta's" views about the coming season's baseball prospects. Broderick was with him like a shadow on the short walk to his duty station in the records office where DiSalvo picked it up and worked beside him through the afternoon. Throughout, the only sour note was Broderick's overt animosity; the others treated Bolan as if he were a longtime friend. Beneath the smiles, however, he could feel a strain of tension. And he had no doubt that each man was wondering if they had moved too quickly with "Lambretta," trusting him too soon. They were prepared to move against him at the slightest sign of deviation from the plan, and knowing that, the warrior also knew he had no choice. At any cost, he must attempt to get off-base and alert his allies in the field.

It was approaching four o'clock, and he was winding down his shift when Rafferty popped in, all smiles. "'Bout ready?"

Bolan didn't have to feign confusion. "What's the story?"

"Little pregame bash to loosen up the troops," the sergeant told him. "Nothing heavy, understand. A couple of drinks, a little native poon to take the edge off. Whatcha say?"

It was an offer Bolan literally couldn't refuse. If he declined, the sergeant would insist, suspicions mounting to the danger level, pressing until Bolan acquiesced. It was a test, of course; no field commander sent his men out on a binge the night before a crucial mission. Somewhere up the line someone had questioned "Frank Lambretta's" mettle and had decided to provide him with a handy length of rope. At this point, Bolan had two options: he could hang himself, or he could reverse the tables, use the line to haul himself out of his personal dilemma. They were taking him off-base to test him. And in the process, they were granting Bolan one last opportunity to put his mission back on course.

ON HIS SECOND TRY, Blancanales still got no answer on Katzenelenbogen's line. Politician gave it up, uncertain what the ringing silence might portend, but ready to accept the worst. He had been blown with Gadgets and Lyons, either of whom might now be dead. The Phoenix line had been unmanned since ten o'clock the previous evening, and he wasn't about to risk a call to the United States. If he was on his own, fine. Pol had played it out that way before, and he could make it work again.

Mulling over options since his first attempt to contact Katz, the Able warrior knew that he had reached the only workable conclusion. It was far from safe, but the alternatives were suicide or worse: surrender. Subsequent attempts to reach the Phoenix team had also failed, each failure reinforcing Pol's original decision, stiffening his personal resolve.

He had decided to stick with Machado's team. Some of them would surely know about Ruiz and Esperanza by this time; they would have picked up rumbles, rumors of another gunman at the scene, and one or two might have an eye out for "Rosario Briones," even now. He didn't plan to make it difficult for them to find him. Quite the contrary: he was on his way to see Luis Machado personally.

It would require finesse, but that was why he had been nicknamed Politician. If Anastasio Ruiz had been alone, or acting with some group outside Machado's clique, it might be possible to pass the shooting off as jealousy. How could Pol know anything, if questioned, of foreigners who might, or might not, have been shot to death in a hotel downtown? Besides, how could such matters possibly relate to Esperanza's death or Ruiz's obvious insanity? He had been forced to kill Ruiz in self-defense, he'd explain, and had been hiding in the meantime, conscious of the fact that he would be a hunted man. Sure, the police could by now have descriptions of him on the street, but he was more concerned with friends of Anastasio Ruiz, the possibility of lunatics or traitors threatening Machado's rule within the local Contra movement.

If Ruiz had learned anything, and had shared his information with Machado and the others, Blancanales would be dead before he had a chance to offer them his spiel. All things considered, it was still the best he had to offer, and he couldn't bear the thought of abandoning Mack Bolan in the field. There might be little he could do from this point on, but he would give it everything he had, and screw the consequences to himself.

He knew Machado's address and wasn't surprised to find the modest house ablaze with lights despite the early-morning hour. Bad news travels fast in any language, and the Contra chief was clearly braced for trouble. Pol detected sentries on the front porch and knew there would be others spaced around the small frame house. He wondered if they had been primed to kill on sight, but decided that it didn't really matter either way.

They spotted Pol at fifty yards, one lookout swinging up a twelve-gauge pump gun while his partner disappeared inside the house. Pol never broke his stride. He was already close enough for them to cut him down at will, and they would surely open fire if he should change his mind and try to run. Instead, he held his jacket wide, revealed the automatic slung beneath his arm and slowly raised both hands above his head. The guard appeared confused, but he was steady as a rock, the riot gun unwavering as Blancanales closed the gap between them.

The gunner's backup reappeared, a squat Detonics .45 in hand, and beckoned Pol to join him on the porch.

Once there, he was subjected to a thorough frisking while the sentry with the shotgun covered both of them. His autoloader was removed and tucked away inside the *pistolero's* belt before his captor prodded Pol inside.

Machado, Raúl Gutierrez and a dozen other stone-faced men were waiting for him in the parlor. Gutierrez's grief about his sister was evident. The other scrutinized "Briones" with undisguised suspicion.

Machado broke the ice. "I did not think that you would come here."

"Where else should I go?"

"You bring disaster to this house. It might have been more prudent to escape."

"Escape from what?" He feigned amazement. "Can it be that you are uninformed of what has happened?"

"We are well informed," Machado told him stonily. "Two of our trusted comrades have been slain."

"Unfortunately, only one was worthy of your trust. The other has betrayed you and the movement with deceit and treachery."

Raúl Gutierrez bristled and took a stride toward Blancanales, but the others held him back. Machado stepped between them, glowering at Pol. "Explain yourself, Rosario."

Politician swallowed hard. He didn't have to fake the swelling of emotion in his chest.

"You know of my regard for Esperanza. We were lovers. I do not deny it. It was my desire to marry her as soon as possible. I knew Ruiz had eyes for her, that he was jealous...but I never knew that he was loco. Last night...I...Esperanza never had a chance to save herself. I shot Ruiz in self-defense and to avenge her death."

Raúl had ceased to struggle, listening to Blancanales speak. "Ruiz killed Esperanza?"

"*Sí*. You thought... that I...?" He spread his arms and spluttered outrage at the stony faces that surrounded him. "Ballistics tests will show the truth. You have my pistol. The police have Anastasio's. But do not wait for any tests! If you believe that I would kill this woman, whom I loved as life itself, then shoot me now. You have the weapons. I demand it!"

Raúl Gutierrez stared at Blancanales for another moment, than shook his head and turned away. "Ruiz was jealous. I have known this and did nothing to prevent my sister's death."

Machado placed a hand upon the grieving Contra's shoulder. "There was nothing to be done. A jealous man is unpredictable. His anger is like lightning, here and gone. You must not blame yourself."

The angry silence in the parlor broke at last. Machado's troops began commiserating with Raúl, a cautious few of them extending hands to Blancanales, welcoming him back into the fold. He felt the tight knots in his stomach slowly loosening and knew that it was still too early for congratulations. He was momentarily secure, but he was still a long way short of wrapping up his mission with the Contras. Their involvement with McNerney's force was still obscure, the nature of their mission—if they even had an active role—concealed from Pol. He would need more, and quickly, if he was to salvage something from his risky grandstand play.

"Inquiries must be made," Machado told him. "By this afternoon, police reports should be available, as you suggest. If they support your story, you will take Ruiz's place, at my right hand. If not..."

He didn't have to state the grim alternative. Pol knew precisely what would be in store for him if his story didn't hold.

CALVIN JAMES STRAIGHTENED his tie one last time and examined himself in the full-length mirror. The uniform fit well enough, which was all he could ask for in the circumstances. Higher rank, they told him, had been unavailable, and he received the word with his usual good grace.

"Your mama."

James wasn't precisely thrilled with his assignment—going in without the paperwork to back him up if he got bagged—but it already beat the hell out of tailing Contras, pulling shift around the clock because they didn't have enough damned guns to go around. It wouldn't matter in the long run, anyway, he finally decided. If he *did* get bagged, his ass was grass, and that would be the end of it. The people they were up against weren't about to check his papers if they caught him huddling with Bolan. They would count him out, no questions asked, and all the background in the world was useless when it came to stopping bullets.

And at one level he was very pleased with the assignment. It would be good to see the man again, make sure that he was safe and sound. Make that as safe and sound as anyone could be in his position, dancing with the devil on the rim of hell. One dip, one slip, and you were crispy critters, but the big guy seemed to like it that way, on the edge.

James hadn't stopped to think about his options if Bolan wasn't safe and sound. If someone had already tumbled to his act, for instance, lining up a little surgical removal prior to game time. It was going on five days without a word, and that was too damned long for Calvin's taste. The usual rules of play were hit-and-git, but this one put the rule book through a shredder from the start. What kind of freaking world had it become when you were playing off against your own team half the time?

The kind of world that needed able warriors, sure. And Calvin James was ready from the git-go. Able, ready and most definitely willing.

He was prepared to lay it on the line tonight, for Bolan, for the mission, just as he had laid it on the line a hundred times before in situations every bit as tight. Whatever happened, James was ready to accept the final consequences and deal with any sacrifice that was demanded on the way to victory or death. You either played the freaking game for keeps, or else you might as well stay home.

With any luck, he would be able to make contact with the Executioner among the myriad cantinas, cathouses and assorted dives that drew Tegucigalpa's servicemen and tourists after nightfall. Failing that, he would be forced to go on-base. He had papers that should get him in if no one on the gate was in a picky mood. But getting out again could be a problem. And on-base the odds of being spotted by the enemy were infinitely higher.

Still, the Phoenix warrior knew that he would do whatever was required. Calvin James had never run from any confrontation in his life, and he wouldn't be starting now.

The dicey part was going in unarmed. He had convinced the others that a boot knife was in order, that no serviceman abroad was ever really naked to the world, but it would only help him if the fight was hand-to-hand. At present Calvin didn't know the number of the enemy, their faces or their names. But, so what? They'd be dealing with a mean cat, the party animal.

First up, the easy part: he had to hit as many bars as necessary, seeking Bolan on the streets. When he was finished there, convinced that every possibility had been exhausted, James would think about the problems that awaited him on-base. Right now the toughest job ahead of him was keeping down a couple dozen watered drinks while tracking Bolan through the red-light district of Tegucigalpa.

Smiling, Calvin James knew he was equal to the task. If he had to search among the fallen sisters of the street, why, he could handle that as well. Perhaps there were fringe benefits to his profession, after all.

But at the end of it lay death for someone, possibly himself. And Calvin James, the party animal, could be a lethal predator when he was cornered, when the smell of blood was in his nostrils and the enemy had been identified. If Bolan had been tagged already, it would be his job to bring the message back and help the others map out their alternatives. It was his duty. But there was nothing in the book that said he couldn't kick some righteous ass along the way.

And if the big guy had been tagged, then his killers had already booked their next dance with the party animal.

A dance of death, with Calvin James to call the tune.

☆ 24 ☆

The imitation Yankee rock band didn't know its Buddy Holly from its Grateful Dead, but Bolan didn't mind. The "music" did its job as background noise, allowing him to think while Rafferty and his friends attempted to converse above the racket. Bolan caught a snatch of dialogue from time to time, but they were keeping it innocuous in public, talking booze and women for the most part, with a few trajectories and calibers thrown in. To any casual observer, it would seem to be the sort of conversation held by fighting men around the world. If the hypothetical observer noted Bolan's moody silence, it would likely be ascribed to large quantities of beer.

In fact, the Executioner was stone cold sober. That was no mean feat, considering the rounds of warm *cerveza* purchased by the others, but adrenaline was keeping Bolan's thought processes crystal clear. He had to lose his shadows soon, long enough to find a telephone and place the call. So far they had been taking turns, accompanying Bolan to the bar or cigarette machine; on two occasions, Vince DiSalvo had trailed him to the rest room, running murky water in the pitted sink and whistling while Bolan had used the toilet.

Now, to make things worse, they were collected in a smoky dive that seemed to have no telephone at all. Bolan glanced at his watch. It was approaching ten o'clock.

He didn't know how late the others planned on hanging out, but if their strike was scheduled for the next day, they would be heading back to base within the next few hours, blowing any final chance he had to contact Able Team or Phoenix Force. His pent-up anger and frustration sent a fresh surge of adrenaline through his veins. He longed to put his fist through Broderick's face, then work his way around, smashing each in turn until they couldn't stand. It would accomplish nothing in the long run, but he thought that it would make him feel just fine.

"It's gettin' late," DiSalvo said to no one in particular. "What say we go an' find some *señoritas*?"

"One more round," the sergeant countermanded, flagging down a waitress who was clownish in her heavy makeup. Holding up a hand with fingers splayed, he yelled, "Five *cervezas*, honey, *por favor*." She slipped away before his probing fingers could insinuate themselves beneath her skirt.

"You're lookin' peaked, Frankie. What's the matter?" Rafferty was eyeing Bolan from the far end of the table, peering through a haze of cigarette smoke.

Bolan forced a drowsy smile. "Nothin'. I just gotta tap a kidney."

"Hey," DiSalvo said, as if on cue, "I need to see the Indian myself. Let's go."

Bolan drained his beer and stood slowly, letting his shadow lead the way this time. Once in the crapper, he could take out DiSalvo and make his exit through a window, find a way to reach his backup... but the problem would be magnified if Bolan made his move too soon. A deviation from the game plan now might ruin everything. Instead of folding up their tents, the plotters would regroup, ride out the coming storm and cut their losses by discarding various subordinates. He could begin to tag them, of course, but he was sure to miss a few.

And nothing less than a clean sweep would satisfy the Executioner. Somehow he had to find a way to reach his backup without jeopardizing everything that he had worked for in the past five days.

The impact of a reeling body staggered Bolan, jostling him against a nearby table and rattling the beer mugs held by four marines. He pivoted to find a khaki-clad soldier staring at him, then recognized Calvin James instantly and knew that he was saved.

"Watch where you're goin', man," said the Phoenix warrior.

"You watch it, boy."

"I ain't your boy."

"That's obvious. I would've taught you better manners."

"Honky bastard!"

James came at him in a rush, fist cocked, and Bolan sidestepped just enough to save his face, big knuckles grazing past his cheek as James collided with him. Both men went down together, flattening the nearest table beneath their weight. Marines and beer mugs scattered with a crash, eclipsing the imitation rock and roll, the lame band limping to a halt as things began to come apart.

They rolled together on the gritty floor, which was awash with beer. Bolan pummeled Calvin, pulling punches, wincing at the impact even though his adversary did the same. He felt someone groping at him, struggling to separate the two combatants when a fist came out of nowhere, flattening the would-be peacemaker.

"Gotta make this look good," Calvin muttered, breaking free and scrambling to his feet. The Executioner was right behind him, dodging as a kick was fired in the direction of his face. He caught James's ankle, twisted sharply and brought him down. Already breathing heavily, he made it to his feet before the black man could recover.

Suddenly DiSalvo had him by the arm. "Let's shake it, Frankie. Leave the jig. We gotta split."

Bolan shook off the watchdog and waded into James as he rose in turn, fists flailing. One of those big hands connected solidly with Bolan's cheek, the jarring impact lighting flares of pain inside his skull. He staggered, found his footing once again and bored ahead, ignoring blows that landed on his arms and shoulders.

Bolan knew he might not have another opportunity. He had to pass the message, beneath the watchful gaze of Rafferty and friends before it was too late. He tackled Calvin, wrapped his arms around the newest member of the Phoenix team's waist and toppled with him to the floor.

James twisted under Bolan, his free hand scrabbling at the wooden floor, his brand-new uniform smeared with dirt and beer. The Executioner had one arm locked around his throat, a simulated choke hold bringing Bolan's lips in line with Calvin's ear.

"Tomorrow," Bolan whispered above the shouts and jeers of patrons grouped at ringside. "San Felipe. Airborne strike."

He gripped a table leg and made as if to swing it overhead, but lost his grip before he could complete the move.

"What time?"

One of the big guy's hands was splayed across his face, as if to gouge his eyes. "Don't know."

It was the best he could do. James whipped an elbow into Bolan's ribs, and Bolan doubled over, gasping, showing more reaction than the impact merited. James seized the opening and wriggled free, already on his feet when one of the marines came charging at him from the sidelines.

"Nigger bastard!"

James ducked the clumsy roundhouse, thankful for the opportunity to throw a solid punch this time. A big right hand impacted on his adversary's nose and upper lip, releasing crimson jets from flattened nostrils. Following the right with a destructive left, he dropped the leatherneck and swiveled back to look for Bolan in the spreading melee.

All around him men in uniform were squaring off by race or branch of service, throwing punches in a general free-for-all. A bottle of *cerveza* whistled past his ear, and Calvin ducked, arm raised to shield his eyes as it exploded into fragments on the wall behind him. An air force pilot stumbled into Calvin, took a stunning elbow in the chops and staggered out of range again, hands cupped around his lacerated face as blood drooled between his fingers.

Somehow Bolan had been swept away in the confusion. Calvin spent no more time pondering it. He sought an exit, conscious of the fact that he couldn't afford a confrontation with MPs just now. He had to deliver a message of the utmost urgency, and nothing must prevent his carrying the word to Katz and the others.

James was heading for the john when suddenly his path was blocked by Bolan's former escort. Snarling, reaching down for what could only be a boot knife, he was primed to strike when Calvin's heavy boot exploded in his groin. The weasel folded, instantly forgetting all about the blade as he collapsed to hands and knees. The

Phoenix member kicked him in the ribs, then scrambled past him toward the sanctuary of the rest rooms.

He was alone, the other tenants having emptied out to join the spreading melee in the barroom proper. Crossing to the nearest window, Calvin cranked it open with an effort, rusty hinges chattering in protest. Standing on a filthy sink that groaned and shifted underneath his weight, he punched the screen aside and scrambled through into the alleyway outside.

His uniform was a mess, but it didn't matter now, unless the MPs spotted him before he cleared the scene. Somebody in the dive was bound to call for reinforcements, if they hadn't called already, and Calvin didn't plan to stick around and meet the cavalry. He had to contact Katz as soon as possible and pass on Bolan's message.

San Felipe.

Airborne strike.

Tomorrow.

It was more than they had going in. James only hoped that it would be enough to see them through.

BOLAN DROVE AN ANGRY FIST into the face that popped up before his eyes like a target in a shooting gallery. He hadn't seen the man before, had no idea who he was or what he hoped to gain by rushing at a stranger in the middle of a barroom brawl. The meet with James had been an unexpected bonus, but it might be a disaster if he lingered any longer and got arrested at the scene.

He glanced around for Vince DiSalvo and found him crawling through the fray on hands and knees, head hanging like a beaten dog. He reached the fallen soldier, dropping two more strangers on the way, and helped him slowly to his feet.

"Who was that nigger?"

Bolan shrugged, one arm already looped around DiSalvo. "Never saw his ass before."

"I think the bastard ruptured me."

"You'll be all right. Let's shake this dump."

The others caught up with them halfway to the exit with DiSalvo slowing Bolan down. As Broderick and Steiner took the limping soldier off his hands, Rafferty seized Bolan's arm. "We didn't need this shit tonight," he growled.

"We didn't *need* to make the rounds at all," the Executioner replied. "Would you prefer I let some drunken shithead put me in emergency receiving?"

"Frankie didn't start it, Jase," DiSalvo said. "It was the shine."

"I see that spook again, he'll wish I hadn't," Steiner vowed.

"Forget him. He's long gone."

DiSalvo snarled, "I'm not forgettin' anything."

They hit the sidewalk running, Broderick and Steiner carrying DiSalvo between them, his arms around their shoulders. They were half a block away and flagging down a taxi when the first carload of helmeted MPs pulled up outside the bar, disgorging burly figures armed with riot sticks.

"That's too damned close for me," the sergeant grumbled, settling in beside the taxi driver.

"What about the *señoritas*?" Vince DiSalvo asked.

"Forget it, man. What were you gonna use, your good intentions?"

"Hey, he didn't kick me *that* hard."

"Hang it up, all right? You're gonna feel like shit tomorrow as it is. And we've all got a busy day."

The Executioner slumped back, relaxing. He had passed the word, and for the moment that was all that he could do. The rest of it was up to Calvin James, the other men of Phoenix Force and Able Team. If all of them were still intact and there was time for them to organize a hot reception for McNerney's team at San Felipe, fine. If not, then it was back to Bolan, battling the odds. He still had no idea how many guns were going on the raid; for all he knew, McNerney might have armed a full battalion. He was counting on a smaller force—the larger numbers made for more severe logistics problems—but he would have to play the cards as they were dealt this time. There would be no more opportunities for Bolan to improve his hand.

Tomorrow...and he didn't even know what time. They might be setting out at dawn, but Bolan doubted it. The sergeant's casual insistence on a night of drinking indicated that the strike was timed for later in the day, perhaps tomorrow evening. Whatever, any time his allies gained was time in which they could prepare themselves to meet the enemy. He didn't envy Katzenelenbogen or the others, bracing for a confrontation with a hostile force of unknown numbers, coming at them out of nowhere, with the crucial zero hour still unspecified. With any luck at all, Politician might have gathered further details from his post inside the local Contra movement, but the Executioner couldn't afford to count on luck tonight.

He had already used his up. Meeting Calvin James had been a fluke, and Bolan knew from grim experience that flukes didn't repeat themselves. Whatever breaks the warrior got from here on out, he would be making for himself. And anything his adversaries wanted from him, they would have to take.

The Executioner had done as much as he could do, without reverting to combat mode, and there was enough time for that once they were in the field. There would be ample time for killing at San Felipe.

☆ 25 ☆

It was going to be a great day. Michael John McNerney could feel it in his bones. This day was etched into his destiny... but he would take precautions all the same. A visionary might put his faith in destiny and fate, but only idiots forgot to keep their options open when their hopes and dreams were on the firing line. Whichever way it went today, McNerney would be covered fore and aft. He liked to think it was impossible for anyone to take him by surprise.

The plan was virtually foolproof, but he knew from experience that anything could happen. You never knew where the next hard break was coming from, and no amount of advance planning could ever totally eliminate the factors of coincidence and chance. If things blew up at San Felipe, McNerney would be ready with his alternate contingencies.

None of the orders or arrangements for the San Felipe strike were written down, so there would be no files to shred or burn in case of a disaster. Half a dozen loyal subordinates could link him with the strike, but none of them would be in any shape to testify if things went sour. It was those above him, his "superiors," who worried Mike McNerney most. Experience had taught him that the higher ranks were only theoretically composed of better, tougher men. In fact, he thought his allies on the general staff might fold if pressure was applied, and once the dominoes began to fall, no one was safe.

He had prepared himself for flight from the beginning, recognizing human nature, understanding that no man was absolutely worthy of his trust. Betrayal was an ugly fact of life in military and clandestine service; every war had seen its traitors, and in peacetime anyone could play the Judas game. McNerney's cash was in a numbered Swiss account, untouchable by Justice or the IRS; he owned three passports and kept his bags perpetually packed and ready. If he couldn't disappear on a moment's notice, he could come damned close, and once he shed his uniform, McNerney was prepared to lead pursuers on the wild-goose chase of a lifetime.

They could never hope to second-guess his backup plan. The scheme was too audacious, straining credibility. If his own participation was exposed, they would be waiting for a bug-out, counting on a run for parts unknown. A counterthrust would never cross the enemy's collective mind, and that was why McNerney knew that it would work. The sheer audacity would see him through, and in the end, when the dust had settled, when a grateful nation heard the call to arms, he would be recognized at last for what he was: a hero and a true American.

Ironically his nominal superiors in Washington had never grasped the full potential of the plan they had conceived. They were content to topple the Ortega forces and reinstate a pro-American regime, but they refused to take the plan a bold step toward its logical conclusion. They wouldn't acknowledge the necessity of minimizing amateur, civilian oversight of military operations in the field. When pressed, they shied away from any implication of dramatic shifts in government, the relocation of supreme authority in military hands.

McNerney, on the other hand, wasn't intimidated by the thought of taking swift, decisive action to eliminate civilian enemies. Regardless of their offices and salaries, their mandate from the people, they were men of flesh and blood. They all had weaknesses, and they could be removed in an emergency without a cumbersome resort to ballot boxes. Never one to think in revolutionary terms, McNerney saw himself as a conservative, committed to the preservation of original American ideals. If Washington and Jefferson had meant the nation to go Communist, they never would have called America one nation under God.

McNerney had the will and the power to save America from her elected leaders. Traitors, every one of them, betraying God and country in the name of liberal ideals, conspiring openly with Third World scum to weaken the foundations of Western civilization. In her darkest hour of need, America still had a hero waiting in the wings, and he would save her yet. If the raid at San Felipe came off as planned, it would be easier, of course. But if the strike team failed, McNerney was prepared to forge ahead toward his final goal. He didn't crave the Oval Office for himself, but if a grateful population should demand it, he would serve. It was a soldier's duty.

He finished packing documents into his briefcase, locked it and retrieved a bottle from his desk. The bourbon scorched his throat at first, but he was used to it, and soon the sweet, familiar warmth was spreading through him, easing tension, building confidence.

McNerney would succeed because he had to. It was necessary, even preordained. The general was hardly a religious man, but he believed in a guiding hand behind the scenes. That hand was guiding him today; that great, omniscient mind was interested in America, in Mike McNerney. For the moment it would be enough. A single, dedicated man could do the rest.

YAKOV KATZENELENBOGEN pushed the wide sombrero back on his forehead and scanned the village square of San Felipe. At a glance, the marketplace looked normal, even though the crowd was smaller than expected for a Saturday. It would require a closer look, some thought, to figure out precisely what was wrong, and Katz was counting on his adversaries being in a hurry, dropping from the sky without benefit of any reconnaissance. If they had time to scrutinize the drop, they would be sure to realize there were no women shopping in the square, no children darting in and out among the market stalls.

A call to Washington had put Brognola on the line to State, from whence had come a limited approval to involve Honduran military personnel. The explanation Katz had offered to authorities was sanitized—a group of mercenaries with Americans aboard was prepared to strike at San Felipe and create a border incident for purposes unknown—but he had managed to secure cooperation in removal of the village's inhabitants. Some twenty families altogether, they were safely quartered at a government facility outside Tegucigalpa. Troops had scoured the surrounding countryside, alerting farmers and their families to stay at home this Saturday, postponing any errands to the local market.

Checking out the plaza now, Katz scrutinized the soldiers in their peasant garb with rifles hidden underneath serapes, submachine guns hidden under tables in the market stalls. On such short notice they had gathered only eighty men, two-thirds of them now "shopping" while the others posed as vendors, trading produce, yard goods, tools, the bare necessities of rural life.

He was informed that on a normal Saturday as many as five hundred persons might be crowded into San Felipe's central plaza, and the gruff Israeli worried that the present token turnout might alert his enemies. Even if they failed to note the lack of women in the "crowd," McNerney's raiders might become suspicious of the tiny gathering and pull back until they could investigate. His only hope lay in the firm belief that they were working on a deadline, which could be lost forever if the mission was postponed. If Katzenelenbogen's enemies were racing with the clock, they might be careless, eager for a go regardless of the target's dwindling size.

Without a firm idea of hostile numbers, Katz was ill at ease with the security arrangements, but he had no time for new provisions now. They had the date and target for McNerney's strike, but zero hour was a mystery. The strike force could appear at any moment, or the day might turn to darkness while they waited, chafing at the silence of the forest. Katz believed the raiders would attack by daylight—it made sense, logistically, and most of their intended targets would have left the marketplace for home by sundown—but he could be wrong just as easily. The waiting game wasn't his favorite, but he had no choice. And while he waited, he couldn't afford to risk their marginal advantage of surprise by shuffling his troops around the square in public view.

Of course, the troops weren't precisely his. There were proprieties to be observed, but the commander was an officer who knew his limitations, and he had been courteous to Katz, amenable to the Israeli's plans for distribution of his troops. The men of Phoenix Force were salted here and there around the plaza: Manning at the table of a produce booth, a Colt Commander primed and ready in his lap; McCarter drifting through the crowd, a slouching peasant with an M-16 and frag grenades concealed beneath the folds of his serape; Rafael Encizo lounging in a doorway on the far side of the square, a wicker basket at his side containing two LAW rockets and an MM-1 projectile launcher. Above Katzenelenbogen's head, Calvin James was seated in the village's only second-story window, commanding the plaza with an M-60 machine gun, ready to begin the dance of death.

Katz prayed that they could bring it off without unnecessary loss of friendly lives. There were so many unknown variables that he couldn't even start to estimate their odds. If the strike force should divide en route and catch them in a pincer movement, they could be annihilated on the spot. If the guerrillas opted for a secondary target, or the Executioner had been deliberately misinformed, their effort would be wasted. So many things could still go wrong....

But Katzenelenbogen was a man of faith. Despite the cynicism beaten into him by years of covert battlefields around the world, he still believed in good and evil, in the proposition that it mattered to the universe which side prevailed. There was no guarantee that good would triumph, certainly—he could have cited countless contradictory examples—but he believed that right and decency must hold the upper hand. If there was any justice in the world, his enemies would find him here, today, as scheduled. From that point on, the Phoenix warrior thought that he could take it for himself.

THE JEEP RIDE FROM TEGUCIGALPA to the forest clearing took an hour. Mack Bolan rode with Rafferty, DiSalvo at the wheel. Behind them in the second vehicle,

Tim Broderick drove, with Steiner riding shotgun and Captain Fletcher Crane behind them, stoic as a mannequin throughout the trip.

The Executioner had been surprised when Crane had arrived to see them off that morning; his surprise had bordered on astonishment when he had learned that Crane was coming with them to command the strike force personally. Somehow Bolan had imagined Rafferty in charge, perhaps a Contra officer or two, but now he saw the depth of General McNerney's personal commitment to the operation. Crane didn't seem delighted with his mission, but he wasn't bitching, either. Like a hundred other officers in Bolan's own experience from Vietnam, he seemed to look on combat as the province of the grunts, a territory that commissioned officers invaded at their peril, only during times of absolute necessity.

Today, apparently, was such a time.

The man-made clearing was approximately sixty yards across, a careless oval etched out of the forest with machetes, axes, sweat and muscle. Something like a hundred Hispanics were waiting for them when they got there, dressed in olive drab fatigues that bore the insignia of Daniel Ortega's Sandinista Front, divided into squads before a line of helicopters, rigged and painted to simulate a Soviet design. They wouldn't pass inspection by an expert, but Crane was clearly not expecting to encounter any aircraft engineering types in San Felipe.

Bolan scanned the somber faces and recognized Luis Machado from his photos in the press, the mug shots still on file at Stony Man. Crane's "mercenary" troops were Contras, then—or, at the very least, included soldiers from Machado's camp. McNerney had enlisted them somehow, with dreams of liberation for their homeland, promises of cash and arms, whatever. With his basic admiration for the Contra freedom fighters, Bolan wished Machado had remained aloof and independent, but the die was cast, and there could be no turning back.

Another too-familiar face, and Bolan frowned as Blancanales fell in step behind Machado, moving out to greet the new arrivals. Politician carried folded uniforms, while two men behind him labored beneath the load of boots and weapons as they moved toward the jeeps.

"Our gear," Crane told them after wrapping up the small talk with Machado. "*Spetsnaz* issue, guaranteed. You've got five minutes to exchange your uniforms and weapons, gentlemen."

They changed in silence, Blancanales smiling grimly at the Executioner when no one else was watching. In the tiger-stripe fatigues and heavy leather boots, an AK-47 in his hands, Mack Bolan almost felt the part. When Crane had passed the hat, collecting GI dog tags and substituting simulated Soviet ID, the transformation was complete.

"One man inside each chopper with the Contras," Crane informed them, angling a thumb back toward the line of waiting aircraft. "Rafferty will ride with me."

"Yes, sir."

"All right, let's saddle up."

Machado's troops began boarding, twenty soldiers to a chopper. Bolan tried to catch Pol's flight, but Steiner beat him to it, and he shuffled on past Broderick to board the last one in line. He knew it wouldn't matter in the end; they would be going in together, and a moment more or less should make no difference to the outcome of the strike.

If Calvin James had been successful in delivering his message to the others, someone should be waiting for them when they landed. He couldn't anticipate the character of their reception, but he hoped that Katz and company were able to evacuate civilians from the line of fire. In any case, it would be a bloodbath.

Pol's presence in the strike force was a plus, but without a hot reception on the ground, the odds would still be more than fifty guns to one against them. Alone, they had no reasonable expectation of survival, but they still might have an opportunity to spoil the afternoon for Crane and his commandos. And regardless of the outcome, Bolan knew that Mike McNerney wouldn't walk away from this one. Somehow, someone would be waiting to punch the general's ticket, no matter what went down in San Felipe. Bolan would have liked the job himself, but he was otherwise engaged.

They lifted off in tandem, one aircraft from each end of the line, so that his chopper was the second one aloft. Below them, backwash from the cargo copter's rotors whipped the trees into a dancing frenzy. When all five whirlybirds were airborne, number one stopped circling and chose its course, running low and arrow-straight above the dancing treetops. Bolan felt his stomach start to roll and double-checked the morning sun's position, feeling sudden agitation as he realized that there was no mistake.

The raiding force was heading south.

Toward Nicaragua.

LANE TRAVERS TOOK THE PISTOL from his desk drawer, pulled the magazine and checked its load, then replaced it in the Browning's grip. Never fond of guns, as were so many cowboys in the Agency, he realized the fact of their necessity and knew an empty gun was no damned good to anyone. If he was forced to kill, as he had been on two occasions in the past, the man from Langley meant to be prepared.

The paranoia that was eating at him was McNerney's fault. Some small degree of it was occupational, but he was generally immune to the neuroses that had plagued so many of his comrades through the years. He had good reason now to be afraid—for his career, and for his life. If the McNerney plan fell apart, and there was every possibility it might, his ass was on the line with all of those who played a much more active role in the arrangements. Someone with a hard-on for McNerney might not pause to differentiate between the bosses and the peons when the shit came down, and Travers was prepared to make his break at the first sign of trouble.

He had had no luck in tracking down Rosario Briones or his shadows, and Travers privately admitted to himself that he had blown it. He would never find them now, and that was fine. The man from the CIA was satisfied with that as long as they made no attempt to locate him. The last thing he needed was a vendetta on his doorstep, just when he was making ready to evacuate the premises.

He might be wrong about McNerney's strike. There was a chance that it would go on schedule with a minimum of interference. Travers thought the Sandinista casualties might be a problem: if the populace of San Felipe was unarmed, how could they hope to kill the necessary number of attackers? He had no doubt whatsoever that McNerney's troopers would arrange strategic "accidents" for several of their comrades, but if anybody from the networks or the major dailies looked too close, well, it might seem peculiar that half a dozen Sandinistas had been shot by their own men and left behind to point the finger at Ortega's team.

No matter. They were in the middle of it now, with choppers in the frigging air already, and it was a bit late to change the game plan. Travers closed his eyes and wished a storm might blow up out of nowhere, bring the strike force down in Nicaragua and be done with it. From the beginning he had favored a direct approach against Ortega rather than the convoluted scheme devised by Mike McNerney and his backers in the Pentagon. He understood their methodology, of course, and as a leading troubleshooter for the Company, he had no qualms about deception, but McNerney still seemed to be going at it in the most roundabout way. With equal effort they could have tagged Ortega in Managua, landing counter-revolutionaries on his fucking doorstep as a birthday present. They could be achieving something instead of circling the jungle, homing in on several hundred unarmed peasants in Honduras.

Travers checked his watch and slipped the pistol back inside his desk drawer. There was still time left before he had to pack. And if the news was good, he might not have to run at all. The Company's man was unaccustomed to the luxury of optimism, and the recent series of events hadn't encouraged him to see the world through rosy lenses, but things might not be as bad as he had first suspected. He had missed Briones and his backup. But so what? If he had scared them off while the operation rolled ahead, then he had done his job. His dead hitters were untraceable to any contact with the Agency. As far as the police or anybody else suspected, he was personally clean.

Unless, of course, they had been following Ruiz the past few days and he had been observed by someone in his last meetings with the "martyred" Contra officer. Someone *might* know, and that mere thought was all it took to bring the throbbing headache back, a pulse of stabbing pain behind his eyes.

Too old. He must be getting too damned old for this intrigue, Lane Travers thought. Today would be as good a time as any for the break, while he still had the strength and courage to pursue another life, while there was still another life to be pursued.

Tomorrow might be too late, and Travers wasn't even banking on this evening. He could wait another hour or two until he got the first reports from San Felipe, making up his mind when all the evidence was in his hand. But it felt sour, even now, and Travers knew instinctively that he was sitting in his office for the final time.

A savvy agent knew when it was time to cut and run, and Travers was among the best at what he did. When all else failed, survival was his specialty, and he intended to survive McNerney's mess at any cost. God help the bastards who were sent to take him out.

"YOU SURE YOU'RE UP TO THIS?" Schwarz asked again.

"I'm sure," Carl Lyons told him, slipping one arm, then the other, into shoulder rigging and stooping to lift his Python from the bed. He checked the load and snugged the cannon in its holster, grateful for the comforting, familiar weight beneath his arm. He felt a stab of pain when he began to pull his jacket on, but ignored it.

He would have rather gone with Katzenelenbogen and the others to prepare a hot reception for McNerney's raiding force at San Felipe. Lyons knew his wound had given Katz some second thoughts, but in the last analysis they needed someone in Tegucigalpa, tying up loose ends. It was important that the raiding party be destroyed, but if the brains behind the operation got away...

Stateside, Brognola and his pals in Justice would be waiting to coordinate their move against McNerney's backers in the Pentagon and the CIA. The Ironman wished them luck, immediately thankful that he didn't have to play the diplomat in all of this. The game was so much easier when it was open season on your enemies, when they were bought and paid for in advance, like General McNerney and his contact in the local office of the CIA.

Once Hal had wired the photos, Katz required no more than thirty seconds to pick out the agent who had been in touch with Anastasio Ruiz. The bastard's name was Travers, and his closest friends at Langley had been on the White House hit list as participants in the attempted coup. They would be taken care of at the other end, by other operatives, but Travers was henceforth the private property of Schwarz and Lyons. Smiling at the thought, the Ironman was already looking forward to their meeting. He could hardly wait to introduce himself...and put a bullet through the traitor's smiling face.

With any luck, he wouldn't have a crew around him when they met. The Able warrior wouldn't be deterred by reinforcements, but he hoped to keep it nice and simple, with time to spare for their unscheduled appointment with the brigadier.

How many other officers on-base had been involved? The open question haunted Lyons, but he had no way to pin the numbers down. When Bolan finished mopping up at San Felipe, he might have some idea who the other players were.

McNerney was the key, from Lyons's point of view. If one or two of his subordinates slipped through the net right now, they would be running for their lives, exposed for what they were and powerless to resurrect the operation. Someone else could tag them later, though Lyons was still hoping for a perfect score. It would be nice to wrap the mission up today.

Frowning, Lyons realized that he was jumbling priorities, forgetting the necessity of taking matters as they came. First, they had to wait for word from Katz at San Felipe to be certain that McNerney's raiders kept their date. From there, while Katz and company were fighting for their lives, they would be free to deal with Travers, saving Mike McNerney and his cronies for dessert.

Soon, now.

But for the Ironman it couldn't be soon enough.

☆ 26 ☆

Ninety minutes from Tegucigalpa, the lead chopper circled wide, doubling back onto a northwesterly course, and Bolan let himself relax a little. They would come at San Felipe from the south to simulate a Nicaraguan point of origin, in case survivors should escape to tell the tale. Whatever happened now, at least they were headed for the proper target.

Bolan ran through his limited options once more. He could attempt to seize the chopper he was riding in and slaughter twenty Contras—and the pilots, too, if they wouldn't cooperate at gunpoint. Having done that, if he could pull it off in such cramped quarters and without disabling the ship, propelling all of them to fiery death among the trees below... what then? The choppers were strictly for transport; none of them were armed as far as Bolan had been able to tell. Once in control, he would be forced to trail the others to their target zone, or play the role of kamikaze, picking one of the remaining whirlybirds for a collision that would shatter both.

Bolan cleared his head of futile speculation. He was aboard for the duration, and he would have to play it cautiously on touchdown. Minimizing the civilian casualties was a priority, of course, but if he fumbled or showed his hand too quickly, he might be cut down without the chance to rescue anyone at all.

At least he had Politician handy. Blancanales would be worth a dozen guns in any close encounter...if he lived. The landing zone was one more unknown variable at present: if his message had reached Phoenix Force in time, there might be a reception waiting for them on the ground; if not...then Pol and Bolan would be on their own.

He scanned the trees below and caught glimpses of muddy river winding through the jungle. Bolan had a general idea of where they were, but he couldn't have put his finger on a map with any certainty. It had been ninety minutes out, but San Felipe was some twenty klicks south of Tegucigalpa, which would mean a shorter backtrack. In the meantime, there was little he could do but wait.

To occupy his mind, he double-checked the AK-47 that he had been issued for the raid. It was a standard paratrooper's model, unremarkable, with half a dozen backup magazines. That gave him two hundred and ten rounds in all—or two rounds per enemy if he was forced somehow to tough it out alone.

There was no way on earth that Bolan could surprise a hundred men at once when he was virtually surrounded. It was patently ridiculous, but there was every possibility that he might have to try.

Another twenty minutes, and the copilot peered around the bulkhead, flashing Bolan and his Contra team the thumbs-up signal, grinning. "ETA five minutes," he announced, voice barely audible before the rotors whipped his words away through open doors on either side.

Five minutes left, and it would be time to do or die. The warrior knew that he might have no options when they hit the ground at San Felipe.

It might damned well be do *and* die, regardless of the course of action Bolan chose. It might already be too late to salvage anything from a horrendous situation. Braced for anything, he snapped the AK-47's safety off and slipped his index finger through the trigger guard. Whatever happened on the ground, he meant to take a number of the hostiles with him. Beyond that, it was anybody's game.

A flash of open ground below, and Bolan craned his neck to see the village drawing closer. Hacked out of a jungle clearing, it was larger than he had imagined... but the crowd collected in the central plaza was considerably smaller. Had they been forewarned? Had Bolan's message gotten through to Katz in time? What else was there about the villagers below that struck a sour chord in Bolan's mind?

All men.

He saw it as his chopper settled slowly into contact with the earth. And he was ready when a storm of small-arms fire erupted in the plaza, angry hornets peppering the aircraft, whispering among the members of the strike force. In place of an idyllic shooting gallery, McNerney's team was looking at a hot LZ, and they were taking hits as they scrambled to unload.

The warrior braced himself to leap for daylight, conscious of the fact that San Felipe's riflemen wouldn't know him from Adam. He was just another enemy within the free-fire zone, and if he made it out alive the Executioner would have to make it on his own.

McNerney's choppers came in with the sun behind them, rotors whipping at the humid air. From his position on the south side of the plaza, Yakov Katzenelenbogen watched them hover briefly, fanning out, descending. His Honduran troops were instructed to let the whirlybirds touch down before they opened fire; if any of the troops got trigger-happy and opened up while the enemy was still airborne, they might escape, and Katz didn't intend to let his quarry slip away this time.

Two of the aircraft were down, disgorging soldiers as the others settled gracefully to earth. Katz slipped the Colt Commander out from under his serape, thumbing the selector to autofire. Around the plaza, "peasants" gaped in evident confusion at the soldiers pounding toward them across open ground. Most of them were Hispanics in olive drab, but two or three were taller, Anglos dressed in tiger-stripe fatigues. Katz tried to pick out Bolan's face, or Pol's, but they were nowhere to be seen.

The last of the assault ships settled gingerly to earth, and Katz was swinging up his autorifle when the big M-60 cut loose overhead. He saw three of the Hispanics stumble, sprawling in the dust, and hoped that Calvin knew who he was shooting at. Another heartbeat and the plaza had become an echo chamber for what seemed to be a hundred weapons, all firing at once. The native troops were hauling out their hardware, dropping prone or firing from the cover of the market stalls, while their assailants opened up on the run, advancing behind a screen of automatic fire.

Katz sighted quickly down the barrel of his weapon and dropped the foremost Anglo runner with a three-round burst across the chest. He didn't pause to watch the dead man thrashing in convulsions on the ground; too many other targets were demanding his attention at the moment, bearing down upon him in a screaming human wave.

Downrange, one of the helicopters exploded in a clap of heavy metal thunder, spewing arcs of burning fuel in all directions. Katz had time to catch a glimpse of human torches scrambling from the wreckage, then incoming rounds were peppering his shelter, forcing him to answer with his own fire.

There was no time to think of Pol or Bolan now. If they were with the raiding party, they would have to look out for themselves. He popped two more commandos, wondering as they fell if they were Contra troops or mercenaries. It didn't matter either way, the gruff Israeli realized. Whatever their philosophy, they had already crossed the line, becoming predators, and it was Katzenelenbogen's job to take them out.

He broke from cover, dodging toward the nearest market stalls. Around him, some of the Honduran troops were taking hits, collapsing in untidy piles, their crimson blood soaking into the dusty ground. How many had they lost already? And how many hostile guns were still arrayed against them?

Sliding behind a stand that offered gourds and vegetables for sale, Katz knew they were fortunate the helicopters were unarmed. If the choppers had had mounted rockets, cannon, even light machine guns, it might have been all over now. They could have swept the plaza from the air, reducing San Felipe to a pile of smoking rubble. If the enemy faced any disadvantage at the moment, it resided in the Phoenix warriors' moment of surprise. On foot, their only means of transportation critically at risk, the raiders would be fighting with divided minds, a part of their attention necessarily focused on the mechanism of withdrawal.

Their plan hadn't been to capture San Felipe, after all. The game was hit-and-run, with maximum civilian casualties and a convenient fade to parts unknown. Confronted with a military force barely half their size, with one of five evacuation ships already blown to hell, some members of the strike team must be having second thoughts. And worried soldiers had been known to hesitate at crucial moments, risking life and mission while their thoughts strayed into areas of personal security. It was an edge that Katz was counting on as he maneuvered for position, crawling past another fallen friendly, looking for an open field of fire.

He craned around the stall, prepared to risk a shot, and felt the heat flash as a second chopper went to hell on rolling thunder. Jagged portions of the rotor blades careened across the plaza, scything hostile troops and friendlies alike.

Whatever happened now, McNerney's raiders had to level San Felipe to save themselves. They had to wipe out every trace of opposition, every witness to their deed. The grim alternative to total victory was death.

So, too, with Katzenelenbogen and the men of Phoenix Force. So long as one of their assailants lived, the job wouldn't be done. And death would be a sorry substitute for victory.

GARY MANNING DROPPED THE ROCKET launcher's empty tube beside its mate and reached behind him for the heavy MM-1 projectile launcher. Chambered in 40 mm with a twelve-round capacity, the weapon resembled nothing so much as a bloated tommy gun of 1920s vintage. Loaded and operated like a revolver, the MM-1 could mix its ammo, anything from harmless smoke to high-explosive rounds. This time the tall Canadian had backed up three HE cans with as many buckshot rounds, the six remaining chambers primed with razor-edged fleschettes.

Weighing in at eighteen pounds when fully loaded, Manning's weapon had no noticeable recoil. Tracking past the blazing wreckage of the choppers that his LAWs had already taken out, he sighted down on number three and put a high-explosive round directly through the windscreen. A ball of fire rolled out of there, consuming man and machine, the fuel tanks following in secondary detonation heartbeats later.

Manning was already sweeping on, aware of hostile gunners closing on his flank. He pivoted to meet them with a buckshot round and swept them off their feet with forty pellets, each equivalent to .30 caliber. Their twisted bodies thrashed together briefly, then lay still.

Returning to the choppers, Manning drew a bead on number four, already squeezing off as frantic figures in the cockpit tried to get her airborne. Ripping through the cargo bay, his HE load went off amidships, cut the whirlybird in two and left it sagging like the broken carcass of a prehistoric dragonfly. The pilot and his backup were attempting to evacuate when Manning hit them with his second buckshot charge and dropped them in their tracks.

Too easy.

Swinging toward the final helicopter, watching it disintegrate, a flaming skeleton with scarecrow figures dancing in the fire, he wondered why no troops had been detailed to guard the transport. They hadn't expected opposition on the ground, of course, but still...

Too easy, yes. As if the raiders—some of them, at any rate—were *supposed* to die in San Felipe.

Manning had no time to puzzle through the riddle before a flying squad of gunners hit him from his blind side. No one had detailed a guard to watch the choppers, but deprived of transport now, some of the raiders were intent on getting even with a pound of Manning's flesh. Their probing fire was eating up the doorway that sheltered him, and in another moment he would have to move or lose it all.

He moved, the launcher chopping out a path with buckshot and fleschettes. The little razor-sharp darts had been designed to slice through body armor, and his opposition wasn't wearing any. Caught on open ground, the foremost of them took three rounds at point-blank range, evaporating on their feet. The rest were having second thoughts, but Manning didn't give them time to sort it out before he emptied the launcher, almost in their screaming faces, blowing them away in rags and tatters.

He dropped the MM-1 and tugged his mini-Uzi out of shoulder rigging, chambering a live one and moving out to join the dance. So many hostiles left, so many friendlies down, and Manning knew that it could still go either way. The fight for San Felipe wasn't in the bag yet.

They could still lose it, and the Canadian had no desire to think about the repercussions of defeat. If anything, the slaughter of Honduran troops would raise more heat than if the victims were civilians. It would be a clear-cut act of war.

And back in Washington, those undecided congressmen would hear McNerney's message loud and clear. They would be voting arms and troops, along with cash, if Manning and his comrades couldn't stem the tide right now.

Aware of everything at stake, he moved out through the drifting smoke of burning helicopters, searching for the enemy.

A SHOCK WAVE FROM THE HELICOPTER'S detonation lifted Blancanales off his feet and hurled him forward on his face. Somehow he kept his grip on the Kalashnikov as air was driven from his lungs, each sucking breath repulsive with the stench of burning fuel and human flesh.

He had no fix on Bolan, no idea why peasant villagers were sporting small arms in the village square. As a precaution, he hadn't been told their destination until they were airborne, but Machado obviously had been counting on an easy in-an-out. Instead, they had come down into a firestorm, and their transport had been blown to hell, eliminating any option of escape. The set was going sour, and while opposition was encouraging, Pol knew he ran a risk of being killed in San Felipe.

Someone leaped across his prostrate form, intent upon the cover of a nearby building, but a bullet intercepted him and hurled him backward over Blancanales. Cursing, Pol kicked free of the deadweight and scrambled to his feet, desperately searching for some cover of his own. He saw three Contras, huddling some fifty feet away beside the tiny village church. One of them waved for him to join them, and Politician sprinted forward, thumbing off the safety of his AK-47 as he ran.

The three of them were firing at a clutch of market stalls as Blancanales closed the gap. They were secure in his allegiance to their cause, oblivious to death approaching in a friendly uniform until he hit them with a burst from the Kalashnikov and dropped them in their tracks beside the house of God. A sour taste was in his mouth, and this time it had no connection with the smell of burning oil or bodies. Crouching next to the remains of three dead men whose final error had been trusting him, Politician scanned for other "allies" he could kill in an attempt to shave the odds.

There was no guilt. The crime was theirs, and yet...

Sighting down the AK-47's barrel at another pair of Contra soldiers, Blancanales thought he might be on the verge of understanding Judas. Squeezing off, he cut down the two guerrillas and left them kicking in the middle of the dusty plaza.

Across the square, he saw one of the *spetsnaz* troopers closing in on the market stalls. Could it be Bolan? There was too much intervening distance, too much smoke and dust between them for Blancanales to be sure, so he held his fire. The plaza was alive with other targets anyway, and one man made no difference.

Except that everybody counted, sure. If they were to succeed in stopping Mike McNerney cold, it had to be a clean sweep. No stragglers, no strays, no MIAs. A single miss was tantamount to failure. If the bastards got away to start from scratch or spread the fiction of a Sandinista border raid against Honduras, then McNerney and his backers would have won.

A couple of the "peasant" gunners had his fix, and they were laying fire on his position now, their bullets chipping at the wood and stonework of the church. He sent a burst in their direction, high enough to miss and low enough to keep their heads down, wondering how long he could continue the charade before he had to kill a friendly. He was an enemy, for all they knew, and they would do their best to nail him if they could.

Breaking from the shadow of the church, Pol dodged across an open no-man's-land, bypassing fallen Contras and defenders alike. He had traveled thirty feet when something struck him in the shoulder with sufficient force to knock him off his feet. This time he dropped his rifle and had to scrabble after it with numbed fingers. White-hot pain was flaring in his shoulder now, warm blood coursing down his arm, and Blancanales knew he had been tagged.

It didn't matter who had shot him. Either way, he was a dead man if he gave the sniper time to try again. He snared the AK-47, staggered to his feet and veered in the direction of what seemed to be a blacksmith's shop. Incoming rounds snapped at his heels as he slid into sanctuary, huddling in a corner, trusting masonry to keep the bullets from him while he probed his wound.

It took a heartbeat for Politician to realize that he wasn't alone. Almost afraid to look, he raised his eyes...and found himself looking down the muzzle of an M-16 assault rifle, held by one of San Felipe's "peasant" defenders.

"You look a sodden mess," McCarter told him, lowering his autorifle. "Who's your tailor?"

"GI Joe," Politician answered testily, his free hand raised to staunch the flow of blood from what appeared to be an ugly shoulder wound. "What brings you here?"

"Cal got the word from Striker late last night. We weren't sure if Machado's people would be in on it."

"You live and learn."

"Assuming that you live."

A stray round ricocheted around the inside of their sanctuary and snapped back out again the way it had come. McCarter scanned the plaza, saw two Contras closing on them from the left and dropped them with a ragged figure eight.

"How bad's that shoulder?"

"Bad enough, but I can fight."

"Take these."

Removing his sombrero, he passed it to Blancanales and watched the Able warrior perch it on his head with bloody fingers. Shrugging out of his poncho, McCarter draped it over Pol to hide his wound and part of his Sandinista uniform.

"The locals here don't know you," he remarked. "Stay put. Play dead, if possible. If not...well...I'll be back when this is finished."

"Thank you, Mother."

"Bloody cheek."

He made another rapid visual and broke from cover, running in a crouch and cutting down another pair of Contras on his short dash to the market stalls. After the first bold rush, both sides had settled in to fight a different kind of battle, sniping at their enemies from cover where it was available, retreating where it wasn't. San Felipe's plaza was an open grave. At least two dozen leaking corpses littered the ground in McCarter's line of sight. There would be others, certainly, and he began to wonder who—if anyone—was winning.

It would be a victory of sorts if they wiped out the raiding force, regardless of the friendly casualties. McCarter planned on walking out of San Felipe on his own, and it was difficult to visualize himself as any kind of sacrificial lamb. He might well die before the day was out, but he wouldn't be going meekly, on his knees.

One of the taller Anglos emerged from cover. McCarter snapped his rifle up, delaying for a moment as the "Russian" turned to glance across his shoulder, verifying that the target wasn't Bolan. Satisfied, he stroked the trigger of his M-16 and put a three-round burst into the gunner's face.

No sign of Bolan yet, and it was only luck that he had stumbled onto Blancanales in the midst of all this chaos. Knowing Striker might be dead already, McCarter still didn't give up hope. Until he saw the body for himself, there was a chance.

Tired of waiting, the Briton braced himself to make another dash from cover through the killing grounds. His war was waiting for him out there in the open, and the former SAS commando didn't plan to keep it waiting any longer.

☆ 27 ☆

Travers knew instinctively that it was time to go. His contact on McNerney's team confirmed the loss of radio contact with Crane's strike force, and that could only mean deep trouble for all concerned. The pilots weren't under radio silence; in fact, they had been ordered to talk as much as possible, impersonating Sandinistas, during and after the raid on San Felipe. Silence was the worst news possible. It might mean loss of pilots, radios or even helicopters. The man from Langley didn't want to think about those soldiers stranded in the jungle, miles from anywhere, with real-life Sandinistas on one side and Honduran troopers on the other.

Some of them would talk if they were captured. That was guaranteed. Machado's men weren't professionals; their patriotic zeal was counterbalanced by a lack of preparation for the grim realities of fighting a clandestine war. The Contras might be hell on raiding villages, ambushing enemy patrols, but when the interrogation started heating up, they often broke. For every one who'd held his tongue, there was another anxious to confess his sins, say anything at all to ease the pain.

None of them knew Lane Travers. He had met Machado once, in passing, but his secret link with Anastasio Ruiz had been the problem, now effectively eliminated by the clumsy bastard's death. But they could lead interrogators back to Fletcher Crane, perhaps to Anthony Falcone, and from there...

If something had gone wrong in San Felipe, then McNerney was in jeopardy, and everyone around him stood a chance of going down. Each moment wasted brought them closer to exposure. Sick to death of waiting, Travers was determined to evacuate before the enemy had time to get a fix on his position, his identity. There just might be sufficient time to make it work.

He finished riffling the desk drawers, thankful that he kept no critical material on hand. There were two stops to be made before he split, at home and at his bank, but he should still be clear and running by the time the shock waves from today's adventure reached Tegucigalpa. In the wake of San Felipe, there would be a certain measure of confusion while authorities went through the wreckage, checking for IDs and looking for a scapegoat. Travers would be grateful for anything at all to buy him extra time.

He pocketed the automatic pistol and finished stuffing papers into his briefcase. He wouldn't miss anything about Honduras: weather, women, work, had all become extremely tedious of late. McNerney's strange diversion had relieved the general monotony a little by replacing tedium with creeping paranoia. Travers would be glad to shake both feelings and put the sweaty place behind him and begin afresh.

He might try Switzerland. He had to stop in Zurich as it was to raid his cash reserves, and if he found the atmosphere accommodating, Travers thought that he might shelter there awhile. It wouldn't last of course, not if McNerney's backers in the Company were still at large. They would be looking for him high and low, employing all their contacts in an effort to eliminate potential leaks.

And if they fell? What then? Would federal investigators find his name on file, connected with the bungled Nicaraguan operation? Would they seek him out for questioning, or simply post a kill-on-sight beside his name?

No, Switzerland would never do. Once he had tapped his numbered bank accounts, the man from Langley would be forced to find himself another hiding place outside the NATO sphere of operations. Somewhere in the South Pacific might be nice. He knew that there were islands to be had at bargain-basement prices if you had the contacts. Lane Travers paused, envisioning himself as King of Traversland, the sovereign ruler of his own domain, and wondered if the CIA would find him there.

He shook his head, emerging from the momentary reverie. He didn't even know precisely where "there" was yet. Before he let imagination run away with him, he had to deal with priorities. And survival through the next few hours topped the list. Once he had cleared Tegucigalpa and booked himself a European flight, he could begin to think about the future. Until then, he was walking on the fringes of a combat zone, and any slip might put his ass directly on the firing line.

It was McNerney's fault, together with the other bastards who had cooked up this scheme in the first place. He had been a fool to play along with them, but it had sounded like a winner at the time. Now, with the clarity of hindsight, Travers realized that there was nothing he could do to save the operation. He would be damned lucky if he could find a way to save himself.

His secretary was at lunch, and Travers passed her vacant desk without a backward glance. He wouldn't bother leaving her a note. She had been fair in bed, but this was no damned time for sentiment. Let her assume that he was out on an assignment. That way, if anyone came asking after him, they might waste hours waiting for him to appear.

His bags were in the car, and he wouldn't be going back to his apartment. It was early yet for any stakeouts, but he wasn't taking chances. If the San Felipe set had gone to hell, there was no telling who might be involved, what information they might now possess. For all he knew, some other faction of the Company might be involved. That kind of convoluted shit was big at Langley, playing off both ends against a middle that was never perfectly defined.

For just a moment, Travers wondered if he might be making a mistake. The loss of contact with McNerney's raiding party might mean anything—or nothing. Communications had been known to fail for reasons other than destruction of the radio or operator, and yet the whole damned thing felt wrong somehow.

No point in stalling. If he wasted too much time, it might be too late. He left the light on in his office, left the door wide open. From appearances, he might have just stepped out to get a cup of coffee.

They made great coffee at his favorite restaurant along the Zurichsee. If Travers never heard from any spokesman for the Company again, it would be too damned soon.

MACK BOLAN FED A FRESH CLIP into the Kalashnikov. Crouching in the shadow of a bullet-punctured market stall, he listened to the sounds of battle echoing around him, wondering if either side had gained a clear advantage yet. The ambush had been professional, but the Honduran troops had been outnumbered from the start.

He could see a number of them sprawled around the plaza now in awkward attitudes of death.

Deprived of transportation when the choppers blew, McNerney's raiders were committed now to victory or death. Retreat would be impractical while any of the local troops survived. The strike force couldn't risk the possibility of yet another ambush in the forest by a larger force of regulars. For all they knew, Honduran reinforcements might be on the way already, moving in to close the trap behind them.

Across the square two Contras burst from cover, running zigzag patterns toward the village church. He raised his AK-47, sighted on the leader, ticking off three heartbeats as he firmed the shot, and put a single round between the runner's shoulder blades. The impact pitched him forward on his face, and Bolan knew the man wasn't about to rise again.

His comrade hesitated, breaking stride, a fatal error given the situation. Looking back across his shoulder, he was braced to run again, when the Executioner's next round exploded in his face and took him down. His body quivered for a moment—short, chaotic messages imparted from his shattered brain to dying muscles—then lay still.

How many down? How many left to go? They had begun with something better than a hundred guns, against perhaps two-thirds as many on the ground. Both sides had taken heavy casualties, but Bolan had no idea of numbers, either way.

Upstairs, across the plaza, the machine gun opened up again, raking the open ground with short, measured bursts. He risked a glance, saw muzzle-flashes in the darkened window, angled toward a line of market stalls and knew that there would never be a better time to make his move.

Charging up and out of cover, Bolan pounded toward the nearest buildings toward what seemed to be a sort of general store. The windows had been shattered, the facade defaced by small-arms fire, but it was standing, and the stout adobe walls provided more protection than the flimsy wooden stalls.

Behind him, the upstairs gunner saw him and swung his weapon right around to bring the Anglo runner under fire. Bolan wondered which of Katzenelenbogen's men might be about to kill him. Twenty feet to go, less now, and Bolan's lungs were on fire, his pulse a driving hammer in his ears. He heard the big M-60 sputtering, a long burst eating up his tracks and gaining, gaining...

Suddenly a human silhouette rose before him in the vacant window of the store, an AK-47 angling across his shoulder, pointing at the buildings opposite. Bolan veered a few degrees off course and hit the wooden door full tilt, bursting through and collapsing on the littered floor as Jason Rafferty laid down a burst of cover fire from his Kalashnikov. The opposition raked his window with a burst of 7.62 mm, but Rafferty had already gone to ground, cursing under his breath.

"We fucked this, Frankie. Man, I'm tellin' you, we royally fucked this up."

"What happened to the others?" Bolan asked him, winded.

"Crane and Steiner bought it right away," the sergeant answered, craning for a glance around the plaza, ducking back before he could become a target. "Broderick's over by the church...or, anyway, he was, the last I saw of him. I haven't seen DiSalvo."

"That leaves you and me."

"I guess." And something in "Lambretta's" voice alerted Rafferty to danger, made him turn to face the Executioner, his automatic rifle tracking, hesitant but ready. "Jesus, you're with *them*."

The move was slick and fast, but he was covered from the jump and really had no chance at all. A stunning double punch ripped through his chest at point-blank range, the impact lifting Rafferty and slamming him against the nearest wall. From there, he slid into a seated posture, exit wounds inscribing traces of himself upon the pale adobe wall.

Bolan pulled the AK-47 from the sergeant's twitching hands and held the rogue soldier's head up, one palm cupped beneath his chin. He waited for the dying eyes to focus on his face.

"Fu-fucking Judas. I thought you were an American."

"I need names," he said. "The buffers between Crane and McNerney."

"I can't hear you, man."

"One chance to clear the slate. You haven't got that long."

"Go fuck yourself, okay?"

The sergeant blew a crimson bubble, shivered, and the light went out behind his eyes. Retreating to the doorway for another look around the plaza, Bolan left him there, still seated with his back against the wall.

It had been a long shot, but he had to try. It would be left to others now to name the players in Tegucigalpa. Bolan was preoccupied with matters of survival, scouting for the rogue Americans who were still unaccounted for. Whatever else went down in San Felipe, he was pledged to save the honor of the Green Berets and remove this stain with cleansing fire. He would confirm the kills on Broderick and DiSalvo, or die in the attempt.

"HEADS UP. Is that the guy?"

Schwarz double-checked the mug shot to be sure. "Bingo."

"Where the hell's he going?"

"How should I know?"

Lyons had a hand inside his jacket, tugging on the holstered Python, ready for the tag before Schwarz stopped him.

"Hey, not here."

"Why not?"

"Too public. Anyway, I want to check that bag he's carrying."

"Forget his bag," the Ironman groused. "He's gonna get away."

"We're on him, man. This piece of shit's not going anywhere."

Across the street, Lane Travers had already stowed his briefcase in the front seat of a dark sedan, and he was climbing in behind the wheel. If he had made his two-man audience, he gave no sign.

Carl Lyons fired the rental's engine as their quarry left the curb, proceeding in the opposite direction. Lyons gave him half a block, then cut a tight, illegal U-turn in the middle of the street, arresting traffic as he powered after Travers.

"Not too close. You'll spook him."

"I know what I'm doing."

"There, he's turning."

"I can see, okay?"

"Stay with him, there."

"You want me *closer*, now?"

"You think he's headed for the airport?"

"Maybe."

"If he is, we've got an open stretch a few miles farther on."

"I know that."

"We can take him there."

"I should have tagged him when I had the chance."

"Too risky. This is better."

"Yeah, unless he fucking gets away."

"Relax. We've got him covered."

"He might be connecting with an army out here."

"No. He's running."

Travers took the cutoff to the airport, and they followed him, immediately losing most of the surrounding traffic. He was leading by perhaps a quarter mile when Schwarz checked out the rearview mirror and decided it was clear enough.

"Let's do it."

Lyons stood on the accelerator, changing lanes and coming up on Travers from the driver's side. The target didn't appear to recognize his danger, holding steady at an even sixty miles per hour, both hands on the wheel, his eyes fixed on the road ahead.

"Come *on*, already!"

"Frigging back seat drivers."

They were still accelerating, pulling up to pass, when Travers saw them. There could be no mistake about it. Just a sidelong glance, at first, and then he did the classic double take, alarm as visible as acne on his face. He punched it, but the Ironman had him, already pulling out into the lead, the rental trembling at seventy-five, its speedometer needle edging toward eighty.

Lyons cut the wheel hard left, across the other lane, and even though he braced himself, Schwarz bit his tongue when they collided with the target vehicle. He tasted blood, but ignored it as he rummaged for the big Beretta underneath his jacket.

Travers lost it heartbeats after impact, jamming on his brakes and locking them, his four-door rolling through a cloud of dust across the shoulder of the highway, nosing down into a ditch. Lyons swerved the rental to a standstill and was out and running as the engine died, the Python in his hand. The windshield of the government sedan was seamed with cracks where Travers's head had cracked against the glass, but Lyons wasn't taking any chances. Standing three feet from the driver's open window, leaning in to skin-touch range, he slammed a Magnum round through Travers's temple, speckling the seat and dashboard with the target's brains.

"Case closed."

"Not quite."

Schwarz circled to the other side and opened the passenger door, making sure to smear his fingerprints in the process. The agent's bag was dripping, but it wasn't locked, and Gadgets spent a moment riffling the contents, finding nothing that related to McNerney or the raid on San Felipe.

"Well?"

"No go. If anything was written down, he stashed it somewhere else."

"So let's get moving. We've got places to go and people to do."

"I'm coming, dammit."

Lyons cut another U-turn, jounced across the grassy median and headed back toward town. He whistled as he drove, and Gadgets wondered if the wet work wasn't getting to him, just a little.

Christ, sometimes Schwarz wondered about himself, and more than a little. He began to wonder if there weren't limitations to the violence that a human being could observe, in which he could participate, without surrendering humanity. At what point did the killing cease to be a duty and become a pleasure?

Not yet, though. The very fact of his concern was proof, at least, that Gadgets hadn't crossed the line. Not yet. Today he was still all right. And so, he thought, was Lyons.

Tomorrow, if it ever came, would take care of itself.

CALVIN JAMES STITCHED another short burst through the nearest market stall and sat back, scanning the plaza. It was a charnel house down there, the dead and dying sprawled together, some of them in tidy rows where automatic fire had dropped them on the run, others scattered in an abstract pattern. James had accounted for a number of them with the big M-60, and he knew there would be more before a cease-fire was declared. Below him, firing was sporadic but intense, with pockets of defenders and attackers trading rounds across the square.

He wondered briefly whether anyone had thought to call for reinforcements. James wasn't convinced that they were winning, even though the enemy had lost his transport, even though he wasn't going anywhere just now. The tide could turn at any moment, and it didn't take a genius to realize the battle wasn't over while a single enemy was still alive and armed.

A flying squad of "peasant" soldiers trundled into view below him, and he recognized McCarter in the lead. James tracked them, waiting for the opposition to reveal itself instead of simply throwing rounds from every side. He needed targets, dammit, or he wasn't any good at all.

One of McCarter's men went down. Another. That left five, and they were veering toward the church, toward cover, when a skirmish line of Contras suddenly materialized downrange. Their point man was a tall American in tiger-stripes, and all of them were pouring automatic fire into McCarter's squad. James saw two more defenders fall. A third—was it McCarter going down?— and then he had his finger on the big M-60's trigger, firing in response.

His heavy NATO rounds ripped through the enemy as if they were made of straw. Two down, then three. The tall American was ducking, dodging, but the effort was too little, far too late. James held the bastard in his sights and poured it on, a rising burst that pinned the target and somehow kept him on his feet and dancing while the slugs tore into him.

James lifted off the trigger and watched the two surviving Contras dive for cover, running for their lives. He saw McCarter on his feet, blood soaking through one pant leg as he tried to drag a wounded friendly off the field. They made it, and James could only wish them well. He wondered if McCarter was the only one to take a hit so far. With all the lead and shrapnel flying in the plaza, it would be remarkable if none of them were killed in the exchange.

As for himself, there was more killing to be done. He heard the Contra gunners when they crashed in on the floor below him, knew the friendlies wouldn't bother coming up. With boot heels pounding on the wooden staircase, angry, frightened voices drifting to him through the open door, James lifted his machine gun, tucked it underneath his arm and turned to face the enemy.

Two gunners led the way, and he knew there would be others in the stairwell, bringing up the rear. He hit them with a spiral burst that pinned them to the wall. Behind them, the adobe wall was pocked with bullet scars and smeared with blood.

James chased them with another burst to clear the landing, edging through the doorway with his M-60, belts of ammunition draped across his shoulders. Scattered rifle fire erupted from the stairs, most of it peppering the ceiling. Towering above them on the landing, James released a stream of autofire that swept the stairway clear of life, depositing the riddled corpses of his adversaries in a heap below.

There were no further sounds of opposition from the ground floor now, but James knew he would have to watch his back. The Contras had him spotted, had recognized the threat his machine gun posed, and there was every chance that they might try again to root him out. He dared not let them catch him by surprise.

He heard more firing in the plaza, punctuated by grenades as one side or the other launched a drive against the opposition. Shrugging off the danger, knowing it would take some time before the raiders decided their patrol had bought it and worked up sufficient nerve to make a second pass, Calvin James returned to his position at the window. In the square below, he saw a squad of Contras, blood and dust discoloring their olive drab, begin a loping drive against the nearest pocket of defenders. Tracking with his weapon, James resumed the hunt.

☆ 28 ☆

Michael John McNerney finished threading the silencer onto his Walther automatic pistol, then placed the weapon in his lap. One final chore before departure, and he would be glad to have it all behind him. His travel documents were safely stowed inside the briefcase on his desk: a passport with his photo in the name of Ernest King; a driver's license and assorted other documents created to substantiate the false identity; sufficient cash to keep him mobile and well fed for several weeks in the United States.

It wouldn't take that long, of course. What Mike McNerney had to do was best done quickly, striking while the iron was hot. There would be charges, countercharges and recriminations in the media for days when news of San Felipe leaked, as it was bound to do. But some powerful Americans were going to support the action that McNerney and his sponsors had attempted. Some of them were not averse to the suggestion of a military government, with suitable protections for free enterprise, of course. You couldn't be conservative enough to please the fat cats, just so long as business was defended, unions penalized and price controls avoided like the plague.

The backup plan was risky, even suicidal, but McNerney was convinced that it could work. *Would* work, if he could keep his wits about him, let his dedication to a free America shine through each word, each deed. The people would support him, not the ravening minorities who sat around all day with both hands out for charity and drugs, but real Americans of substance, those with an interest in their nation's future. His approach would shock them at the outset, but with time the true Americans would realize that radical techniques were necessary sometimes. If an arm or leg was gangrenous, you didn't spend a fortune trying to revive the lifeless tissue. You cut the bastard off, and it was time for some corrective surgery to help the body politic as well.

In this case, though, instead of whittling away at rotten toes and fingers, butchering the body piecemeal, Mike McNerney would be starting at the top.

By half past four, the general had given up on news from San Felipe. Something had gone drastically, irrevocably wrong. He knew that much at least; his field commander would have reported on his progress, otherwise. In reality, he didn't care what had befallen Fletcher Crane and company. There were a handful of scenarios available, and all of them spelled trouble.

Evacuation was the only answer, with a fallback to his secondary plan. He had devised this one alone, without assistance from the "brains" at Langley and the Pentagon. His backers had no inkling of his scheme. For all their patriotic posturing, the noises that they made behind closed doors, they were a stinking pack of hypocrites, afraid to go the extra mile, incur the added risks involved in modern warfare. Everything was fine as long as they were safe within their lavish offices, dictating orders to some flunky in the field, but it was something else entirely when they were required to sacrifice and put their asses on the line.

McNerney had been using them, their pull, their cash, from the beginning. In ignorance, they had imagined he was under their control, but he would shortly disabuse them of that notion, with a vengeance. If he fell, he didn't plan to go alone. And if he pulled it off... well, they would soon be sniffing after him, attempting to ingratiate themselves with his administration. Let them try. It would be humorous to watch them play their scenes before he brought the curtain down.

McNerney had a list of traitors, armchair patriots who talked a mighty battle on the golf links at the country club, but who were nowhere to be seen on D-Day. He knew who they were: military officers who hedged their bets against a possible defeat, withdrawing critical support in time of direst need; assorted federal spooks who played both ends against the middle, juggling the action and competing on behalf of their respective interests; "patriotic" businessmen, more interested in money than in ideology, who dealt with enemies and friends alike until they could no longer tell the difference.

McNerney's list was long, and growing longer by the day. Once he was in the driver's seat, there were some changes to be made, and heads would roll. He liked the mental imagery, and wondered if it might not be a good idea to find himself a guillotine. Public executions had a sobering effect; he knew that much from Nam, and what could be more public than a televised decapitation on the White House lawn?

The thought appealed to him... but it would have to wait. He was a long way from the Oval Office, and there was business to be taken care of in the meantime.

Fletcher Crane and his Berets had slipped beyond McNerney's grasp. With any luck at all, they would be dead in San Felipe, permanently silenced by whomever or whatever had derailed the mission. Travers would be dealt with by his own team, if they had their wits about them; if they missed him first time out, he could be counted on to save himself and disappear. That left one problem for McNerney to eliminate, and even as the thought took shape, the problem stuck his head through Mike McNerney's open door.

"Excuse me, General," said Major Anthony Falcone, "but your duty officer is out."

Of course he was. McNerney had insisted on it, shutting down the office early with a lame excuse the sergeant had been happy to accept. The brigadier put on a plastic smile and said, "Come in."

Falcone's face was deeply etched with worry lines. "I'm sorry, sir. There's still no word."

"It's not your fault. Sit down."

"Yes, sir."

"We have to face the music, Major. Something has gone wrong. It's time to cut our losses."

"Sir?"

"Beginning now."

Falcone's mouth dropped open when he saw the silenced Walther, and McNerney put his first round through those oval lips, the impact puffing out Falcone's cheeks. Rounds two and three punched the major's chest, dark crimson blossoming beneath his campaign ribbons, pooling in his lap.

McNerney set the automatic on safety, put it in his briefcase and closed and locked the office door behind him when he left. Falcone would be waiting for the duty officer in the morning, a little something extra to begin the day, and by the time he was discovered, Mike McNerney would be stateside, making preparations for the activation of his backup plan.

No one could stop him now.

FROM HIS POSITION in the blacksmith's shop, Rafael Encizo had a field of fire including roughly half the plaza. It was infinitely preferable to his first position in the market stalls, where the incessant cross fire had cut through flimsy wood as if through paper, but the Phoenix warrior feared he might have moved too late.

Encizo had sustained two hits while sprinting from the stalls to relative security behind the stout adobe walls and brickwork of the blacksmith's forge. One of them was a graze beneath his arm, but he wasn't concerned about it despite the smear of blood that stained his peasant shirt. The other round had gone right through his thigh, with damage to the fat femoral artery, and while he had used his web belt as a tourniquet, he had only slowed the bleeding. At the present rate, he thought he might lose consciousness within an hour.

In relative security he scanned the village square. The quickest route to medical evacuation was through annihilation of the enemy, and so he searched for targets, ready with his autorifle as he searched the shadows, double-checking the dead and dying on the field of battle. Any movement might betray an enemy in hiding, but the last three "targets" had been friendly: David McCarter limping with a leg wound, and two Honduran troopers dodging for cover near the church. The firing had abated temporarily, and Rafael was conscious of the distant throbbing in his leg, aware that any great delay in mopping up might cost him his life.

Assuming that it would be the friendly troops who did that mopping up. Thus far Encizo had no evidence that they were winning. OD uniforms were numerous among the dead, but there had been more gunners in the strike force to begin with. Rafael could draw no conclusions from a random body count, and the behavior of the scattered friendlies he had seen, intent on diving for cover, gave no cause for optimism.

If the enemy was winning it, his leg no longer mattered. They would come for him in time, and whether he was comatose or conscious, it would make no difference if the odds were on the other side. The blacksmith's shop was San Felipe's most secure facility, but it wasn't designed for armed defense, and they could take him if they tried.

A head appeared around one corner of the village store, ducked back and reappeared to make a second scan. Another moment passed before three members of the raiding party broke from cover, darting toward the market stalls in single file. Encizo followed them with his M-16 as they came closer to their destruction.

His first round took the leader low and side to side, above his belt line, drilling vital organs as it tumbled through resistant flesh. The runner stumbled, tried to make a go of it on hands and knees, but found his legs wouldn't respond. Before he had a chance to scream, round two ripped through his face and silenced him forever.

Hurdling his fallen comrade, runner number two had almost reached the safety of the stalls, but Rafael squeezed off and brought him down. The guy thrashed like a mackerel out of water, and Encizo left him to it, tracking after number three. A round between the shoulder blades propelled the next guy into impact with the bullet-punctured siding of the nearest stall. Rebounding, he toppled backward, sprawling lifeless in the dust.

Encizo swept his rifle back to number two and found the guy inert, no longer struggling with death. On the far side of the plaza, firing had intensified, as if in answer to his own. Some of the rounds chipped brickwork overhead and ricocheted around the shop before they spent their force. He spotted muzzle-flashes in the shadows, but held his fire. He was afraid of wasting ammunition and endangering his comrades if he indiscriminately sprayed the plaza.

But his time was running out. The trouser leg below his wound was saturated with blood. Already Rafael could feel a creeping dizziness betraying his determination to remain alert.

A slender figure blundered through the entrance to the blacksmith's shop, out of breath from running. In a heartbeat, Rafael picked out the OD uniform, the Hispanic features so much like his own, and then the enemy was hauling up his AK-47, startled by the presence of another in his would-be sanctuary.

Holding down the trigger of his M-16, Encizo nearly cut the guy in two. His enemy was crucified by armor-piercing rounds, propped upright by the stunning impact. When Encizo let the trigger go, his lifeless adversary toppled slowly forward.

And it could be that easy. Any gunner from the plaza might come waltzing in, overrunning his position. In his present state there was damned little Rafael could do to keep them out.

But he could kill them, sure, while energy and ammunition still remained. When he ran out of cartridges...well, he would ponder that one when it happened. In the meantime, he was still alive, still in the middle of the fight. And anything the bastards wanted from him, they would have to take by force.

"YOU SURE I LOOK ALL RIGHT?"

"You're fine."

Carl Lyons checked the rental's mirror once again and made some adjustments to his bogus uniform. According to the emblems on his collar, he was now a colonel in the U.S. Army; campaign ribbons on his jacket indicated that he had enjoyed an active and industrious career. The slacks weren't a perfect fit, but he could live with it for any length of time required to close McNerney's case.

"I don't like going in unarmed."

"You're not unarmed," Schwarz said. "Your piece is in the attaché, right next to mine."

"I feel unarmed."

"You'll live."

"Let's hope so."

Finally satisfied with his appearance, Ironman Lyons climbed behind the wheel again and put the car in motion, powering along the narrow access road to reach the highway, turning south, in the direction of the army base and Brigadier General McNerney. It was time to roll the bastard up, and Lyons had been looking forward to this moment for a week. He wasn't about to be distracted by the throbbing of his wound or the relatively small discomfort of his too-tight slacks.

McNerney and his various subordinates should still be waiting for some word from San Felipe. In the worst scenario, with someone on the strike force sounding an alarm, it still would take some time for news to reach the base, allowing Schwarz and Lyons room to make their tag before the general and his cronies could pursue evasive action.

That had been the theory, but Lane Travers, the Company agent, had been running when they'd taken him out, and McNerney might have taken some precautions on his own. The thought made Lyons nervous, and he goosed the rental, suddenly intent on making better time. They had too many problems now without him dawdling.

Too many unknown variables, for instance. Going in, they still had no fix on any possible subordinates involved. It stood to reason that the brigadier would have his buffers, but Lyons didn't know if there were two or twenty men between McNerney and the firing line in San Felipe. One thing was apparent: they couldn't take on the whole damned base, regardless of the Ironman's sudden yen to do precisely that.

McNerney was the key, the mover, and they had their orders. Basically the plan required them to identify the players, but they were still to make the tag, even if McNerney failed to play along. The guy was dead no matter what, and he would know it going in, which automatically reduced the chances of securing his cooperation. And it stood to reason; if you were positive some asshole planned to blow your brains out, why on earth should you provide him with the names of other targets from among your friends? The more he thought about it, Lyons was convinced that it would be impossible to close the net airtight around McNerney and his pals. Unless some names could be secured in Washington.

The sentry on the gate was courteous as he requested their ID and thorough as he studied it. You couldn't fault the kid for being taken in by forgeries from Stony Man. They were the real thing, after all, prepared from blanks supplied by DOD for use in covert missions. If he tried to back-check, they were covered all the way to Hal Brognola's allies among the joint chiefs of staff.

The sentry handed back their bogus paper and passed them through. Signs showed the way from there, and in another moment they were parked outside McNerney's command post, double-checking hardware prior to tagging their man. Aware that stealth might be essential, Lyons opted for a mate of Schwarz's Beretta 93-R, equipped with silencer. Discarding the attaché case, both Able warriors tucked their hardware under military jackets, patting down the bulges as they made the short walk to McNerney's office.

It was empty.

The reception room was vacant, though the lights still burned. Beretta in hand, the Ironman tried McNerney's private door and found it locked. Without a moment's hesitation, he applied his boot heel to the lock and followed through immediately, his weapon out and tracking.

In the general's private office they were greeted by the dead. He was—had been—a major, and his polished nameplate bore the name Falcone. Lyons didn't know the guy, but he realized that he was looking at a late and lamented member of McNerney's team. The brigadier wouldn't be dropping officers at random, not unless his mind had snapped completely, but he might be shutting down his pipeline to the Contras, covering his tracks in such a way that no one would be left to testify against him.

Except that leaving bodies in your private office was an awkward way to prove your innocence. More likely, he was trimming out deadwood, ensuring silence with regard to some escape route. Falcone had become a liability with the snafu at San Felipe, and the price had been his life.

"We're late," Schwarz said unnecessarily.

"One down," the Ironman answered, moving toward the office door.

"We've lost him."

"Maybe not."

The two Able warriors found McNerney's quarters after stopping once to ask directions. They marched directly to his door. There was no answer to the chimes, and Gadgets held the fort while Lyons circled, found a window left unlocked and wormed his way inside. Together, pistols drawn, they searched the general's rooms and found them tidy, Spartan, empty.

"Shit."

"The airport?"

"Christ, who knows?"

"We'd better check it out."

"I guess."

But they had lost him. Schwarz was right, and Lyons knew it in his gut as they retreated to the waiting car. The bird had flown, and there was nothing they could do to bring him back again.

"God*damn* it!"

Gadgets frowned. "I know exactly what you mean."

HIS SHOULDER THROBBED—in fact, it hurt like hell—but Blancanales had stopped the bleeding with a compress tucked inside the wound. The effort had necessitated stripping off his shirt, and he was covered by McCarter's poncho, intent on looking like a friendly if he could. The AK-47 was a problem, but if no one looked too closely, Blancanales thought he might survive.

Emerging from the shelter of his doorway, glancing rapidly in each direction, Pol decided on his move. He had observed four Contras moving cautiously as they had disappeared inside the village's sole two-story structure.

On the second floor, Calvin James was manning a machine gun, visible from time to time as he leaned out to reassess the battleground, and Blancanales reasoned that the enemy was bent on closing out his game. Another team had tried it earlier, and they had bought the farm, but Calvin was busy now, engaged in pinning down a rifle squad while Katz and Manning tried to flank on the far side of the plaza near the church.

Pol made his break, ignoring angry protests from his shoulder, dodging in and out of doorways as he ran. Along the way assorted riflemen threw rounds in his direction, but he had no way of telling if his change in "uniform" had made a difference. In any case, there would be enough time to check it out upon arrival at his destination.

Another twenty yards to go. He stumbled once, but saved it with an outstretched hand, hot slivers knifing through his shoulder down into his chest. Ten yards, and he was concentrating on the doorway now, prepared for anything as he burst through into sudden shade.

Three of his enemies were halfway up the stairs, the fourth apparently detailed to stay behind and watch their backs. But he wasn't doing very well at it. He was still gazing after his retreating comrades when Politician staggered in and took him unaware. The AK-47 stuttered, blowing him away, the muzzle climbing, tracking, almost of its own accord, as Blancanales raked the staircase. Twisting, falling, trying to return fire as they died, the Contra troopers came down in a tangled heap, their bodies piled on others bunched around the bottom of the stairs.

Above him there was a sudden, ringing silence from the sniper's nest. A shadow filled the doorway there, stretched out across the landing, and Calvin James ducked into view, prepared to hose the floor with his M-60 if a hostile presence was revealed. The Phoenix warrior visibly relaxed when he recognized Blancanales.

"Guess I owe you one," he said.

"Forget it. I was thinking I might hang out there awhile."

Above him, James was smiling. "Welcome to the Y."

He disappeared, returning to his window and the field of death below. Alone again, Politician stripped the nearest body of its ammunition belt and found himself a place from which he could command the door and windows simultaneously. If the end was coming, he would meet it here.

MACK BOLAN LOBBED his last grenade in the direction of the market stalls and saw two Contras airborne, arms and legs flailing before they struck the ground dead. A third man staggered from the smoking wreckage, both hands clasped against his face, and Bolan cut him down before he took a dozen strides.

He had located Vince DiSalvo moments earlier and had scratched him off the list. A burst of automatic fire had riddled the traitorous soldier from knees to eyebrows. And that left Broderick.

If Rafferty had seen Broderick near the church, he might still be there, or in the immediate vicinity. Another forty yards of open ground, and Bolan would be crouching in the chapel's shadow. Emerging from his cover into daylight, Bolan was acutely conscious of his own vulnerability, and he braced himself for the impact of a shot between his shoulder blades.

Still intact, he made it to the church and waited for a moment, crouching near the door, alert to any sounds inside. Unable to be certain with the crack of scattered gunfire all around him, Bolan made his move into the narthex. Here, the light was filtered through a stained glass window set above the altar.

Bolan moved into the sanctuary, then froze again as he detected movement near the altar. He was braced when Broderick emerged from the concealing shadows, carrying his autorifle ready at his hip.

"I didn't know you were a prayin' man," he said.

"I have my moments."

"Yeah. I guess you're havin' one right now."

"It's over, Broderick."

"Not yet."

The warrior knew it was hopeless, but he had to try. "I need the names of your superiors."

"I guess you haven't noticed, Frankie, but I'm the best there is."

And Broderick's weapon was already winking flame when Bolan caught him with a blazing figure eight across the chest, the impact lifting him completely off his feet and draping him across the altar. Dying, Broderick wouldn't release his grip on the Kalashnikov, its last rounds shattering the chapel's stained glass window, raining multicolored fragments on his face and chest.

New footsteps in the ringing silence, and the warrior swiveled, ready to confront his enemies. Instead, he spotted Yakov Katzenelenbogen closing in from the narthex.

"You all right in here?" the Israeli asked.

"So far."

"We're done out there."

He listened, conscious of the fact that there was no more gunfire in the plaza. Seeing Katz before him, he wasn't required to ask the outcome, but he wondered at its cost.

"How bad?"
"Let's say we won."
"I wonder."

☆ 29 ☆

McNerney had an hour at New Orleans International before he had to catch his flight to Baltimore. He had considered flying into Dulles as a gesture of defiance, but discarded the idea as foolish, realizing that the airport might be covered with a blanket of security by now. If they were thinking clearly—and they had been, long enough at least to edge him out at San Felipe—they would know he wasn't running. He had never run from anything since childhood, and his military record would describe an officer who never called retreat, attacking relentlessly until the enemy surrendered or was finally annihilated.

They would cover all the options, certainly. His former proximity to South America would set the assets hopping in Bogotà, Rio, Buenos Aires. There was a quaint hotel in Acapulco he had favored for vacations, and he could imagine Feds in polyester suits and mirror shades stampeding through the halls, accosting any white-haired man they found and making asses of themselves.

They might as well be checking Hong Kong or New Delhi, and he put the problem out of mind. Security in Washington was his immediate concern, and while they couldn't know the details of his backup plan, they would be conscious of his so-called friends and allies in the area, the men from Langley and those members of the general staff who had encouraged him to make his dream a bold reality, supplying cash and the necessary hardware. Would they all be in the net before he reached the capital? McNerney hoped so, smiling at the notion of their fraud exposed, their phony patriotism held up to the purifying light of day.

He had no sense of being used, manipulated. Rather, *he* had been manipulating *them*, capitalizing on their desire for a "free" Nicaragua to work a little magic of his own. While his "superiors" were building castles in the air and slicing the hypothetical pie to their own specifications, he had worked for rather different goals. Ortega's ouster would have been the signal for a broader revolution—no, a counterrevolution—as the people of the Third World learned to wage relentless war against the Communists. Their example might have sparked some similar resistance on the home front, made things hot for parasites in Washington, but there were different ways to get the same job done.

Like knocking off the President, for instance. At Baltimore-Washington International, he rented a nondescript Buick sedan, using his bogus Alabama driver's license and a phony credit card, both in the name of Ernest King. The sweet young thing on duty didn't bother checking out his card, and he was on the road in twenty minutes, ticking off the thirty-seven miles that separated Baltimore from Washington, D.C. En route, he found a roadside shop that dealt in sporting goods, made several purchases and stowed his parcels in the Buick's trunk.

The basic plan was simple: find the President of the United States and execute him as a traitor to the people. Afterward, assuming that McNerney was alive, there would be ample time to state his case and rally stalwart patriots to his defense. Specifics were a different matter; lacking any real idea about the presidential schedule, he would have to bide his time, collecting information from the media, selecting the most advantageous time and place to strike.

The time wasn't a problem. He had sufficient cash to carry him for several weeks, if he didn't indulge himself with lavish suites and six-course meals. The press would keep him posted on his target's movements, and he would be waiting, watching, when the inevitable moment arrived. Despite a prior brush with sudden death, the President refused to be confined and mothered by his Secret Service detail. He was still accessible, still vulnerable to a gunman with determination or someone with absolute commitment to his cause.

He might be able to complete the tag within a day or two, but if he had to wait for two weeks, three, it would be worth his time. A lag might even help, allowing guards to grow complacent and convince themselves the danger was illusory. Whichever way it played, McNerney was prepared to die, if necessary, to attain his goal.

Historians and analysts contended that no single man was indispensable within the democratic system, that assassination of a President changed little in the long run. They were wrong of course. In 1865 the death of Lincoln shattered plans for peaceful readmission of the late Confederacy to the Union, bringing on the violent period of Reconstruction. McKinley's murder in 1901 had elevated Teddy Roosevelt to the White House, ending an era of laissez-faire big business and inaugurating the age of the muckraking trustbusters. In 1963 a rifle shot in Dallas canceled plans for troop withdrawals from Southeast Asia, paving the way for overt American military involvement in Vietnam.

Elimination of a President changed everything, hell, yes, and this time would be no exception. This time the tide was running out on liberals and socialists, the welfare state reformers and their goddamned pacifist associates in Congress. How they loved to criticize South Africa for "violating human rights," ignoring flagrant genocide in Laos, Cambodia, Afghanistan. How quick they were to cut off military aid for Contra freedom fighters, all the while expanding trade agreements with the Soviets, the Red Chinese.

America was slowly waking up and questioning the actions of its leaders. Mike McNerney was prepared to sound a general alarm—and more, to take the first decisive step toward reclamation of a government of, by and for the people. Naturally it would require some time before the people were prepared to wield their newfound power. Expert supervision was required, and who was better able to provide that necessary guidance than a professional leader of men?

McNerney was a natural. If he survived the next few days, the people would elect him President by acclamation. He was certain of it. Just as Washington had been the father of his country, Michael John McNerney would be named the nation's savior. Snatching victory from sure defeat, he would make history at one fell stroke. And afterward...

Well, afterward would take care of itself. A strategist by training and by inclination, he knew well enough that he must deal with first things first.

And first up was the President.

A SMALLER GROUP HAD GATHERED in the briefing room at Stony Man Farm. Of the original collection, five weren't in evidence; Encizo, Lyons, Blancanales and

McCarter were recuperating from their wounds in sick bay, under orders from Brognola, while Kurtzman's assistant, Barbara Price, was busy running crucial traces through the farm's computer system. Bolan missed them all, in different ways.

He sat beside Grimaldi, having finally soothed the pilot's irritation over being left out of the action in Honduras. Gadgets sat to Bolan's left, and facing them across the table sat the three undamaged operatives of Phoenix Force. They all looked glum, a mood that had affected even Kurtzman, in his usual place beside Brognola.

Katzenelenbogen broke the ice. "Go on and spell it out," he growled. "How bad?"

"It could be worse," Brognola told them all. "We made a clean sweep on the home front, anyway. Caught the bastards with their pants down and rolled them up without a fight. One general bit the bullet, otherwise they're being handled through administrative channels."

Each member of the team was perfectly aware of what might happen in "administrative channels." On occasion individuals might be declared incompetent, confined to mental institutions from which they were never likely to emerge. Some others simply disappeared, their paper trails suggesting love affairs, embezzlement, a planned escape to parts unknown. A few had tragic "accidents" in public places, serving as the ultimate example to a handful in the know.

"Honduras?" Manning asked.

"We can't be certain yet, but from appearances McNerney was the only one to slip the net."

"Goddamn it!" Schwarz was obviously bitter and embarrassed by his failure.

"Let it go," Hal ordered gruffly. "There was no way to anticipate the play. He had us going in."

"We could have tagged him first instead of going after Travers."

"Only at the risk of an abort, in case you made the touch too soon." Hal shook his head. "I hate to disappoint you, Gadgets, but there isn't any room for blame on this one. These things happen."

"Sure." The Able warrior didn't sound convinced.

"Our problem now is tying up loose ends. We've got McNerney's hometown covered. Ditto half a dozen relatives and friends, if you could call them that. So far we're sucking wind. He's not about to call a family reunion when he knows that every badge in the United States is looking for him."

"Is it public yet?" Katz asked.

"A sanitized report is being issued even as we speak. We've got him on the FBI's Top Ten for interstate flight to avoid prosecution. The charges are listed as murder and sabotage. For public consumption, he's been linked to terrorist activities of the Aryan Nation."

"That fits," Calvin said.

"Close enough. He's down as armed and dangerous, with all the usual quotes about how no one's going to bring him in alive. Nobody wants to study this one, gentlemen. He's bought and paid for."

"Any idea where he'd run to?" Manning asked.

"We're most concerned right now about D.C."

"How's that?"

Brognola frowned. "We have three individuals matching McNerney's description on a flight out of Honduras to New Orleans on the day it all went down. Two of them have been traced and cleared. The third name was a phony—Ernest King—and Mr. King made a connection into Baltimore that evening. We were pretty sure he couldn't have been carrying, and on a hunch we started checking gun stores in the area. A place called Hubert's off U.S. 95 near Scaggsville has the records of a major sale to Ernest Michael King. The salesman still remembers him because he came in right at closing time."

"He had a Maryland ID?" Calvin asked.

"Not necessary," Hal reminded him. "The '86 revisions to the Federal Firearms Act permits a purchase out of state on long guns."

"What exactly did he buy?" Schwarz questioned.

Brognola checked the shopping list in front of him. "A Winchester Security Defender twelve-gauge pump with pistol grip in place of shoulder stock. One hundred rounds of double-ought in three-inch Magnum loads. A Sako Finnbear, chambered for 7 mm Remington Magnums, with a Bushnell sixteen-power target scope attached. Four boxes of the Remingtons. Let's call it eighty rounds."

"Assassination?" Bolan asked.

"Right now, I wouldn't rule it out," Brognola said. "He's got the tools."

"So, button up the Man," Grimaldi said, "and keep him under wraps until we have this sucker in the bag."

"Which could be never," Katz responded, "if he's waiting for his shot."

"He's got to show himself sometime," Schwarz put in.

"With ample money, he could stay submerged for months," Katz told them. "Does anybody here believe the Man is going to make himself a prisoner because of what *might* happen?"

"We've suggested that he take an unannounced vacation at his ranch," Brognola said. "He categorically rejected the idea."

"So, turn the game around," the Executioner suggested. "If you can't conceal the target, put it on display and make it irresistible."

"I'm listening," Brognola said.

"Present McNerney with an offer that he can't refuse. Announce the President's location, leave security at status quo and throw in something for the kicker."

"Such as?"

"Oh, well, let's say a Soviet ambassador, for instance."

"Bogus?"

"Naturally."

"You have someone in mind to play the role?"

"Well, he would have to fit the mold, as far as general age, authoritarian appearance, general sour disposition."

"Hey, I've got it," Kurtzman beamed, one hand already resting on Brognola's shoulder. "Someone perfect for the part."

Hal glowered at him, steered the conversation back on track. "You can't expect the Man to cut White House security."

"I wasn't thinking of the White House," Bolan answered.

"Oh?"

"Camp David."

There was silence for a moment as the other warriors chewed it over, searching for a weakness in his plan. They didn't need to mention its most glaring problem—namely, that if there was any error in planning, any actual—opposed to perceived—weakness in presidential security, McNerney might be able to achieve his goal, take out the chief executive and leave them all up the creek without the proverbial paddle. In that eventuality, they would be coconspirators in the assassination of a U.S. President.

"I hope there's more to this," Brognola said.

"There is," the Executioner assured him.

For most of half an hour, Bolan spelled his plan out in detail, refining it as he went along, smoothing the rough edges until everything meshed. When he finished and sat back, the others stared at him and at each other for a long moment of silence.

It was Hal who finally broke the ice. "You don't want much, now, do you? I don't know if I can get this past the Secret Service."

"Get it to the Man, Hal. Bodyguards are paid to follow orders."

"This is very risky."

"Give me an alternative."

But there was no alternative, and Bolan knew it. The President wouldn't submit to house arrest for untold weeks or months, and if McNerney was already stalking him, they had to flush the would-be killer out before he had an opportunity to choose the killing ground himself. It was a sucker play, but it could work, and at the moment Bolan couldn't think of any other decent options.

"Shit. I'll see what I can do," Brognola said. "Is there anything else?"

He was already on his feet, moving toward the door, and no one tried to stall him by prolonging the debate. With their decision made, the hardest part was still ahead, and none of them were envious. It was Brognola's task to make the President of the United States expose himself, become a sitting target for the madman who was stalking him. And he was running out of time.

"I'M SORRY TO DISTURB YOU at this hour, sir."

The President dismissed Brognola's apology, driving at the heart of their mutual problem. "Have you got a handle on McNerney yet?"

"No, sir, but we're still convinced that he's in Washington and armed with weapons suitable for close- or long-range assassination."

"I see."

"I hope you'll reconsider my suggestion—"

"No," the commander-in-chief cut him off. "I won't run out to California and hide like some intimidated child. This administration will not live in fear of irrational enemies."

"Very well, sir. Striker has suggested an alternative."

"I'm listening." The Presidential voice was curious, yet wary.

Hal outlined the plan in simple terms, including his participation, that of Bolan and the able-bodied men of Stony Man. When he had finished, there was momentary silence on the other end.

"I think your plan has merit," the President said at last. "I'll have my press secretary make the appropriate announcements. Let's call it day after tomorrow."

"Yes, sir. We'll be there."

"I hope so. It wouldn't be the same without you, Mr. Ambassador."

The President was laughing as he cradled the receiver, but Brognola didn't share his levity.

It was goddamned risky any way you cut it. Bolan might have figured all the angles, covered all the odds, but there was still a lethal wild card in the game. Assuming that McNerney took the bait—a very hazardous assumption, in Brognola's mind—there were a thousand things that could go wrong. He might slip past the several layers of security or have an ally up his sleeve whom they would never recognize until it was too late. Assuming for a moment that the Man had been mistaken in his own assessment of the D.C. sweep, granting the remotest possibility of other plotters still at large, the odds were drastically revised, and in favor of their enemy. If Mike McNerney had an inside man...

Brognola pushed the morbid thought away. He was becoming paranoid with age. The President had covered everything in Washington, with some assistance from the chiefs of staff and loyal supporters at the top in Langley. If Brognola started seeing shadows now, imagining a plethora of enemies around him, he was beaten well before he took the field.

For now, it was enough to know that Bolan and his other trusted men were on the job. Together with the normal complement of Secret Service agents, it would have to be enough.

Please, God, he thought, just let it be enough.

BARBARA PRICE FOUND "Colonel Phoenix" walking in the open fields behind the ranch house, hands thrust deep into his pockets, studying the tree line. She was fifty yards away when he turned to face her with a distant smile.

"I'm sorry. Would you rather be alone?" she asked.

"Not really."

"Good."

The smile was warmer now, as she drew closer, but there was still a certain hesitance about him. Barbara wondered if it was the mission or herself that bothered him the most.

"A penny for your thoughts."

"You wouldn't get your money's worth," he said.

"You were all brilliant in Honduras."

"Were we? Forty percent casualties, and we missed the fox completely."

"Still—"

"What brings you to this kind of life?" he asked her, taking Barbara by surprise.

She shook her head. "You'll think it's corny."

"Try me."

"Sure, okay. In college half the people in my classes had their eyes fixed on a dollar sign. The other half spent all their time deploring our society. It took a while, but gradually I became convinced there must be something in between."

"Such as?"

"A sense of values. Oh, I don't mean God and apple pie necessarily. But good and evil, right and wrong. I guess I started feeling that I ought to stand for something."

"It can be a lonely life."

"I used to think so."

Bolan searched her eyes, and Barbara held his gaze, unblinking. "You were right the first time," he told her.

Barbara shook her head. "I've changed my mind." She hesitated, searching for precisely the right words, then screwed up her courage to begin. "I talked to Aaron while you were away. I tricked him into talking, I'm afraid. He didn't tell me everything, of course...a lot of it was need-to-know...but he filled me in on some of the details about...about April Rose."

"I see."

He hadn't sounded angry, so she forged ahead. "I know that I was prying, and I *do* apologize, but... well, I had to know what drove you out. I mean, this project, this facility, was *yours*. You walked away from all of this. I had to understand that. Please forgive me."

"Nothing to forgive," he told her, sounding like he meant it. "Anyway, what happened here was only part of it. Sooner or later I would have had to leave, regardless."

"Now I'm confused again."

"Join the club." His smile seemed genuine, if sad. "Did Aaron tell you anything about... before?"

She shook her head. "I didn't push him. As I said, the rest of it was strictly need-to-know."

The soldier frowned. "I'd say you have a need."

And in the next hour he enlightened her. About a family torn by debts and lies. A father driven to the point of desperation. The surviving son, a veteran of other killing grounds, who found a lethal enemy already waiting for him on the home front. He regaled her with the thumbnail version of an everlasting war, a life in hiding that was interrupted all too briefly by a season at Stony Man Farm. When he was finished, Barbara knew who she was talking to, knew all that he had suffered, and it broke her heart.

"I remember the news of your 'death,' in New York."

He grinned. "The reports were greatly exaggerated."

"So I see."

"You must have been in high school at the time."

"Not quite."

"A prodigy?"

She laughed. "You guessed it."

The man whom she knew as Phoenix turned to face her in the twilight. "I'm old enough to be your father," he informed her.

"Sorry. All of us were psychoanalyzed before we got our postings to the farm, and I have no confusion in that area."

"I see."

"From personal experience, I'd say you're very capable."

"And if tonight is all there is?"

"Then let's not waste it, hmm?"

The soldier took her hand and led her back in the direction of the farmhouse.

IN HIS MOTEL ROOM, off the Jefferson Davies Highway in Arlington, Michael McNerney sat upright in bed, watching television. His face was on the screen, blown up to nearly twice life-size, a somber portrait that had been strategically cropped to eliminate most traces of his military uniform. The charges had been sanitized as well, avoiding any mention of the San Felipe raid, Central America or the army in general. They had him down as some kind of demented neo-Nazi, and McNerney gave them points for thinking on their feet. He was amused to see that he had made the FBI's Most Wanted list.

Next up, a story that intrigued him even more. The President was leaving Washington next morning for Camp David, where he would confer with Soviet ambassadors for several days. No firm agenda was available, but local newsmen speculated that the list of topics for discussion might include Afghanistan and arms reduction.

Turning off the TV set, McNerney paced the narrow room for several moments, lost in thought. He wasn't worried by the broadcast of his picture or the artificial charges lodged against him. It was disconcerting that they had already blown his alias as "Ernest King," but he was registered at the motel as Arnold Greenglass, and he doubted that the slob-ass on the desk would watch—or comprehend—the television news. He should be safe tonight, and in the morning he was moving, anyway.

The presidential story was of greater interest to McNerney, and the germ of an idea was stirring in his mind as he walked back to the bed, reclining with his eyes closed, thinking through the problems and advantages of what he had in mind.

He knew Camp David better than the average American who scans the highway maps of Maryland in vain for any sign of the chief executive's retreat. Some years ago he had accompanied a senior officer from Washington to the presidential hideaway, delivering a message from the Pentagon. From the abbreviated clips he'd seen on television here and there, the general layout of the buildings at Camp David hadn't changed, and after flying in that once, McNerney was convinced that he could find—and penetrate—the camp's perimeter.

There would be guards, and if the FBI had traced him to the capital as "Ernest King," security around the President would be redoubled. Still, it might be worth the risk, an opportunity to bag the greatest traitor in the nation, even as he huddled with acknowledged enemies of the United States. With any luck he might succeed in bagging all concerned, driving his point home with a vengeance.

It had all the makings of a historic moment, and McNerney smiled to himself as he began to work the angles out. By dawn, just before fitful sleep surprised him, carried him away, the brigadier was confident that he could penetrate Camp David, kill the famous men inside *and* make his getaway.

It was essential, after all, for the savior of America to live so he could fulfill his destiny. He had so much to do before they brought him down, so many enemies to vanquish yet. And there was no time like the present to begin.

☆ 30 ☆

The limousine had diplomatic plates and tiny Soviet flags mounted on each fender above the headlights. It was armored, stem to stern, with tinted windows guaranteed to stop .50 caliber rounds at a range of thirty yards. The tires were puncture-proof, and the limo's undercarriage was sealed against explosives, toxic gas or flames. Hidden gunports in the several doors provided passengers with the option of returning hostile fire when feasible.

Sequestered in the rear, with Katz and Gary Manning facing him from folding jump seats, Hal Brognola felt ridiculous. He didn't even recognize Grimaldi up front, with the chauffeur's cap pulled low across his brow. The suit and bulky overcoat, in European cut, felt awkward, out of style. Brognola glowered at the passing countryside, imagining himself as a performer in a grade-C gangster movie.

"This will never work," he growled. "Whose idea was this, anyway?"

"You *know* who," Katz replied. "Relax, already. You don't even have to speak the language, chief. Just put in an appearance, sit around here looking Russian until someone tries to blow your head off, then we take him."

"Swell. As chief of Soviet security, you give me loads of confidence."

"We aim to please, comrade."

"How much longer?"

"Twenty minutes, give or take," Grimaldi answered from the driver's seat. "We're getting there."

"My luck, the bastard will be on-site, waiting for us."

"Not a chance, sir," Manning told him. "Secret Service has been running sweeps around the clock since the announcement. No one's broken the perimeter."

"What makes you think McNerney will get through?"

"He wants to," Katz replied. "If we're on target with this yo-yo's thinking, he's committed to the death. He won't be put off by a few security precautions."

"Oh, so it's a few now, is it? Jesus, I hate feeling like a sitting duck."

"You've got the safest duck pond in the world," the gruff Israeli said. "Once in, McNerney won't be coming out again."

"The President?"

"Is safe and sound in Washington, as per the plan. A team of Secret Service men drove the limo and a tail car up this morning, early. From appearances, they had no tail."

"He might be here already."

"Possibly, but there's no visual on the compound from outside. He'd need an airlift, and we've got that covered, five by five."

"No chance a watcher could have made the decoy team this morning?"

"Negative. They went in black, without exterior exposure."

"Well, that's something. Now, if I can make the bastard think I'm Russian, we may have a chance."

"No sweat," Katz grinned. "You bureaucrats all look alike."

Hal didn't join the laughter of his bodyguards. Conditioned to accept the risks of hazardous assignments, wounded more than once in confrontation with the ever-changing enemy, he worried not so much about himself as over how McNerney might react if he was foiled...and then escaped. Katz had described the chief executive's retreat as totally escape-proof, but they were already counting on McNerney to break *in*. That done, if he wasn't eliminated on the grounds, there seemed to be no prima facie reason why the goddamned guy couldn't break out again.

The key was tagging him on-site before he had an opportunity to cut and run. The President wasn't at risk this time, but if McNerney knew that he had been deceived, if he should slip the net, they might not have a second chance to draw him off his target. He would almost certainly be extra cautious, choose his time and place with greater care...or would he lose it, detonating like a human time bomb in some shopping mall or supermarket, taking down as many innocents as possible in an expression of his rage?

The possibilities were endless unless they nailed him here.

"I hope we're squared away," Hal said to no one in particular.

"We're set," Katz assured him.

"Let's run it down again."

"Okay," Katz said, sighing. "At 8:15 p.m we'll lose power over twenty-three square miles, including Camp David and two nearby communities. A story will be phoned in to a deejay just outside the zone, to cover radios in cars, transistors, everything like that. According to the scoop, a trucker dozing at the wheel took out a power station on the interstate. Repairs are under way, etcetera. We give our man two hours. That's his window. If he's on the scene, he'll use it. If he's not... well, then we're playing with ourselves."

Hal frowned. "We're dealing with a goddamned brigadier. He'll know the camp has backup generators."

"Did have," Katz corrected him. "At 8:19 the backups will kick in for thirty seconds and then fail, spectacularly. Write it off to faulty maintenance, whatever. These things happen."

"Now we're stretching."

"So? We're dealing with a lunatic who wants to kill the President and anybody else available. He's rational?"

"He may be crazy, but he isn't stupid."

"It'll work."

"I hope so."

"Striker's betting on it."

"Hell, we all are."

And Brognola's frown became a scowl. It wasn't only Bolan riding on the line this time. With power down, the camp was vulnerable to McNerney, and to anyone he brought along with him. Despite the double complement of Secret Service agents, despite three special warriors on the grounds and three more ready at his side, Brognola knew that they could lose it here. Two hours was a lifetime, with a madman on the prowl, and anything could happen in the darkness of Camp David, stripped of its electric fences, sensors, TV cameras and alarms.

McNerney wouldn't find the President tonight, but he might find Brognola. He might find the house staff, varied agents of the Secret Service, men of Phoenix Force and Able Team. God willing, he would find the Executioner instead, and it would be all over.

McNerney had no firm idea of how to breach the camp's defenses, but he knew he had to try. His target was inside, together with the Soviet ambassador, a symbol of the evil that endangered all Americans, the very values of the nation that he loved with all his heart and soul. Regardless of the danger, he must find a way inside the enemy encampment and strike his blow against the godless traitors who were ruining America.

From his initial visit to the camp, McNerney knew about its lethal fences, eight feet high and topped with razor wire, electric current adequate to barbecue a brontosaurus coursing through the "innocent" chain links. He knew about the inner line of sensors, with their knee-high beams invisible to human eyes, which sounded an alarm inside the compound any time the beams were broken. Other sensors, closer to the presidential home away from home, were sensitive to pressure on the ground itself, and television cameras provided Secret Service guards with views of the surrounding property from every angle.

It should be impossible for him to make his way inside, conduct his business and escape intact...but he was bound to try. He hadn't come this far and dared this much to simply turn his back and walk away.

With darkness, he prepared himself to scout the camp's perimeter on foot. His hands and face were blackened with cosmetics, snowy hair concealed beneath a stocking cap. His turtleneck and jeans were black, as were the sneakers on his feet. The Winchester Security Defender, with its pistol grip and eighteen-inch barrel, hung across his back, available when needed with seven rounds of buckshot in the magazine and one already in the firing chamber. The Sako Finnbear, shoulder slung with muzzle downward, held five rounds of 7 mm Remington Magnum with 175-grain Core-Lokt slugs. Remington advertised its Core-Lokt rounds as the "ultimate mushrooms," with destructive power capable of stopping most big game. With a muzzle velocity of 3,250 feet per second, the Magnum rounds would strike their target with three thousand foot-pounds of explosive energy at a hundred yards. They should be adequate, McNerney thought, for what he had in mind.

Around his waist, across his chest, he carried bandoliers of extra ammunition for the shotgun and the rifle. Ideally he wouldn't be squaring off against the Secret Service team in residence, but conditions were far from ideal. He would be lucky to walk away from this one with his life, McNerney realized...and still, he had no choice.

He was making a final equipment check, prepared to lock his car and leave it, when he noticed something indefinably out of place. Searching the tree line of Camp David, he pondered the problem for a moment and was almost ready to blame an attack of nerves when he turned around and glanced back in the direction of the nearest crossroads village.

It was dark, the combination grocery store and all-night service station black as pitch, where lights had blazed a moment earlier. A good mile farther on, almost beyond the rim of sight, McNerney thought he could recall a power pole in someone's front yard, but he couldn't be sure, for now the highway was in utter darkness.

Slipping back inside his rental car, immediately grateful that he had removed the dome light's tiny bulb, he turned the ignition key to permit use of the radio without starting the engine. Pushing buttons on the radio, McNerney finally found a country station that sounded clear and reasonably close, then waited through the final bars of a song, hoping for some mention of what seemed to be a local blackout.

When the deejay came on, McNerney first mistook him for another country singer, twangy voice and "jive talk" rhythm grating on his nerves. The words were music to his ears, however, as the jock announced a sudden power outage covering the best part of a county. Some damned fool had wrapped his semi around a power pole or some such nonsense, and crews were rushing to the scene.

The blackout made no difference to McNerney, since the Secret Service had their own auxiliary power in the compound. Still, it could facilitate a getaway if things progressed that far. He left the car, hiked twenty yards into the woods and found the high electric fence with warning signs suspended from the razor wire. As if to emphasize the danger, little floodlights had been mounted with Danger signs, ensuring that nocturnal trespassers and nearsighted fools had fair warning before they fried themselves on the wire. The brigadier was pondering a method of avoiding any such disaster when the floodlights flickered, dimmed and finally went out.

He froze, alert to any sign or sound of danger. From the middle distance, in the direction of the compound proper, he could hear a momentary sound of sizzling, like bacon in a skillet, followed by the muffled crump of an explosion. Waiting in the darkness, he wondered if somehow, providentially, the backup generators had failed... and if snipers in the trees were ready to cut him down.

It still could be a trick, he knew, although it seemed to be elaborate and pointless. Even granting that they knew his mission, would the Secret Service strip a President and foreign delegates of all security to trap him here? It struck him as improbable, and yet...

He found a fallen tree branch, three feet long, and took it to the fence, propping one end on the ground at arm's length and allowing it to fall. It struck the chain link squarely with a thin metallic twang... but without the shower of sparks and the crackling sound McNerney was expecting.

So the fence was down, for whatever reason. And if the fence was down, so were the sensors, TV cameras, all the rest of it. Whatever the explanation, whatever the risks, McNerney couldn't afford to pass up his golden opportunity.

He withdrew a pair of cutters from his belt. They were insulated, just in case, but he wouldn't have need of insulation now. With deft, decisive strokes, he cut a three-foot hole in the chain link, closing it behind him with a twist of wire to fool the casual observer and preserve the circuit if they got their juice back while he was inside. He would have other problems in that case, but one of them wouldn't be a warning alarm sounding from the ruptured perimeter.

Inside, he brought the stubby riot shotgun up and flicked the safety off. His rifle was for distance work, where he would need precision for the kill. Close up, in darkness, there was nothing better than a scattergun to make your enemies think twice about attacking your position. Moving through the trees, alert for hidden booby traps or sentries, Mike McNerney felt that he was on the verge of a historic moment. Darkness at the house would make his final task more difficult, of course, but it would also hamper Secret Service agents trying to protect the President and his Russian houseguests.

At ninety yards he saw the flashlights, heard disgusted voices calling back and forth around the compound proper. Someone was cursing the backup generators, their mechanics and assorted nameless peons whose heads were bound to roll come daylight.

Edging closer, he could see the outline of the presidential residence, the smaller generator building, other hulking shapes that he remembered as garages and quarters for the staff and Secret Service. It was too damned dark for him to pick out any faces, but he knew the President and Soviet ambassador weren't out there with flashlights, roaming through the shadows. Somehow he would have to penetrate the house...or lure his prey outside.

He was working on a notion, thought it might succeed, when he was conscious of a rustling sound behind him. He was about to pivot and face the coming danger when a soft voice stopped him in his tracks.

"Don't try it, man. One move and I'll be pleased to blow your ass away."

CALVIN JAMES WAS BORED until the lights went out. He knew the game would wait for darkness, and his circuit of the camp's perimeter before they "blew" the generators was a waste of time. He had completed maybe half the distance and was closing on the eastern curve of the property when it went down—a flash, produced by welding torches, and a smoky bang whipped up by Gadgets and the Stony Man special effects department. Camp David went as dark as if someone had thrown a switch—which, in fact, they had. The power could be instantly restored at any time, but barring contact with the enemy, and hopefully a kill, they would be dark the next two hours. Waiting.

James was good at waiting, hunting in the dark. In basic training he had endured the tired, old "nightfighter" gibes from redneck Southern boys, the jokes about how "you can never see ol' Cal at night unless he blinks his eyes or smiles." In time, his talent had become apparent, and the two or three who'd clung to prejudice, continuing to taunt him, had eventually learned respect a different way while dining on a knuckle sandwich à la James.

Tonight his senses were especially alert. This one was big time, even with the President removed from danger miles away. If a fanatic like McNerney could attempt to set the world on fire, then add the murder of a chief executive like icing on the cake, no one was truly safe. A man of few words under normal circumstances, Calvin kept his feelings to himself, but that didn't negate existence of those feelings. He believed in all the things that stirred a soldier's blood and made him risk his life for love of country. If that was corny or old-fashioned, no one had convinced the Phoenix warrior yet. And no one ever would.

He had no idea of how their quarry might attempt to enter. No one knew for certain that McNerney was in Maryland, much less on-site, but if he was and took the bait, he would be forced to cross the fence somehow. James was still pondering the question, several moments later, when he found the entry cut and repaired with twists of copper wire.

He had a radio, but he was also under orders not to use it casually, in case McNerney might be listening. The standing orders were to hit on sight and call for reinforcements only if the bastard rabbited, or if a single gunner couldn't do the job. Supremely confident, James turned from the fence and started tracking Mike McNerney on a relatively straight run toward the compound. He was going for it in the darkness, as predicted, closing fast. McNerney hadn't been inside for very long—five minutes, tops—when James had found his point of entry on the wire, and he couldn't have gone too far—unless he knew the place of course.

James cursed the sketchy nature of McNerney's bio in the files. They had his service record with all the physicals, promotions, commendations, reprimands, but they were too damned short on details. Had he ever visited Camp David? Had he ever scrutinized the compound from the ground or air? Did McNerney have a better picture of the grounds in mind than his pursuers?

Picking up the pace as much as silence would allow, James flicked the safety off his CAR-15 and set the weapon's selective fire switch for full automatic. In the darkness and the undergrowth, he might not have an opportunity to make the perfect shot, but he would hose the bastard down, cut him into ribbons and make damned certain that he didn't rise again.

Ahead of him he saw a black-clad figure crouching in the shadow of a weeping willow, staring at the house. He knew instinctively that it was neither Schwarz nor Bolan... but he couldn't be entirely certain.

Another step, and James cursed silently as thorny bushes snagged his clothing and made a rustling sound like night wind in the leaves. No point in further stealth—he was already blown—but still he wasn't sure. Downrange, the crouching figure shifted, turning.

And that was when James uttered the warning.

The target moved despite the caution, pivoting and going down all in a single, fluid motion, even as he raked the shrubbery with a string of 5.56 tumblers, clipping leaves and empty air. The shotgun blast was thunder in his ears, and James was driven backward by the impact of a dozen buckshot pellets, finger locked around the trigger of his CAR-15, still firing at the sky.

Reclining on a bed of moss and leaves, with ringing silence in his head and blessed numbness in his legs, James thought, So this is what it's like to lose it. This is what it's like to die.

A human silhouette loomed over him, the face obscured by shadows, hatred shining through the narrow eyes. The Phoenix warrior lost his grip on consciousness and followed swirling darkness downward to a place of everlasting night.

AUTOMATIC FIRE, immediately punctuated by a shotgun blast. Mack Bolan waited for a moment, fixing the position and direction in his mind, expecting the announcement of a kill to crackle from the compact walkie-talkie at his waist. Another precious moment ticked away, and then the rush of thin, metallic voices was eclipsed by the methodical explosions of a big-game rifle.

What had the bastard found to shoot at in the darkness? Even with a night scope—which McNerney hadn't purchased from the Scaggsville shop, but which he might have picked up somewhere else—his targets would be limited to Secret Service agents and the silent buildings of the compound. He could never hope to score a hit by firing blindly through the shuttered windows into darkened rooms. And yet, if there was no alternative, if he had watched his plans dissolve like tissue paper in the rain, McNerney just might try it.

The warrior moved, already homing on the sounds of combat as sporadic small-arms fire responded to the Sako Finnbear. Cranking out five more of the explosive Magnum rounds, the hunting rifle was a giant quarreling with impertinent pip-squeaks, shouting them down. But he couldn't hold out forever. Against Calvin James and Gadgets, Katz and Manning, all the Secret Service men, there was no realistic hope of Mike McNerney getting out alive.

Ignoring odds, extrapolating angles, Bolan veered off course, as if to intercept a runner. There were no more 7 mm thunderclaps, and if McNerney had an ounce of common sense remaining, he would be retreating, breaking off and heading for his exit as if his life depended on it. Which it did.

At night, with trees and undergrowth to baffle sound, distances could be deceiving, but the Executioner relied upon his instincts and a lifetime of experience in jungles all around the world. There were a hundred different ways his man might run, but there was only one track that would finally take him home. Attempting to invade the hunter's thoughts, he opted for a downhill track, through scattered trees and shrubbery, which would eventually take him to the fence two hundred meters away.

With eighty yards to go, he caught a fleeting glimpse of movement in the undergrowth, a darting silhouette against the darker outline of trees. He whipped his Colt Commander up and fired a short precision burst, not taking time to aim. The tumblers were clipping shrubbery, drilling tree trunks, when his quarry answered with a shotgun blast and Bolan went to ground, facedown among the fallen leaves.

At this range, McNerney's Winchester pump was as dangerous as Bolan's autorifle. Each round held a dozen buckshot pellets, each the rough equivalent of a .32 caliber bullet, and the stubby barrel spread them in a conical pattern, covering as much as three square feet at thirty yards.

The soldier wriggled on his belly, searching for another angle of attack. Ahead of him, he heard the quarry moving, looking for a new position of his own. Two blasts in rapid-fire cut through the ferns above Bolan's head, forcing him deeper into the grass and leaves. Before he had an opportunity to return fire, a crashing in the underbrush told Bolan that his prey was breaking for the fence.

Cursing, Bolan scrambled to his feet and gave chase. They were down to the wire now, literally, and if McNerney cleared the fence, they were back to square one.

Pounding through the darkness, sharp limbs whipping at his face and chest, Bolan clawed the walkie-talkie free of his belt and mashed the transmission button.

"Bring the power up!" he barked, not caring if McNerney heard him now. "Electrify the fence!"

CUT AND BLEEDING after running his gauntlet through the trees, McNerney reached the fence and found his exit waiting for him. Dropping to his knees, he ripped the twists of wire away and clawed the chain link back with desperate fingers, crawling through on hands and knees. Behind him, in the darkness, he could hear an angry voice dictating orders, but he couldn't grasp the words.

He cleared the open gap and was rising to his feet when sparks exploded all around him, crackling on the dew-damp grass. Somehow they had restored the power, but it didn't matter now. If anything, it was a blessing, for the hunters would be trapped inside the compound, unable to pursue him without running around to the main gate.

Incredibly McNerney knew he had it made. He had escaped. No matter that his mission was a failure. He was still alive, and he would try again until he got it right.

He ran downslope, following the natural line of a grassy ravine, hidden from the viewpoint of a gunner in the trees behind him. Let the bastard try to climb the fence or use his exit hatch. One brush against the crackling wire, and he would fry. They could shut the power off again, of course, but every second wasted only strengthened Mike McNerney's lead.

The rental car was dead ahead, a crouching shadow in the filtered light provided by a quarter moon. No more than fifty yards, and he would slide behind the wheel, put all of this behind him. Later, when he was completely safe, there would be time to analyze the play, find out why it had gone wrong. Had they been waiting for him? Or had he, in his exuberance, merely stumbled into the camp's normal security precautions?

No matter. Twenty yards now to the car, and he was slowing, catching his breath, when a shadow detached itself from the trees on his right, moving swiftly on an interception course.

"That's far enough!" the watcher shouted, leveling some kind of automatic weapon from the hip. They fired together, and McNerney staggered with the impact of a bullet ripping through his shoulder, reeling, going down. Before he fell, he fired a second shot, one-handed, and the faceless gunman toppled, sprawling on the grass.

He might be still alive, but Mike McNerney didn't give a damn. Ignoring the flares of pain from his wounded shoulder, he scrambled to his feet, lurching toward the car. Somehow he found the keys in his pocket the first time, unlocking the door and slumping behind the wheel. He was about to key the ignition when he caught the tiny, whirring sound, so like an insect's trilling, somewhere close at hand.

And Mike McNerney knew that he was dead. Before he dropped the keys, before he pivoted in the direction of the open driver's door, he knew it was too late. There wasn't even time to scream as rolling thunder ripped his world apart, consuming him with righteous fire.

"CUT OFF THE POWER!"

"But you said—"

"Goddamn it, cut the power! Now!"

"We roger that."

The lethal, crackling fence fell silent, and Mack Bolan wriggled through the exit port provided by his enemy. He felt extremely vulnerable, exposed, until he gained his feet again, and even then the shadows threatened him.

The soldier had a choice. McNerney might have run toward the north or south, but northward lay the highway and potential places of concealment for a vehicle. He turned in that direction, knowing that if his selection was in error, he had blown it, finally, perhaps forever. Having missed McNerney here, there might not be another chance to bring him down before it was too late.

Gunfire added urgency to Bolan's stride. A shotgun blast, a burst of autofire, an answer from the twelve-gauge. Someone, somehow, had attempted to waylay McNerney, but the warrior wasn't betting on their chances of success. He had already learned a new respect for his adversary, but that respect only amplified the need to bring McNerney down.

Ahead of him, the sudden flash of an explosion lit the trees, immediately followed by the sharp, concussive sound. Bolan started running toward the firelight, slowing as the flames resolved themselves into the form of a shattered automobile. From fifty feet away, their heat was stifling.

A movement on the grass to Bolan's right brought him into a crouch, the Colt Commander tracking into target acquisition. Seated on the grass, his features visible in the reflected light of dancing flames, was Hermann Schwarz. Despite the intervening distance, Bolan caught a glint of crimson on his camouflaged fatigues.

"What happened, Gadgets?"

"I was working the perimeter, outside," Schwarz answered, grinning crookedly behind his combat makeup. "Found his car and decided that I'd wait for him in case he made it out."

"How badly are you hit?"

"I guess I'll live."

The Executioner was frowning, curious. "I didn't hear the burst that tagged his fuel tank."

"That's because I never fired one," Schwarz replied. "The bang was waiting for him when he opened the driver's door. A five-second tension-release fuse...just in case."

"The doomsday fallback."

"Now you're talking."

For the first time in a week or more, Mack Bolan felt like smiling. Calling up the medics, he could feel a weight of worry lifted from his shoulders, evaporating into thin air. Their ETA was five, but he and Schwarz could wait. For now, it was enough to read tomorrow in the flames.

EPILOGUE

"You were superb, as always."

"Thank you, sir."

The presidential limousine was air-conditioned, roomy, but Mack Bolan still felt claustrophobic as he sat beside Brognola on the jump seats.

"No telling where that madman might have popped up next." The chief executive frowned, showing genuine concern. "I trust your people are receiving proper care."

"Yes, sir," Hal answered for him. "Gadg—uh, Schwarz, was wounded in the side and shoulder. James took several buckshot pellets in the legs and groin."

"Good Lord!"

"No lasting damage, sir. Bethesda's best assure me everything will be in working order when they're finished."

"Well, thank God for that at least." He turned to Bolan once again. "This may not be the time or place, but I was wondering if you've had time to reconsider my proposal."

"I've considered it."

"And?"

"Sir, my quarrel has never been with you."

The Man dismissed his statement with an airy wave. "I know that, son. If someone sold me out the way they did to you...well, dammit, someone nearly *did.* I understand your feelings, but I need an answer all the same."

"I couldn't come back to the team full-time," he said at last. "I need the kind of stretch you just don't find in uniform."

"I see." The President seemed genuinely saddened.

"However, in the proper circumstances I might be available from time to time."

"On call, you mean?"

"We'd have to take it one job at a time. No promises."

"You run a greater risk outside," the President reminded him unnecessarily.

"Yes, sir."

"I can't protect you while you're on your own."

"You can't protect me on the farm," the Executioner replied.

"I understand. But if we need to get in touch with you—"

"Hal has the number of a service that I use. I check in twice a day." There was no need to mention brother John, no need to make the government aware of his existence.

"All right," the President agreed. "About that pardon..."

"That's not necessary, sir."

"I think it is."

"You'd just be wasting time," the soldier cautioned him. "This time tomorrow, I may be a criminal again."

"There should be something—"

"I don't want permission, sir. The action justifies itself. I'll take my chances."

"Very well. But if you ever want for anything..."

"I'm getting by."

"Yes, I guess you are." The President was openly bemused. "Can I at least give you a ride?"

"It's taken care of, sir."

They shook hands all around, and Bolan put the presidential tank behind him, striking off across the parking lot through autumn sunshine. The Turbo Z was waiting for him on the far side of the lot, its engine idling, with Barbara Price behind the wheel.

"How did it go?"

"All right."

"That's it? 'All right'?"

"We understand each other."

The lady shook her head and smiled.

"Fair enough. Where to?"

"You mean, my place or yours?" It was the soldier's turn to shake his head. "I haven't got a place."

"Oh, yes, you do."

Without a backward glance, she put the Turbo Z in gear and took the warrior home.

MACK BOLAN, SUPERHERO

DON PENDLETON's
MACK BOLAN
Sudden DEATH

**An assassin is programmed to kill.
His target is programmed to die.**

Mack Bolan is back in action! His enemy... himself!

In this seventh SuperBolan, a series of political assassinations is sweeping Europe – but the US president is closely protected at a meeting of European leaders.

Who could imagine that his greatest defender will be his assassin – that Mack Bolan is programmed to kill him?

Bolan must overcome the programming and uncover the brilliant terrorist group behind this fantastic plot. Will Mack Bolan be able to fight back this time?

Widely available from Boots, Martins, John Menzies, W.H.Smith and other paperback stockists

Pub. October 1987 **£2.5**

GOLD EAGLE

MACK BOLAN, SUPERHERO

DON PENDLETON's **MACK BOLAN** — TERMINAL VELOCITY	 DON PENDLETON's **MACK BOLAN** — FLIGHT 741	DON PENDLETON's **MACK BOLAN** THE EXECUTIONER — STONY MAN DOCTRINE (BIGGEST BOLAN BESTSELLER!)
£1.95	£2.50	£1.95
MACK BOLAN — DIRTY WAR	 DON PENDLETON's **MACK BOLAN** Resurrection Day	 DON PENDLETON's **MACK BOLAN** DEAD EASY
£2.50	£2.25	£2.50

...lethal, killing machine ...atched in merciless ...ombat against the ...rces of evil through ...ese six action ...acked 'chapters' ...f the story so far.

GOLD EAGLE

Widely available from Boots, Martins, John Menzies, W.H. Smith and other paperback stockists.

THE TAKERS
JERRY AHERN
£2.25

A gripping story in which the legends of the past could shape the future.

DEATH LANDS: Pilgrimage to Hell — JACK ADRIAN — £2.75

DEATH LANDS: Red Holocaust — JAMES AXLER — £2.25

The aftermath of the nuclear holocaust – the fight for survival in a living hell stalked by fear.

VIETNAM: GROUND ZERO — ERIC HELM — £1.75

VIETNAM: GROUND ZERO — P.O.W. — ERIC HELM — £1.95

The saga of an American Special Forces Squad embroiled in the bloody violence of Vietnam.

Widely available from Boots, Martins, John Menzies, W.H. Smith and other paperback stockists.

GOLD EAGLE

The fifth book in America's most dramatic
Vietnam story

A U.S. Army Special Forces camp is threatened
when an American sergeant turns renegade

VIETNAM: GROUND ZERO
SOLDIER'S MEDAL

ERIC HELM

The trigger-finger tension of Vietnam continues...

Listening Post One is overrun by the Vietcong. The entire squad is slaughtered except Sergeant Sean Cavanaugh, who escapes.

Guilt-ridden, Cavanaugh's nerve cracks. Fatally flawed by his experience Cavanaugh is a time bomb waiting to explode.

Captain Mack Gerber, Commander of Camp A-555, suspects the Sergeant's secret and realizing his mental state could endanger the lives of those with him Gerber is faced with only one choice – find and kill Cavanaugh!

Widely available from Boots, Martins, John Menzies, W.H. Smith and other paperback stockists.

Pub. March 1988. **£1.95.**

GOLD EAGLE

RUSSIA HAS LAUNCHED THE ULTIMATE WEAPON

WAR ✱ MOON

TOM COOPER

The new espionage superthriller from the author of *Triad of Knives*

A sophisticated orbiting space battle station. The Russians have it. The U.S. want it.

The White House wants Natasha Smirnova, the genius behind War Moon, on their side. And they are using one of their most brilliant nuclear engineers, Chris Carmichael, to get her.

But Smirnova has been ordered to use every weapon she possesses – as a scientist and as a woman – to make sure Carmichael defects to Russia. Whilst they face the ultimate test of love and loyalty, their respective nations grapple in a desperate struggle to survive.

As the core of the Soviet power structure crumbles, murder and manipulation become the only rules in a frantic contest where both sides are playing for keeps.

GOLD EAGLE

Widely available from Boots, Martins, John Menzies, W.H. Smith and other paperback stockists. Pub. April 1988. **£2.95.**